THE PIG FARMER'S WIFE

LaVonne Misner

ISBN: 979-8-218-18405-6 (paperback)

Published by LAM Haub Press

Names: Misner, LaVonne, author.

Title: The pig farmer's wife / LaVonne Misner.

Description: [San Diego, California] : [LaVonne Misner], [2023] | Includes bibliographical references.

Subjects: LCSH: Women—Fiction. | Sex discrimination against women—Fiction. | Women's rights—Fiction. | Families—Fiction. | Farmers—Fiction. | Self-realization—Fiction. | Self-actualization (Psychology)—Fiction. | Women—Employment—Fiction. | Minnesota—Fiction. | Feminist fiction.

Classification: LCC: PS3613.I84476 P54 2023 | DDC: 813/.6—dc23

I dedicate this book to my daughters,
Carol and Sara.

ACKNOWLEDGEMENTS

Thank you to

- Beta readers: Mary Agne, Cindy Bassuk, Jennifer Bolden, Kathy Louv, Jeannie Mayfield, Paulette Millander, Carol Misner, Lynn Owens, and Lyba Vinitsky.
- Critique group members: Rob Bachman, Jennifer Bolden, Julie Burke, Sheila Fisher, Pamela Sanders, and Larry Weiner.
- Author, friend and writing role model, Richard Louv.
- Writing instructor, Tara Gilboy.
- Joe and Allan Peterson, who shared their memories of growing up on the family pig farm during the 50s, 60s and 70s.
- Jerry Garfield of the Steele County Historical Society.
- Ken Benson for technical assistance.
- Katy Sigler for the cover design.
- Sandra Yeaman for the copy edit.
- Most of all, thank you to my husband, Tom Olson, who continually supported and encouraged me in this endeavor.

PART I

1931–1950

1

INNOCENCE OF YOUTH & HARD REALITIES

"For most girls growing up, the most important degree was not your B.A., but your M.R.S."

— RUTH BADER GINSBURG

Papa interpreted my birth as an omen of greatness because I was born in 1931, the same year *The Star-Spangled Banner* became our National Anthem. But Mama, in her own practical way, scoffed and called that just a bunch of nonsense.

"Never mind about omens and such," she told Papa. "Our Gertrude only needs to grow up to become a proper young lady, so stop putting grandiose ideas in her head."

Papa never openly contradicted Mama, but he never changed his mind either. Instead, he smiled and gave Mama a little kiss on the cheek, which caused Mama to blush and say, "Honestly Herman, you're incorrigible."

I loved both my parents, Papa for his charm and Mama for her down-to-earth practicality. Together they made a perfect team. They had come to the United States before I was born, and with them they brought their strong German work ethic and a modest inheritance which they invested into a small convenience store in St. Paul, Minnesota.

My earliest, and perhaps my fondest memories, are of the days when I scurried around in that store with the ease of a dust mote.

"May I help you find something?" I remember asking customers in my sweetest voice as I swished my satin skirts to maximize the rustle of the fabrics. "I'm seven, and I know where everything is."

"You're not seven," Mama always corrected. "You're six, or five," or whatever age I was at the time. Then she'd give me her special look, the one only Mama and her furrowing eyebrows could project. But I'd pretend I didn't hear her and scamper off to greet the customers, enticing their smiles or winks. Sometimes they'd even pat me on top of my head, as if I was a puppy dog.

But I always liked it best when Papa tended the store, because under his watchful eye, I was allowed to do grownup things like ring up sales. I loved seeing the surprise on customers' faces when they saw me, a diminutive girl, doing something they expected only grownups could do.

One time, I remember trying to show Papa how extra helpful I could be by restocking the shelf of corn that had become somewhat depleted. I went into the storeroom where we kept the extra inventory and placed three cans of corn in my doll carriage. Then I pushed the carriage into the store and stood on my tippytoes to lift each can onto the empty space next to the other cans of corn.

When Papa saw what I was doing, he told me I needed to *face* the cans when I added items to the shelf, and then he showed me how to do that. Immediately I saw how much better the shelf looked, so I ran back into the storeroom to get two more cans, but in my haste, I dropped one.

"Gertrude!" Papa's voice bellowed out. "Did I hear a can drop?"

"Yes, Papa, but it's okay. I picked it up."

"Gertrude, bring the can you dropped to me, please."

Sheepishly, I walked over and handed him the can.

"Do you see this dent?" he asked, turning it around to show me. "People won't buy dented canned goods. So take this to your mother and explain how it happened. We'll be eating this corn for dinner tonight."

That was such a memorable lesson. Each and every day I learned something new, and by the time I was a teenager I was capable of handling any and all tasks needed to run the store. Papa had even taught me how to take inventory and reorder stock.

Meanwhile, Mama instructed me on all the things she thought a young lady should know. Things like how to dress modestly, sit with my knees together, and how to present myself. *Should*, it seems, was Mama's most important word. Never, however, did either she or Papa ask me what I might like to be, or what I may want to do when I grew up. And truth be told, I very likely wouldn't have known what to say had either of them asked, because I was never encouraged to worry my *pretty little head* about such matters.

My job, as Mama so often reminded me, was to find a suitable husband, one with whom I could walk down a church aisle wearing a beautiful white dress. Preferably someone who would be a college graduate and able to meet his financial obligation to take care of his family.

Much to Mama's dismay, however, I wasn't particularly interested in boys, at least not until I was in college, and that's when I met George, my first potential husband candidate. He was standing behind me in the coffee line in the student union, and when I heard him mumble something, I turned to inquire what it was.

"I just asked how your day is going," he said with a smile that displayed the most beautiful set of white teeth I had ever seen. I smiled back, mesmerized by how impressively straight his teeth were, all lined up in a perfect row, just like Mama's pearl necklace she wore to church on Sundays. Not at all like mine, with my eyeteeth sticking out like tusks.

In an effort to be flirtatious, a skill I hadn't had much practice with, I tipped my head coyly and told him my day was going very well. "How is yours going?" I asked in return.

"Mine is going well too," he answered, looking pleased with himself, as if he'd just eaten the last piece of cake. "But" he added, "it'll be even better after I get a cup of Joe in me."

I giggled, which was another thing I wasn't accustomed to doing, and put a little extra effort into standing up straighter.

Then he invited me to join him at the empty booth where he'd piled his books.

I paid for my own coffee, waited for him to get his, and followed him to the booth like a newly adopted puppy. On the way, I learned his name was George, and together we slid across the leather cushions of the booth.

Unable to think of what to say, I heard myself blurt, "I'm new to college and I'm surprised to see how crowded it is here."

"Ahh," he said, sounding confident and knowledgeable about such matters, "It'll thin out in a few weeks when everyone is hunkered down in the library."

I nodded, acknowledging my understanding, as we launched into nervous chatter while my feet took on a life of their own, jiggling and flexing back and forth under the table. In spite of my anxiety, I realized I was having a great time, so much so that I was shocked when I glanced at my watch.

"Holy cow!" I blurted out, feeling a warm blush of embarrassment for my unsophisticated outburst. Then I forced myself to add in a calmer voice, "I need to get to class."

"Oh," he sputtered. "But we've barely had a chance to get to know one another. Would you be interested in going out with me on Friday?"

"Sure," I agreed and jotted my phone number down on a paper napkin before scurrying off to class. That evening George called to confirm our date and get my address.

In preparation for the big night, I washed and starched my crinolines before leaving for school that Friday, letting them drip dry over the bathtub all day. When I got home from school, I buffed my penny loafers until they glowed and searched in the cash drawer for two shiny pennies to insert into the leather shoe pockets. Then I washed my hair in a nicely scented shampoo and rolled it onto orange juice cans. When my hair was dry, Mama combed it out into a perfect flip. She also polished and buffed my fingernails.

"Good grief," Papa said at the precise time George was due. "Did a Mac truck pull up in front, or is there a car out there without a muffler?"

"It's probably my date, Papa."

"Your date! Can't that boy afford a muffler?"

"I don't think he has much money, Papa. Remember how you used to tell me how poor you were when you were young?"

"That was Germany," Papa grumbled. "This is America!"

After planting a quick kiss on Papa's cheek, I hurried into the store to greet George, hoping Papa wouldn't make too big of a deal about his loud car. I found George perusing the snack food aisle and invited him through the privacy curtain that led to our private living quarters, where Papa immediately began questioning him.

"Tell me, son," Papa said, "where do you expect to be working after college?"

I was dying a thousand deaths, but George took my father's interrogation all in stride, calmly answering each question. Strangely, Mama never made a peep, not a single word slipped from her lips. She just continued stitching her embroidery, acting as if she was no more interested in the conversation than what a pile of clean dishtowels might be. Yet I knew she was listening, evaluating, and cataloging George's every word.

Finally, Papa must have run out of questions because he smiled and said, "Well, okay then, off the two of you go."

I sighed with relief and led George back toward the front door of the store, but before stepping through the privacy curtain, I took one quick glance back, just in time to see Papa give me a quick little wink.

"Mind your feet now," George said, opening the creaky passenger door of his Volkswagen for me.

I slid onto the seat, shocked to see the floorboards had been replaced with two narrow wooden slats, each barely as wide as my shoes.

"Sit tight now," he said, closing the door behind me before jogging to the other side of the car. Then he reached inside the open window, shifted the car into neutral and began pushing it down the street. I was stunned by what he was doing, but before I could even comment, he opened the car door, leapt inside, slipped the clutch, and put the car in gear, causing it to roar to life.

"Okay," he said with a huge grin and a little out of breath. "We're off!"

"I see that."

George offered no explanation, simply saying breathlessly, "I heard the movie at the St. Clair Theater is pretty good this week. Would it be okay if we go there tonight?"

"Sure," I answered. "That'd be fine. I guess I'm up for most anything." I watched the pavement whizzing past my feet.

Based on the condition of George's car, I began to suspect the cost of two movie tickets may be a large expenditure for him, which caused me to guess further about how he was able to afford tuition. But I appreciated his easy manner, his gentleness, and the fact that he wasn't a greaser, someone who wore skintight black pants with a pack of cigarettes bulging from a rolled-up sleeve. I still didn't know if he drank beer, or if he would try to put his hand inside my blouse, but I knew those things would reveal themselves all in good time.

"Do you live on campus?" I asked, in an attempt to make light conversation.

"No. I live with my aunt in Highland Park. She took me in after my parents died, and so long as I'm in school, she lets me live with her rent free. It's working out pretty well for both of us, I think, because I do the heavy chores for her, things like cutting the grass and shoveling the snow."

"That must be nice for both of you."

"Yeah! It is for the most part. But, if there's a party or something special on campus, the guys usually let me crash on one of the sofas at the Ag. Frat House. But I'm not a paying member, so I try not to take advantage by overstaying my welcome."

An awkward silence lingered as I tried thinking of something else to say, but before the silence became uncomfortable, George patted the dashboard and said, "I think I may have enough money next month to paint old Nellie here. I've been thinking some shade of blue might be nice. What do you think, Gert? Do you have a color preference?"

"Sure," I said. "Blue would be good. Would you paint it two shades or keep it all one color?"

"Not sure yet. That'll be something to consider."

Not only was George's car noisy and needed help to get started, but it didn't have a lick of paint on it, only the flat, rust-colored undercoat. It was without a doubt the ugliest car I'd ever seen, and I was fairly certain very few girls would be willing to be seen in it.

George found street parking close to the theater, and we arrived in time for us to see the Porky Pig cartoon and the newsreels:

- The US launched the Explorer satellite!
- The Soviet Union launched Sputnik 3!
- The USS Nautilus Reached the North Pole!

As soon as the lights dimmed and *Cat on a Hot Tin Roof* rolled onto the screen, George put his arm around my shoulder. I flinched when I first felt his touch, but then I felt a smile creep across my face as I willingly snuggled into the contour of his arm.

The movie was great, both gripping and emotional. So much so, that when the theater lights came back on, I was a little sorry when George removed his arm. With the other attendees, we shuffled up the aisle to exit the theater, discovering it was snowing outside. Big soft fluffy flakes, illuminated by the streetlights, fluttered from the ink black sky. Visually, the scene was Christmas-card perfect, and the ground that had previously appeared unkempt had a fresh blanket of pristine white snow, creating both a beauty and a quiet tranquility to the air.

"Are you up for a plate of fries?" George asked with a grin as wide as his face could hold, displaying all his beautiful teeth again.

"Sure." I pulled the collar of Mama's jacket up tight around the back of my neck.

We stepped out into the nippy air and leapt across Snelling Avenue without waiting for the stoplight to change. The new clean snow made everything seem quiet, with the only sound being that of the crunch of the snow beneath our feet. We ducked into the St. Clair Broiler, stomped the snow off our feet, and scanned the room for an empty booth.

"Evening, George," a waitress said as soon as we slid into a booth near the back while George and I were still in the process of removing our jackets.

"Evening, Maggie," George answered. "We'll have a plate of fries and two cherry cokes."

"You know the waitress by name and the menu by heart?" I asked in surprise after she left.

"Yeah! Sometimes I wash dishes here on weekends. So how did you like the movie?"

"I loved it, but it wasn't anything like I expected it to be from the title. I thought it would be about cats, you know, the actual animals. But Elizabeth Taylor was wonderful in it! She's so talented and beautiful!"

After an awkward moment where neither of us said anything, our fries and cokes arrived.

"Wow!" George said, popping a hot fry into his mouth. "They're fast tonight."

"You know," I said, as I sipped my Coke, "I see you on campus and in the student union, and I heard what you told my parents about your studies, but I'd love to hear more about what you're studying."

"Well, like I told your father, I'm working toward a degree in agriculture."

Mesmerized by his kind eyes and dashing smile, I listened without interruption.

"My parents used to have a little farm in southern Minnesota. We all loved that farm, but we just couldn't keep it up or compete with the big guys. You know, the corporate giants."

I nodded to encourage him to continue talking.

"My parents were crop farmers: corn and soybeans. But, as I said, the small ma and pa farms don't have a chance of making a living anymore. So they sold the land and moved into a little retirement home closer to town until they died. But I suspect they died of broken hearts because the farm meant everything to them. What about you? I see you walking to class in those cute little skirts, but I don't know anything about you except that you have great legs. What's your major and what are you studying to become?"

"What am I studying to become?" I parroted, astounded by the question. "Well, I don't know what I'm studying to become. I never thought about it that way. I'm just taking a bunch of Home Economics classes. I have a class in textiles where we're learning to name fibers by examining them under a microscope. And I've learned how to refinish wood and make draperies and reupholster furniture, but I don't know what any of that will help me become. That's an interesting question. No one has ever asked me that before."

"Well, maybe you should think about it because I'll just bet you are the smartest girl in all your classes."

"Not really." I tried to follow Mama's advice to avoid sounding too smart around boys. But somehow I couldn't help myself and added, "I do have a test in Art History tomorrow."

"Wow! Tomorrow? Really? Are you ready for it?"

"I think so. It's just a lot of memorizing."

After a pleasant evening, we held hands and strolled back to his car while enjoying the snow that was still falling. I cringed when I realized George would need to start the car in the same manner he did earlier in the evening. I suspected the slippery ground would make jogging next to it a lot more dangerous.

As it turned out, getting the car started was a small matter compared to the fact that the heater didn't work, which meant the freezing cold air blew up onto my bare legs where there were no floorboards. The drive home was also extremely slow because of the black ice hidden beneath the snow, which caused the car to fishtail every time we hit a patch. What had begun as an enjoyable evening had quickly morphed into one of misery. I could hardly wait to get home and into the warmth of my bed.

As we neared the store, I was surprised to see people I recognized standing outside, all lined up along the curb. Most were our neighbors and customers. I also saw a florescent-vested policeman standing in the middle of the street directing traffic, directing the cars to turn around.

"Something must be very wrong," I said. "Why would our neighbors be outside on a night like this? And why aren't the cars being allowed to continue down our street?"

"Yeah!" George said. "I was wondering the same thing."

As we got closer to the intersection where the police officer was redirecting cars, George rolled down his window and asked, "What's up? What's happening?"

"There's a fire in the store up ahead, son. You'll have to turn around here and go down a different street because this street is going to be closed for some time."

"What did he say was on fire?" I asked as George began rolling his window up.

"I think he said the store was on fire."

"The store? Our store? Is that what he said?"

"I think so," George answered as he began turning the car around. Then I saw smoke and flames shooting up into the sky.

"Stop the car!" I screamed. "I need to get out!"

I opened my door and leapt from the still rolling car, intending to find my parents, but I was blocked by a second police officer.

"You can't go down that street, miss," he said.

"I have to," I said. "I live at that store, and I need to find my parents?"

"Hey, Joe!" he said to his backup, while preventing me from moving any further. "Get that Red Cross lady over here."

But when he looked away for a second, I used the opportunity to burst past him and I began running as fast as I could toward the store. I slipped and stumbled a couple of times because the pavement was slippery and full of slush. I also began coughing in the putrid acrid air, but I ignored all of that and kept running forward toward the store. I heard the police whistles and heard people yelling for me to stop, but I ignored all of them and kept running as fast as I could through the icy wet slush.

"Stop that woman!" a deep husky voice yelled. "She's heading directly into the fire!"

But I didn't stop. Instead, I shouted, "Mama, Papa, I'm coming!" I nearly lost my balance a couple of times, but with determination, I managed to stay upright and kept going. Then, all of a sudden, when I was about to crash onto the slushy wet pavement, one of the police officers did catch up with me, and he grabbed the sleeve of my jacket.

"Okay, miss," he said as much out of breath as I was. "Let's just calm down here so we can get this all sorted out. Shall we? We need to let the firefighters do their jobs, and there's nothing any of us can do to help them. Our job is to stay out of their way. Understand? They're doing the best job they can to put the fire out, but it's not an easy one because there are propane tanks in there."

The words were barely out of his mouth when I heard and felt the impact of two explosions.

"That's a couple more of them exploding now," he said. "Which is why you have to stay here. Okay? You'll only get in the way and slow their work down if you get any closer. Do you understand?"

Propane tanks? Of course there are. We keep propane tanks out in the back of the store for our customers' outside grills.

2

DESPERATE EMPTINESS

"You will lose someone you can't live without, and your heart will be badly broken, and the bad news is that you never completely get over the loss of your beloved. But this is also good news. They live forever in your broken heart that doesn't seal back up. And you come through. It's like having a broken leg that never heals perfectly, that still hurts when the weather gets cold, but you learn to dance with the limp."

—Anne Lamott

This can't be happening! It just can't!

I understood what the policeman was saying, and of course, I wanted to allow the firemen every opportunity to extinguish the fire, but I also desperately needed to find my parents.

"Hello," a woman said, appearing from the crowd, guiding me away from the chaos. "I'm Mrs. Duddelson. I'm with the Red Cross and my car is right over there." She motioned toward some type of compact vehicle that was barely visible in the dark. "Let's go over and get in it, shall we, dear? I'll turn the heater on while we talk."

I followed her, hoping to learn more about the fire and the

whereabouts of my parents, but I also knew I was allowing myself to be seduced by the mention of her car heater.

"Gertrude," she said once we were in her car and the heater was blowing full blast, "both the store and the apartment out in back are burning."

Dah! I already knew that.

I smiled and said, "I just need to find my parents, especially my mom." I explained how upset my mother got when she didn't know where I was. "Mom will just fret and stew and make Papa's life miserable until she knows I'm safe."

There was a long silence while Mrs. Duddleson sat silently staring at me. It felt as if her eyes might burn holes right through me. Then she blinked, pursed her lips, and said, "We don't think your parents made it out."

"Made it out of what?" I asked, feeling a little cocky now that I was somewhat warmer and thawed out.

"Gertrude, there's no easy way for me to say this, but your parents very likely died in that fire."

I heard the words, but they sounded as if they were part of a movie script, something too preposterous to even contemplate.

"What?" I asked, feeling as if my world had just exploded. "Did you say you think my parents are . . ." I couldn't finish the sentence. Something had taken my breath away, so I paused and started over. "Are you saying that you think my parents are dead?"

"Yes," she said, nodding her head in the affirmative with a sad puppy dog expression as she reached across to open her glove box and retrieve a box of tissues, setting it on the seat between us.

I looked at the box and slowly raised my eyes to meet hers. Only this time, I glared at her with the hatred of a lioness who might have just learned her cub had been recently eaten by prey. A rage I had never experienced before gurgled up from someplace deep within me, a feeling I didn't know how to manage. And yet I stayed sitting in her car, as rigid as a statue, soaking up the heat that was coming from the small vents on her dashboard.

"Do you have relatives near here," she asked, oblivious to the growing hatred I felt toward her. "Is there somewhere I can take you tonight?"

"Relatives?" I growled in a voice I didn't recognize as my own. "No! I don't have relatives! None! I don't have any relatives at all! I only have my parents, and I don't believe they are dead! They escaped from Germany when times were really difficult for them, which is more than any of us could have done, and they would certainly escape a fire! They wouldn't stay there and die. I'm done with you, whoever it is you claim to be."

With that outburst, I shoved the car door open and ran toward the store, back to where the firefighters were working to put out the fire.

"Where do you think you're going?" another policeman shouted at me when he saw me lifting the yellow barrier of plastic tape. "You can't come in here," he said, physically guiding me back outside the line of tape.

"Don't touch me," I shouted, shrugging his hand off my shoulder! "My parents are in there and I have to help them get out!"

"No, miss! You're not going anywhere near that fire."

"Didn't you hear me?" I said. "My parents are in there!"

He refused to acknowledge what I had said, and yet I knew from his expression that he'd heard me. But that only caused him to keep a closer eye on me.

I was so frustrated and confused that I didn't know what to do, so I paced back and forth like a wild animal in an enclosed cage. Fifty feet in one direction, and fifty feet back in the opposite direction while ice water seeped into my loafers. In a mere blink of time, my feet were numb, and yet strangely they ached. Still, I continued pacing, ignoring my discomfort from the cold and the ironic blistering heat on my face, not to mention the putrid odor from the smoke.

Icicles crackled on the back of my neck where my hair had frozen into sticks, and my bare legs became so cold that I lost all feeling in them, except for my upper thighs where my mesh crinoline sliced into my most tender skin around my panty line. In a futile attempt to supply some warmth I rolled my bobby socks up, but they were so sodden that they refused to stay up, forming heavy clumps that sagged at my ankles.

Just when I thought I couldn't be any more miserable, that Mrs. Duddleson, the Red Cross woman, reappeared and flapped her lips at me with more lies.

"Go away," I said. "I don't want to hear anything you have to say. Leave me alone!"

"Gertrude," she said, in a measured calm that I found disgusting because she was obviously pretending to be a professional instead of a nutjob who preyed on vulnerable people. "I know you're upset with me right now, and I'm sorry if I dropped that information on you too quickly, but it's the truth, and I didn't think there was any point in giving you false hope."

I heard the shortness of her breath as she tried keeping up with my pacing. Finally, she said bluntly in a loud voice, "Gertrude, your parents are gone! And as hard as that is for you to hear, there is no easier way for me to tell you."

I stopped my pacing, turned, and shouted directly into her face. **"I don't believe you!"**

She looked startled by my outburst but quickly switched back into that same measured tone that was really pissing me off. "I'm sorry, but I'm only trying to help you."

"There you are," George said, jogging toward me from the darkness. "I was afraid I'd lost you. The cops wouldn't let me park anywhere near here, but I finally found a spot a few blocks away. Have you found your parents yet? They're very likely roaming around here looking for you like I was."

"This woman says they're dead," I told him.

"Dead?" George gasped. "But they didn't seem frail or anything. Surely, they would have left as soon as the fire started. Wouldn't they?"

"Of course they would! She's just a lunatic. Ignore her."

Along with the other spectators, the three of us kept our vigil. We stomped our feet and clapped our arms in an effort to stimulate circulation. We listened to the flames crackle and roar as they reached for the sky in defiance of the torrents of water the firefighters were dousing them with. Suddenly I felt warm, hot actually, and I began removing my jacket.

"What are you doing?" crazy lady said, reaching over to prevent me from taking my jacket off.

"What's it to you?" I said. "I'm hot."

"No! You're not hot! You're experiencing hypothermia."

On cue my teeth began chattering and I could no longer control or minimize my shivering.

"I have a blanket in my car," George said. "I'll run back and get it, but please don't move 'till I return."

I was confused and couldn't understand why George would want a blanket, but I remember nodding my head in agreement.

When the fire was out and the firefighters began loading their trucks, I asked the police officer closest to me if I could go into the store now to search for my parents. "They're probably out in the back," I told him through my chattering teeth. "Out by the alley."

"No, miss," he said. "I'm afraid not! We're waiting for the coroner to remove the bodies. No one's going in there for a very long time."

"What did you say? Did you say there are bodies in there?"

"Yes, two people died in there tonight."

"Two people? Did you say two people died in the store?"

"Yes," he said and added, "I can't imagine that it's a pretty picture in there."

"Where am I?" I asked, finding myself in a bed, naked under a white cotton nightshirt that I'd never seen before in my life.

"You're at the YWCA," crazy lady answered from across the room. "You fainted and we brought you here."

"We? Who is we? Who brought me here?"

"Your boyfriend and I brought you here. He carried you in and I made the arrangements."

"Where are my clothes? And who undressed me?"

"Your clothes are drying on the table across the room." She avoided the second part of my question. "Your shoes and socks are under the heater. Everything was soaking wet."

Am I having a nightmare?

"I sent your boyfriend home. You can talk to him tomorrow."

What the heck! Have I been kidnapped? Who does she think she is to be telling me who I can and can't talk to?

"I've arranged for you to stay here until we get everything sorted out."

Sorted out? What is she talking about? I tried focusing on what she was saying but it was difficult because I was so frightened and con-fused. *Who is this woman, and what is she going to do to me next?*

"I know you don't like me right now, but I'm here to help you. This is my job, and I've done things like this before. So for now you'll just have to trust me."

Trust her! She undresses people for a living, and I'm supposed to trust her?

"I've put together a small box of toiletries for you. They're in this pouch, things like a toothbrush, toothpaste, shampoo, soap, and deodor-ant. You can get meal coupons for the cafeteria from the front desk."

She tried handing me the pouch of sundries, but I refused to ac-cept it.

"Okay," she said. "I'll just leave it here on the table for you. My phone number is on a calling card inside."

I watched her set the small pouch on the table next to my underwear.

"The bathrooms are down the hall, and there is a payphone on the wall next to them. Do you have any questions?"

"Yes! Where are my parents?"

I saw her shoulders slump, but she didn't answer my question. After what seemed a long silence, I gathered up my courage to ask, "Are they dead? Are my parents really dead?"

"Yes, Gertrude. They are," she said in a softer voice.

Her eyes looked sad, but I still hated her. I wondered if she knew how much I wanted to hit her, or pull her hair and dig my fingernails into her face, to do whatever I could to make her take back her words?

Our eyes locked, but she looked away and dragged the chair over to the window, where she turned her attention away from me and sat watching the falling snow. I continued sitting on the edge of the bed, glaring at the back of her head, thinking of all the ways I could hurt her. Finally, after what seemed like forever, I stood and walked over to stand next to her. We exchanged a look but neither of us said anything, each turning our attention to the silent fluff falling from the sky as it dressed the trees, the parked cars, and a large mound off to the left of the lot which was nothing more than a dilapidated Dumpster. But the snow made everything look clean and presentable. Even the Dumpster began looking as if it was a large chunk of alabaster waiting to be sculpted into something of beauty, which caused me to guess about the size of the chunk of marble Michelangelo may have used to carve The Pieta. *I wonder if it might have looked something similar to the Dumpster.* And then, I guessed about the likelihood of there being a question about The Pieta on tomorrow's art test?

Silently, I chastised myself for thinking about school, knowing instead I should be asking a thousand questions about my parents and the fire.

Yet, I really had only one question, a single selfish question, one I was ashamed to ask, but finally mustered the courage to do so.

"What's going to happen to me?" I heard myself whimper.

Instead of answering, Mrs. Duddelson stood and left the room, returning moments later holding two cardboard cups. "Here dear," she said handing one to me. "Let's try to get something warm into you."

I appreciated the warmth of the cup in my hand as I sipped the sweet hot chocolate. And then, I broke down and cried, finally accepting the reality of my parents' death.

"Gertrude, I'll try to answer all your questions tomorrow, but right now, I think you and I both need to get some sleep. I'd like to give you a sleeping pill and when I come back tomorrow, we can begin making plans. Would that be okay with you?"

I nodded my agreement, swallowed the pill, and asked no more questions. I watched her pick up her handbag and step toward the door, surprised by how heavy my eyelids felt.

"Good night, Gert. I'll see you in the morning."

She switched off the light and I barely remember hearing the click of the door as it closed behind her.

3

FACING THE WORLD

"I do not wish women to have power over men, but over themselves."

— MARY WOLLSTONECRAFT

I woke in a mass of bedsheets, confused, and lost in an unfamiliar bed in a strange room, with tiny snippets of the previous night gradually resurfacing as I struggled to reassemble the pieces.

I remembered my date with George and recalled seeing my father wink at me before I left with George in his loud car. And I recalled the missing floorboards in his car. How could I ever forget? And I remembered the movie we saw too, and how pleasing it was when George put his arm around me in the theater. And I felt myself smile when I recalled how George held my hand when we dashed across the street to a small diner, where we talked and ate fries. Those were all lovely events.

So, what went wrong? And why am I here instead of at home in my own bed?

I rubbed my eyes, massaged my temples, and tried to pull together the pieces, struggling to dredge up the portions of the night that I was having difficulty recalling.

Suddenly, it all came flooding back: the fire, the smoke, the cold, and my missing parents.

Oh my God! My parents! Did I ever find them?

Visions of the fire returned, and I remembered running toward the store while it was burning.

I think a police officer stopped me. Why would he stop me if I was only trying to find my parents? And why would he prevent me from doing that? I remember screaming at him. *Did I really scream at a police officer?* Why would I do that?

I remembered being cold, so very, very cold. And I remember ice water soaking into my shoes, and there was a strange woman bothering me, insisting my parents were dead.

DEAD! Are my parents dead?

Can that be true? Or did I dream that? Was that just a nightmare as a result of sleeping in this strange bed? But why am I here and not home in my own bed? I vaguely remember letting that woman give me a sleeping pill.

Why would I do that? And was it really only a sleeping pill? What if it was one of those bad drugs, like that LSD stuff I've read about, the illegal stuff that causes people to jump out of windows? Good grief, have I been kidnapped, drugged, and locked in here?

I bolted from the bed and lunged for the door.

Escape! Run before that woman returns and gives me more drugs.

My head spun in fright, nearly sending me to the floor, causing me to grope my way back to the bed, where I clung to the mattress until my head stopped spinning.

Breathe! Breathe in! Breathe out!

As the reality of the previous night slowly returned to me, I heard what I thought was an animal moaning in pain, shocked to realize the hideous sound had come from me.

Breathe! Slowly! Breathe in—breathe out.

When I was able to sit up without feeling dizzy or nausea, I saw my clothes draped over a table and chair across the room. My puffy crinoline looked as if it were about to perform a ballet, while my poodle skirt and sweater lay crumpled next to my exposed under-wear. Slowly, I crossed the room, dressed, and padded barefoot down the hallway in search of a bathroom. When I returned to my temporary room, I looked around more carefully, seeing what the room did and did not have, discovering it had no creature comforts other than the bed, not even a radio. What the room had was glaring sunlight that poured uninvited through the large window with no shade or draperies. Everything outside glistened with brilliance and whiteness that bounced off the surfaces with such intensity that it was painful to look outside without sunglasses. Even the branches of the pine trees were heavily ladened with snow that matched the sterile whiteness of the walls and mirrored the bleakness in my heart.

What am I supposed to do? Is there anyone I should call? If so, who would that be? There must be something I should be doing. But what?

I sat on the chair feeling lost and confused, searching for guidance or direction. Finally I remembered I was scheduled to take a test at school that morning.

I should call someone and let them know I won't be in class today? Yes, I'll call my friend Mary and tell her what happened and where I am. Hopefully she will invite me to come live with her until I know what I'm going to do.

With a renewed mission, I found my coin purse still neatly tucked in mother's jacket and exited the room in search of a payphone. I found one at the end of the hall and was relieved to have remembered Mary's phone number. I placed a dime in the proper slot and dialed.

"Hello, Mary?" I said with a shaky voice. "It's Gert." I launched directly into the reason for my call. "Mary, I'm in a bit of a jam." I explained to the best of my ability what had happened.

"Oh my gosh," she gasped. "Mom mentioned something about a fire in the Midway District, but I had no idea it was your store. It was even televised on the news last night. Well, I was about ready to leave for school. Do you want me to tell the professor you won't be in for the test today?"

I closed my eyes and bit back my tears.

"Yes, Mary, tell the professor I won't be in today, and tell her why too. Would you do that for me?"

"Sure, Gert. I'll tell her first thing, just as soon as I get to class."

I heard the click of the phone as Mary hung up, realizing she didn't even request a call back phone number or ask where I was. Wouldn't a friend have invited me to her home?

I returned to room number ten, my room for now, and threw myself back onto the bed with grief sliding right in behind me, wrapping me into its arms of anguish where I cried until the muscles across my shoulders ached.

Somehow, I managed to return to the bathroom, where I showered without a washcloth and air-dried myself without a towel by standing in front of the wall-mounted hand-dryer. I dressed and tried removing the white salt stains from my stiff leather loafers by dabbing at them with a wad of wetted soapy toilet paper, not unlike what my mother used to do when she washed the milk mustache off my face when I was a child.

Unfortunately, the salt stains didn't come off as easily as my milk mustache did. Another pair of shoes were ruined by water stains.

Like a robot, I checked the pockets of my mother's jacket and found the breakfast coupon the woman gave me last night. Without knowing what else to do, I took the elevator downstairs in search of coffee, where I saw a stack of newspapers on the counter of the front desk. The headline caught my attention with several black and white photos preceding a lengthy article.

"Arson Fire in Midway District—Two People Dead"

"Oh," I gasped and grabbed the counter to steady myself.

Just then, that Mrs. Duddleston woman appeared and put her arm around my waist to supply support. Our connecting eyes said it all, a communication of recognized pain and understanding.

"Could I have saved them if I wasn't on a date?" I asked her.

"You might have died with them."

I nodded, acknowledging the validity of her statement. "Do you think they suffered?"

"Don't go there, Gert. It won't help you and it won't change anything. We need to assume they fell asleep in the smoke. Try not to focus on the macabre. No one knows for sure what actually happened, and it won't do you or them any good if you focus on anything worse."

Again, I nodded without comment.

"Have you eaten anything?" she asked.

I shook my head, "No."

"Well, should we go in and get a cup of coffee and a little something to eat? Would that be good?" She guided me toward the cafeteria.

I watched as the server placed a bowl of oatmeal in front of me along with a cup of coffee, but I nearly gagged at the site of the lumpy gruel and pushed it aside where I didn't have to look at it. Coffee was all I could get down. After several cups, I began feeling better.

"Gert, we have a lot to do today and none of it is going to be easy. I know you haven't had an opportunity to mourn the loss of your parents yet. And in some ways, I suspect you may still be trying to accept that they're gone. I wish I didn't have to rush you with any of these things, but the reality is I need to help you concentrate on the things you're going to need right now."

I didn't comment on what she was saying, instead I nodded my understanding.

"You'll have time to mourn your loss later. Actually," she paused and took my hand in hers, "Gertrude, you may find you never stop mourning the loss of your parents, but I can promise you this. In time the pain will recede. Each day will become a little easier. But right now, we need to focus our attention on how you're going to live without them. I'm sure that's what they would have wanted for you. Don't you agree?"

My practicality helped me acknowledge the wisdom of her statement. And unlike the way I'd felt about her the previous night, I began appreciating her orderly manner and I welcomed her guidance. I knew I needed to have someone tell me what to do, because I no longer trusted my own thoughts or feelings. Mrs. Duddleson had become my strongest ally against the world. She provided me with vouchers for the Piggly Wiggly grocery store, where I could buy a few needed hygiene products, and she gave me several vouchers for the Salvation Army located across the street where I purchased a couple changes of clothing.

The biggest bonus of all was an insurance policy she was able to unearth from some bureaucratic records office, an insurance policy my parents had on the store. She contacted the company and made an appointment with an adjuster. On the day of the appointment, she drove me to his office with the hope of accessing money from the policy for me to live on.

"My condolences, miss," the adjuster said, leading us into his office. "Bad situation with your parents and all that." He motioned to the chairs he wanted us to sit in.

"Well, let's see here." He sat behind his desk, searching through several stacks of papers. "Ah yes. Here it is. It's Gertrude, isn't it? Your name. It's Gertrude, right?" He looked up with an expression that made me realize I was just one of the many little nuisances he'd be dealing with that day.

"Yes," I answered, nodding in the affirmative, acknowledging that Gertrude was indeed my proper name.

"I know this must be a bad time for you right now, but no need to worry because we'll get this all straightened out one way or another. Now, do you have a brother, uncle, or grandfather with whom we could transfer the funds from your parent's insurance policy?"

"No. I thought you already knew I don't have any relatives. It's just me."

"Ah yes, so I did. Hmm. I see." He looked perplexed.

"Couldn't you just put the money into a bank account for me to draw upon as I need it? Because, you see, I don't have any other money to live on. Actually, I won't be able to survive at all without the insurance money."

"No, I'm afraid not, little miss. It needs to be a male member of your family. Besides, you're not even a legal adult yet. You're still several months shy of being twenty-one, and even then, you'd still need a male family member to manage the account. You know how it is. Could there be a male guardian someplace you may have forgotten about? Perhaps a trusted friend of your parents, someone you may not have considered before." He looked up at me over his half-glasses.

"No, there's no guardian. It's just me."

He gave out a sigh, finally saying, "Well, I guess I could appoint a bank advocate to act on your behalf, but of course, he'd take a pretty good share of the money just to facilitate the account. Unfortunately, if we went down that path the money would become depleted fairly rapidly." He leaned back in his swivel chair. "Or have you considered getting married? We could release the money to a husband. Yes, a husband would certainly work! You could do that, you know! Just get yourself married. You're an attractive enough girl. That would certainly be the simplest way to deal with this."

Mrs. Duddleson hadn't said anything during the entire meeting, but when she saw me become flustered by the suggestion of my finding a husband, she spoke on my behalf.

"Thank you," she said to the adjuster. "We'll have to think about this." She shook his hand and guided me out of his office.

"Do you want to talk about the meeting?" she asked when we arrived back at her car.

I shook my head, and she didn't push the matter further. She started her car and we drove back to the YWCA in total silence.

I was fighting hard to prevent myself from breaking down in tears, determined to not give in to opening that floodgate again, feeling as if I'd already done enough crying. Now it was time for me to take charge of myself.

When we arrived at the YWCA, she parked in front and asked if I'd like to have her go upstairs with me.

"No, I think I want to be alone. But thank you." I opened the car door, climbed over a pile of freshly shoveled snow along the curb, and dragged my heavy feet up the icy sidewalk toward the front door of the YWCA.

The front door felt heavy to me as I entered the building. Once inside I carried my broken spirit across the lobby and headed directly to the elevators without stopping at the front desk. I was relieved to find the lobby empty, as I was in no mood to exchange pleasantries with anyone.

The elevator door opened, and I pushed the button for the second floor where I headed to the payphone at the end of the hall. I opened the phone booth door, sat down, and inserted my last dime into the proper slot before closing the door behind me. Carefully, I dialed a phone number I'd only recently memorized.

"Hello, George?" I said when he answered his phone. "Could we meet? I have something I'd like to talk over with you."

4

THE MORTGAGE LIFTER

"The Secret of change is to focus all your energy—
not fighting the old, but on building the new."

— SOCRATES

I had always balked at Mama's urgings to date when I was in high school, cringing at the thought of it because most of the guys had only one thing in mind, my breasts. Of course, I never told Mama my reason for avoiding boys in high school because I knew she would have been shocked, and I would have found the entire conversation totally embarrassing. But the reality is, I've had no earlier dating experience. George is the first guy I ever dated, and he was respectful, and he seemed interested in me, and that will have to be good enough. He even asked me what I was studying to become, which surprised me because I didn't know how to answer him.

I like him. Actually, I like him a lot. But do I love him? I don't know. I'm not even sure what love is supposed to feel like.

What I do know is my dream of wearing Grandma Gertrude's wedding dress, as Mama had done when she married Papa, the dress Mama kept in blue tissue paper in its own special box tucked under her bed, is a dream that can't be fulfilled. And the day I thought would be the most special day of my life, a day when my heart would burst with joy and happiness, a day when Papa would beam with pride as he walked me down the aisle isn't going to happen either. Neither will Mama be glowing with happiness as she sits in the front church pew, with a tear of joy in her eye. None of those things are going to happen. Those dreams are dashed forever and will remain an unfulfilled fantasy that vanished with the fire. Instead, I will marry George as a matter of practicality, wearing an inexpensive cream-colored dress I bought from Goodwill. And George, in all likelihood, will be wearing a poorly fitting sport jacket borrowed from someone at the frat house.

I scolded myself for yearning for things that could no longer happen and finished dressing for my wedding. Then I folded my few meager belongings and placed them in a reused Piggly Wiggly bag before rolling down the top of the bag to make a makeshift handle. I took one last glance at my YWCA bedroom, stepped into the hallway, and closed the door behind me before clicking across the marble floor in my Goodwill heels as I walked toward the elevator. I pushed the button for the lobby and headed to the front desk.

"I'm checking out today," I told the desk clerk. "Actually, I'm getting married."

He accepted the key silently with a nod.

I nodded back and stepped outside. George's car was sitting at the curb in front of the building. Carefully, I ambled down the icy sidewalk, trying to avoid turning an ankle because I wasn't used to wearing heels. I opened the car door, got in and tucked my Piggly Wiggly bag down into my lap. George's and my eyes met, but neither of us said anything. I wondered if he was having second thoughts. He stepped out of the car and pushed it a short distance to get it started and then we drove to the courthouse in silence, each of us contemplating the enormity of what we were about to do. Moments later we were standing in front of the Justice of the Peace.

"Do you, Gertrude, promise to love, honor, and obey . . .

"Do you, George, take this woman as your wedded wife, to love and to honor . . .

I hardly heard what the overweight man in the black robe said. I only knew we slipped plain gold bands onto each other's fingers and promised to love, honor, and obey. When George kissed me, I made an extra promise, I vowed to never look back, rationalizing this marriage couldn't be much different from arranged marriages all over the world. George seemed nice enough, and I did genuinely like him. In time I hoped I would love him.

After the wedding we went to his aunt's house.

"Welcome, my dear," Auntie said, giving me a light as a feather peck on my cheek. "George told me about your troubles, and I hope my humble home will provide you some much needed respite."

Then, she turned to George and said, "Go on George, take your wife's things upstairs."

To me she added, "Feel free to have a little look around, dear, and then you should get yourself washed up. I'll have dinner on the table shortly."

Ever so gently I cupped both her gnarled hands in mine and thanked her for letting us, me in particular, stay there.

George carried my Piggly Wiggly bag up the steep narrow attic steps, and I followed, holding onto the wooden handrail as I carefully navigated the steep stairs in my heels. I saw the single closet, which was packed with George's clothes, and searched for a couple of empty wire hangers so I could squish my few belongings into it. The entire room wasn't much larger than my room was at the YWCA and had a peaked wooden ceiling with exposed joists lining the roof of the house. A single bed was tucked under the sloping ceiling on the same side as the closet, while a large oak desk, cluttered with books, sat in the center of the room where the ceiling was highest. On the spine of one book, I saw the word "Fertilizers," on another was "Farm Management," and a third was about "Animal Nutrition." A broken lopsided desk drawer had papers spilling out, and a heavy oak chair was pushed into the knee hole. A bare light bulb hung over the desk from someplace up high at the peak of the ceiling. I slipped off my mother's leather jacket and hung it over the back of the desk chair.

On the wall opposite the bed was a large trunk. It looked as if it might be a cedar chest, but I didn't ask about it, assuming I'd have plenty of opportunity to explore its contents later. The single rectangular window, opposite the stairs, had a tan pull-down shade but no curtains. The view outside was the street below. Both the floor and the walls were unfinished wooden slats. My inspection, and my move into the attic room, took only a few moments.

Meanwhile, I could hear Auntie setting the plates on the table downstairs, and she began putting the food out as soon as George and I descended. Dinner conversation was light. I told her about my parents, my happier times in the store, and a little about the Home Economics classes I was studying in college. Somehow, I couldn't bring myself to tell her about the terrible way my parents died, but I suspected George had already explained all of that to her. She instinctively knew I wasn't ready to talk about any of that. Instead, she shared tales of her own, stories about financial hardships that she and her late husband faced when they were first married. I suspected she was trying to offer us hope.

The evening may not have been what most brides might expect on their wedding night, but it was warm and loving, and I appreciated Auntie's kindness and her welcome.

Just as George and I were about to go upstairs for the night, she said, "I hope you'll be all right up there. If you need anything just ask, but quite frankly my dears, I'm deaf as an old bat at night. I sleep pretty soundly you know." She winked at George, but I suspect it wasn't meant for me to see.

Once upstairs, George and I stood staring at the narrow bed, a metal frame thing with a thin mattress atop a mesh frame. A brightly colored woolen blanket of wide red, green, and yellow stripes covered it.

"Umm, gosh," George said blushing, which caused me to laugh.

Realizing it had been a long time since I had something to laugh about, I said, "We'll make it work, George. Don't worry, it'll be okay."

I changed into my Salvation Army nightgown, climbed into bed, and moved as close to the wall as I could, trying to leave space for George. He slid in behind me, wrapping his arm around my waist, mostly, I suspect, to avoid from falling off the outer edge of the bed.

"I feel like a pimento in a stuffed olive," I chuckled.

We giggled and eventually fell asleep, each trying to avoid moving our nested bodies, as neither of us thought Auntie was quite as deaf as she professed. Over the next few days, our bed nesting skills improved.

On Sunday I woke to a gloriously empty bed, one that offered all the room I wanted to stretch, as George had already gotten up. I rolled over, fully intending to go back to sleep, until I smelled something wonderfully sweet wafting up from downstairs. I got up, descended the steep staircase, and found George and Auntie at the breakfast nook, each reading separate sections of the Sunday newspaper.

"Good morning, everyone," I said. "What smells so delicious?"

George jumped up to give me a peck on the cheek and said, "Auntie made cinnamon rolls. They're in the kitchen. There's fresh coffee too."

"Help yourself, dear," Auntie added. "They need to be eaten while they're still nice and warm."

In the kitchen, I poured myself a cup of coffee and put a big gooey cinnamon roll onto a saucer before carrying both to the breakfast nook where I joined George and Auntie.

"This looks like a great hot-dish recipe," Auntie said, scanning the Home Section of the paper. "Hand me those scissors, will you, George? I think I'll clip this one out."

George did as she asked as he continued reading the want ads. I saw he was focused on the *Land for Sale* section.

"Look at this, Gert," he said. "There's a pig farm for sale in Steele County. I think we should drive down and take a look at it. We might be able to afford it once your insurance money is released."

"A pig farm!" I laughed, thinking he was joking."

"No, I'm serious. I'd like to see it."

"You do realize, I don't know anything about pigs, absolutely nothing at all. As far as I'm concerned, a pig is just walking bacon or a pork roast that a person prepares for a fancy Sunday meal. That's what I know about pigs. And besides, didn't you say your parents lost a lot of money farming, that the small family farm couldn't make it anymore?"

"My parents were crop farmers, Gert. This is a pig farm!" He said it as if he thought I'd grasp the difference.

"Ah," Auntie said, putting the newspaper down. "A mortgage lifter."

"Yes! Exactly!" George said.

"A what?" I asked, totally confused.

"Pig farms are referred to as 'mortgage lifters'," Auntie said, "because they are so lucrative that the owners are able to pay off their mortgage in a relatively brief time."

"Gert, this would be live animals," George explained further. "Animals aren't hampered by the weather like crops are. Animals just keep living, growing, and thriving regardless of the summer heat, torrential rains, or snow. They don't care if the land becomes bone dry, because they just drink out of their trough and continue eating whatever they're fed. They keep growing and growing 'till they go to market. It's perfect, Gert! It's everything I've ever dreamed of having."

"Oh," I said, feeling completely out of my element.

George called the phone number in the ad, and that very afternoon we drove to Steele County to visit the pig farm. He jabbered the entire trip as I listened to his one-way conversation, wondering what my parents, or Mrs. Duddleson for that matter, might have said about buying a pig farm.

I remember Mama telling me there would be things I would need to accept after I got married, things that a husband might not approve of about my young girlish attitude, but I was fairly certain, even she never dreamt it could involve a pig farm.

"This is just so exciting!" George kept repeating with a grin so wide that his face was totally dominated by his teeth. "I never dreamed I'd be able to get my own farm, not this early anyway. I hope they'll be fair about the price. Hopefully, they're desperate to get out from under it all as my parents were. Because a farm is a lot of work, especially when folks get older, and I got the impression over the phone that these people have been at it their whole lives. Most folks hope they'll have a son or two, someone who'll want to take over the farm. But sometimes there is no son, or the son may not be interested in the farm. Anyway, this is a great opportunity for us!"

His nonstop repetitive chatter was becoming more irritating with each mile we drove.

After several hours George suddenly exited the highway, turning onto a narrow two-lane county road lined with square and rectangular fields on both sides of the road. Some were green, others were tan, each was of a different texture. I had no idea what any of them were, nor was I inquisitive enough to inquire about them, but I knew I was smiling because the fields looked like a living quilt.

I was further amazed when George turned off the country road and entered a small side road, as all the roads looked alike to me. After a bumpy, muddy five-minute drive, trying to avoid as many water-filled potholes as we could, a mailbox nailed to a wooden post materialized amidst the endless rows of crops. Sure enough, the farmer's name was painted on the side of the box, with an arrow pointing toward the farm.

"How did you know to turn here?" I asked.

"I was reading the mile markers."

His matter-of-fact answer implied I shouldn't have had to ask such a silly question.

We bounced over more potholes and slowly drove up a long driveway. He was trying to avoid hitting the dogs who were barking and running circles around George's loud car. He parked on a gravel area near the front of the house and opened his car door.

"Don't, George!" I said. "Those dogs will bite you!"

"They're not going to bite me, Gert. They're just excited to see people."

"How do you know that?"

"Just look at them. They're wagging their tails."

"Oh," I said, embarrassed but still not completely convinced that the dogs were harmless.

George reached down to pet them before he came around to my side of the car to open the door. With caution I stepped out. The black and white fluffy one at once jumped on me, putting its muddy paws on the front of my skirt.

"Patsy!" a woman standing on the front porch shouted. "Get down and get over here! Yes, both of you. Come on now."

Upon hearing their owner's voice, the dogs loped over toward her.

"Now go lay down," she said, pointing her finger in the direction she wanted them to go. Then she turned to us, shaking her head. "I'm so sorry about that," she said and wiped her hands on her apron as she stepped down off the front porch. "Those dogs don't mean no harm. They're just excited to see people. I'm Susan. Are you the folks who called about seeing the farm? Come on up to the porch. I'll call my husband. He won't be but a few moments; he's just down with the pigs."

George and I seated ourselves in large wooden rocking chairs on the porch. When Susan's husband arrived, she disappeared into the house, reappearing moments later with a pitcher of fresh squeezed lemonade and a plate of oatmeal cookies.

I sat quietly, rocking ever so gently while listening to the men talk about pigs: how many they had, how often the pigs reproduced, their genetic improvement over the years, and the current market price for hogs. I was further confused when the conversation turned to a discussion about corn and oat fields. And they talked about the current Department of Agriculture rules and regulations. I heard every single word, overheard the name USDA mentioned several times, but didn't understand any of what they discussed. I knew how to run and manage a store, how to take inventory, and how to buy wholesale canned goods. I also knew a lot of household and domestic skills. But all the talk about USDA rules and regulations concerned things I had no knowledge of. I was bored with the entire conversation. But then, when they invited us inside to tour the house, my interest perked right up. The inside overwhelmed me. I'd never been inside such a grand spacious home before. Each room was beautifully furnished too. Auntie's house was nice, but nothing like this.

The kitchen was immense, as were the equally impressive appliances, all neatly lined up along one wall. The gas stove had six burners with two ovens. There was a long rectangular table covered with an embroidered tablecloth, with six tall straight-backed chairs neatly tucked in place, three on each side. In the center of the table sat a large ceramic bowl filled with lemons.

On the wall opposite the appliances was a deep white sink with a long side drain. A pump handle was mounted on the back. I wondered if it was used for pumping well water, but I didn't think it was my place to ask.

Off to one side of the kitchen was a tiny room, about the size of a closet. But unlike a closet, it had a second door, which I assumed led to the working part of the farm, as I'd noticed there were boots lined up on a mat, jackets hanging on wall hooks, and the outline of hand tools painted on one wall with hooks to hold the tools.

The combination living room/dining room, found off to the other side of the kitchen was huge, twice the size of my parents' entire living space behind the store. The dining room had a round oak table with six more chairs, all positioned neatly around it.

The adjoining living room had a massive stone fireplace that extended all the way up to the ceiling with easy chairs placed on each side. A country print covered the chairs, with a pleated skirt hiding the chair legs, and a matching sofa sat opposite them. Next to the sofa was a maple rocker with a knitting basket sitting on the floor.

There was a television too. It had aluminum foil wrapped around a rabbit ear antenna, and was positioned on a low table in such a manner as to accommodate viewing from most of the seating in the room. Behind the living and dining rooms I spied two bedrooms and a bathroom. Susan led us upstairs where we saw two more bedrooms, each neatly made up and decorated. One had a blue theme. The other was yellow.

I loved the house and couldn't imagine ever living in such a spacious grand home. I was so enthralled with looking at everything in the house that I hadn't noticed the men had disappeared. Not until Susan and I returned downstairs did I notice they were gone.

"Where did my husband go?" I asked, alarmed to realize George was nowhere in sight.

"The menfolk are out in back looking at the animals. Should we return to the porch, or did you want to have a peek at the pig pens?"

My answer was a smile, as I returned to the porch where I repositioned myself in the same rocking chair I'd sat in earlier.

"I'll bring out more lemonade," Susan said. "It's so pleasant sitting outside these last few warm days of autumn."

While she was busy inside, I looked out at the property with renewed interest. The yard had several large oak trees, each dropping red, orange, and yellow leaves on the spacious manicured lawn. The dogs that had previously frightened me were sprawled on their sides in a spot of dappled sunshine, no longer interested in me.

"Here we are," Susan said, setting the pitcher down on the table behind us.

To make small talk, I said, "It doesn't look like you've had any snow here."

"No, not yet," she said. "But I heard they got some up north in the cities. We're just a little further south, you know. So the winters down here aren't as severe as up north."

"Hmm," I said, nodding my head in acknowledgment as I continued sipping my lemonade.

"Folks up north always have it worse than we do down here."

I smiled and continued nodding, choosing not to elaborate on the snowstorm that had recently taken place the night my parents died in the fire.

Instead, I changed the subject and told Susan her lemonade was fantastic.

"Thanks," she said. "Glad you like it. The lemons are from our local Piggly Wiggly in town."

I was running out of trivia to talk about and felt relieved when George and John returned from the pig pens. I saw George wipe mud off his shoes in the grass. Then they shook hands and George thanked them for their hospitality.

"I'll be in touch," George added.

We returned to the car and headed for home. "Well?" I asked. "What happened?"

"We settled on a price. And I told them we'd buy it as soon as I get your insurance money."

"You decided that all by yourself, without waiting to even talk it over with me?"

"What's to talk about, Gert? You knew why we were coming here. I negotiated a fair price. It's a done deal. They're even going to leave most of the furniture because they're moving across country to an apartment in Washington, DC, where their daughter lives."

I found myself twisting my wedding band on my finger, stunned by what had just happened, causing me to become increasingly irritated by George's rickety car as it rattled along the highway sounding more like a stack of metal pots nested precariously in my mother's cupboard.

What have I gotten myself into? Doesn't George respect me enough to even discuss with me how my money is going to be used?

The realization that I had lost all control over how my money was going to be used was a shock, because not until that moment was I aware that my money belonged to George from the moment he married me. I, of course, had no way of knowing if George negotiated a good deal or not, because even if he told me the price, I didn't know anything about the value of farm property. Neither did I know where to find such information. I knew how to run a convenience store, but I knew nothing about farms.

We were both deep in thought on our trip back home, and George was reluctant to discuss any of the financial details with me.

"George," I finally spoke up. "You do realize I've never seen a live pig up close, don't you?"

"Well, you'll be seeing a lot of them once we own them." He chuckled and patted my knee. "And we'll be growing a little corn and oats too, but just enough to feed the pigs, not a huge field for market purposes."

"George, I don't know how to grow *anything*, including oats and corn. Oats in my experience are something I measure out of a round Quaker Oats box when I want to cook breakfast. And corn is something I pick up from the corner vegetable stand in late summer, or, in the winter, I buy it in a can, cans that were previously on grocery store shelves."

"You won't be doing the growing, Gert. I'll be the one doing that. We grew a lot of it on my parents' farm, so that's going to be the easy part."

The easy part? I shuddered to think what he considered the hard part might be.

As I was mulling that over, George sprang one more surprise upon me.

"Oh, by the way," he said, "there are two cows that come with the property too."

"Cows? I thought it was a pig farm."

"It is a pig farm, Gert, but there are a couple of cows that come with it too. John said he uses a hand separator to collect the cream after he milks them and sells the cream to the local creamery. They use it for butter. But the real kicker is that he mixes the leftover skim milk with the pig slop, which he claims makes his pigs bigger and healthier than the competition. He says it's the milk that helps him get top dollar for his pigs. Isn't that interesting? I'd have never thought of that!"

"Pigs, cows, corn and who knows what else you haven't told me, George. Don't you understand? I don't want any of this! None of it! I want us to use my money to buy another convenience store, like the one my parents owned, possibly we could even purchase a larger one than theirs if we are able to find one for sale. I know how to run a store, George. I'm good at it, but I don't know anything about farming."

"Gert, we can't buy a store because I don't know anything about them. I wouldn't know the first thing about managing a store. What I know is farming. You knew that when you married me. All my training has been about farming. That's what I know, and you've married a farmer."

What have I done? Why would it be more outlandish for me to expect George to learn how to run a store than it is him to expect me to learn about farming? Is that so unrealistic? And if we do this farm thing, does that mean we will both be dropping out of school? I guess it does if we are planning to run a farm, hours away from the University.

Well, this may be George's dream, but it was **not** mine!

The crawl of time and the loud silence between us as we drove back to Auntie's that day was torture, not to mention a whole lot of confusion on my part.

5

FARM LIFE

"Happiness is not a goal. It is a byproduct."

— Eleanor Roosevelt

That night at Auntie's we remained polite with each other but in a stiff manner, hardly talking at all other than to ask if someone would pass the salt or something like that. I'm sure Auntie felt our tension, but she pretended not to notice. When it was time to go upstairs, George and I repeated the order we'd gotten into the bed the previous night as we pretended nothing had changed. I got into the bed and moved all the way to the wall so George could get in behind me. I thought we might discuss the situation more once we were in bed, but that didn't happen. In fact, I was surprised at how quickly George fell asleep, but not me. Oh no, not me! My head remained busy, jumping this way and that with one conflicting thought after another. I tried to lie still, but my busy brain fired like rapid gunfire.

I listened to George's steady even breathing, not knowing if I admired his ability to sleep or hated him for it.

I swear, that man falls asleep the moment his head hits the pillow.

I wondered what Mrs. Duddleston might have to say about this.

Would she encourage me to follow my husband's lead, to go along with the purchase of the farm and start my life anew? Maybe I should call her in the morning to get her feedback. Still, I hated the idea of bothering her knowing she was likely helping someone else, someone who may be as desperate as I was that first night when she first helped me. What could she do anyway? She couldn't end my marriage.

Could she? And if she could, would she be able to get my money back for me?

I took a deep breath, exhaled slowly, and wished I could bend my knees. Ever so little would help, just enough to ease my back. Instead, I forced myself to remain plank still and wondered if pig farmers were allowed to count sheep.

Okay, stop it now! Things could be a lot worse. I've just got to make this work.

What was it Mrs. Duddelson said? Let's see. I think she told me, that in her experience when people have an intimate relationship with death, they can sometimes look upon it as a gift, if they let it. She told me I should let my parents' death teach me how important it is to live, and to live my life well. I'm sure she's right about that, but does it have to involve pigs and cows?

I sighed softly, pushing a pesky stray hair away from my face, a hair that had been tickling my nose.

I'm not even sure how I'm going to handle being married and having a husband make all my decisions for me. I guess that's what Mama meant when she used to scold Papa for letting me have so much freedom. Being a wife is going to be difficult enough, but I can't even imagine how I'm going to learn how to deal with farm life!

I brushed that same pesky hair away from my nose for the second time, or maybe it was the third, finally drifting off to a fitful sleep.

A few days later, George went to the bank and signed the required papers to buy the farm. Because I was still not happy about the purchase of the farm, he told me I didn't need to go with him if I didn't want to. So I stayed home and pouted. We moved into the farmhouse the following day.

Luckily, the sale included nearly all the household furnishings, making our physical move into the farmhouse extremely easy. The only items we moved ourselves were George's college books and our few articles of clothing. Even that was mostly George's stuff because I still only owned a few secondhand items from the Salvation Army, all except for my mother's suede jacket.

After our move, I watched George work with the animals, determined to learn how to deal with the creatures. I decided I didn't have to like them, I only needed to know how to deal with them. By emulating George, I learned how to mix the slop, feed the pigs, and milk the cows. And after getting knocked down a couple of times by the overly zealous hungry creatures, I learned how to outmaneuver them when I brought their slop pail down to the pens. The cows were easier. I just needed to clamp the machine to their teats and the machine did all the work. The only problem with the cows was that they expected to be milked on a very precise daily schedule.

It was no surprise to me that the task I was most skilled at was that of keeping track of our finances. I set up a ledger book and logged our expenses (animal food, vet bills, etc.) I also listed the exact number of pigs we owned, kept track of how rapidly they grew, and quickly discovered what age was the most profitable time to sell them. George was impressed when I showed him my account book and he let me manage all of our expenses while he did the lion's share of tending to the day-to-day tasks.

Surprisingly, the thing I was most unprepared for was the social life expectations when local residents began dropping by the farmhouse unannounced to visit. They came uninvited at any old time of day, but mostly they arrived mid-morning. They'd show up at our door with leaflets and pamphlets in hand, each pitching some organization or worthwhile cause.

I felt pressured to be properly dressed and always prepared for these impromptu visits, which was counterproductive to what I thought I should be doing to help George and the animals.

The first of the visitors were three women from the Ladies' Guild.

Then, there were several who stopped by to issue an invitation to the Extension Club meetings, and there was Mrs. Peterson, the widow who lived on the adjacent farm. She, at least, brought a jar of homemade strawberry jam when she stopped in to introduce herself.

But my most memorable visitors were the local minister and his wife. They rang the bell on our front porch the same as all the others. But when I opened the door, he and the Mrs. were both looking up into the sky with their arms straight up in the air.

I gasped when I saw them.

"Good morning, Mrs. Johnson," the minister said with a melodious voice. "It's a glorious day for God's work, is it not?"

"Indeed, it is," I said, trying to refrain from laughing.

Then as they lowered their arms, he said, "The Mrs. and I just stopped by to welcome you to our church."

I must admit they did bring a smile to my face. In fact, I had to pinch myself to avoid from laughing out loud. I invited them into our living room, brewed a fresh pot of coffee, and brought out several slices of coffee cake that I'd made the previous day.

"Will the Mister be able to join us?" the minister asked as I set the tray down with only three cups.

"No, he's out in back milking the cows and tending to the pigs. He has to keep them all on their schedule, you know."

"Ah, yes. The animals are God's creatures too. Aren't they? Yes, indeed they are."

This entire time, his wife sat silently next to him. She didn't drink any coffee or reach for any of the refreshments I'd set before them. She just sat there wearing the same smile she'd arrived with, as if her face might break if she stopped smiling.

Meanwhile, the minister drank his coffee in gulps and talked nonstop.

"Did you sing or play the organ in your previous church, Mrs. Johnson?" he asked.

"No, I never learned how to play an instrument, and I haven't sung anything since high school."

"Well, how about Sunday school? Have you taught Sunday school?"

"No, I'm afraid I haven't done that either. In fact, I wasn't very involved in our church. I did attend with my parents occasionally, but my family wasn't really very active with the church. Occasionally I sung with the choir for some of the holidays, but that's all."

"Pity," he said, "yes indeed it is, because we could use another Sunday school teacher, and our organist is getting up in years so she could use a backup now and again. Yes indeed." He clicked his tongue to the top of his mouth. "It really is a shame you can't help us with either of those things. Indeed, it is."

I didn't know what to say, so I just smiled and watched him reach for his wife's coffee cake and devour it.

He washed the last bit of it down with his coffee and cleared his throat. "Well, do tell us, Mrs. Johnson. What can you contribute to our church? There must be something you can do."

He didn't wait for me to answer. Instead he launched into the next phase of his one-way conversation.

"Of course, there's always the Ladies' Guild. They can always use help visiting the sick and infirm. They also knit baby hats and booties for our new mothers, and of course there's the orphanage at the other end of town. Those children can always use mended clothing and knitted items. Oh, yes, I'm sure you have many talents you'll be able to contribute. We just need to discover what they are."

When I didn't offer to put another pot of coffee on, he stood in preparation to leave. On the way to the door, he repeated the times of the Sunday services. Finally, just as they were stepping out onto the front porch, his wife spoke for the first time.

"Thank you for your hospitality," she said in the tiniest little squeaky voice I'd ever heard come from a grown woman.

The next day the church choir director came roaring up the drive on his motorcycle.

"Mrs. Johnson," he said in an excited rush just as I was about to go out to the pig pen. "So sorry to just pop in like this, but our minister mentioned that you did some singing before you came here. I'm so hoping to learn you're an alto. We desperately need one more alto in our choir."

I set the pig slop bucket down. "I'm so sorry to disappoint. I'm a soprano, not an alto."

"Ah, I'm so sorry then for interrupting your day."

I watched his hopeful smile evaporate. With that he slid his goggles back down over his eyes and roared back down our driveway.

That was our last impromptu visit, which was a huge relief because I began feeling sick every morning. By noon I felt better, but again in the evening certain aromas seemed to bring on more nausea. I found I could either cook dinner or eat it, but I couldn't do both. I could only eat something if I hadn't previously smelled it. A trip to the doctor informed me I was pregnant.

"It's just a simple case of morning sickness," the doctor said.

I drove home thinking there was nothing simple about it at all, and I wished more than ever that my mother were alive to counsel and guide me.

I gave birth to a healthy eight-pound boy. George was ecstatic, as was I, and from the first moment I held our newborn son my heart swelled, filling all the voids I'd been missing since the fire. Our son gave me a reason to feel happiness again.

Our baby was perfect—Dr. Spock perfect. We named him Jason Herman Johnson, Jason after George's father and Herman after mine. He was healthy, strong, and alert and I loved holding him. There were times early on when I sat rocking and nursing him a lot longer than needed just because I enjoyed gazing at the wonder of him. When his eyes began to focus on things, I watched him reach up trying to touch my nose, grab the portable mobiles above his crib, or grasp a rattle a few inches from his hand. He was bright and inquisitive, and I loved watching his eyes when they followed me around a room.

When he first rolled over, I clapped my hands in joy. When he learned to sit up, crawl, stand, and finally take his first steps, I hovered over him, ready to protect him from his inevitable fall. My life was so wrapped up in our beautiful son, that when he had his first birthday, I wondered where the year had gone. And then, in what seemed like no more than a blink, he was a toddler and lost all interest in spending his days with me, preferring to follow his father around the farm, doing the things men and boys do, which left me with a profound sense of loss.

My duties shifted from being Jason's cheerleader to becoming his and George's housekeeper, cook, and bookkeeper. But then, one day when Jason was older, he brought a runt piglet into the kitchen.

"Mom," he said, holding a tiny piglet in his hands. "Where are my old baby bottles?"

"What do you want with a baby bottle, Jason? And why is that piglet in the house?"

"It's a runt, Mom, and the sow is refusing to nurse it. She just wants to let it die."

"Well, let it die, Jason. That's nature's way. The sow knows what she's doing. She needs to reserve her milk for the piglets who have the best chance to survive. You know that. You shouldn't try to fight Mother Nature."

I had learned a few things since living on the farm and one of them was to never bring an animal into the house, especially one that will eventually go to slaughter.

"No!" Jason stuck his chin out in defiance. "I'm going to nurse and take care of it myself. And I'll find my old baby bottles by myself too."

He stomped upstairs, still holding the small creature in his hands while searching for his old bottles. Why I'd saved them I have no idea.

"Jason," I shouted upstairs, relenting upon my earlier statement. "I think they're in the yellow bedroom closet."

When Jason returned to the kitchen with bottle and piglet in hand, he filled the bottle with cow's milk, still warm from the cow, that he'd left in a container on the back porch, and let the little creature guzzle greedily. When it was full and seemed content, he put it into a small nesting box he'd already hauled up from the barn and pushed the box into a far corner under the kitchen sink away from any draft.

"I'm going to call her Priscilla," he said, covering the little creature with one of his old baby blankets.

The piglet had a good appetite, I'll give it that, but why I let Jason disregard my stance on keeping animals out of the house was a puzzle even to me. I suspect it was because I knew Jason would want to spend more time with me at the house if he was caring for a piglet. Whatever the reason, I let him keep the tiny creature, and I even found myself feeding it during the long stretch when Jason was in school. When Priscilla was large enough to eat solid food from a pig trough, Jason returned it to the adolescent pen with its siblings. But he made it perfectly clear to both his father and me, Priscilla was not ever to be taken to market and sold. She was his pet and had become a pig with status.

I must admit I agreed with Jason on that topic, because I too had become attached to her. She'd developed a personality more like that of a loyal dog, looking up at both Jason and me with loving trusting eyes. I'm embarrassed to admit that I missed her when she was large enough to be with the others out in the pen.

6

POWERLESSNESS

"We realize the importance of our voice when we are silenced."

— MALALA YOUSAFZAI

I'm not sure where all the years went, but Jason seemed to have shot up overnight. He'd become tall, strong, and handsome and would begin his senior year this fall.

Classes weren't scheduled to begin for a couple more weeks, but the school was holding tryouts for the football team today, and Jason had been talking about applying for the team all summer. I worried needlessly for the better part of the day, hoping he wouldn't be too terribly disappointed if he wasn't selected.

"Mom, Dad," Jason said as he bounced through the kitchen screen door linebacker style, letting the door slam behind him, again. "I made the team! I did it! Practice begins tomorrow!"

"Congratulations," George answered from the mud room off the kitchen, where he'd already parked his boots on the mat and was in the process of emptying his pockets from the tools he'd carried with him that day. "I know you're excited, but good God, Jason, do you always have to let the door slam behind you every time you enter this house? It's enough to knock your mother's plates off the wall."

I'd heard the same script for years and simply shook my head, knowing nothing would change. Jason would continue slamming the door and George would resume his admonishments.

"Sorry, Dad, but making the football team is, well, it's just the best thing that's ever happened to me. I'm so jazzed I can hardly stand still!"

"That's all good and fine, son, but don't think for one moment that you can slack off from your duties around here just because of football. The animals won't care if you're some big fancy football jock or not. They just want to be fed each day."

"Yeah, I know, Dad. About that . . ."

I immediately heard the change in Jason's voice, but George hadn't picked up on it yet. He was still concentrating on methodically placing his tools on their proper pegs where he'd circled the outline of each one on the wall. It was a ritual that never varied.

"Well, you see, um, football practice starts in three days. And ah, it'll go on every day right up until school starts, and for the rest of the season too." He paused to let the statement settle.

"What are you trying to say, Jason?" George asked, finally stepping stocking footed into the kitchen now that he had returned all his tools properly to their specific peg.

"Well, it kind of means I won't be able to go to the State Fair with you this year."

Silence, stone cold silence, sucked the oxygen from the room, leaving the three of us standing rigid as garden posts in the middle of the kitchen. No one spoke for what felt like an eternity.

Finally, Jason broke the silence. "But I'll still get up early and do my chores each day. I just won't be able to go to the fair with you this year. That's all."

"Oh!" George grinned with a grin like the Cheshire cat slowly creeping across his face. "Now that does present a different kettle of fish, now don't it?" He looked directly at me. "Well, I'll just have to take your mother with me this year."

"Me!" I gasped. "Oh no! I don't think so! That's a man's trip. The trip to the fair isn't for me!"

"What do you mean it's a man's trip? You're as good with the pigs these days as we are. Anyway, it'll be fun, just the two of us, like it used to be."

"No, George, it was never the two of us with the pigs and you know that! It was the two of us *before* the pigs, but not *with* the pigs. I do what I need to do with them. I can manage them, but just barely. You know very well they are not my favorite creatures!"

George just tipped his head, smiling and pointing his crooked index finger at me in his cocky, overconfident manner. "Yup, Gert, you're going to the fair with me this year."

"No, George, I don't want to go! I don't ever want to go near that corner where my parents died, and I know we'd have to drive right past it. Besides, I look forward to my alone time here when you're gone. That's when I'm able to begin my next quilt. I don't want to go with you."

George's mannerism and tone immediately changed from one of humor to cold authority. "Gert, it's time you got over that fire. That happened twenty years ago, and I doubt if you would even recognize that intersection anymore because it has changed so much. And as far as your two weeks are concerned, well you just won't have them this year because I need you to be with me. And I don't think that's too much to expect from you!"

Jason slithered out of the kitchen, mumbling something about going to his room to study the football manual. I'm glad he left because it's not good for a child to see and hear his parents quarreling.

George avoided further eye contact with me and stepped over to the sink to wash up. His expression had become stone hard, and I saw the muscles clench in his jaw as he dried his hands.

"Call me when dinner is ready." He turned to head toward the living room. "I'm going to catch a little of the news."

He exited the kitchen, leaving me standing in front of the stove to cook his dinner and stew in my anger. Once again, I'd lost control over my own destiny.

When dinner was ready, I called both of them to the table, hoping George may have mellowed and that we'd be able to discuss the trip further. I thought if we talked about it, we'd find some other workable alternative. But there was no discussion at the table about anything at all, not about the fair, not about the football tryouts, and not about any of the animals. There was only an uncomfortable silence as George and Jason each inhaled their food and left the table as soon as they'd finished eating.

My stomach tightened as I wondered why I always made life more difficult for myself than it needed to be. Why didn't I just go with the flow and accept things the way they were. But no, I had to get stubborn and say I didn't want to go to the State Fair with George, knowing full well I'd have to relent and give in eventually anyway.

And then I began to wonder, did other wives argue with their husbands, because I couldn't recall there ever being a real disagreement between my parents. My girlhood recollection was of them mostly trying to please each other, but surely there must have been little spats between them as well.

Heck, even the Electrolux ads on television claimed wives glowed with happiness when they were taking care of their family, especially when they were using an Electrolux. Well, I didn't have an Electrolux, but even if I did, I doubted vacuuming would thrill me because I've never found satisfaction in cleaning and devoting my existence to mundane matters, regardless of the appliance or tool I use. And I hated feeling powerless and having so little control over my destiny. I've always wanted to be more than a human machine to be plugged in when needed. I wanted some purpose or meaning to my life and future, and escorting a truckload of pigs to the fair wasn't something I wanted to do at all.

Gradually, however, over the next few days, I worked at mellowing my attitude. Eventually I warmed to the idea of making the trip by forming my own agenda for the times when George wouldn't need my help.

On the morning of our exodus, the day before the State Fair opened, all three of us were up at the first gray of daylight. To assuage his guilt for bailing on this trip, Jason had already loaded the pigs into the back of the truck without being asked to do so. While he was finishing up George kept firing last-minute instructions at him. I couldn't resist chuckling, because not until then did I realize how uneasy George was about leaving Jason in charge of the farm. Logically we both had the utmost confidence in our son, but this was the first time he would be left entirely alone in complete control of everything.

"I know, Dad!" Jason kept saying. "I know all of that. You've been telling me all those same things for the past week. Don't worry. I've got it all under control. Just go. Have a good time."

"Yeah, sorry, Jason. I know I sound like a broken record. You know I have complete confidence in you though, don't you? But there are ever so many things that could go wrong, and besides. Well, I'm going to miss you." He slapped Jason lightly on the shoulder. "It's always just been the two of us on this trip, ever since, oh gosh, since you were eight or ten years old, I guess."

"I know, Dad, but stop worrying because nothing's going to go wrong. Just go, have a good time. The rest of the pigs, cows and those nasty chickens of Mom's will all be fine."

"Nasty chickens, indeed," I said, raising one eyebrow at him much like my mother used to do with me. "You still have to feed them, you know. You can't skip feeding them just because you don't like them."

"I know," he said with that silly little grin of his, as he wrinkled his nose at me in a playful gesture. "Don't worry. I won't forget to feed your devil chickens."

I gave him a hug and told him again about the prepared meals I'd placed in the freezer for him. "They're all individually packaged. Just remove one each morning and place it in the refrigerator. That'll give it enough time to thaw, and it'll be ready for you to pop into the oven by the time you want to eat at dinner time. Let it bake for about 30 minutes at 350 degrees."

"I know, Mom! You've told me all that before and you have it all written down, and no, you don't need to worry about your nasty chickens. I swear though, they don't like me."

"That's because you tantalize them, Jason, and you know you do. Just try to be nice to them for a change. You might be surprised."

I gave Jason a big hug before climbing up into the cab of the truck where I'd repositioned my large leather bag that I'd previously parked on the seat.

George tossed his duffle bag behind his seat and climbed into the driver's side of the truck.

"Where's your suitcase, Gert?"

"I don't have one. Instead, I've organized everything I'll need for a few days in this bag. I even managed to stuff in my rolled-up quilt, the one I'm planning to enter in the quilting competition. It's at the bottom of the bag."

George looked at me bug-eyed and slack-jawed. I knew he was trying to absorb what I had said. Then, he closed his mouth and swallowed, but he continued looking at me with a confused expression.

So, I explained further. "I won't need very much for the first few days, George. Just a few essentials, and I've put those on the top of my bag. Once everything is set up, I'm planning to go shopping. I'm going to buy all new clothes for myself. I might even buy one of those new chemise dresses, you know, the ones with no waistline. They've become very popular with the ladies at church."

George blinked but still looked confused, so I continued. "I need to buy a new suitcase too, George, because the handle of my old one is broken and falling off. But don't worry, I'll wait until we have the pigs all settled before I go into town."

"Really!?" George said with a gasp. "That doesn't sound like you, old girl. Am I to assume you have the money for all this?"

"Yes, I have my egg money."

"Well, blow me over with a feather. I would never have guessed such a thing from you. But, good on you!"

George gave a little whistle and shook his head before giving it a slight scratch, allowing himself a moment or two more to think about what I'd just told him. Then he cleared his throat, turned the key in the ignition, and didn't utter another word before driving off.

7

THE TRIP

"Risk is trying to control something you are powerless over."

—Eric Clapton

George bounced the wheels of the truck onto the uneven pavement of the narrow country road at the end of our property line. It was a section of road where the highway department had recently added blacktop curbing. The curbs were supposed to prevent vehicles from flying off the highway and skidding into the surrounding farmland, but, in my opinion, the curbing made the highway doubly hazardous for wide trucks such as ours, because if a wheel so much as touched one of those curbs, the truck was tossed toward the middle of the road and into oncoming traffic. Even in my small DeSoto I hated driving on this section of road, and I could only imagine how challenging it was for George to drive our wide truck.

Just as I pondered that thought, a wheel must have touched one of those curbs, because I felt the truck lurch toward the center with no warning. Luckily, George had a good grip on the wheel and kept control, but I could hear the pigs vocalizing their displeasure from the jolt.

"Shit!" George said. "I hate this section of road! I hope to bloody hell nobody's coming the other way, especially another truck or piece of wide farm equipment."

"I know what you mean. I don't even like driving this section in my little car."

"You'd think it might get easier over time. But it never does."

I murmured something of support while trying to avoid distracting him, realizing he needed to remain totally focused.

While George drove, I settled in as comfortably as I could with the silence, enjoying the rare treat to sit perfectly still without jumping up to begin another task. I had nothing to do but enjoy watching the farms glide past my window as I listened to the sounds of the tires on the pavement and the pigs complaining in the back. As I gazed out the window, I noted what others along the road had done with their barns, the height of their remaining crops, and the condition of the already harvested fields. Fields of yellow, green, and tan where the land was flat and never seemed to end. All seemed serene and peaceful until I smelled something awful.

"Phew! Did we just run over a skunk?"

"Yup," George said. "He was already dead, and I couldn't avoid running over him, probably got hit sometime last night."

At 6:30 George turned on the radio to listen to the farm report on WCCO, 830 on the dial. At home, our clock radio was set for that station as our morning wake-up call.

30% chance of thunderstorms, then sunny and hot. Low of 72 degrees Fahrenheit.

Closing market prices:

- *Corn is trading at $1.54 per bushel – down 5%.*
- *Wheat is trading at $2.40 per bushel –up 22%.*
- *Pork bellies trading at $63.85 – up 8%.*

After the weather and farm market report *The Prairie Home Companion* show came on with the melodic voice of Garrison Keillor. We both enjoyed Garrison's local humor and the spoofs featuring The Kitty Boutique and Ralph's Pretty Good Grocery Store with the motto of "if we don't have it, you don't need it."

As the day wore on and the sun climbed higher in the sky, the temperature in the truck rose as well. It had been chilly when we left that morning in the near dark, but now the air began feeling clammy.

"I brought a thermos of coffee and a jar of lemonade, if you'd like either?" I said, as I removed the thermos and jar from under my seat where I'd stashed them.

"That sounds pretty good, Gert, and mighty nice of you to do that too."

"It was a simple thing to do, George." I handed him the thermos of coffee. We took turns drinking directly from it.

"Yup, really nice." George passed the thermos back to me. "I'm glad you came with me this year, Gert. Remember how it was when we were young? This is like it used to be before we bought the farm and before Jason was born, just the two of us going down the road together enjoying each other's company. It's going to be a 'funny moon' for us, Gert."

"A funny moon, George? What on earth are you talking about? There's no such thing as a funny moon."

"You know, Gert, sort of a honeymoon, but it's going to be more fun." George laughed, thinking he'd said something terribly brilliant considering we'd never had a honeymoon in the first place.

"That's nice," I chuckled, realizing I was indeed beginning to enjoy myself. "That was nice of you to say that."

After a long, comfortable silence, I inquired about the signs I was seeing along the side of the road.

"They don't mean much. They're just advertising for Burma Shaving Cream. Some of 'em are pretty clever though. I suppose you never get out this far and haven't had much of a chance to see them."

We began reading the signs together, anticipating when the next one would appear, as they were usually spaced one mile apart:

The Midnight Ride
Of Paul
For Beer
Led To A
Warmer Hemisphere

—Burma-Shave

Ashes to Ashes
Forest to Dust
Keep Minnesota Green
Or We'll All Go Bust

—Burma-Shave

Soon we were both laughing and reminiscing about our dating years, a time prior to the fire and all the pressures of the farm. George and I finished the thermos of coffee and began sipping on the lemonade, passing that jar back and forth to each other as well.

"How come you agreed to marry me?" I asked him out of the clear blue. "I know you could have held out for one of those pretty girls because you were very handsome, you know, and funny too. I knew some of the girls who flirted with you, you know. Was it just the money from my insurance? Was that the only reason you married me?"

"No, Gert, it wasn't just the money. Although that did come to us at an opportune time. Those other girls may have been pretty, but they had nothing but fluff between their ears. I wanted a gal who was more than that. I wanted someone who would be my partner, someone I could buy a farm with, and someone who would stand by me. And anyway, who says you weren't pretty? You were just as pretty as any of any of them."

I felt myself blush as I took another sip of lemonade.

"What about you, old girl? Why did you marry me? I was never as smart as you were in school, and I had that old car, and let's face it, there weren't many girls who would be happy about moving to a pig farm in Southern Minnesota."

"Well," I said, "I never really dated anyone before, and you were the only person who ever asked me what I wanted to become someday. No one had ever asked that. Anyway, a couple of those other guys you hung around with were real jerks. Remember Robby? He was terrible to all us girls."

"Yeah, I know." George laughed.

"What's so funny about that?" I asked.

"Oh, I was just thinking about the time Robby had that snake in his bed."

"Oh, that's right. We all heard about that. That was the funniest thing ever! I always wondered how it got there."

"I put it there," George said.

"You put the snake in Robby's bed? It was you? How did you do that?"

George could hardly stop laughing as he told me about the incident from his college days so long ago.

"Well, one day I found this harmless little garter snake. I picked it up, not knowing what I was going to do with it. I put it in my jacket pocket and never mentioned it to anyone. In fact, I forgot about it being in there, but that night I was staying at the frat house and Robby started acting up and being a real jerk to one of the other guys who lived there. Robby began picking on him just because the guy was smart and wore glasses. Robby was dumb, you know, and he never felt comfortable being around anyone who was smarter than him. Anyway, this little guy wore thick glasses, and he was very smart and nerdy, and Robby just kept picking on him and picking on him. We were all fed up with listening to him, and I know we all felt sorry for the little guy, but we also knew if we tried to stick up for him, Robby would just keep it up and things would just get worse."

"What was his name, the little guy with the glasses? Because I don't remember anyone like that. I thought all those guys were just a bunch of goof-offs."

"Yeah, I guess most of us were, but not this guy. He was smart. I can't for the life of me remember his name. It was a common name like Bill or Jim, or something like that, but anyway, I remembered the snake I'd put in my jacket pocket earlier that day and I checked to see if it was still there, and sure enough, it was happily curled up as far down as it could go. I gently lifted it out and let it twist around my wrist, but I didn't show it to anyone. Instead, I searched for a big safety pin and put it through the back of the snake just above its tail. Then I pinned the snake to the sheet inside Robby's bed, way down under his covers where his feet would go. All the guys were telling him to knock it off and go to bed because we were sick and tired of hearing his rude remarks. No one knew about the snake, so everyone just went to bed like they did every night and I curled up on the sofa. When Robby got into bed, I guess that old snake started to curl up around his feet because Robby came charging out of bed like he was a locomotive. He flew into the hallway yelling and screaming with eyes the size of saucers. He tried to find out who did it, but no one knew, and I never told anyone about it. Well, not until now."

"George Johnson!" I gasped. "I can hardly believe you would do such a thing!" I took another gulp of lemonade and almost choked trying to stifle my laughter.

"I sort of felt bad for what I did to the snake, but I never regretted doing it to Robby."

I was still laughing at George's admission of guilt with the snake when I heard him say, "OK, little miss perfect. It's your turn. What did you see in me?"

"Well, when my parents died in that fire, you were the only person who showed me any kindness. Some of the neighbors said things like, 'I'm so sorry for your loss,' and my school chums said what they thought they should say, but none of them invited me to live with them or make any effort to help me. They just parroted things they thought was proper to say. You and Mrs. Duddleson were the only people who seemed to care about me. You showed me kindness, George. That's why. You showed me love."

A comfortable silence settled in the truck as we finished the last of the lemonade, each reflecting about how and why we married each other. I tucked the empty jar under the seat and broke the silence. "You know this suede jacket I'm wearing was my mother's. I love it because it was hers and because it's so soft and supple. I wouldn't have ever spent the money to buy anything this nice for myself. Mom's friend, Mr. Schneider, made it for her when she lived in Germany, and she let me wear it on my date with you that night, George, and now it's the only thing I have left of her."

"It looks good on you, Gert. I'm glad you have it."

"You know, George." I changed the subject. "I wasn't happy when you insisted I go with you on this trip. You didn't ask me or even discuss it with me. You just told me that I would be going with you."

"I could see right away from your expression that you didn't want to come with me, Gert, but when Jason couldn't come, there was no other alternative. I knew I'd need your help, but what I didn't get was why you didn't want to come? Aren't we having a nice time, and aren't you glad you came now?"

"Well, yes, I am having a nice time. In fact, I'm enjoying our time together more than I expected, but still, I wish you had asked me instead of just telling me. Can't you see the difference in that?"

"What difference would it have made? We both knew you'd have to help me if Jason couldn't come."

"I suppose that's true, but still there's a big difference between being asked and being told. That's all I'm saying. A girl likes to be asked occasionally, instead of always being told what she needs to do. Besides, Jason had a choice too. He could have opted out of football if he wanted to. You didn't give me a choice, George. That's all I'm saying. It would have been nice to have had a choice."

"Hmmm, I don't really see much difference there, Gert old girl, because the outcome woulda been the same either way. What I can't figure out is why you aren't proud of Jason? Most mothers wouldn't want their sons to give up a chance to play football. Sometimes I just can't figure you out."

"I didn't say I wanted Jason to have to give up football. I'm just saying that sometimes I'd like to have options too. It's only respectful,

George. Seems to me that I never have options. I'm always just waiting on the two of you."

"Hmmm, now, that just doesn't make any sense at all, Gert. In fact, Jason couldn't figure out why you made such a big deal out of it. He thinks you don't want him playing football."

"Really? Why would he think that? I never said I didn't want him to play football. And if he thought that, why didn't he ask me about it himself? And why are the two of you talking about me behind my back? I don't gossip with Jason behind your back. That's not right, George! Don't you see the difference between being respectfully asked about something as opposed to being told what to do? Are both of you that thick?" I took a deep breath in an effort to calm down, feeling more hurt and angrier by the moment.

Neither of us spoke, each listening to the uncomfortable silence growing between us. Finally, I said, "I need to find a lady's room!"

"Jason and I usually wait until we get down the road a bit further. Do you think you can hold on for another half hour or so, Gert?"

"**No**, George! I *do not* think I can hold on for another half hour. I need to find a lady's room in the *next* town."

George kept driving but offered no response. I saw the muscles in his jaw tighten as we each kept our own counsel, each deep in our own thoughts. I listened to the sound of the tires pounding on the pavement and the grunting of the pigs in the trailer behind us. I didn't know how long George would stew about my chastising him because this was new territory for both of us. But I had a more urgent problem. I needed a bathroom so badly that at that moment I didn't care what George felt or thought about anything.

When the next exit appeared, George pulled off the highway and drove up to a gas station. It was one of those combined stations with a small convenience store inside.

"They probably have a public toilet in there," he said.

I had my makeup kit in my large tote, so I grabbed the entire bag, opened the door, and jumped out of the truck, almost running into the store. I scurried past a huge statue of a bear just outside the front door, but I gave it no more than a brief glance in my haste. Much to my dismay, the door of the lady's room was locked, but I could hear there was someone inside. I waited uncomfortably outside the door, shifting my weight from one foot to the other, hoping I'd be able to hold on. When the woman finally exited, I dashed in, peed, washed my hands, and slapped on a little lipstick and rouge. I was feeling a little kindlier toward George as a result of my relief.

I'd already made my point, so I decided I'd try to soften the tension when I got back into the truck because I had to admit, other than our last little confrontation, I was enjoying our time together. The best part was reminiscing about our school days, because at home we only talked about pigs, cows, and farm matters.

I tucked a few stray hairs behind my ears and took one last glance at myself in the mirror before exiting the lady's room. *Not too bad, old girl.*

8

GEORGE

"Destiny is a name often given in retrospect to choices that had dramatic consequences."

—J.K. ROWLING

While George waited for Gert, he puzzled over her behavior. All her talk about being asked, versus being told, made no sense to him at all, causing him to guess whether or not she might be feeling ill or coming down with a cold or something. But those thoughts were interrupted by a guy shouting at him.

"Hey, you there," the guy said. "You with the swine! You have to move your truck so the rest of us can get up to the pumps."

George saw the voice had come from a guy in a shiny red convertible.

"Gotcha," George said. "Pretty nice car you've got there!"

The guy didn't answer, leaving George to conclude he was very likely an asshole who thought of himself as a bigshot in the town.

Not wanting to tangle with him, George drove toward the back of the store, intending to circle around it and come out on the other side, figuring that way he'd be facing in the right direction to enter the highway as soon as Gert returned. But, as luck would have it, he couldn't because there was a camper parked behind the store, blocking his way.

Well, this is a fine kettle of fish.

Thinking he had no other choice, he drove down a narrow country road, expecting he'd drive a short distance and turn around at the first opportunity.

He heard the pigs voicing their displeasure with the situation because the county road hadn't been adequately maintained and had an assortment of potholes, thus causing the truck to bounce on the pavement. A sign indicated he was driving on County Road 14, a road leading in the direction of the neighboring state of Wisconsin. But George had no intention of driving that far. He planned to turn around long before reaching the Mississippi River and crossing into Wisconsin.

Unfortunately, there were no places for him to turn, and he found himself driving a lot farther than he had intended. The further he drove, the more agitated and frustrated he and the pigs became. He saw several turnouts for cars, but none large enough to accommodate his truck.

Then, when he saw a road sign indicating the town of Havana was up ahead just a few miles, he thought he'd drive into town and turn around there. But before he saw the town, there was another sign stating: *Come Back to Havana Soon.* Where the town was, he had no idea. So with no obvious alternative, George kept driving. When he came upon a farm, he pulled into the driveway, assuming most farms had large U-shaped driveways to accommodate turns for large vehicles. Unfortunately, this farm had a locked gate across his road, thus preventing George from driving any farther.

"*Shit! Shit! Shit!*" he said, pounding the steering wheel in defeat.

Okay, take a couple of breaths and decide what you're going to do, because sitting here and berating yourself isn't going to help.

Noting there wasn't a lot of traffic, he thought he might have enough time to back up and make a three-point turn. It would be a little tricky, but he decided it was worth the gamble. He waited until the road was clear and began his maneuver as quickly as possible by gunning the engine as he backed out onto the road. Unfortunately, the road was too narrow for the maneuver, causing his rear wheels to slip down into the drainage ditch on the opposite side.

"*Shit!*" He pulled back across the road into the farmer's driveway, in just the nick of time before a couple of tailgating cars whizzed past him.

Whew! That was a narrow miss! They would have broadsided me, sure as shooting, killing themselves and all the pigs too. Okay, I've got to have another think on this.

After allowing himself a few moments to calm his jangled nerves, George decided his only choice was to get back onto the road and continue driving in the wrong direction, thinking he would come upon another town fairly soon, where he'd be able to drive around a block and return to where he knew Gert would be waiting for him.

He checked the long mirrors on both sides of the truck. "Okay, Priscilla, sorry about this but here we go, old girl."

He gunned the accelerator, bumped the wheels up onto the pavement and resumed driving in an easterly direction, heading farther and farther away from where Gert was waiting for him. Once he was back on the road, he tried to make up for lost time by becoming a little heavy footed on the accelerator.

He passed another road sign which said the town of Claremont was ahead.

"Let's hope it's close," he mumbled to himself, "hopefully no more than ten minutes away."

As he entered Claremont, he came upon a funeral motorcade, escorted by a police officer. The officer motioned for George to accommodate the procession by pulling over to the side, thus allowing the funeral to have priority. George obliged as he watched the motorcade make its slow journey from the church to the cemetery at the opposite end of town.

As the mourners passed in an unbroken procession, he noted the occupants of the cars were holding handkerchiefs over their noses rather than using them to blot teary mournful eyes, thus telling George his pigs were defecating more than usual because of all the stress they'd been experiencing and were very likely giving off an undesirable stench.

George waited, not so patiently, hoping the officer wouldn't issue a ticket for dripping slop on this town's tidy main street. He'd heard stories about how some of these small towns required out-of-towners to return at a later date to pay their fine in person, and George wanted to avoid that hassle at all costs.

When the funeral procession ended, and the officer motioned for George to move on, George felt a great sense of relief, noting that the officer had turned a blind eye, or nose in this case, to the pig residue left behind. Relieved by the outcome, George barreled forward, ignoring the cluster of blackbirds feasting on some type of roadkill ahead. Confident that the birds would scatter as soon as his truck approached, he sped forward, ignoring them.

"Damnit all," he muttered as he sped over the roadkill. *"I swear, those skunks smell a lot worse than a little pig slop."*

While focusing on his mission to get back to Gert, George berated himself for being in this situation in the first place. In doing so, he neglected hearing the warning signs the truck had been giving out for the past several miles. And not until he saw a wheel roll independently past him into a ditch did he realize he was in trouble due to a broken axle.

The cab of the truck lurched sideways, tumbling over onto its side. George was tossed in multiple directions, his head bouncing first against the side window, then slamming into the steering wheel before bouncing back again against the window.

Meanwhile, the bed of the truck where the pigs were riding had untethered itself from the cab and toppled onto its side, where it began skidding down the road unguided, thus creating a ghastly scraping sound and a kaleidoscope of colorful sparks. George was horrified by what was happening, knowing his pigs would be terrorized.

Finally, the pig section of the truck came to an abrupt stop when it tumbled into a ditch fifty feet ahead. Not until then did the scraping sound of metal stop, and that's when everything became eerily silent except for the screaming of the terrorized pigs.

"It's okay, Priscilla," George said faintly, in a feeble attempt to calm the pigs. "It'll be alright."

9

GERT'S WAIT

*"Woman is like a tea bag—you never know how
strong she is until she gets in hot water."*

—ELEANOR ROOSEVELT

I hurried from the lady's room, knowing I'd been inside much longer than I intended, but when I stepped out the front door, I didn't see the truck. I looked in both directions and when I didn't see George, I thought I must have exited through a different door than the one I had entered. Puzzled by that likelihood, I returned to the bathroom area in search of a second entrance but discovered there was none. There was only one door, which led to the parking area where the gas pumps were. Upon exiting the second time, I scanned the lot more carefully in search of the truck, relieved to see the large statue of the wooden bear because I recalled having passed it on my way into the store earlier.

Oh, for heaven's sake, George is probably parked along the side someplace in the shade, trying to keep the pigs from getting overheated.

With that in mind, I checked both sides of the building, discovering he wasn't parked at either side. Then I thought he might have parked up near the highway, perhaps in a truckers' area, so I walked over toward the highway only to discover there not only was no truck stop, but George wasn't there either.

Surely, he wouldn't have left without me! Of course not! Why would I even think that?

Still, I found his absence puzzling and wondered if he might have made a run into town to pick something up. Could he have mentioned something I didn't listen to in my haste and urgency to find a lady's room? Well, whatever it is, I knew I'd just have to wait, thinking he wouldn't be much longer.

There were no chairs or seating available, only a small narrow bench attached to the wooden bear. Thinking it was better than nothing, I ambled over and perched on its edge while reminiscing about the morning.

I have to admit, the entire trip was a lot more pleasant than I had expected. In fact, it's actually been nice talking about our college days, back when we were young, because at home all our conversations are about farm matters. This entire day has been surprisingly pleasurable until I brought up how hurt I was when George didn't give me a choice about going with him. But really, I don't understand why that was so hard for him to grasp. Doesn't he realize how seldom I get to do something just for myself? He didn't even try to understand what I was telling him because he's so wrapped up in what he and Jason need or want? I don't think he appreciates or has any idea of what I do for them, or with our finances either, how I make sure everything gets paid when he buys whatever he wants without even telling me about it.

I took a deep breath to exercise patience, knowing there was no point in getting all worked up over any of this. But as the day grew longer and the narrow bench became increasingly uncomfortable, my patience began growing shorter, and my attitude soured. And the longer he was gone, the more concerned I became about what he might buy, because as of late he'd been making a lot of expensive purchases for which I hadn't budgeted. In fact, the barn is full of gadgets, and newfangled pieces of machinery that he's hardly ever used after having bought them. They just sit there taking up space while it becomes my responsibility to figure out how we're going to pay for them.

My derriere was getting fatigued on that narrow bench, so I stood and began pacing. *I don't suppose George even considered that I might also have enjoyed seeing what this town has to offer. No, of course not!*

As my irritation grew, I paced with increased vigor. Unfortunately, the faster I paced, the more irritated I became, and suddenly I realized my actions were launching curiosity from the locals. So after a few strange looks, I curtailed my agitated tempo in an attempt to be less conspicuous, realizing people were looking at me quizzically, as if wondering what this out of towner was doing hanging around in front of one of their establishments. Heck, I know I've given a few of those looks to strangers who loiter in our town too. At least the glances of these people are still only of curiosity and haven't reached a level of disgust or disdain.

As the temperature increased, so did the heat radiating up from the blacktop pavement, causing the bottoms of my feet to burn through the soles of my leather shoes. That was another reason to curtail my pacing, so I returned to the narrow bench and continued waiting. While sitting there, I refocused my attention on the bear that towered over my head, by examining the details of the carving. It was magnificent and had been carved with such detail that it almost looked as if it had fur. The bear's arms were carved in such a manner to offer a sort of perch, or chair, a small person could climb up into and sit if they were so inclined.

I was pleased when a little boy, perhaps five or six years old, ran over and looked up at me quizzically with his big baby blues, asking without saying a word if he could climb on the bear. I smiled, stood, and roughed his blond curls, remembering how my Jason looked at that age, and how customers in my parents' store used to pat me on my head when I was that age. The boy's mother and I watched him climb up onto the narrow bench and then up into the bear's arms, where he brushed out the dry leaves that had settled there. Then he reached up and touched the bear's amber glass eyes that sparkled in the sunlight. It was a delight to hear the boy's laughter and a great diversion from my boredom. When he tired of exploring the bear, he jumped down to the blacktop pavement in one grand leap, luckily without injury, much to the visual relief of his mother, who was anxiously hovering. The two of them left holding hands while excitedly talking about what he could see when he was up that high.

After the boy and his mother left, I had nothing to do but continue exploring potential reasons for George's absence, and that was when I began speculating on the possibility that something might have happened to him. But I couldn't imagine what that might be. If he had felt ill, surely, he wouldn't have driven off. He would have waited for me to return to the truck. And no one would have kidnapped him with a truckload of pigs. That thought was just too ridiculous to even consider.

Even my speculations were sounding foolish, so I stopped second-guessing the situation and continued waiting.

As the sun rose higher and the temperature and humidity increased, I began feeling a bit nauseated. Thinking I might be dehydrated, I returned to the bathroom area where there was a bubble fountain mounted on the wall. I drank all I could and ran cool water over my wrists before returning to my position in front of the store. When I returned to sit next to the bear this time, I thought more about the possibility of George being in some sort of trouble. But again, I pooh-poohed the thought because if George were in trouble, it would have been the gossip of the town with all those pigs. Everyone who came in here would be chattering about it.

Then I wondered if this could be one of George's little jokes, like the one when he put the snake in that Robby kid's bed? Could he be trying to make a point about something, or teach me a lesson because I told him I didn't think it was right for him to deny me a choice about this trip?

Well, it better not be that, is all I have to say, because if it is, I'm not finding any of this funny. No siree, there's nothing funny about this at all!

I uncrossed my legs and sat up ramrod straight, a position I used to take when I was irritated about something in school. The mere thought of this possibility being one of George's, jokes infuriated me. Parched, hungry and fuming, my head began pounding. A quick glance at my watch told me it was 1:30.

With hunger poking at me, I entered the store to explore my food options, finding my choices were Hostess Fruit pies, Baby Ruth candy bars, an assortment of uninteresting cookies, Cracker Jacks, or ice cream on a stick. I bought a cherry fruit pie and a candy bar. After eating them, I felt better, ignoring how frivolous my food selections were. Normally, at home, I'd never allow myself to eat such things. I suppose, in some way, that made them special.

Feeling somewhat better, I noted a flutter of anticipation every time a truck approached. I watched how the tall grass and seedpod tips swayed in perfect unison as trucks lumbered past the gas station, thus creating an amazingly attractive yellowish-green wave. But each episode was another false alarm.

With nothing to do but wait, I watched a fat, orange-bellied robin hopping along the narrow grassy patch in front of the gas pumps, tipping its head while listening to the ground. Finally, I saw the bird pull up a fat wiggly angleworm that was writhing and curling itself in all sorts of contortions, in its attempt to escape. But the robin efficiently jerked it down its gullet.

Moments later, a guy in a long fancy turquoise car stopped to let his dog out to do its business on that same small sliver of grass. The guy watched his dog leave a steamy poop exactly where the robin had recently found its feast. When his dog jumped back into the car, the guy flipped his cigarette butt onto the ground next to the poop and drove off.

All was quiet for a fairly long stretch of time, until a jalopy crammed with teens pulled up to the traffic light a few yards down the road. I might not have noticed them if they hadn't been playing their music so loud, but as soon as the car stopped at the light, they hopped out while leaving the ignition running. They laughed and talked all at once as they ran to the other side of the car and jumped back into a different seat before the traffic light changed. Then they sped off with squealing tires and left two black rubber marks on the road. I'd heard about that game at one of our last Extension meetings.

One of the mothers told us she caught her son playing it. She said the kids called it Chinese Fire Drill, and when I heard about it, I thought surely she was exaggerating, but apparently, she wasn't.

All I could think about was the stupidity of the game, as I'm sure those kids could find something more productive to do with their time! I suppose they think is a *gas* or a *blast,* or whatever slang they use these days, and I was grateful to not be one of those parents who would have to pay for the tires on that car, because I knew my Jason would never do anything like that.

10

SHERIFF HICKS

"The most common way people give up their
power is by thinking they don't have any."

—Alice Walker

Unbeknownst to Gert, Sheriff Hicks was sending George to the hospital in an ambulance while she was waiting for him. Then, the sheriff had the challenge of rounding up the pigs and getting them off the road before they caused another accident.

The Dodge City TV crew was on site, filming the entire accident.

Most people found the entire pig episode hysterically funny, unlike farmer Jones, who was not pleased to be standing around helplessly watching the pigs decimate his corn crop. There was nothing amusing, as far as Jones was concerned, about any of this. He'd worked hard to plant those rows of corn, and he'd planted them as a cash crop, not as pig food. The more annoyed and frustrated farmer Jones became, the faster he chewed his gum, popping another stick of Juicy Fruit into his mouth every few minutes. Faster and faster, he chewed.

"Those critters," Sheriff Hicks said to his deputy and the farmers standing by to help, "are the most stubborn ornery creatures I've ever met."

"Yep, I agree with that," Mr. Slatter said with a slight grin and a little tip of his impressively wide-brimmed hat.

Mr. Slatter was a cattle rancher who'd settled in the county a few years back. He volunteered to help because, as one of the newer members of the community, he was still trying to win acceptance from the old-timers, the ones who'd lived in the area their whole lives, many being second- and third-generation farmers. He also had the equipment to haul the pigs and the space to board them, that is, if the sheriff could get the ornery beasts up into his truck.

Meanwhile, the pigs scattered themselves in every direction on both sides of the highway, rooting and eating everything in their path. It was a mess, and of course very humorous to the casual onlooker, especially for the TV crew, who were capturing every moment of the escapade because excitement like this hardly ever happened in Dodge Center. Still, there was nothing amusing about it for those who were trying to coax the pigs to walk down the road and up into a strange cattle truck. Pigs, the sheriff and the farmers learned, have minds of their own. They went when and where they wanted to go, which was not up a plank into Mr. Slatter's truck that smelled of cattle. When the pigs didn't want to move, they simply laid themselves down and rolled onto their sides with a big huff, making the situation dangerous, because if one of the men lost his footing on the uneven wet turf, or if they fell just as one of the pigs decided to lie down, the guy stood a good chance of becoming crushed, because even the smaller pigs likely weighed close to 400 pounds and could squash a man with its weight. No one wanted to take a chance of stumbling or falling in or around one of those beasts. And the threat of slipping on the tall grass or losing one's footing increased as darkness approached when the evening dew came rolling in, causing all vegetation to become slippery.

"I think you're supposed to talk to them," Slatter said.

"Talk to them? Is that what you said? I should talk to a pig?" Sheriff Hicks tossed his cigarette butt to the pavement and crushed it violently under his steel-toed boot.

"That's what I hear," Slatter said. "They're supposed to be smart, and I've heard people say you can talk to 'em."

"Well, what are you waiting for? Go ahead and talk to them. Tell them to get their fat bellies down the road and to march up that ramp of yours into your truck. Go ahead. Just tell them what they should do. Jeez, this one must weigh six hundred pounds. Okay, pig. I'm going to talk to you really nice like. See? I just need you to walk over there with me to that nice truck. See it? That nice truck is going to take you to a farm where you'll be comfortable all night. Okay?"

Priscilla, the lead pig, paid no attention to Sheriff Hicks, deciding instead to let her latest meal digest. She lowered her great girth into the ditch, rolled onto her side, and looked content, considering the crash of the truck and all.

"Maybe if I poke her with a stick, I could get her to move," the sheriff said. "You got a stick in that truck of yours?"

"No, but I've got an electric cattle prod. Do you want to try it? I don't know if it'll work on pigs, though."

"Well, anything is worth a try. Get it for me, will you?"

Sheriff Hicks tried it on Priscilla, which caused her to become angry. Very angry! She stood up, made a loud noise of protest, and pushed the sheriff down into the ditch with such violence that he at once vowed not to try using the cattle prod ever again. Even farmer Jones couldn't avoid a little chuckle at seeing the fright in the sheriff's eyes when the pig charged him.

"Shit!" the sheriff said, getting back onto his feet while brushing the fresh grass stains from his pants leg. He walked back to his patrol car with a bit of a limp and called into the station.

"Sally, listen here. This is Sheriff Hicks. I'm out here with this pig situation and I'm going to have to close the highway for the night. Have the boys put up roadblocks at both ends, and get a detour set up using the back county roads. We've got traffic backed up both ways down the highway, so we'll need a couple of extra guys at each end to guide the first cars through. I don't want to take a chance on having one of those cars hitting one of the pigs, and I'm not going to be able to remove them until morning. The pigs will just have to survive out here overnight on their own. And the Accident Scene Analyzers just finished up. They'll be bringing the report in to you soon, but I can't even get a wrecker out here to clear the truck off the road until after I get these damn pigs out of here."

"Yes, sir," Sally, the traffic controller, said, trying to keep a professional voice, because she too was watching the whole pig fiasco play out on the evening news on the small TV she kept hidden in her office. "I took the information from the guy's driver's license. His name is George Johnson, and he lives in Olmsted County, so I contacted the Olmsted County Sheriff and reported the accident. The local sheriff went out to the address and discovered it was a small pig farm. He said a kid named Jason was taking care of the farm while his parents were away. Anyway, the kid was pretty shaken up when he learned about his dad's accident, so the sheriff gave him our phone number, and he called a little while ago and said he'd be here in the morning."

"How's the pig farmer doing, Sally? Does it look like he's going to make it?"

"I don't have an update on his condition, but I thought you'd like to know that the kid asked how his mother was. I didn't know what to tell him. Was there a woman in the truck? I thought it was just one guy."

"No." Sheriff Hicks groaned. "We didn't find a woman, but I'll go take another look."

He signed off his patrol car radio, took out a second flashlight, and walked down to the truck in search of another person, hoping he wouldn't find a dead female they had previously overlooked.

11

GERT'S EARLY EVENING

"I've been accused of being cold, snobbish, distant. Those who know me well know that I'm nothing of the sort. If anything, the opposite is true. But is it too much to ask to want to protect your private life, your inner feelings?"

—Grace Kelly

"Gol dang it, George! Where the heck are you?" All afternoon I'd been listening to the monotonous twang of the cicadas.

As evening approached, I found myself fascinated by the clouds, how wispy they were as they swept across the sky, painting the melon-sized sun as it slowly slid toward the horizon.

Gradually, the cicadas began to silence themselves. Unfortunately, that's when the mosquitoes appeared from their slumber, and they're the nastiest beasts on earth. The one that just bit my ankle is already causing a rivulet of blood to run down onto my foot. Searching my pockets, I found a slightly used paper napkin to blot at the blood.

"Do not scratch it!" I told myself, knowing that scratching mosquito bites was a good way to get an infection, as I surely didn't want to add an infection on top of all this, whatever *this* is.

What on earth can be taking George this long. I can't imagine what is going on in that man's head?

I began pacing again while swinging my arms to discourage other mosquitoes from landing on me and wondered what I would do if George didn't come back for me at all. The mere thought of that sent shivers up my spine. But why? Why would George suddenly decide to leave me here? He may have his faults, but holding a grudge isn't one of them. For the most part, he's a gentle soul. Of course, he can be a little thick in the head, but I've never known him to be cruel, and I would never have expected this from him. But then, I don't suppose anyone ever wants to think such a thing is possible from their husband, and yet here I am, and *the proof is in the pudding,* as the saying goes.

As I continued pondering my situation, I began recalling stories about husbands from some of the women at church. One told us about the time her husband drove to the Twin Cities and bought a brand-new Cadillac convertible. "A fancy two-toned straight stick," she told us. "One I don't even know how to drive. I didn't have a clue he even had a hankering for a convertible because he never mentioned anything about one before, or about getting a new car either. He just drove off one day and brought it home. I still can't figure it out. Why would a corn farmer who lives in Minnesota where the winters are freezing cold, want a convertible? It makes no sense at all. Now, doesn't that sound like he's gone bonkers or crazy to you?"

As I thought about that conversation, I reconsidered calling Jason, thinking George may have gone daft too. Maybe he needed my help. Jason could use my DeSoto to come for me and help me look for George. I think I may even have a full tank of gas in it, although I can't actually remember when I last filled it. But, if he left right away, he could be here by 10:00 p.m., or not much later.

Remembering a pay phone next to the bathroom, I returned inside. I was relieved to see the phone was exactly where I had remembered seeing it, because it reinforced the fact that I wasn't the one who'd lost their mind.

I opened the bifold door of the phone booth, sat on the cool metal seat, and lined up three dollars' worth of change on the stainless-steel counter. As was my nature, I organized the coins in order of their value, nickels with nickels, dimes with dimes, and quarters with quarters before picking up the receiver. After dropping a dime into the right slot, I carefully dialed the farmhouse number while listening to the mechanism rhythmically ratchet back after having dialed each number. When I confirmed I had dialed all the right numbers, I let it ring exactly ten times, finally realizing Jason was likely still at football practice.

Then I realized I wouldn't know where to tell him to come for me, because I had no idea where I was.

As I pondered that, I decided I didn't like the idea of having Jason driving alone after dark anyway. Heck! He's still an inexperienced driver, and anything could happen to him on those dark, narrow country roads at night. Besides, I wouldn't be able to reach him until very late, because after football practice, he would still have all the farm chores to do before returning to the house. So no, calling Jason isn't a practical solution.

I could call our neighbor, Margaret Peterson, but I'd still have to ask a total stranger to tell me where I am. Not only that, but I hate the idea of having Margaret know anything about this. And she'd want all the juicy details too. She wouldn't be happy until I told her every little minutia about George's desertion, and then she'd probably embellish it and blab it to all the ladies back home. Nope, I'm not about to confide in her because I don't think I can trust her. Anyone who jiggles their bosoms in front of menfolk like she does isn't trustworthy. And I know George takes notice of her too, because more than once I've heard him whistle after she left our house. One time I heard him say, "Whew, that woman is built like a prized heifer."

Nope! I don't trust Margaret Peterson, not one little bit. In fact, I sometimes get the impression she has her eye on George as her prize. Ha! Some prize! But in spite of my being really upset with the scoundrel right now, I'm not ready to let her march in and take him away from me either. At least not yet. Besides, this isn't anyone else's business. Whatever is going on between George and me is for us to deal with, and it's no one else's business.

Papa used to stress the importance of family privacy with me quite often. In fact, the first time he talked to me about it, I was only six or seven years old. I had worn holes in the bottom of my new patent leather shoes, and instead of scolding me, he used it as an opportunity to explain how important privacy was.

"Your dress-up shoes were never made for play activity." Which hadn't been obvious to me until I saw the holes I'd worn in the bottom, holes large enough for my white stockings to show through. He told me to remove my shoes and give them to him. I watched him trace the outline of the bottoms of my shoes onto a piece of cardboard from the back of a writing tablet. Then he cut along the line and slipped the cutouts inside my shoes.

"There," he said. "Now your shoes will look as good as new on top, but the bottoms will need to be camouflaged. So save these shoes for church, and when you wear them, keep your feet flat on the ground. That way, no one will know there are holes in the bottom. We never want to let people know our vulnerable areas, Gert. Do you know why? Because people will take your worst secret and make it work against you. That's why. Now, go out and play, but change into your everyday shoes. These shoes are strictly for church."

He kissed my forehead and sent me outside, but the memory of that conversation only reinforces my determination to solve this problem without outside help. I don't know how I'll do it yet, but I'm not going to call my neighbor or anyone else. Whatever is going on between George and me will remain between us with no outside snooping.

With renewed determination, I began to suspect George may not return for me until Labor Day, or even the day after Labor Day. I considered taking a room down the street, but decided that not only would be expensive, but George wouldn't know where to find me. So I decided I should stay put, exactly where I was.

Just as I began feeling comfortable with my decision, I had a frightening encounter with two teenage boys. They arrived in a beat-up jalopy with music blaring from their rolled down windows. They stepped out of their vehicle with an arrogant strut, and as they got closer to me, I saw both had a splattering of freckles and unruly reddish manes. One was taller than the other, but both advanced toward me with an unmistakably challenging gait, obviously looking for trouble, anything to spice up their boring empty lives.

"Hey, old woman, what you got in that big bag? You got anything in there for me?" The tallest of the two taunted. "We'll just come on over and take a little look, that be okay with you?"

Old woman indeed! I'm not old! Those young whippersnappers don't know anything about me at all.

Runnels of sweat ran down from my armpit, and I didn't know what I should do.

What was wrong with those boys? Didn't they have any manners at all?

I shrank away, clutching my tote bag closer to my chest, when just then, a blue Nash station wagon pulled into the gas station with a family inside. The woman passenger stepped out of the car, with her two small children in tow, and headed into the store. The children were chattering excitedly about the color Lolli they each planned to buy, and I ran into the store behind them.

"There are two big boys bothering me, and I'm just waiting for my husband to come back and pick me up." I finished my one long, barely coherent sentence directed to the woman with the excited children.

The woman stopped walking, turned, and looked at me. I guess she could hear how terrified I was. She didn't say anything immediately, but then she called out to the store manager.

"Hey, Carl, the Hooligan boys are harassing this woman while she's waiting for her husband. Can you get them out of here?"

"What's that, Alice?" a male voice from the cash register area answered. "Did you say it's the Hooligan boys again? I tell you, school can't start fast enough for me. Those boys are just bored and when that happens, they become troublemakers. I'll have a talk with them and shag them out of here. I can't have them scaring my customers."

"Thank you, so much," I told the woman in a softer calmer voice.

"You're welcome. Those boys are a problem for everyone, but Carl's a good guy. He'll move them on their way. I don't think they'll be a bother to you anymore."

True to Alice's word, the boys were gone when I returned from the lady's bathroom, which provided me with the opportunity to resume sitting next to the bear while I contemplated what I should do. While examining my lack of options, I noted how dusk was bringing in a completely different clientele, mostly a young, single crowd. As I sat there watching the local people come and go, I also watched the fireflies sparkle and light up around me.

I wondered if Jason might be sitting on the porch, watching the fireflies after his chores tonight. That was something the three of us did fairly often together on these fall evenings.

In spite of the total uncertainty of my situation, my tension relaxed as I recalled the years when Jason was young, back when he captured the fireflies and put them in pickle jars. They'd light up the entire jar, creating light similar to a lantern. Of course, all of them were dead by morning, but there always seemed to be a new batch for him to capture the following night.

Those were good days!

As dusk seeped in deeper, I sat there doing absolutely nothing about my situation. Instead, I watched the last of the daylight slipping away, leaving a mere dusting of light as both the foot traffic and vehicle traffic began tapering off. When I heard my stomach growl, I returned to the store to buy another fruit pie and an ice cream, and I took both outside to eat while sitting next to the wooden bear.

Then Carl, the owner of this gas station and convenience store, turned off his lights and stepped outside with a cigarette hanging on his lip. I felt my stomach lurch when I heard the click of his key turn in the lock.

"Criminy," he said, startled to see me sitting next to the bear, licking my sticky fingers. "Are you still here?"

"Yes, I'm just waiting for my husband. He'll be back any minute now."

I knew better of course, but I still wasn't comfortable telling anyone about my situation, finding it humiliating and, quite frankly, embarrassing.

"Well," he said, pausing briefly with ribbons of smoke escaping from his nose, "I've already locked up. Are you sure you'll be okay out here by yourself? There's a small rooming house down the street if you need one. I don't know if they're full or not, but it'd be worth checking out."

"Thank you, but that won't be necessary. My husband won't be long now."

He hesitated, took another deep drag as he was contemplating what to do about me. He must have decided to not let me become his problem because he finally said, "Well, okay then," and flipped his ash onto the pavement before walking over to his car.

I watched his tired, sagging body cross the parking lot. Then I heard the crunch of his tires on the pavement as he slowly drove away.

12

CARL

*"Don't ever wrestle with a pig. You'll both
get dirty, but the pig will enjoy it."*

—Cale Yarborough

Carl walked into his house, kissed his pregnant wife, and rubbed her round belly. "How's our little guy doing in there?"

He stopped at the refrigerator, removed a can of Schlitz, popped the metal tab, and went into the living room where he planned to wait for his dinner. He flipped on the TV, turned the dial to Channel 5 news, and adjusted the aluminum foil on the rabbit ear antenna before kicking his shoes off and sitting in his easy chair, putting his tired feet up onto the worn footstool as he did every night.

That night the news wasn't about the economy, bombs being tested in the Nevada desert, murders, fires, or weather. It was about pigs! Sheriff Hicks was trying to remove a bunch of them from a county road near Wisconsin.

Carl burst out laughing.

"Martha," he shouted to his wife who was in the kitchen preparing his dinner. "You've got to see this? Some fool pig farmer rolled his truck, and the sheriff and his men are chasing pigs all over the road. What a circus! I can only imagine what a mess those fool pigs are making of that farmer's cornfield."

PART II

HAPPENINGS 1973

13

GERTRUDE'S FIRST NIGHT

"You may encounter many defeats, but you must not be defeated. In fact, it may be necessary to encounter the defeats, so you can know who you are, what you can rise from, how you can still come out of it."

—Maya Angelou

I tried choking back the sinking nauseating feeling that washed over me as I watched Carl's taillights exit the parking lot. Knowing I was totally alone in this desolate place brought on a full-blown blubbering sob. My shoulders shook and the muscles across my shoulders tightened into knots as salty tears flowed down my face, dripping off my chin. I'd been alone before, but never like this. Not at night in an empty parking lot in the middle of who knows where, with only a couple of dark buildings in sight.

The nighttime insects continued their buzzing, and the hungry mosquitoes remained eager to make me their evening meal. I felt as if I was living in a horror film, except this was no movie set and there were no cameras rolling.

After wailing uncontrollably and feeling totally sorry for myself, I finally cried myself out of tears and mopped my face with the sleeve of my shirt, while berating myself for not asking someone to help me when I had the opportunity to do so.

What in the world was I thinking! I should have done something hours ago.

I closed my eyes, partly to allow my vision to adjust to the diminishing light, but also in defeat and submission. When I opened them, the pit of my stomach clenched when I thought I saw arms of doom reaching out along the pavement to grab at me. But then I realized, the shadows were the silhouettes of oaks and elms lining the parking lot, the very trees whose leaves were offering a soft whisper and marginally welcome breeze.

The gentle movement of air was welcome, but still not enough to prevent the mosquitoes from landing on me. My only defense against them was my own movement, so I continued swinging my arms as I paced back and forth. Timidly I peered around the corner of the building, where in the diminishing light I could barely see the litter: empty pop bottles, paper bags, wrappers, and cups, all of it was trash, no boogie men in sight. Sauntering back in front of the bear to the other side of the building, I took a similar peek, seeing much of the same: trash and ominous darkness. Rebuking myself for not being proactive about my situation, I returned to the bear and sat next to him on the bench.

"This is absurd," I said aloud while scratching the itchy bites on my ankles and arms. Seconds later, I stood again and resumed my pacing, as it was my only defense against the ravenous creatures. I paced back and forth with flailing arms, noting how quickly the glow on the horizon was fading. The earlier half-ball, peach-colored sun was becoming a mere fringe of purple as it slipped further below the horizon. Soon, there was nothing but darkness.

Seconds later, without sound or warning, cones of brilliance from security lights flooded the parking lot, garishly amplifying the ugliness of greasy shimmering oil slicks. Cockroaches, previously feasting on spilled food, scampered away in search of darkness, while the crumpled white cylinders of cigarette butts strewn about on the pavement lay defiantly exposed. The lights aroused the nighttime insects from their daytime slumber, causing them to sizzle and snap like fat in a frying pan as they were drawn to their demise by flying into the hot bulbs. The surprise of the light was such a jolt, that rather than offer me comfort, the lights intensified my anger and disgust with this whole situation.

Twenty-two years of being married to that man and apparently, I've never really known him. It was cruel what he did to Robby with that snake and cruel to the snake too. And now he was being cruel to me.

With newly aroused anger, I kicked the bear's huge foot when I passed him.

"Ouch! That hurt!" I yelled.

Just then, from somewhere above in the trees, came a hoot from an owl.

"Oh, did you hear that Wilkes?" I asked the bear. "That is your name, isn't it? It's what's carved on your foot, so I figured that was your name."

Hearing the owl brought me a sliver of comfort because it reminded me of a particularly precious night from long ago, back to a sticky hot night not unlike this one when I was very young. I'd gotten out of bed that night, intending to tiptoe into the store where I planned to stand in front of an open freezer door, the one where Papa and Mama kept the ice cream. But Papa was sitting in the dark in his favorite chair and caught me in the act.

I remember being startled when I heard him ask me what I was doing out of bed, but he didn't scold me. Instead, he invited me to climb up onto his lap. I rested my head on his chest, where I could hear the beating of his heart as he stroked my hair.

"You know, Gert," he said, "Life isn't always easy, sweetheart. But if you're healthy and you're alive, then you must learn not to complain, at least not about something as small as a hot night."

I remember soaking up his love as I sat in his lap while he reminisced about his boyhood in Germany.

"Your mother and I had many difficulties when we were growing up, Gert. We haven't always had these nice luxuries that you take for granted. In fact, when I was your age, my parents received ration cards for things such as gasoline, sugar, shoes, and even bread. But even then, just because we may have had a ration card for something, it didn't mean we had enough money to buy it. When I was a child, sweetheart, I was hungry all the time, simply because we didn't have enough money to buy the food we needed. And then, when the war came, everything got even worse. I used to glean from my neighbors' victory gardens, just to avoid starving, but I never felt completely safe from starvation until we got to America."

"What's gleaning mean, Papa?"

"Gleaning, sweetheart, means picking up the leftover vegetables from other people's gardens, things they didn't feel were worth harvesting. I'd eat all I could and bring home anything else I could carry to my mother. She made meals from anything I could find. I hope you never have to be exposed to the conditions your mother and I had to endure, but I think it's important for you to realize that a few hot and sticky nights aren't really so bad. So let's just sit here and think about all the good things we have until we get sleepy enough to go back to our beds. What do you think, Gert? Would that be a good idea?"

That was such a long time ago, and I hadn't thought about that night for ages, but hearing the owl tonight triggered that memory, because I not only recalled Papa's words and love, but I also heard an owl outside our window that night so long ago. An owl not unlike the one that had hooted here in this parking lot.

"Wilkes," I said as I walked past him this time, "that owl we just heard? That's a signal for us to be brave because he's going to keep us safe tonight."

When the owl hooted again, I slowed my pacing while seeing how my shadow was growing longer behind me.

"Wilkes," I asked, "would you mind if I snuggled up with you tonight? You don't mind? Oh, that's good. Somehow, I didn't think you would."

I sat down next to Wilkes, wishing the bench were a little larger and not so hard. But, after giving it further thought, I decided to climb up into the rounded curves of the bear's arms, where I was about as comfortable as any adult could be while sitting on a wooden carving.

My mother's jacket served as an inefficient pillow, and the quilt I'd made intending to enter it into the State Fair competition served as a barrier from the insects as well as the damp evening air. But the night was far from quiet, as there was the continual sound of bugs zapping in the security lights, and the whine and screech of feral cats on both sides of the building. I saw a wrapper of some type skip loudly across the parking lot and get hung up on the corner of the building until it freed itself and joined its cousins in the dark dungeon of hell on the side of the building. Eventually, the security lights dimmed, allowing the moonlight to paint a path across the tarred parking lot. The night remained alive with noises and changing visions, but the sound that provided me with comfort came from the owl, an owl I couldn't see but knew was up there watching over me. As I listened to its hoots, I recalled another piece of wisdom from Papa. It was from when I was in college when I didn't feel prepared to give a speech in one of my classes.

He told me all I needed was a little courage. "And courage," he said, "seldom means a person is brave. It simply means we've learned to deal with our fears." He was right about that too, because when I got up in front of my class that day, I'd forgotten all about my shaking knees and sweaty palms. I began speaking and sharing all the information that I'd prepared, and it all flowed out. Not only did the class clap for me, but my professor gave me an A.

And I knew Papa's wisdom was going to give me the courage I needed to help me get through this night as well. With that final thought, I closed my eyes and dosed off to sleep.

14

THE FOLLOWING MORNING

"The question isn't who's going to let me; it's who is going to stop me."

—Ayn Rand

"**G**ood God! Are you dead?" I heard a male voice ask as I simultaneously felt something poke at my leg.

"Ouch!" I said, startled awake, finding myself looking into the face of the frightened store owner.

"Well, at least you're not dead!" He jumped away from me, as if I was the aggressor and not him.

He looked as stunned as I felt, but at once saw his relief when he realized I wasn't a dead body draped over the wooden bear in front of his establishment. Still, he was visibly upset at finding me sleeping there.

"No, I'm not dead."

I may not have been dead, but I was extremely startled, and jangle-nerved, as I hadn't expected being caught off guard like that. Instead, I intended to approach him with my proposal in a far more reserved manner. Not like this at all.

I slid off the bear, adjusted my clothing, and tucked my hair back behind my ears while he demanded to know what I was doing there.

"Well, sir, apparently my ride won't be picking me up for about two weeks, so I'm going to have to wait here until he comes for me."

"Two weeks!" he shouted. "Oh no! Absolutely not! You can't sleep in front of my store for two weeks!"

With that, he turned his back to me and strutted across the lot toward the store where he unlocked the door and escaped inside.

I suspected he was trying to compose himself while simultaneously giving me the impression of his authority, just as I was trying to show a calm, nonplussed control of myself. Neither of us were doing a very good job of fooling even ourselves, let alone one another. I had formed a plan in my head last night, planning to approach him with it in a much more composed manner than this. But, in spite of our rocky beginning, I mustered up all my bravado and followed him into the store, where I continued our conversation.

"No," I said, "I don't suppose I can sleep outside again. But I had a lot of time to think last night, and I realized I could sleep inside your store, out in back, in the storeroom."

He glared at me, obviously shocked to hear such an absurd and brazen assumption on my part. But I didn't give him a chance to speak and continued presenting my plan.

"I could work for you in exchange for rent."

"Work for me!" His face flushed. "Absolutely not! It's out of the question! There's no place for you to sleep and I don't have a job for you. So you'd best just get moving along and figure something else out."

"That's not true," I countered in as calm a voice as I could manage. "You have a place for me, and you have a job for me too. Your lady's room is sorely in need of a good cleaning, and if the lady's room looks that bad, I can only imagine what the men's room may look like."

"Holy crap. What did I do to deserve this? I don't need any help and I don't want you hanging around here! So just get out of here before I call the cops."

With a final harrumph, he turned his back to me and walked toward the front counter, where he took up his post behind the cash register. I was pretty sure he hoped that by ignoring me, I would leave.

But I wasn't about to let that happen. As soon as he walked away from me, I headed to the bathroom to freshen up. While there, I surveyed what needed to be done to clean it. When I came out, I avoided getting within earshot of him and slipped through the privacy curtain into the back room of the store, where I searched for mops and cleaning supplies. Without saying another word, I hauled all the supplies I would need into the lady's room, where I scrubbed the floor, disinfected the toilets, cleaned the sinks, and polished the mirrors. Then, I replenished the roll of cloth towels and toilet paper.

When I exited the lady's room, he avoided approaching me. Instead, he lit a fresh cigarette, glared at me, and dialed the telephone. I heard him say loudly, making sure I could hear him, "Sheriff Hicks, this is Carl Olson over at the gas station and convenience store at the intersection of highways 65 and 14. I've got a transient woman here who slept outside my store last night, and now she's making a nuisance of herself. Can you send someone over to pick her up?"

I walked past him, pretending I hadn't heard his call to the police, and returned all the cleaning supplies to the back room, making sure I'd replaced everything in the exact location where I'd found them.

"Good God!" Sheriff Hicks said. "Was there a full moon out last night or what? I've got my hands full with this pig situation, and I sure don't need something more to deal with right now. Do you think this woman is dangerous?"

"I don't know, Sheriff. What the heck do I know? All I know is there is a strange woman who slept on that big wooden bear out in front of my place last night, and now she just finished cleaning the lady's bathroom, and I don't know how to get rid of her."

"Why would you want to get rid of someone who's cleaning your bathrooms, Carl? Seems to me you fell into a good thing. Tell you what. I've got all my men helping me with this pig thing. If she isn't dangerous, and if she isn't causing you a problem, just try to hang in there for a few days. I'll get back to you as soon as I can."

Carl hung up the phone with a sigh.

Having not heard the sheriff's side of that conversation, I didn't know what might happen next, but I decided cleaning a bathroom wasn't something I could be arrested for. I considered cleaning the men's room too, but I didn't want to be caught in there if a man entered needing to use it. So I decided to postpone cleaning it until after the store was closed, that is, if I was still here.

The back storeroom was in such a state of disarray that I couldn't help myself from straightening and organizing it. At first, I thought I'd just do a little reorganizing, but before I knew it, I was sorting and rearranging all the stock. There were all sorts of duplicate canned goods stacked in separate areas of the room. Some looked as if they had been there a long time, so I began grouping similar items together, putting older stock in front of the newer stock. Then I dusted all the cans, tidied the rows, and restocked the shelves in the store, almost forgetting about the call Carl had made to the sheriff. And then I struck gold when I found an old army cot tucked behind the furnace. I opened it and found it was sturdy and fairly comfortable, much better than a wooden bear. If I could finagle my way to stay in the back room of the store, it not only would be a cheaper solution to my predicament, but it would provide me with the advantage of being able to stay exactly where George dropped me off, which would certainly simplify his ability to find me when the fair was over.

I was so elated with my discovery that I almost pranced down the street to a small café called The Kitchen, where I rewarded myself with a proper breakfast of ham and eggs. The rest of the day I kept busy organizing and reorganizing the storeroom, enjoying myself so much that I was surprised when I heard myself humming some of the old songs I'd sung when I was a child. The store brought back so many wonderful old memories for me, so much so that I was astonished at how quickly the day had slipped by. And I was completely caught off guard when Carl entered the storeroom with a fist of dollar bills for me.

"Here," he said, offering me the money. "This is for the work you did today. I have to admit you made the place look a lot better, but you have to leave now. It's time for me to lock up for the night,"

"Oh, I appreciate this, but I didn't expect you to pay me. All I want is to sleep on the cot in your storeroom for a couple of weeks."

"What are you talking about? I don't have a cot back there, and no, you can't sleep there!"

"Yes, you do, and why not? Why can't I sleep in your storeroom?"

"Well, you just can't, that's all. I don't know anything about you, and I don't know if I can trust you."

"Look, if I was going to do anything bad to your store, wouldn't I have already done it? Of course you can trust me. You already told me the store is looking better since I've been here."

I knew he couldn't argue that point because the lady's room was clean, the shelves were all full, and the storeroom looked orderly for the first time since who knows when.

Instead of answering or responding, he turned his back on me and returned to the front counter, acting as if he'd just thought of something he'd forgotten to do. I saw how he was struggling with my request and knew his decision could easily swing either way. So I followed him to the front of the store, knowing I needed to say some-thing to tip the scale in my favor. In my very pleasantest voice I said, "It will just be for a few days, two weeks at the most."

With a reluctant groan he finally agreed, but added, "Once I lock the door, you'll be locked inside all night. Are you sure you're okay with that?"

"Oh yes. That's no problem at all. I'm perfectly fine with that." I mustered as much bravado as I could while trying not to think about how my parents had died in their beds, unable to escape the fire in our store twenty years earlier. I gave him my best pretend smile and a nod before stepping back through the privacy curtain leading to the back room. I sat on the cot and waited to see what might happen next. Then I heard the click of the key in the front door and knew I was locked in for the night.

I removed my quilt from my tote bag, spreading it out on the cot before kicking off my shoes. Then I stretched out full length with a sigh. I heard the squeak of Carl's car door as he opened it and then the slam when he shut it, followed by the start of his engine. Next, I heard the crunch of his tires driving across the gravel on the side of the building. Finally, the only sound left was the hum of electricity from the refrigerators and freezers where Carl kept milk, beer, and popsicles.

All the way home Carl stewed and fretted about what he'd agreed to. While waiting at a stop light, he almost returned to the store to tell that strange woman she'd have to leave. But before he knew it, he was pulling into his driveway.

"What's wrong?" Martha asked as soon as he entered the kitchen door.

"Nothing's wrong. What makes you think there's something wrong?"

"I know that look, Carl. Something's bugging you, so you might just as well tell me what it is."

"Well, it's nothing really. I just agreed to let a woman sleep at our store for the next few nights."

"You did what? What woman? Why would you do that?"

"Well, when I got to the store this morning, she was sleeping on that big wooden bear out in front. Seems she's waiting for someone to pick her up, but they've been delayed and won't be here for a couple of weeks. So she asked if she could sleep in the store."

"What are you up to, Carl? If you have some sweet little hussy on the side, that you think you can court right under my nose with a story like that, you must think I'm pretty dumb. I remember what a Casanova you were back in high school, and you can't start pulling something like that on me. I may be pregnant and big as a house right now, but I'm not dumb. And I'm not going to put up with you keeping a skirt on the side. Have I made myself perfectly clear about that?"

"Martha, it's nothing like that. She's not my girlfriend. Good God, she's an ugly scrawny thing, pushy too. I just felt sorry for her. That's all. It'll just be for a short time, a few days at the most and then she'll be gone and on her way.

"No, Carl, she won't be gone in a few days. She'll be gone tomorrow! I'm going to the store with you in the morning, and I'm going to let her know she needs to pack her bags and move on because there is no room for her here at all."

Carl cowered in his armchair, watching the evening news while waiting for his dinner. Neither of them wished to discuss it further. Martha set his dinner plate on the table with a thud and said, "You can wash your own dish tonight. I'm going to bed."

Carl ate his dinner alone while Martha did a slow, angry burn alone in her bed.

As the marital drama was taking place in Carl and Martha's home, Gert organized the cleaning supplies for the second time that day and carried them to the bathrooms. She emptied the trash, washed the containers, and put in clean liners. She scrubbed and disinfected the toilets, polished the sinks, and removed all the graffiti from the backs of each toilet door and walls before climbing up on a ladder to change the dusty flickering fluorescent light bulbs. Finally, she scrubbed, paste waxed, and buffed the entire floor of the store. When she finished, she smiled with pride at seeing the results of her efforts, as both the store and the bathrooms were clean to her standards.

15

JASON

"You have to accept whatever comes and the only important thing is that you meet it with courage and the best that you have to give."

—Eleanor Roosevelt

"Mrs. Peterson," Jason blurted into the telephone. "The sheriff just left here and told me my parents were in an accident. Dad's in the hospital and our pigs are running loose on the highway. I'm calling to ask if I could borrow your truck to drive up and collect the pigs, because the sheriff said our truck is pretty much destroyed."

"Oh, my lands!" she said. "Of course you can use our truck. Did the sheriff say how badly your parents were injured?"

"No, just that Dad was in the hospital. He didn't say anything about Mom, so she may not have been as badly injured."

"Oh, my lands alive! I saw the sheriff's car drive past the house and wondered where he was going."

"I'd like to leave tomorrow morning at first light," Jason said, "if that'd be okay with you."

"Of course, dear. You can get the truck now if that suits you. That way you can get it gassed up and ready to leave as early as you want. Is there anything else I can do to help?"

"No, I don't think so. Just your truck is all I need. I'll get the animals here all taken care of before I leave in the morning. Thanks, Mrs. Peterson. I appreciate this, and now that I think about it, I think you're right. It would be a good idea for me to come and get the truck now if that's okay with you."

Jason jumped onto his motorcycle and rode over to the Peterson farm. He parked it in the barn and retrieved the truck key from Mrs. Peterson before driving into town to fill it with gas. When he returned home, he fed the animals their evening meal and picked a bunch of apples, putting them in a basket on the front seat of the truck.

As planned, he fed the animals again early the following morning, before first light. Then he tossed a pitchfork and shovel into the back of the truck. He put his brown bag with bologna sandwiches next to the basket of apples. Then he headed down the county road till it joined US 65. Following the sheriff's directions, he headed north until he reached county road 14, where he made a right turn and drove to the address of the sheriff's office. With an empty trailer and his adrenaline pumping, he arrived at Sheriff Hick's office by mid-morning.

"The sheriff is out trying to get the pigs rounded up," Sally the county dispatcher told Jason when he arrived at the office. "He's trying to prevent them from causing another accident and destroying some poor corn farmer's crop, but I don't think he's having much success." She chuckled. "Do you think you'll be able to get them rounded up, or corralled, or whatever one does with pigs?"

"Yes, of course I will."

Sally wasn't sure if she should be impressed by his confidence or put off by his arrogance. *Youth*, she thought, and gave him directions on how to find the sheriff and the pigs.

Jason was so focused on the pig mission that he was out the door before turning to ask, "How are my parents? Our sheriff told me Dad was injured and in the hospital, but he didn't say anything about my mom."

"Yeah, well about that," Sally said. "Yes, your dad is in the hospital, and you can see him whenever you want, but we don't know where your mother is. We don't think she was in the truck during the time of the accident."

"What?! Well that's just plain crazy because I watched them leave together!"

"That's all I know." Sally raised her voice as Jason was already marching heavy footed out the door, letting it slam behind him.

Jason wrestled with trying to decide what he should do first. Should he go to the hospital to see his dad, or should he round up the pigs first? He decided to drive out to the accident site to round up the pigs and learn more about what happened before heading to the hospital.

When he arrived at the scene of the accident, he was horrified to see his family truck in two parts, with both sections lying on their sides. He pulled up next to the cab part, where several police officers tried to prohibit him from parking. But when Jason explained who he was, and that he had come to collect the pigs, they welcomed him.

"Can you tell me where I can find Sheriff Hicks?"

"Hell yes!" one of the officers said. "Hick's is going to want to see you! That's for goddamn sure! Just walk down the road a little further. You'll see him in the cornfield on the right trying to coax the pigs out."

Jason walked in the direction the officer pointed but wasn't at once able to see the sheriff because he was so well camouflaged in the thick corn crop. But Jason could hear him.

"Come on, nice piggy. Now let's get out of the farmer's cornfield." Of course, the pig wasn't paying any attention to the sheriff. Neither did it stop Priscilla from digging up those delicious stalks of corn. "Look," the sheriff said, "I'm trying to talk to you real nice like, but you're about the most obstinate creature I've ever set eyes upon. Just stop eating and digging up the goddamn plants!"

In spite of the accident, the costly damage to the truck, and the worry Jason had for his parents, he couldn't help but chuckle at the ridiculousness of seeing a full-grown man, a man in uniform no less, looking and sounding so frustrated and inept around a few pigs. It was funny, no matter what the circumstance.

"Hello, Sheriff," Jason said. "I'm Jason Johnson and those are my pigs."

When the sheriff heard Jason, he exited the cornfield by carefully stepping down into the runoff ditch before leaping over the standing water. Then he took another big leap up onto the blacktop.

"Am I ever glad to see you," the sheriff said as he reached out to shake Jason's hand. "Are you going to be able to get these pigs out of here?"

Jason looked so young that the sheriff had his doubts, but he hoped he was wrong. He would *love* to be wrong and have the kid remove the beast from his road and get them out of the farmer's corn crop asap, because farmer Jones was getting testier and testier about the decimation of his corn crop. With each new conversation, the old farmer popped another stick of Juicy Fruit into his mouth and, if you asked the sheriff, he'd say the farmer was beginning to look a lot like one of the pigs.

"Sure, I can round them up," Jason said. "I'll just drive up here and load them up."

"Yeah! Sure kid, you do that," the sheriff said with a groan, thinking the kid was being a smart-ass.

With that, the sheriff lit another cigarette, his fifth or sixth that morning. He'd given up smoking last year, but the stress of this pig escapade caused him to fall back into the old habit. He was halfway through this pack, and it wasn't even noon yet. He waited for Jason to drive his truck forward. Then he watched the kid drop the back gate and slide a narrow wooden plank out, securing one end to the back of the truck. It formed a ramp that led into the bed of the truck. Then, the sheriff watched Jason remove a bushel of apples from the cab of the truck and lift it up onto the truck bed before hopping up into the bed with the ease of youth. Jason tossed the apples all around in the back of the truck, all except for one, which he held high in his hand for the pigs to see.

"Chewy, chewy, chewy," Jason said in a high-pitched voice.

When the pigs heard him, they stopped eating the corn, lifted their heads, and began walking toward the truck where Jason was standing. Jason showed them the apple in his hand a second time by holding it high in the air. One by one, the pigs began walking toward him.

"Chewy, chewy, chewy," Jason repeated in a high-pitched voice. The biggest one led the pack and began running toward Jason.

"Jesus! Look at how fast that beast can go?" Sheriff Hicks said under his breath, completely astonished, thinking it was one of the funniest sights he'd ever seen. *I didn't know pigs could run!*

When Priscilla, the largest pig, reached the truck, she didn't even hesitate. She just walked up the plank and got into the truck, and all the other pigs followed her. They began eating the apples and acted as if nothing unusual had happened.

Jason slid the plank into the back of the truck and secured the back gate.

"What will you do with the truck?" Jason asked.

The sheriff stood with his mouth agape, in awe at seeing how easily Jason was able to get the pigs to walk up the plank and get into the truck. "What, son?" Hicks asked, still amazed at what he'd just witnessed.

"What will you do with the truck?"

"Oh, the truck. Well, what would you like me to do with it? I was planning on having it hauled off to the scrap heap. But I suppose there might be some good parts left on it. Do you want to see if it can be salvaged? I can have it hauled to a mechanic if you would prefer. I don't care where it goes, I just have to get if off the road."

"Yes, have it taken to a mechanic and give me the address. I'll stop by there later to see how badly it's busted up and find out how much it will cost to get it repaired. I'm going to head to the hospital to see my dad next. And I don't understand about my mom being missing. Can you fill me in on that? How is that possible?"

"Sorry, son. We've searched all over this area. Your mother simply isn't here. I have no idea what to tell you."

"But that doesn't make any sense, Sheriff! None of this makes sense. She can't have disappeared into thin air!"

I don't know what to tell you, son. Go see your dad. Maybe he will be able to tell you something. If you find anything out, stop by my office before you head home. Hopefully, we'll have some answers by then."

Jason drove toward the town, stopping at a local vegetable stand along the way to make another purchase for his pigs.

"Hi," Jason said to the roadside vendor. "Do you have any castoffs you could sell really cheap? I have a bunch of hungry pigs in back."

"Yeah, there's some rotting fruit and vegetables behind the tarp. You can have all you want free of charge. In fact, it'll save me from having to load it up and bury it when I get home. So help yourself. Take all you want."

With the use of the pitchfork and shovel, Jason tossed all the rotten fruit and vegetables into the back of his truck for the pigs. Then, he drove into town and parked under a shade tree a few blocks from the hospital. He locked the truck, walked to the hospital, and asked what room his father was in. When he entered the chilly room, he was surprised to see how small his father was in the hospital bed, all tucked under a white blanket. His dad had always seemed bigger than life on the farm, but here he looked frail and shrunken, with a tube in his nose and another taped to his arm, each connected to machinery with rhythmically beeping lights.

Jason saw his dad was trying to say something, so he leaned in closer, trying to decipher what he was trying to say.

"It's okay, Priscilla," his father whispered. "It's okay."

Jason realized his dad was unaware of where he was and was still trying to calm the pigs.

"Dad, I'm here. Can you hear me? It's Jason, Dad. You're in the hospital and all the pigs are safe. Where's Mom? Tell me where Mom is." Jason held his father's hand.

His father didn't respond and seemed to think he was still in the truck.

"Okay, Dad, just rest and get better. I'll be back tomorrow. We can talk tomorrow. Okay?"

Jason knew he had to get the pigs home, and he preferred to do it before dark, but he made a stop at the sheriff's office before hitting the road.

"Were you able to get any information from your father?" the sheriff asked.

"No," Jason said. "He isn't responding at all. But none of this makes any sense. I can't figure out why he was east of Highway 65 in the first place."

"Do your parents have relatives out in these parts?"

"No, neither of them have any relatives at all. My mom's parents died in a fire before I was born, and Dad's parents died when he was still in college. I'm not aware of any relatives or connections out here at all. This is the first year I wasn't with him. Mom went with Dad this year instead of me, but there's still no reason for them to have come this way. You've got to find her!" Jason pleaded in an increasingly loud voice.

"Calm down, son. Let's begin with a description of your mom. What's her full name and what does she look like? Height, coloring, and distinguished markings. Stuff like that."

"Her full name is Gertrude Johnson," Jason said, "and she's a tiny little woman, can't weigh much more than a 100-pound sack of feed, 135 lbs. tops. I guess she's average looking, you know, she's my mom, so I'm not sure what I'm supposed to say. She's certainly the kindest person anyone could ever want to know, sweet, kind, and generous, and she's shy. Everyone loves her. She's the best mom anyone could ever ask for."

As Jason spoke, the truth of what he was saying, and the pressure of the whole situation caused him to break down. He pulled a large handkerchief from his back pocket to mop his leaking eyes and blow his nose.

"That's okay, son. I understand how difficult this must be for you. I know you need to get those pigs home, but I presume you'll be back here within the next few days. Why don't you bring a couple of pictures of your mom with you the next time you come. That way we'll have something for a missing person's report. Meanwhile, I'll ask around to see if there's a new person in town. We'll find her. Don't you worry. We're very good at what we do."

"Do you have a lot of people missing?"

"Well, no, you're right. This is actually highly unusual. In fact, it's the first missing person case I've ever had. People don't usually just go missing." He stood. "We'll keep in touch, son."

Jason realized that was his cue to leave. They shook hands and Jason added, "I'll be back tomorrow, Sheriff, because you've got to find her."

Now there's a really nice kid, the sheriff thought as he watched Jason exit his office. *We should have more kids like that around here.*

Jason drove west on Highway 14 until he reached the gas station with the big bear carving, which was on the intersection where he turned onto Highway 65. When he was no more than a few miles from his farm, he stopped at the local gas station to refill the gas tank. At home, he unloaded and slopped the pigs, hosed out the back of the truck, and drove it to the Peterson farm to return it.

Rapping lightly on the kitchen screen door, he announced himself.

"Thanks so much for letting me borrow your truck." Jason handed the key to Mrs. Peterson. "I really appreciate it. I've gassed it up and hosed it out." He remained on the other side of the half-opened screen door.

"That's what neighbors are for, Jason. I'm glad I was able to help out. Did the truck give you any problems?"

"No, it ran perfectly."

"And how are your folks doing?"

"Dad's not doing well at all. He's in the hospital, but I don't think he knows it. In fact, I don't think he even knew I was there. He keeps mumbling to Priscilla, our big old prize pig, and seems to think he's still in our truck."

"I'm so sorry, Jason. And what about your mom? How is she holding up with all of this?"

"That's just the craziest thing! No one knows where she is. She seems to have disappeared." Jason felt as if he had the weight of the world on his shoulders.

"Disappeared? What do you mean? Didn't she leave the farm with your father?"

"Yes, I watched them drive off together."

He paused to bite back the tears he wasn't ready to release, wishing there were something for him to put his fist through, anything to help relieve his frustration while struggling to maintain his composure in front of Mrs. Peterson.

"None of this makes any sense," Jason said. "The sheriff wants me to bring him a picture of Mom so they can make a missing person poster, but I don't know if I'll be able to find one because Mom was always the one to take the pictures. She never liked being in them. But I'm going to look for some anyway when I get home. I'll be able to take my motorcycle tomorrow, so I won't need the truck again, but I really appreciated borrowing it today."

Jason didn't want to talk anymore. He just wanted to leave as fast as he could and hit a wall or something in the privacy of home. But he didn't get away fast enough, because Jessica, Mrs. Peterson's high school daughter, appeared next to her mother wearing freshly applied makeup and a big flirty smile.

"Hi Jason," she said. "I told your homeroom teacher you wouldn't be registering on time this year because your parents were in an accident, and that you borrowed our truck to go pick up your pigs. Should I tell them you won't be in school tomorrow either?"

Jason simply couldn't hold his anger or frustration any longer. "And did you go to my football practice for me too, Jessica? Did you? Did you do that?" Jason shouted at her.

"Well no. Why would I do that?" Her eyes welled up.

"What gave you the right to go to my homeroom teacher? Stay out of my business, Jessica! Do you hear me?"

He stormed away from the Peterson's back door with heavy feet and an even heavier heart, stomping all the way to the barn to retrieve his motorcycle. He gunned it up and sped down the road toward home.

As he did this, Jessica ran upstairs to her bedroom with black rivers of freshly applied mascara flowing down her face.

"That Jason Johnson is terrible! He's mean and I hate him!" She shouted to her bedroom walls and wept into her pillow.

16

MARTHA

"And though she be but little, she is fierce."

—WILLIAM SHAKESPEARE

Martha sat stewing in the car the following morning as she waited for Carl to finish up in the bathroom. The whole situation with this pushy broad who slept in their store last night upset and worried her. Martha wasn't only concerned about the potential damage a woman like that could do to the store, but it disturbed her to think that Carl had allowed it in the first place. Something just seemed a little fishy about the entire situation, and she had every intention of finding out just exactly what it was, suspicious that there was likely a lot more to the story than what Carl had told her. Either way, she was going to insist upon getting Carl's Jezebel moving on her way. She'd make it perfectly clear that Carl was *not* going to be that woman's next sugar daddy.

Having dressed in somewhat of a rush, she checked her lipstick in the visor mirror and fluffed her hair by running her fingers through it while she waited.

The longer Martha waited, the angrier she got. By the time Carl finally exited the house and approached the car, she had worked herself up to full steam of anger, causing her to flip the visor up with a snap.

"Oh," Carl said, looking as surprised as he felt when he discovered Martha had been waiting for him. "I didn't realize you were serious about going to the store this morning."

"I told you that last night, Carl. Apparently, you didn't listen very well."

Noting her tone, Carl said no more. He lit his first cigarette and started the car, driving to the store in silence, as neither of them seemed in the mood to listen to the radio or discuss the matter further. Martha listened to the pounding of her heart and the hum of the tires on the pavement, while Carl drove and tried not to think about anything at all.

When they arrived at the store, Carl pulled into his usual parking spot, got out of the car and walked to the front door, leaving Martha to fend for herself.

Well, that's a fine hullabaloo, Martha thought. *He could have at least asked if I needed help getting out of the car. Does he think it's easy for me to maneuver this late in my pregnancy?*

She struggled unassisted to exit the car while keeping an eye on her scoundrel husband, watching him put his key in the lock, open the door, and step inside. Then she heard him yell, "Holy shit!"

"What's happened, Carl?" Martha clumsily speed waddled into the store behind him.

"Did you know our floor was green?" he asked.

Following his gaze, Martha looked down, amazed to see the linoleum had been washed, waxed, and buffed until it glowed, showing its natural variegated color of green. It was, as they say, *clean as a whistle*, hospital clean.

"Carl," Martha whispered. "Do you think we should be walking on it?"

Before he could answer, they heard a woman's voice coming from the lady's bathroom.

"Good morning," the woman said and walked toward them as she tucked a strand of loose hair up into a bun.

"Good morning to you too," Carl said. "Did you wash and polish this floor last night?"

"Yes, do you like the way it turned out? I had to use quite a lot of your solvent to work the dirt away from the corners, but I was pretty pleased with the end result."

"I'll say," Carl said. "I haven't seen this floor look this good since, well I don't know when. By the way, this is my wife, Martha, and I'm sorry but I don't remember your name."

"It's Gert," she said while pumping Martha's hand.

Martha was completely unprepared for this Gert woman, as she expected her to look like a tart with heavy makeup. But this woman was nothing of the sort. Martha could not have been more surprised to find herself shaking the calloused hand of a plain, industrious woman with a skinny, pointy nose. *She's a strange one, but she's apparently willing to work for her keep, and just one look at her assures me she isn't a threat to my marriage.*

Martha's attitude toward this Gert woman changed completely. "Carl tells me you're planning to stay here for a few days, is that right?"

"Yes, if I can," Gert answered. "It'll just be until my husband can come back for me, sometime around Labor Day."

"Oh." Martha smiled at the words Labor Day, because to Martha, the only Labor Day this year would be the day her baby was born. "Well, if you're going to be staying for a few days you'd better show me where you're sleeping. Carl said something about a cot."

Together the women toddled to the back room where there was another surprise waiting for Martha.

"What did you do back here?" Martha asked. "I can hardly believe this is the same room. It looks so much larger and it's all neat and tidy."

"I hope it's okay with you. I just sorted the canned goods by product and date, putting the items that need to be sold first in front and on top of each stack."

"You did all that? It looks so different. All the clutter made the room appear to be a lot smaller."

"I hope you're not unhappy that I did it."

"Unhappy? No, I'm just amazed that's all. Is this where you slept?" Martha walked over to the cot when she saw it in the far back corner of the room.

"Yes. It worked out really well and I really appreciate being allowed to stay here."

"Was this quilt back here too?" Martha pointed to a quilt neatly folded at the foot of the cot.

"No, the quilt is mine. I made it."

"You made this quilt?"

"Yes, I did. I've won prizes for some of my quilts."

Martha looked at the quilt more carefully, running her fingers over the fine stitching, admiring both the detail and blend of colors. "When did you make this, and how long did it take you?"

"Oh, I've worked on this one the better part of last year. It takes a long time to do a quilt with this much detail."

"May I unfold it?"

"Of course." Gert helped Martha spread it out across the cot for further inspection.

"This is really beautiful." Martha stepped back, admiring it as a whole piece, seeing it more as a work of art than a mere quilt.

While Martha continued her inspection of the quilt, Gert explained how she had planned to enter the quilt in the State Fair. "That is until I found myself stranded here at your store."

"Hmmm." Martha hardly listened to what Gert was explaining to her. "I wouldn't mind learning how to make a quilt. Nothing this difficult, of course, but perhaps something simple, like a small baby quilt. Do you think you could teach me while you're here?"

"Sure. A baby quilt wouldn't be difficult. It just takes a little patience and planning."

Suddenly Martha got an idea. "Don't move," she said. "I'll be right back."

Martha began waddling back into the front of the store, but stopped, turned, and said, "Would it be okay if I called you Miss

Birdie? It just seems like you're an industrious little bird who flew in here. Would that be okay with you?"

Gert just smiled in surprise, not knowing how she felt about the nickname of Miss Birdie.

Assuming the name change was okay, Martha lumbered out of the storeroom and ambled toward the cash register in search of something. When Martha found what she was looking for, she toddled back to the storeroom where the new Miss Birdie remained standing in wait for her.

"Come with me, Miss Birdie." Martha held a key in her hand. "I'm a little out of breath from hauling this stomach around, but it'll be okay."

Gert followed Martha out the back door and together they stepped over to the camper that was parked behind the store. By holding on to both sides of the door jamb, Martha was able to hoist herself up to the door, unlock it and step inside.

"Come on," Martha said, motioning for Miss Birdie to follow, "but watch your head. It's got a low ceiling."

Gert followed and together they stepped further into the camper, a combination kitchen-living room-bedroom configuration.

"Carl and I used to travel in this a lot when we were first married. But now, with the responsibility of the store and with me being pregnant, we don't use it at all anymore, so I think you should sleep in here instead of on that old cot. We can take the sheets and towels to the laundry and get them freshened up. And when we come back, we can talk about quilting. What do you say? Wouldn't this be better than the cot?"

After removing the bedding and towels, Gert insisted that she be allowed to carry them so Martha could use both hands when she exited the camper. Together they returned to the front of the store where Martha asked Carl for the keys to the car.

Carl's eyes enlarged with surprise, but he handed her the car keys, afraid to ask any questions after her anger about this woman the previous night. He heard the two of them giggle and watched from the store window as they loaded the bedding into the back seat of the car.

Women! Who can figure 'em?

The women had barely driven away when the store phone rang. "Convenience store and gas station," Carl said.

"This is Sheriff Hicks getting back to you about that transient you called about yesterday. Is she still there?"

"Oh yeah." Carl groaned, realizing how much his life had changed overnight. "She's still here alright."

"Well, do you remember that pig accident I was dealing with out at the Wisconsin county line?"

"Yup, couldn't forget that, Sheriff. It made for some pretty good news watching that night."

"Yeah, very funny, Carl. Anyway, the point is, the truck driver is in the hospital, but he has a teenage son who insists his mother was in the truck with his father. And now the mother is missing. Her name is Gertrude Johnson. The kid says his mom is a tiny little thing, and I got the impression she may be a real good looker. Anyway, the kid says his mother doesn't weigh much more than a hundred pounds, 'not much more than a hundred-pound bag of pig feed,' is how he put it. Anyway, I figure a woman that small very likely has all the curves in the right places, if you catch my drift."

"Yup, I hear you, Sheriff."

"Anyway, the kid says his mom is a shy little thing, a gentle soul, and he's pretty broken up about the fact that she's missing. Too bad too because he seems like a nice kid. Anyway, I know your place is quite a distance from the county line where the accident took place, but I wondered if your transient might be his missing mother."

"I sure wish she were, but I really doubt it. I can't remember what she said her name was. It might be Bertha, or something like that, but let me assure you, there is nothing good-looking or shy about this woman. She's all angles and sharp elbows, and she's bossy as hell. My wife calls her Miss Birdie, and for some reason, Martha likes her. Come to think of it, that's a good name for her because she has a long skinny nose and sort of looks like a chicken."

"Okay, that's too bad. I was hoping both our problems might be solved. The kid's pretty broken up about it. He said he usually makes this trip with his father, and that they never come over in this direction. I wonder if the old geezer wasn't chasing some sweet-talking skirt out at the county line because he keeps calling for a woman named Priscilla. When the kid told me his mom's name was Gertrude, I didn't have the balls to tell him about this Priscilla dame. It would break his heart, and I just didn't have it in me to do that to him."

"I see what you mean," Carl said. "I guess you're in kind of an awkward situation there."

"Yeah," the sheriff said. "You know, just maybe, his mother got wind of this Priscilla dame and left with the first fast-talking trucker who offered her an alternative life. If she's really as good-looking as the kid implied, I can't say I blame her. The pretty ones are often a little simple in the head, you know, which makes them vulnerable to fast-talking truckers."

"Yup, could be," Carl agreed.

"Shoot, she could be across the state line and in Wisconsin by now. Then she'll end up being someone else's problem. Okay, Carl, nice talking to you and keep me posted if your stray gives you any grief."

"I will, Sheriff, and thanks for getting back to me."

"We should buy your fabric first," Miss Birdie said, "because we'll need to have it washed and dried before we begin cutting it. That's important because otherwise your quilt can pucker and shrink when it's washed after it's made."

Martha drove to the Five and Dime store, knowing they had a wide assortment of fabrics to choose from. When they got there, Martha found there was such a wide selection of baby print fabrics that she had a difficult time choosing between bunnies, dogs, kittens, flowers, rainbows, or cartoon characters. Finally, she settled on puppies. Then, she picked out two more patterned fabrics with compatible colors and had the clerk cut off the amount Miss Birdie said they would need. Meanwhile, Miss Birdie put the other supplies they would need into their shopping cart, things like scissors, extra-long straight pins, and matching thread.

They dropped the bedding and new fabric off at the laundry, asking that it be washed and dried while they went to the Piggly Wiggly, where Martha bought fresh produce unavailable at the convenience store. While there, Martha greeted an old school friend she hadn't seen since algebra class. The women all beamed and cooed at the friend's infant daughter who was contentedly sleeping in the new black buggy her in-laws had recently purchased for her.

On the way back to pick up the laundry, Martha said, "This is ever so much fun! I'd plum forgotten how enjoyable it is to be active and have someone to do things with."

When the women got back to the convenience store, they sounded like giggly schoolchildren as they hauled their purchases and clean laundry through the store and into the camper. Martha put the groceries away in the half-sized refrigerator while Miss Birdie put the fresh bedding on the bed and hung the clean towels.

"Okay, where do we begin with the quilt?" Martha said, spreading the fabric out onto the small kitchen table.

"Well, let's first begin with what you want your quilt to look like. I always begin with a drawing or a sketch."

Miss Birdie analyzed the fabric and drew several options out on paper, showing Martha the different ways they could display the puppies. Then she figured out the mathematical configurations for each choice.

"Gosh," Martha said, "I didn't know you needed to know arithmetic just to make a quilt. I was never very good with numbers when I was in school. I guess I didn't put much effort into learning them because I figured I was just going to get married, so why bother."

"Women need to apply math for sewing and cooking all the time. And when you make draperies or reupholster furniture, you absolutely need to have basic math skills. It's very important for women to know these things."

"Really? Do you know how to do all those things? Draperies and reupholstering, I mean?"

"Sure, I can do both of them. I used to help my mother do those things when I was very young, and I learned more advanced skills in my college Home Economics classes."

"You went to college?" Martha asked in surprise.

"Only for a short time." Miss Birdie didn't explain why she hadn't completed her degree.

"Wow! Just the same, that's something! None of my girlfriends ever went to college."

Martha and Miss Birdie spent the rest of the day exploring quilting options, measuring, designing, and cutting the triangles and squares for Martha's quilt.

After Carl locked the store, he stuck his head into the camper and said in a stern voice, "Martha, I'm going home now. Are you coming?"

Both women gasped with surprise to see what time it was. "Okay, Carl. I'll be right with you. Just give me a second."

Martha retrieved some of the groceries she'd purchased earlier, leaving the rest in the camper. "I'll be back tomorrow," she told Miss Birdie, "because I want to work on my quilt again." Then, she toddled out to the car with her bag of groceries, the things she planned to cook that evening. Carl was waiting for her in the car with the engine running.

"What's for dinner tonight, Martha? Have you given any thought about what you're going to cook for your husband, who worked all day?"

"As a matter of fact, I know exactly what I'm making for dinner."

When they got home, Carl got out of the car and strutted into the house, once again leaving Martha to struggle on her own, this time with a bag of groceries. She struggled up the back step at the kitchen door, set the bag on the table, and struggled again to retrieve her largest pot from the bottom of the cabinet, noting how it was becoming increasingly more difficult to bend over her huge belly. She filled the pot half full of water, set it on the stove, and lit the burner before dumping in the uncooked pasta. While the pasta cooked, she assembled the other ingredients she'd need. Having made this casserole so many times before, she could assemble it without consulting her recipe. While it baked, she made a salad with her home-grown lettuce, tomatoes, and cucumbers. Dinner was on the table within half an hour.

"Well, that was fast," Carl said as he sat down at the kitchen table with his second bottle of beer. "I was afraid you might think you didn't need to cook tonight just because you weren't home today."

Martha was about to laugh, thinking he was joking, but when she saw his expression, she realized he was serious. She found his attitude offensive but chose, for the sake of harmony, to avoid commenting because she was excited about making the baby quilt and she didn't want George's grumpy attitude to dampen her joy.

"So," she said, "Miss Birdie is helping me make a baby quilt. Isn't that great?"

"I hope you're not telling me you're planning to go to the store again anytime soon."

"Yes, that's exactly what I'm saying. In fact, I'm going with you every morning until I either have the quilt completed, or this baby decides to be born."

17

LIFE GOES ON

"If you don't like being a doormat then get off the floor."

—Al Anon

The following morning Carl hurried with his bathroom routine, intending to get to the car before Martha got any more ideas about going to the store with him. But Martha knew her husband all too well and wasn't going to give him the opportunity to drive off without her, suspecting he would pretend he didn't think she was serious about going with him again. Or, he might say he left without her because it had just slipped his mind. Martha had no intention of giving him the opportunity for either of those excuses, and for that reason, she was in the car before Carl left the house.

"Oh," he said, genuinely surprised to find his wife once again in the car before him. "So, you're serious about this. Do you really want to spend another whole day with that woman?"

"Yes," Martha answered a lot more sweetly than what she felt. "I told you that last night."

Carl cleared his throat, removed the red cellophane strip from a fresh pack of cigarettes, taking his time to peel the thin aluminum covering from one corner of the pack before gently tapping it on the back of his hand. It was a ritual he did with each new pack, but this morning he allowed it to take more time than usual as he grappled to find something he could say to dissuade his wife from spending another whole day with that Miss Birdie woman. Carefully, he tapped the first cigarette out of the virgin pack and placed the coveted cylinder between his lips.

Martha patiently waited, recognizing how hard he was trying to think of something he could say to prevent her from going to the store with him. But, in the end, he didn't say anything at all. He just lit up, inhaled deeply, and tossed the freshly opened pack onto the dashboard, while allowing the lit one to dangle on his lip. He turned the key in the ignition and drove to the store without saying another word, completely unaware of the burlap bag Martha had already placed on the floor of the back seat.

When they arrived at the store, Miss Birdie came running out to greet them. She helped Martha out of the car and removed the tote bag from the back seat.

What the hell! Was that Miss Birdie woman expecting that bag?

Carl noted how heavy the bag appeared and wondered how Martha had managed to get it to the car in the first place. In spite of his curiosity, he chose not to inquire, preferring to let the women think he didn't care one way or the other how a pair of foolish women spent their time. His main concern, had anyone asked, was that Martha may have decided not to cook dinner on the days she was at the store.

Business that day had been particularly good at the gas pumps, which didn't give Carl a lot of time to think any more about the women. And because the women had stayed in the camper and out of sight, he pretty much had forgotten all about them.

When it came time to lock up for the night, he strutted back to the camper and opened the door abruptly, thinking he may catch them doing something he may not approve of.

"Martha," he said with an authoritative tone, before stopping mid-sentence. "Wow, something smells really good in here. What are you cooking?"

The women were so startled by Carl's abrupt entrance that they both jumped as if they'd been caught doing something covert.

"Oh," they answered in unison, "it's dinner."

Martha quickly portioned a serving out for Miss Birdie before transferring the hot pot to the burlap bag that she'd brought it in earlier that morning.

"I'll carry this out to the car for you," Miss Birdie said.

Martha waddled behind Miss Birdie as they walked to the car together, giving each other a little hug after Miss Birdie securely placed the bag on the floor of the back seat.

"I'll see you tomorrow." Martha rolled the window down to let some of the day's afternoon heat out. "That is, unless this baby decides to come tonight."

Miss Birdie nodded, adding, "Carl, will you remove that bag from the car when you get home? Martha shouldn't be lifting anything that heavy. I can lock up for you tonight."

Carl blinked, hardly believing his ears, as it was only a few days ago when that Miss Birdie woman was nothing more than a transient sleeping outside on the wooden bear in front of his store. And now, she announces *she* will lock up? What the hell!

He lit a cigarette, got into the car, and inhaled aggressively. "Is that our dinner?" He scowled as he turned the key in the ignition.

"Yes," Martha answered sweetly. "I've made your favorite dinner for you tonight. We're having pot roast with carrots, onions, and potatoes."

Silence hovered as Carl's appetite whetted, while Martha wisely avoided filling the silence with idle chatter. She knew Carl didn't approve of her going to the store with him, but she also knew he loved pot roast, and that was why she'd cooked it all day in the camper, knowing the long slow cooking process would make it tender and juicy, just the way Carl liked it.

While Martha and Carl ate their dinner, Gert lined her dimes up in the payphone booth, where once again she dialed the farmhouse. Over the past few days, she'd called several times, but never got an answer, which began to concern her.

She hadn't actually planned to talk to Jason because she still didn't know how she was going to explain what his father had done to her, thinking it wasn't good for Jason to have ill feelings about his father. But she wanted to at least hear his voice, thinking she would have a sense of knowing how things were going for her son just by hearing his voice.

Unfortunately, the phone rang and rang, with only the clicks of the party line being heard. They were notorious for being nosey and listening in on others' private conversations.

I suppose football practice is consuming a lot more of Jason's time than any of us initially thought. And of course, there would be games some evenings too, so that may be where he is. I'll try again tomorrow.

With that last thought, she hung up the phone and got on with her evening cleaning chores.

18

MARTHA AND THE BABY

*"Life is not measured by the number of breaths we take,
but by the moments that take our breath away."*

—Maya Angelou

"Wake up, Carl!" Martha shouted, shaking his arm.

"What?" He groaned and rolled over.

"No, Carl! Wake up!"

What? What's wrong and what time is it?"

"My water broke."

"What did you break?" Carl grumbled half asleep.

"My water broke! The baby is coming."

"Oh." He jumped out of bed in his boxers. "What should I do?"

"Help me get to the car. My bag is packed and sitting next to the front door. Put it in the car and take me to the hospital."

"Okay! I'm ready! Let me pull my pants on."

He grabbed his jeans from the closet hook, pushed one leg in and nearly toppled over as he inserted his second leg. Sliding his bare feet into his shoes, he neglected tying his laces to save time. While Carl was stumbling about trying to get dressed, Martha waddled herself, unassisted, to the car and settled herself in the front seat.

"My bag, Carl," she said as her husband opened the driver's door. "You forgot my bag."

"Oh yeah, the bag!" He leapt back into the house and retrieved Martha's small overnight suitcase while trying to avoid tripping on his shoelaces. On the way back to the car, with the suitcase in hand, he realized he didn't have the car keys, so he made a second trip into the house to retrieve them from the hook in his closet. Then, he sped down the highway to the regional medical hospital, where Martha was at once whisked away in a wheelchair.

After parking the car, Carl found the Expectant Father's room where there were already several other anxious fathers pacing the floor, smoking, and drinking copious amounts of strong black coffee. Periodically, a doctor entered the room to announce a birth.

At 8:42 a.m., Martha's doctor stepped in, asking which father was Mr. Olson. Jittery from all the coffee and cigarettes, Carl nearly knocked him over as he leapt forward to identify himself.

"Congratulations, Mr. Olson," the doctor said. "You have a beautiful, healthy girl. She's 8 lbs. 4 ounces."

"It's a girl!" Carl said louder than he intended, "Oh, my gosh." He pumped the doctor's hand. "I'm a dad," he announced to the other unimpressed waiting fathers. "I have a little girl!" He pushed his half-smoked cigarette into the overflowing ashtray.

"Can I see her? Can I see my baby?"

"Yes, the nurse will have her cleaned up and in the nursery in a few minutes. And you can go take a peek through the nursery window down the hall."

"Okay!"

Carl was about to head in that direction when the doctor added, "And Mr. Olson, your wife is doing well too."

"Oh yes, Martha. I meant to ask you that. Should I see her, my wife, I mean? Should I go see Martha?"

"You can see her for a few moments, but then you should probably leave because she's going to need total bed rest for several days."

Carl found Martha's room and stepped in as quietly as a man hyped up on caffeine could manage.

"You did really good Martha! Really, really good! We have a baby girl. Did you see her?"

"No, not yet, but I think they'll bring her in for me to nurse her pretty soon."

"Did we decide on a name, Martha? I don't remember if we decided. I know we talked about a lot of names, but it didn't seem real 'till now. Now it's real, Martha! We have a baby! We have a little girl and I'm a dad! Should we name her after one of our mothers?"

"Let's decide tomorrow," Martha said. "I want to see her before I name her."

"Okay, we can decide later. The doctor told me you need to rest now anyway, so we can talk tomorrow about a name. Gosh, Martha, I can hardly believe it! A little girl! Imagine that. We have a baby daughter!"

Martha smiled, realizing she'd never seen Carl so keyed up before. He was usually so quiet and nonplussed about things. This was a new Carl, and she wasn't sure what to make of it. But mostly, she wanted him to leave, because his clothing reeked of cigarette smoke and his breath was gagging her.

"The doctor said you need to rest, Martha, so I'll just go down and have a peek at our baby. Then I'll come back later tonight. Is that okay with you?"

After leaving Martha's bedside, Carl scurried down the hall toward the nursery. Exhausted and jangle-nerved, he looked through the smudged nursery window at the lineup of little sleeping bundles until he saw a crib labeled *Olson girl*. Inside the Olson crib, he saw a tightly wrapped pink bundle. The nurse rolled the crib closer to the window, allowing him a better look, but all he could see was a fat little pink face with a tuft of black hair sticking straight up on its head. The other babies didn't have much hair at all. Some had a little blond peach fuzz, but most were bald.

He would have liked to count his baby's fingers and toes, just to make sure they were all there with no extra appendages, but he fig-ured the doctor would have told him if there was anything out of the ordinary to be concerned about.

Carl smiled at the nurse, motioning his permission to return his baby to the queue with the others. Then he swaggered down the hall, past the dads' waiting room and strutted as proud as a peacock into the parking lot.

Surprised to find the sun was up, and that the morning air was cool and ever so refreshing, he glanced at his watch while lighting another cigarette, shocked to see the time.

Oh, my God! I'm late opening the pumps. I should have had them open an hour and a half ago.

Fearing that his customers might get comfortable getting gas at one of his competitors, he hit the gas pedal a little heavy as he headed directly to the store.

He would have liked to have a shower, shave, and a change of clothes, but felt it was more important to open the store and gas station.

When he arrived, he was shocked to see the store was already open, and it was running smoothly with Miss Birdie taking care of his customers.

"Good morning, Carl," she said in a cheery polite manner.

"Yes, good morning to you too. I see you've opened the pumps and the store, and you're taking care of my customers."

"Yes. Did Martha have her baby last night?"

"How did you know that?"

"Well, when you didn't come in this morning, I figured that's what happened. Is she okay?"

"Yeah, she's fine!"

"And the baby? Is the baby okay too?"

"Yes, we have a daughter. She's 8 lbs. 4 oz."

"That's a big baby. Congratulations to both of you."

Carl waited for Miss Birdie to step aside so he could take his right-ful place behind the cash register, but she didn't move.

Instead, she said, "I can take care of things here today if you want to go home and get a little shuteye. You may want to shave and take a shower too, and put on some socks. Your white ankles look like a pair of headlights down there."

What a bossy woman! She takes over my store and then tells me to go home and even has the gall to tell me to shower and how to dress.

Gert made no effort to remove herself from behind the cash register. After Carl stood there several more minutes, he began feeling both silly and exhausted. The longer he stood, the worse he felt, realizing his mouth felt like the bottom of a birdcage.

"Well, maybe that's a good idea," he finally acknowledged. "A little shuteye would feel pretty good. If you're sure you can manage things, I think I'll take you up on that. We have a telephone right next to our bed, so I can be back down here in a jiff if you need me. Call if you have any difficulties at all."

With mixed feelings and total exhaustion, Carl drove home and nearly fell into his bed, leaving Miss Birdie in charge of his store and the gas pumps.

19

JASON

"With a new day comes new strength and new thought."

—ELEANOR ROOSEVELT

Early the following morning Jason returned to the neighbor's farm timidly knocking on the back door, having timed his visit so he'd be there before Jessica left for school.

"Good morning, Mrs. Peterson," he said. "Would you ask Jessica to come to the door, please?"

"Good morning, Jason. I have to say I'm surprised to see you here this early, but I don't think Jessica wants to see you this morning."

"I don't blame her. I wasn't very nice to her yesterday. I said some things I shouldn't have, and I've come to apologize. Please, ask her to come to the door."

"Well, okay, wait here, Jason. I'll ask her if she'll come to the door."

Jason brushed dirt and sand away from the top wooden steps with his hand before sitting on it as he nervously allowed what he was about to say to run through his head. He hoped he wouldn't botch things up more if his words didn't come out right. The longer he waited, the more nervous he became. Finally, he heard Jessica's soft voice on the other side of the screen door.

"Hi, Jason. Mom said you wanted to see me."

Jason jumped to his feet as he tried to look through the screen, but Jessica was barely visible from this angle because the early morning sun was glaring off the screen at a peculiar angle.

"I've come to apologize," he blurted out in one big burst of energy. Jessica didn't make a peep, and he wondered if she'd heard him, or for that matter, if she was even still there. What if he was talking to an empty screen door?

Slowly the door opened, and Jessica stepped outside. In a more controlled voice, he said, "I shouldn't have yelled at you, Jessica. I'm sorry. I know you were just trying to help."

Recognizing Jason's stress, she thanked him for coming to apologize, adding, "I appreciate your apology, Jason."

Silence hung stiffly in the air as they both stood awkwardly, Jason with his hands stuffed deep in his pockets, and Jessica wiping hers onto the sides of her skirt.

Jessica was the first to break the silence. "You really hurt my feelings, you know. But after I had time to think about it, I realized you were right too. I shouldn't have butted into your business. So I'm sorry too."

Together they sat on the steps and talked. Jason explained how his mother was still missing and that his dad remained unconscious. "Dad doesn't even seem to know he's in the hospital or that I was there visiting him. It makes me feel terrible."

Jessica told Jason about the things that were happening at school. "We're all mostly doing makeup work for all the stuff we missed last year due to the snow-days."

"Jessica," Jason said, "when you picked up my school assignments from my homeroom teacher, you did the right thing. I was just too much of a jerk to realize it at the time. If you wouldn't mind, I'd like you to continue doing that for me, because while I'm sitting with Dad, I could be reading or studying. In fact, that's the only way I'm going to be able to keep up with any of my classes at all. Would you be willing to do that?"

"Of course, if you're sure that's what you want. I'd be happy to do that."

After a short pause, Jessica asked, "What about football? Do you think you'll have to drop off the team?"

"I'm not sure yet about football. I'm thinking that if I leave the hospital by 1:00 o'clock each day, I could still get back in time for football practice. Of course, I'll have to get up extra early each morning to get the chores done, but I'm thinking I could still do the evening chores after football. Still, it's going to be a problem on game nights, but I'll just have to see how it all unfolds. It's too early to tell yet. But at this point, I'm going to try."

Jason's days were full. He did the morning chores at first light, packed a sandwich for himself, and drove two hours to sit with his dad at the hospital.

"I'm here, Dad," he said each morning. "Can you hear me?"

There was never an answer, but the nurses assured him his dad would know he was there. Apparently, there had been cases of coma patients who reported being able to hear everything around them while locked in that state. So Jason continued talking to his father. He read him all his school assignments: History, English, and even talked the process through when he did math calculations. He was in level three Spanish, and he read that to his father too.

"You know, Dad, if you can really hear me, like the nurses say you can, you might be able to understand Spanish when you come out of this coma. Won't that be a kick?"

At noon each day, he kissed his father on the forehead and said goodbye. "Dad, I've got to leave now for football practice, but I'll be back tomorrow."

As Jason drove down the road each day, he marveled at the wood-carving of a large bear at the intersection just east of where he turned onto Highway 65.

One of these days, I'm going to stop and take a closer look at that carving. I can't imagine how they did it. They must have had to stand on a ladder with a chain saw. Good grief! Just think of how dangerous that must have been.

20

GERT'S LABOR DAY

*"Woman is like a tea bag—you never know how
strong she is until she gets into hot water."*

—ELEANOR ROOSEVELT

The fair always closes on Labor Day, which is only a few days from now, and I expect George will come back for me as soon as he has Priscilla loaded.

Huh! I wonder how he'll act. He'd better not just come prancing in here laughing and acting as if this little stunt of his is a big joke. Because abandoning one's wife is *not* a laughing matter, no matter how well I've adjusted to being here. What if I was still sleeping outside on that bear? I'd have gotten soaked in last night's storm. It was eerie enough hearing the thunder from inside this camper because it sounded as if I was inside a drum.

Still, I could never have imagined how much I would have enjoyed these past couple of weeks. If George thought he was punishing me when he dropped me here, he will likely be sadly disappointed and surprised when he sees how well I've managed. In fact, he couldn't have left me in a better place, because the store has not only been a reminder of happier times from my childhood, but this little camper has turned out to be very cozy and comfortable as well.

Still, I'm looking forward to getting back home to see Jason and my chickens, but I'm going to miss being here as well. Actually, these past few days have been like a vacation for me because there's no one demanding anything from me. But, I'm going to miss a lot of things from here too, especially Martha, because it's been such a treat to have a female companion to share ideas and be able to talk about topics of interest to women. But now that Martha has a baby, her life will be changing too. She probably won't be coming to the store much at all anymore.

Well, I might as well enjoy my last few days here because when I get home, I'll be plunged into all sorts of things, things that have been neglected in my absence. I'll be up at the crack of dawn each day with the chickens, because it seems there is never an end to the list of tasks needing my attention. And I can well imagine the disarray Jason has left the house in.

Well, I may give a good talk about wanting to be leisurely, saying I wished I had a whole day with nothing to do, but leisure has never actually suited me. Besides, if I want to get Martha's quilt finished so she can carry her baby home from the hospital in it, I'd better get up and begin working on it.

With no further procrastination, I got out of bed, stepped into the shower, dressed, and brought a cup of coffee with me into the store. I was surprised to see two cars parked out in front of the gas pumps, waiting for Carl to open, as he was usually here by now.

"Are you waiting for gas?" I asked both drivers.

They answered in the affirmative, so I unlocked the pumps, filled their tanks, and collected the proper fee. Luckily, the first customer had small bills with him and the other had his checkbook.

After they left, I opened the store and stood behind the counter, where I waited for Carl to arrive. While standing there, I noticed Carl had slipped a new state map under the protective glass next to the cash register. I was puzzled by the fact that he'd already defaced it with an inky red circle because he was typically so frugal and picky about things like that. It seemed out of character for him to mutilate a brand-new map.

I had no prior experience with map reading, but found the mark so puzzling that I began studying it. Then it dawned on me. The mark very likely stood for the location of the store. Fascinated by that revelation, I examined the map more closely, scrutinizing the narrow blue and red lines that crisscrossed and ran parallel to each other near the red circle. The thickest and boldest line was labeled US 65, which I knew was the main highway connecting our farm town to the Twin Cities. According to the map, it passed near Albert Lea, Owatonna, and Faribault, all names of towns I heard before. Owatonna was the town closest to the red circle, so I ran my finger down the map along Highway 65 and could see for the first time where our farm was located relative to the store.

I also noticed the map had large blocked off sections with five-digit numbers printed in the center of each one. In the small print on the corner of the map was an explanation of the numbers. They were called Zip Codes, something I'd recently read about in the newspaper. According to the article I read, Zip Code stood for Zone Improvement Plan, which was supposed to make mail delivery more efficient.

Yeah, right. We'll see about that now, won't we.

Realizing for the first time where I was on the map and seeing where our farm was in relation to the store was not only exhilarating, but I found myself feeling a little cocky about my new map reading skills, thinking I could probably even give directions on how to get here now. Of course, I knew that would no longer be necessary because I expected George would be by to pick me up on his way home as soon as the State Fair closed, and that was only a few days from now. But that meant I only had a few more days to finish Martha's quilt, because I knew Martha would like to carry her baby home from the hospital in it. So I worked on the quilt late into the next two evenings and finished it just in time.

The morning of Labor Day, I met Carl in the parking lot as soon as he arrived and asked him to take the quilt to Martha on his next visit.

"I know Martha will want to bring the baby home in the quilt," I said as I handed it to him.

Carelessly, and without commenting on the quilt, he tossed it onto the front passenger seat of the car.

Then he stepped to the back of his car and opened the trunk. "Help me carry these fans in. It's going to be really hot today and we're going to need them."

I helped carry the fans into the store and watched him focus all his attention on strategically placing them in various locations: one at the front counter, one near the fresh produce, and the third in the far corner near the bathrooms and payphone. He was so engrossed in choosing the precise positioning of them that I don't think he even noticed when I left and returned to the camper to tidy it and pack up my few possessions.

I wanted to make sure everything was done prior to when George arrived, because I knew George would want to leave immediately with no time for me to make long goodbyes. When I finished packing my few belongings, I returned to the store, busying myself with miniscule tasks where I still could watch for George.

I considered telling Carl that I'd be leaving later that day, but he was so preoccupied with his fans and the flood of customers coming and going that I decided I'd just introduce them when George arrived, thinking there was no point in making a big deal about it until George was actually here.

I stood tall, and to avoid looking nervous, I fiddled and straightened any little thing where I had a good view of the road. I swept and re-swept around the front door, forcing a smile to appear relaxed. It helped when I saw two young boys climbing on the bear, each daring the other to reach up and touch the bear's glass eyes.

The entire store felt alive and festive that morning, which was further enhanced by the large American flag Carl had mounted near the entrance. The flag flapped grandly in the breeze, letting the public know the store and pumps were open. My heart raced so much with the anticipation of George's arrival that I appreciated all the hustle and bustle of the day because it helped camouflage my anxiety. Yet, no matter how hard I tried to calm myself, I jumped every time I heard a truck ramble down the road. Each so far has been a false alarm, but I continued waiting with both eager anticipation and an unexplained dread that I would find difficult to explain.

I tried thinking about something to help me relax, and in doing so, I reminisced about what I did on hot days like this when I was a kid. Back then, all I wanted to do was to stand in front of an open freezer door in my parent's store, which brought on a smile, because even today as an adult I wouldn't mind standing in front of one of Carl's open freezer doors. In an effort to avoid giving in to that temptation, I refocused my attention by eavesdropping on some of the customer's private conversations. That was how I learned Carl's store and gas station were the only businesses open that day, which I knew would result in record sales for him at both the pumps and the store.

I had forgotten how town people could use their holidays for leisure activities, because on the farm, every day was the same. The animals needed to be fed and tended to regardless of the day. Unlike farm people, town people could take full advantage of their holidays, as seen by the steady flow of people purchasing last-minute items. They bought blocks of ice, cigarettes, pop, popsicles, snacks, lip balm, and fuel for their cars, trucks, and boats. Carl wasn't allowed to sell strong beer because of the Minnesota Blue Laws, but he could sell 3.2 low-alcohol beer, and he was selling a lot of it.

What I found most astonishing of all was the volume of angle worms and grubs he sold, because I knew farm people would never spend money on such a thing. They'd simply dig their own worms for fishing. But Carl kept small white boxes of worms in a cooler next to the milk, beer, and pop, and the town people were buying them at highly inflated prices.

I had always known Minnesota boasted of being the state of 10,000 lakes, because the motto is stamped on the license plate of every car, yet I never realized the full impact of that. Based on the fervor of the last-minute purchases, and the number of boats being towed behind cars and trucks going through the gas station, I realized every one of those lakes were very likely going to be well populated this weekend. There were canoes, fishing boats, power boats for water skiing and boats for sightseeing. And there were even a few pontoon boats being hauled behind trucks on very wide trailers.

I've never been on a boat of any kind and would have loved being able to take a ride on any one of them, as I'm sure it would be a joy to ride around on top of the water and see the sumac, cattails, and reeds that partially camouflage the birds and ducks. And how fun it would be to see what people's cabins looked like along the shore. But today was not the day for me to be lusting after boat rides. Today, my only job was to watch for George.

By midday, the outdoor thermometer was in triple digits. That, coupled with the humidity from last night's thunderstorm, caused the day to be insufferable with both humidity and heat. I knew it had to be even worse for Carl when he was standing on the black tar pavement when he pumped gas. The heat radiating up around his feet and ankles had to be excruciating.

As the locals said, "it was a scorcher of a day."

While wiping sweat from the back of my neck, I tried second guessing how George would act when he arrived.

As the day progressed, I became less and less patient, as a headache began to build. Thinking I might be dehydrated, I glugged down a large glass of water and continued waiting, knowing I had no other choice. When evening approached, I was still waiting. And when it was time to close the store, I finally realized there was nothing left to wait for.

When Carl began locking up, I didn't say a single word, not a good night, not a congratulatory comment about it being a good day for business, not an offer to bring in the flag. I simply couldn't speak.

I returned to the camper, not caring what Carl or any man felt or said about anything. I was exhausted, fed up, and depressed, acknowledging for the first time that my husband hadn't abandoned me for the two weeks during the State Fair, but he had abandoned me forever.

The soles of my feet burned from weariness. My skin was hot and sticky. But my heart, well, my heart was cold and hard as a rock.

Robot style I returned to the camper where I removed the quilt from my bag, brought it to my sweaty face and collapsed onto the bed where I wept, while listening once again to the thunder rumbling in the sky again.

21

JASON THE DAY
AFTER LABOR DAY

"Life shrinks or expands in proportion to one's courage."

—Anais Nin

Like a dutiful son, Jason fed the animals before dawn each morning. Then he drove to the hospital to offer his father comfort and encouragement, each day hoping his father's coma would lift. He felt that would be the only way he'd learn the whereabouts of his mother because both he and the sheriff remained baffled as to where she could be. They asked themselves over and over what clues they were missing, what details were escaping them, yet neither was having any success with putting the pieces of the puzzle together.

In the middle of the night, nine days after the accident, Jason stumbled into the kitchen in his undies to answer the wall-mounted telephone.

"Hello?' Jason said louder than he'd intended, hearing his still half-asleep and changing voice crack.

"This is Doctor Smith," the voice on the other end of the line said. "I'm your father's nighttime attending physician. I'm afraid I'm calling with bad news."

Jason reached over to drag one of the kitchen chairs to him and sat on the cold vinyl.

"Your father," the doctor said, "stopped breathing at 3:02 a.m. We tried resuscitating him, but our efforts weren't successful. We couldn't bring him back."

Jason heard the words, knew what they meant, but somehow couldn't utter a sound. He sat there shivering, wondering what he was supposed to do, ask, or say.

"We all hoped for a better outcome." The doctor heard nothing but breathing on Jason's end of the conversation. "Would you like me to arrange for your father's body to be sent to the mortuary closest to you?"

"Okay, I guess so."

The doctor said something else, but Jason couldn't focus on anything other than knowing his father had died. After hearing that, nothing else mattered because he feared the death of his father also meant he'd likely never find his mother.

Not until after Jason hung up the phone did he realize he was cold, but what did that matter? Nothing really mattered anymore. Not really, because he was no more useful than a broken pitchfork.

He knew he'd taken so many things for granted: trips to the fair with his father, and all the wonderful times they recapped them for his mother when they got back home, embellishing upon the minutia of what he and his father did. Nothing would ever be the same again. Not even the simple act of having someone to share the details of each pig's birth would ever happen again. Now who would he talk to about those things?

His father's body was sent by medical hearse to the Olmsted County Mortuary, where the funeral was scheduled to take place on September 2nd. Over the next couple of days, Jason was asked to decide upon things he never wanted to answer. What casket did he want? Where would the burial plot be? What words did he want on the gravestone marker? What was his preference for music at the service, and who would speak at the service? When it came time to decide upon the flowers, he lost it and broke down into a puddle of misery. It was all way over-the-top too much to endure.

Thank goodness for Mrs. Peterson, who stepped in to offer her maternal guidance and support. She guided him through each difficult decision and also helped prepare him for what he would face on the day of the funeral.

"The funeral," she said, will be in the morning, so people will probably bring food to the house immediately following the service."

"Food!" he gasped. "What for? Why would they do that?"

"It's the country way, Jason. People bring food to these things, and they expect there to be a celebration of life at your house following the ceremony. They'll talk about your father and share their memories of him."

"Do you mean they'll be expecting a party?"

"Well, not exactly a party, but, yes, it is a party of sorts, I guess. But folks call it a celebration of life. Anyway, people will expect you to invite them back to the house after the funeral, but don't worry. I'll help you, and so will Jessica. We'll take care of everything. All you need to do is make sure the refrigerator is fairly empty and the bathrooms are clean. You just show me where your mother's tablecloths are and where she keeps the extra silverware. Jessica and I will take care of the rest."

If it hadn't been for Mrs. Peterson and Jessica's support and guidance, Jason might not have been able to get through the day at all. Their help was invaluable.

Surprisingly, the funeral attendance turned out to be huge, much larger even than what Mrs. Peterson had expected, which meant the gathering at the house was larger than what she had expected as well. People came and went for hours, with the farmhouse phone continually ringing to request driving directions.

"Johnson residence," Jason heard Mrs. Peterson say into the telephone over and over. She'd been giving out directions on and off for the past half hour. She'd hardly hang up from one call when the phone would ring again.

"Hello, Johnson residence, Mrs. Peterson speaking. You'll need to speak up a little more clearly, dear, because I'm having difficulty hearing you."

She held the mouthpiece aside for a moment to supply directions to Jessica who was trying to balance a salad bowl and a meringue pie. "Jessica, darling, put the salads on the sideboard in the dining room. Save the dining room table for the main dishes because we'll need the entire table for them. The desserts can go on the porch table. We'll cut those last."

Mrs. Peterson lifted the phone back to her ear. "I'm sorry, dear. There's so much happening here, that I couldn't hear what you were saying. Could you repeat that, and would you speak up a little louder please?"

Jason saw Mrs. Peterson shake her head.

"Some of these calls are really strange," she whispered to Jason as she placed the mouthpiece on her shoulder to prevent the caller from hearing her comment. She listened a little longer but heard only sputtering and heavy breathing. "Look," Mrs. Peterson said, "if you want me to hear you, you'll have to speak up more clearly because I'm too busy to listen to someone breathing!" She returned the phone to its cradle and got on with arranging food on the tables.

"Who was that?" Jason asked.

"I have no idea. My best guess is that the notoriety of your missing mother has caused a lot of curiosity and pranksters, because I don't think your parents even met most of the people who are here today."

Jason scanned the hordes of people milling through his house, socializing on his porch, and roaming across his lawn. He recognized a few of them. There were members from the church, women from the Extension Homemakers Club, and of course, every farmer in the county who had ever had business with his father was there. The farmers were putting in their appearance out of respect. But there were many he didn't know, and he suspected Mrs. Peterson was correct in assuming they were here for no better reason than to satisfy their curiosity.

The house, the big wrap-around porch, and the front lawn were packed with people and cars. Some even parked up on the expansive lawn Jason had so carefully mowed two days earlier.

The farmers typically shook Jason's hand, awkwardly expressing their sympathy, while each in his own way managed to inquire about Jason's plans for the farm now that his father wasn't there to run it. Women typically approached him with long serious faces, offering platitudes and inquiring about his mother, asking him if he knew where she was. Jason had no answers for any of them.

To get away from all the inquisitiveness he escaped to his private bathroom in his bedroom. He closed the lid of his toilet, sat on it, and hid. Then, Jason realized he could overhear conversations taking place on one section of the porch through the small vent high up on the outside wall.

"What do you think the kid's going to do with the farm?" one farmer asked.

"Don't rightly know about that, Jeb. Seems like a pretty big operation for a young upstart to manage all by himself."

"Yup. That's what I was thinking. Suppose a person who knew

what he was doing might be able to get a pretty good deal on the place."

"Yup, I suppose that could be so. Are you thinking about making an offer?"

"Well, I can't rightly say. I'm not interested in going into the pig farming business, if that's what you're asking. I'm just a crop farmer, you know, been one my whole life, just like my daddy and my granddaddy. Seems to me this land would be pretty good for growing corn and maybe a little wheat or soybeans too, probably pretty rich soil from all those pig droppings over the years. It's worth giving a little thought to. Know what I mean?"

"Yup! You got that right. It's definitely worth giving some thought to, that's for sure."

Jason recognized the sound of a glass bottle carelessly plopped down onto the wooden rail, because he and his father had done the same thing many times. It was a familiar sound from happier times.

"I think I'll just mosey over and find myself another one of them free beers. This one's empty. You want another one?"

"Nah, I've got to get home. The wife's got things she wants me to do today, but it's been nice chatting with you. As soon as I get my last crop in, I'll start going to the coffee shop in the mornings again."

"Yup. Same here. The old gang should all be showing up there by the end of the month."

Shortly after the two farmers vacated that space on the porch, female voices replaced the male voices.

"Does anyone know what actually happened to the woman?"

"What woman are you talking about, Mable?"

"You know, the kid's mother, the old guy's wife."

"Oh, her. No, I don't think so. I don't think anyone knows anything about her. Guess she just got up and disappeared."

"That's pretty weird, don't you think? You never know what kind of strange things go on with people who live out in the boonies like this. Remember that Ed Gein guy in Wisconsin. People were disappearing back then too, and it took the police years to figure out he was killing them and using their skin to cover furniture and lamps. Remember?"

"Geeze, Mable, what made you think of that? That was nearly fifty years ago, and that guy was a whacko creep. Look at this kid. He's just a nice kid who's hurting a lot right now."

"Just say'n you can never tell about the ones who live out here in the boonies. And anyway, that wasn't so far from here if you recall. What if the kid murdered her or something? She might even be buried out here on the farm someplace. And just maybe, the farmer went crazy about it and that's what caused his accident."

"Mable, you're the only one who's weird. That poor kid is probably going through hell right now, and he sure doesn't need any rumors like that getting started. My guess is she just got fed up with living out here on a farm with no other woman around. Maybe she ran off with a lover or something."

Mable found funerals ghoulish in the first place and wasn't about to back down on her macabre speculation. Instead, she changed the subject. "I suppose the kid will inherit the farm. What do you think all this is worth?"

"I have no idea. It just looks like a whole lot of loneliness to me. I can't imagine living out here in the winter. The thought of all the ice and snow along that long driveway, combined with so much isolation, with pigs, nonetheless, would drive me crazy."

Jason overheard more than enough! He was horrified by the gossip and the chilling speculations and would have liked nothing more than to make this terrible nightmare end so he could get back to his normal life. Yet, he knew normal would never exist for him again. He left the privacy of his bathroom, timidly venturing into the living room in search of Jessica. She and her mother had everything under control, and he wanted to tell them how much he appreciated what they were doing for him.

But before he found them, he saw a young boy running up into the side yard screaming something about his sister having fallen into one of the pig pens.

"She wanted to pet the baby pigs," the boy said.

The two youngsters had apparently wandered off when their parents weren't watching. And when the children spied the pen of piglets, the little girl told her brother she thought they were cute and wanted to pet them. She was small enough to slip through the bars of the pen, and to her young eyes, it must have looked like it would be easy to walk across the boards that were floating on the oozing mud to get closer to the piglets. Of course the task wasn't easy at all, and she slipped off and fell into pig muck.

When her brother ran back to the house shouting that his sister was in a pigpen, everyone ran down to watch the fiasco. The girl's father was strong enough to break the surface tension of the muck and pull her out, while the mother kept shouting, "Find her other shoe, dear. Those are her new patent leather shoes."

Upon further questioning, it wasn't clear if the girl decided to wander into the pen on her own, or if her brother had encouraged her because the boy laughed during the entire escapade.

As the father carried his muddy daughter up toward the house, Jason heard her say, "I just wanted to pet the baby pigs, Daddy."

The spectators all thought the scene was humorous, but Jason knew how dangerous it was. That little girl could have drowned in the pig slop because it's sticky and it tends to hold the person down. He also knew her little patent leather shoe would never be found. It belonged to the pigs now.

After the pig incident, people began leaving. Mrs. Peterson had already transferred the leftover food into small containers, which she labeled and dated before placing them in Jason's refrigerator and freezer. Then, she and Jessica washed all the serving bowls, spoons, plates, and containers for people to take back home with them before setting them out on the front porch table. Next to the clean empty containers, she stacked piles of fresh produce from Gert's Garden with a sign inviting people to help themselves to as many of the fresh vegetables as they wished to take back home with them. Jason wouldn't have to think about cooking for himself for several weeks, nor would he have to worry about trying to return empty dishes to people, and neither did he have to wonder what to do with the bumper crop of vegetables from his mother's vegetable garden.

Jason looked at Mrs. Peterson and Jessica with total gratitude because they had taken care of everything.

After everyone left, Jason walked down the hill to sit with the pigs. "Priscilla, you're the only one who knows what happened to Mom. I sure wish you could talk to me."

Priscilla gazed at him with anticipation of food, but when she realized Jason hadn't come to feed her, she rolled over on her side and gave him her best and deepest snort.

22

GERT'S DECISION

"I know God will not give me anything I can't handle.
I just wish that he didn't trust me so much."

—Mother Teresa

I rubbed my pounding temples while peering out the window where only a few hours earlier I was fixated in terror at lasers of lightning streaking across the sky. Retrieving my watch from the bedside table, I saw it was 7:00 a.m., late for me as I'm typically up by 5:30 or 6:00.

Still and all, I'm thankful to be alive after last night's storm. It was bad enough to endure the sound of thunder and crack of lightning, but when the tornado sirens blew the whole situation became a lot more frightening because I didn't have a basement to go down into. Not only that, but I suddenly realized no one would have known who to notify if I had died in last night's twister.

I'll say this though, that storm caused me to wake up to a few things, things I should have addressed more than two weeks ago. I suppose there's nothing like a Jesus moment of fear to help someone like me come to grips with reality. For one thing, it's helped me acknowledge that I've been abandoned, deserted by the one person

I should have been able to trust and rely upon. I'm not proud of my meltdown or my naivete, sobbing like that, and for what? A bum? A scoundrel? Well, no more! From this day forward, I'm going to take charge of myself. It's time for me to get a backbone and do something about my situation.

I marched my throbbing headache to the bathroom in search of the aspirin bottle and began formulating a plan. After swallowing two of the chalky tablets, I returned to the bedroom, picked up one of the wilted magazines I'd already read, and tried in a futile effort to use it as a makeshift fan. But I ended up tossing the useless magazine into the basket next to the bed.

Good God almighty! We've had some hot days on the farm too, but not like this. And I could always get some relief from the heat by sitting on the shady side of our wraparound porch over by the big oak. And there was usually a breeze there too.

After taking a tepid shower, I dressed in my coolest cotton dress, gulped down several cups of strong black coffee, and poured a third one to take with me. I picked up my coin purse and marched to the phone booth with renewed determination, planning to complete my call and get this business resolved before Carl arrived.

I emptied the coins from my purse onto the metal counter and sorted them into monetary order before lifting the receiver. Then I dialed the farmhouse phone number. Not so patiently, I listened to each click of the dial in its rotation, letting it move at its own slow clip to avoid a mechanism error. My stomach felt as if it was doing flips, and the combination of heat and anxiety was causing my deodorant to fail.

After dialing all the numbers, I listened to the ringing on the other end of the line. While it rang, I took a gulp of the bitter black coffee, nearly burning the roof of my mouth.

I can't imagine where those guys could be. Surely, they still aren't doing chores unless one of the animals is sick. I suppose that might be a possibility. One can only speculate about how well Jason took care of the pigs in our absence.

My coffee began tasting bitter, but I drank the last of it anyway as I continued listening, willing someone to pick up the phone.

I hope my chickens are doing okay. They were all healthy when I left, and they were laying pretty well too. In fact, I was getting top dollar for our eggs because the eggs were so large. I bet George doesn't even know where to get the best price for them because he's never paid any attention to them, always pretending they were beneath him. But, if it weren't for my chickens and my egg money, I wouldn't have been able to eat these past two weeks.

The tension was building on the back of my neck again, and I noted how my temples began throbbing. I dreaded the thought of going through all this same anxiety again later, but I also promised myself that I wouldn't procrastinate a single day longer. I would call back later and insist on one of those guys picking me up, and I no longer cared which of them did it. I was fed up with both of them.

I bet neither of them even gave me a second thought during last night's tornado watch. It's disgusting!

I scooped up my coins and returned them to my coin purse before tucking my purse into a pocket of my dress. As I exited that phone booth, I realized I had even more questions than what I had when I woke this morning. But I also had a renewed determination to reach George or Jason and get answers to those questions.

I can't imagine what George may have told Jason when he got home without me. The scoundrel! To think I was so concerned about not involving Jason, and then George just goes home without me anyway. Is it possible that he's lost his mind? Or I wonder if George may have forgotten where he dropped me off? Now, that's a possibility, I suppose. I was about to return to the camper when I heard the newspapers being tossed in front of the store. So I went out to retrieve them. I couldn't lift the whole pile at once, so I split it and carried it in half in at a time. But first I removed yesterday's leftover papers from the counter and tossed them in the recycle box for the Boy Scouts to pick up later. The scouts earned money for their troupe by selling the papers to a company that recycled them for Pelham cloth.

Curious to know how our pigs placed in this year's competition,

I pulled out the Home Section of today's paper and searched for the State Fair judging results. Scanning down the page I found the Swine Winners section, but I was surprised to see our name wasn't listed as winners in any of the events.

I can hardly believe our pigs didn't win anything, not even an honorable mention, because we've always at least placed. And fairly often we'd taken first place. I wondered if something happened to Priscilla.

But I decided I had enough to deal with, without contemplating the health of a pig or the equability of ribbon distribution, so I stopped guessing and considered returning to the camper to get a couple more aspirin. Thinking twice about the wisdom of taking more than what the aspirin bottle recommended, I decided to try focusing on something else. With that in mind, I opened the store and found myself at once busy at the gas pumps, where I maintained a brisk, efficient manner with the customers. I pumped their gas, collected their payment, made change, and sent them on their way, all with little or no small talk.

Between customers I guessed as to why Carl hadn't arrived at the store, assuming he'd likely overslept because Martha wasn't there to wake him and keep him on schedule. I hoped he was beginning to realize all the things she did for him, because like all wives I knew, she did everything she could to make Carl's life easier for him. He was probably used to having her wake him and have his breakfast on the table for him each morning. But now, with Martha at the hospital, he's probably all off his schedule.

When Carl finally arrived, I saw his immediate relief when he saw both the store and the gas pumps open. And yet, I also couldn't help but notice how suspicious he was of me.

I bet he's worried that I may pocket his money for myself. Of course, I'd never do such a thing, but he doesn't know that about me.

"Thanks for opening the store and minding the pumps," he said as he breezed up to the counter slightly out of breath. "Were you able to make change? I don't remember leaving any working cash in the cash register last night."

"That's right. You didn't leave any working cash, but I worked around it because most of the early customers had the proper cash, and then I made change for the others from the first customer's payments. A few of them wrote checks. It's all in the register."

In spite of Carl's thank you and the relief I saw on his face at my having opened up the store and tending to the gas pumps, I was still well aware of his distrust of me. His tone, his expression, and even his body language all reflected how much he resented having me here on the premises. Even the fact that he needed me right now doesn't seem to alter his low opinion of me. But I know I can't afford to be confrontational with him because I'm going to have to rely on his charity a day or two longer than I had previously anticipated.

After Carl took his usual position behind the counter, I returned to the payphone, expecting George would surely be back inside the house by now. Again, I carefully dialed while simultaneously feeling the tension crawl back up my neck. I didn't realize how stressed I was until I broke a fingernail and saw the deep half-moons in the palms of my left hand where I'd been nervously digging my nails into my own flesh.

While listening to the ringing, I practiced in my head what I wanted to say. Still, no one answered. A half hour later I tried again, but this time there was a busy signal, which surprised me, because neither George nor Jason typically used the telephone. So I redialed, thinking I might have dialed wrong.

This time someone answered, but it wasn't at all who I expected to answer.

"Johnson, residence, Mrs. Peterson speaking." I heard Margaret Peterson say into my house telephone. I was speechless! After having practiced what I was going to say to George or Jason, I was completely thrown off guard when I heard Margaret Peterson's voice.

Why would she be answering my house phone? And why was she even at my house?

When I heard noise in the background, I listened more intently. *Did I hear a party taking place?*

Then I heard Margaret say to someone else in the room, "Jessica, put the salads on the sideboard in the dining room. Save the dining room table for the main dishes because we'll need the entire table for them. And put the desserts outside on the porch table."

What!? What did I just hear?

I blinked as I tried to make sense of what I'd heard, and I also heard clicking on the line, which let me know our nosey party line was listening in.

"I'm sorry," Margaret said, returning to our previously brief conversation. "There's so much happening here, I couldn't hear what it was you were saying."

What on earth is going on? Did I really hear her say that? Why would she be talking to me like that? Is she hosting a party at my house?

I was so shocked that all I could do was mumble.

"Look," she said, "if you want me to hear you, you'll have to speak up more clearly because I'm simply too busy to be listening to a prankster!" Then she hung up.

As I listened to the dial tone, my head began to swirl, and I felt faint. So I rested my head against the back wall of the phone booth and tried to sort out what I'd just heard. Did I really hear that? Then, all of a sudden, it all made sense. How could I have been so stupid?

I realized George probably wanted to get rid of me all along so he could start up a relationship with Margaret Peterson, the so-called poor, widowed neighbor lady. And finding a place to abandon me at some faraway rest stop was his perfect opportunity. Hah! I've had my suspicions about that woman all along and now it's finally all coming out!

I remember all the times when she called to ask George to come over and help her with this, that, and a multitude of other little things. And then there were those times when she brought over baked goods and wanted to discuss different planting options with him. I wondered then what she thought George could tell her, because we don't grow crops, just a small field of oats and corn for the pigs, but nothing on a big scale like she was asking about. But George sure was all puffed up about it. He talked about crops with her for hours, as if he was the fountain of farming wisdom.

And all that sweet talk in the truck about when we were in college and the trip being an opportunity for a *funny moon* was just a bunch of poppycock. Boy, did I ever allow myself to be played the fool. Well, *no more*! I'm *not* going to play that game. How naïve of me to be the good wife waiting for my naughty husband to come back for me. What I really don't get though, is how he got Jason to go along with his hair-brained scheme.

Unless Jason is all heart-strung for the daughter. Is her name Jessica? I think so, or something close to that. I wonder if the two women came together as one package. Noooo! Could that be possible? It just sounds too preposterous. But what else could it be? What's very clear is the fact that twenty years of living with George doesn't guarantee me any rights at all.

Heck, I suppose he and Jason can double their profits if they own both farms. Pretty slick if you think about it. Especially since it was my insurance money that enabled George to get started with the pig farm in the first place. So all he had to do to get ownership of the Peterson farm was to hook up with the widow and her daughter. Then he'd have twice as much land and both a crop farm and the pig farm. I suppose that puts both George and Jason in the position of becoming very wealthy farmers.

The image of Margaret Peterson with my George sliced at me like an apple being peeled with a very sharp paring knife, one curled layer at a time, deeper and more exacting with every twist and turn. Seething with anger, I was unaware of the fact that I was still gripping the earpiece of the phone. When I saw it in my hand, I slammed it into its cradle with a vengeance that the phone didn't deserve.

Somehow, I got through the rest of the day, how, I'm not sure, because I not only didn't know what I was going to do, but I wasn't entirely sure *how* I wanted this scenario to end. I hated feeling abandoned and having been played a fool, but after hearing what was going on at the house, I wasn't sure I wanted to reclaim my cheating husband either. Neither was I sure if I wanted to return to the farm, thinking this may be the break that I'd been waiting for, my opportunity to get away from an existence I never wanted in the first place.

23

TRANSITION TIME

"A strong woman understands that gifts such as logic, decisiveness, and strength are just as feminine as intuition and emotional connection. She values and uses all of her gifts."

—Nancy Rathburn

That brief phone conversation totally consumed me, with the words repeatedly churning through my head. I was driving myself crazy with hate and resentment on the one extreme, and relief and elation for my freedom on the other. Finally, I decided it would be best if I focused on something else, something routine and not particularly stressful. With that in mind, I started restocking the shelves. As I worked, I automatically made a list of items that needed to be ordered, and sorted the list by category, exactly the way my father had taught me to do so many years ago. By midday I had the inventory of all the stock complete.

"Carl," I said, walking back into the store, handing him the list. "I did an inventory of your stock and put together a list of things you're low on. You should probably place an order for these items fairly soon."

He looked at me with bewilderment and blinked a couple of times before breaking out into a smile. It was the first time I'd ever seen him smile. Apparently, my doing the inventory both pleased and surprised him, as he seemed genuinely grateful. In fact, it was also the first time he looked at me with respect instead of loathing. I guess he hadn't expected me to do it, especially not without being asked, and I assumed from his obvious delight that he'd been dreading the thought of tackling it himself. Actually, based upon the disorder of the storeroom when I first arrived, I assumed he procrastinated to the point of never getting around to doing a proper inventory at all.

Or I speculated, I wonder if he doesn't know *how* to do an inventory. Now that's an interesting thought! If he doesn't know how, he might find me of greater value than either of us previously thought. Come to think of it, I wouldn't have known how to do a proper inventory either if Papa hadn't taught me.

"Thank you," Carl said, accepting the list I'd handed him. "That was mighty nice of you to do all on your own."

"You're welcome. I appreciate being able to stay here and I'm happy to help. And I can mind the store for you too, if you want to visit Martha sometime today since you couldn't go yesterday." I was fairly certain he had no idea how he was going to visit Martha and take care of the store, because planning ahead was definitely not one of Carl's strong suits.

He didn't directly answer me and acted as if he didn't hear me, but finally he said, "That's very kind of you, Miss Birdie. I'll think about that and let you know."

I suspect he's still a little skeptical of me because, after all, I'm just some strange woman who has become a part of his life by default. Actually, I've been afraid he might begin asking me questions, but so far, he hasn't asked me anything at all. Actually, I don't know what I'd tell him if he asked me anything because at this point, I'm not sure who I am anymore. I don't even know if I'm still married. But what seems perfectly clear is that I apparently no longer have a home on the farm. So until I know what I'm going to do, I need to remain as useful here as possible.

With that in mind, when the next customer occupied Carl's time, I returned to the camper and began cooking his dinner. At 5:00 p.m. I brought it out to him in one of the Corning Ware dishes from the camper.

"Carl, since Martha isn't home, I made dinner for you. You can either eat it here or take it home and bring the dish back tomorrow, so I can return the container to the camper. And I can manage the store for you for the rest of the night if you want to visit Martha and the baby."

I knew I'd made the right move, because with the mere mention of dinner, I saw his expression soften, as I was fairly certain he hadn't given any thought to what he might cook for himself.

He thanked me and at once said he'd like to take the dinner home so he could freshen up before going to the hospital. As he exited the store, with the Corning Ware dish in hand, he smiled and said, "This is really swell of you, Miss Birdie. Yes, really, really swell."

PART III

AWAKENING 1971–1980

24

FOLLOWING THE BIRTH

*"The freedom to lead and plan your own life is frightening
if you have never faced it before. As frightening when
a woman finally realizes that there is no answer to the
question 'who am I' except the voice inside herself."*

—BETTY FRIEDAN

Martha knew she was supposed to stay at the hospital a full ten days following the delivery of her baby. It was the way things were done. But she also saw no reason for it, none at all. She'd been given Twilight Sleep, a combination of morphine to kill the pain and scopolamine to erase all memory of the birth, and she felt fine, actually she felt great. She didn't even know she'd delivered the baby until the nurse woke her and told her she had a daughter. And now Martha was eager to go home, home to her own bed and activities with her new friend, Miss Birdie.

"Tomorrow when the doctor comes in," she told Carl, "I'm going to ask him to release me because I'm going crazy here with nothing to do. And besides," she strategically pointed out before allowing Carl the opportunity to contradict her, "I know it's not good to have our customers find our station closed and the store locked when you're here."

"Actually," Carl said, "that Miss Birdie woman is minding the store for me tonight. She even made a casserole for me for dinner."

"Really!?" Martha smiled in surprise. "That was mighty nice of her!"

A mere four days after having given birth, Martha's doctor reluctantly granted his permission to allow Martha and her baby to go home.

Carl arrived promptly at the designated time, and a nurse placed his daughter in his arms. Immediately Carl stiffened like a piece of cardboard, fearful of breaking or injuring his own baby daughter. Luckily, baby Olson was oblivious to her father's uneasiness and continued sleeping.

While he was holding her, Martha spread the new baby quilt out on the bed and told Carl to place the baby on it. "Just be sure you keep supporting her head."

Carl ratcheted like a wooden puppet with rusty joints and placed his baby in the center of the quilt. Martha couldn't help but smile with tenderness when she saw how carefully he set their daughter down. Then, she wrapped the quilt tightly around the baby and was about to pick her up when the nurse gave both of them a frightful scare.

"No, madam!" the nurse said. "It's too early for you to pick the baby up! I'll do that, or your husband should be doing that. That's why you shouldn't be leaving the hospital this soon. She turned to Carl with a look that could kill. "Here, you can take your wife's overnight bag to the car. Bring the car around to the front door and we'll meet you there!"

Carl didn't need to be asked twice to escape. He at once left the hospital with Martha's small suitcase in hand. He placed it on the back seat of the car and drove to the circle driveway in front of the hospital, where he pulled up to the curb. Martha and the stone-faced nurse were already there waiting for him.

With a disapproving sigh, the nurse lifted the baby from Martha's arms, thus granting her permission for Martha to step out of the wheelchair and get into the car. Not until Martha was seated in the car did the nurse relinquish the baby to Martha's arms.

"Are you comfortable, Martha?" Carl timidly inquired.

"Yes, Carl. I'm fine."

The nurse gave Carl one last scowl and closed the car door with a final harrumph.

Carl wasn't accustomed to being chastised, especially by a woman of authority. He felt as if he was being reprimanded, as if he'd been a naughty child. But he put his feelings aside, put the car in gear, and began slowly driving away from the hospital, trying to avoid any bumps in the road.

Before they even reached the main road, Martha said, "I'd like to stop by the store before we go home, Carl. I want to show our baby to Miss Birdie."

"That's crazy, Martha. I don't think the doctor would have allowed you to leave the hospital if he knew you weren't going directly home and resting. And nurse cantankerous back there would probably eat me alive if she found out I took you anyplace other than straight home."

"No, Carl. I want to show Miss Birdie our baby before I go home."

"That's not being reasonable, Martha. You can't be traipsing around and not resting."

"That's just silly. Stopping at the store for a few moments is not traipsing around."

With great reluctance and a heavy sigh, Carl acquiesced. It was the second time today he felt bullied, and it wasn't a position he liked. As soon as Carl parked, Martha opened her car door and scurried into the store, proudly clutching her new treasure tightly to her chest.

"Wow, look at Martha go. She doesn't even waddle anymore. And she almost has her figure back too, not to mention her energy."

When they entered the store, Carl saw something shocking, something he never expected to see. Miss Birdie's entire face was beaming, and she had both arms outreached as she stepped away from the counter. She was almost glowing with a big, toothy grin spread across her entire face. Her smile was so big that the pink of her gums were exposed.

"Amazing," he mumbled under his breath. "Never saw that woman so much as crack a grin before."

He watched Miss Birdie lift his baby from Martha's arms and begin sashaying in front of the counter with her hips in full motion, in what one might call a dance of sorts as she cooed to the baby.

What Carl didn't know was that his baby was supplying the tenderness and solace that Gert needed at precisely the time in her life when she needed it the most. Neither did he realize a woman never forgets how to hold a baby.

25

MISS BIRDIE WITH MARTHA'S BABY

"The first step toward change is awareness."

—AUTHOR UNKNOWN

"You're beautiful, little one," I cooed. "Do you know that? You're just the most precious little thing ever." I stroked the top of her hairy little head. "And look at all this beautiful hair. Oh, we could put a lot of pretty little bows in that hair."

"She's perfect, isn't she," Martha said, radiantly smiling at her daughter.

"Yes, indeed she is! Absolutely perfect!"

"Thank you," Martha said. "You have no idea how much I appreciate you, first for finishing the quilt and also for cooking dinner for Carl. That was very nice of you."

"Oh, that was nothing, I was happy to do it." I followed Martha to the camper, still holding the baby in my arms. We automatically fell into our usual comfortable chatter, and that's when she told me she'd named her baby Bernadette.

"Bernadette? Gosh, I haven't heard that name in a very long time. Was that your mother's name?"

"No, it's not anyone's name on either side of our families. Can't you guess why I've named her that?"

Without waiting for me to guess, she told me she had chosen the name Bernadette because it was as close to Miss Birdie as she dared get, without causing too much wrath from Carl.

"Really?" I gasped. "You've named your baby after me?"

"Yes." She giggled.

I gave Martha a sisterly one-armed hug because I was still holding Bernadette in my arms, and that's when Martha launched into telling me about her hospital experience.

"I had way too much time on my hands," she said. "And one day, when the nurse was walking me up and down the hall, I saw a book called *The Feminine Mystique* sitting on the table. It was just sitting there and the title sort of tickled my curiosity. So I picked it up and brought it back to my room. At first, I thought I'd just flip through it, sort of scan it you know, just to see what it was about. I thought it might be a little dirty, you know, kinky. But it wasn't like that at all. As you've probably guessed, I haven't done much reading in the past, so for me to get interested in a book is really something. In fact, I can't ever remember finishing a book when I was in school. But this book is different from any of those my teachers wanted me to read. This one feels like the author is talking directly to me, and I read every single page. Some parts I even reread a couple of times, because it's the most exciting thing I've ever come across, and it's opened my eyes to a lot of things. I brought it home with me. I shouldn't have taken it from the hospital, but I want you to read it so we can talk about it later."

Martha retrieved the book from her diaper bag and opened it to where she had previously turned down the corner of a page.

"Listen to this," she said, reading from the book. "*The public image, in magazines and TV commercials, is designed to sell washing machines, cake mixes, face makeup and hair color.*"

I started to laugh when I heard Martha read that, because that was the very same kind of thing Papa used to tell me when I was a teenager and wanted to buy expensive makeup that had been featured in the magazines in our store.

"When I began thinking about it," Martha said, "I realized it's absolutely true. I just hadn't ever thought about it like that before. But this author is right about that, and she's right about a lot of other things too. There's a lot more. Listen to this, *no woman gets an orgasm from waxing the kitchen floor.*"

"You've got to be joking!" I gasped. "Does it really say that?"

"Yup, it does!"

We both broke out into uncontrollable laughter. In fact, we laughed so loud that it woke little Bernadette and she started to fuss.

"Yes," Martha said, as she stuck a pacifier into Bernadette's mouth. "It absolutely does say that, and I think you're going to enjoy this book. After you finish reading it, I want to talk to you about a whole lot of things. The thing is, this author has gotten me to think about how women shouldn't have to be subservient to their husbands. She says we shouldn't have to limit ourselves to staying home and doing housework if we don't want to. She thinks we should be able to do a whole lot of things if we want to do them. And she says we can be partners with our husbands, not just their servants. Anyway, after reading this book, I've decided I'm going to bring little Bernadette up to be a modern woman, not a woman like me who's allowed herself to become totally dependent upon her husband. And I'm going to try to be different too. I'd like to be a partner with Carl, like it says in this book. I don't want to just be his cook and housekeeper anymore." Martha sighed. "I'm so sorry my own mother didn't open up my eyes to all of the possibilities of being a modern woman. I suppose she didn't try because she may not have known there was any other way of being a woman, or if she did know, and if she did try telling me, I probably wasn't listening."

Martha blotted a little slobber off Bernadette's chin. "And now that Mom's passed away, I can't even ask her about it. But you, and this book, have caused me to become determined to bring little Bernadette up to be a lot different from the old Martha. Bernadette and I are going to be stronger, smarter, and more confident. We're going to try to be more like you. I'm determined to become my own individual person. You just wait and see."

I wasn't sure where all of Martha's adulation was coming from, because I certainly didn't feel I'd earned any of it. Heck, I wasn't an independent woman. I was just trying to survive. Nonetheless, Martha's words and excitement were exactly the encouragement I needed to jolt me out of my slump and self-pity. Martha was right. I just needed to find where I was going to fit into society, and I needed to find the new me, a me without George and without the farm.

"Thank you, Martha," I said. "I'll begin reading this book tonight. Then, we can talk about it later."

While Martha changed Bernadette's diaper, I said, "I've been doing some reading too. The other day when the newspapers arrived, and I was about to put the old ones in the box for the Boy Scouts, I decided to read a couple of them. Martha, I was surprised to learn there are a lot of things women are doing in the world today. Just last June a Soviet woman named Valentina Tereshkova became the first woman to go into outer space. Imagine that! A woman going into space! Who would have ever thought such a thing was possible? And that got me to thinking. If she can do that, Martha, we can do things too, not that big, but things just the same. We just have to put our minds to it and stretch ourselves. Together, who knows what we can do? And I also read where President Kennedy signed an Equal Pay Act law."

"Yeah? So why's that a big deal?" Martha slid the plastic panty over Bernadette's diaper. "How will that affect us?"

"Well, what it means, if we take jobs, our employer will have to pay us the same hourly wage as he pays men doing the same job. I think that's interesting, don't you?"

"I guess so, but I don't think I'll be getting my panties in a wad over it, because nobody hires married women in the first place, and they for sure don't hire mothers with infants. Still and all, equal pay is only fair I guess, because a loaf of bread costs 22 cents no matter who buys it."

"Exactly!"

"Well, I'm going to let Carl take Bernadette and me home now, because I'm beginning to feel a little tired. But I'm going to come back in the morning."

I walked Martha to the front of the store and manned the counter and gas pumps while Carl took Martha home.

When Carl returned, I retired to the camper, where I made myself a cup of tea and prepared to curl up with Martha's book. But first I closed the drapes, and as I did so, I saw a small black four-legged creature run under the camper.

Please, dear God, let it have been a cat and not a skunk!

Thankfully, I didn't smell anything, so I brought my tea to the bedroom, curled up on the bed and opened the book, *The Feminine Mystique* by Betty Friedan.

As I read, my brain spun with new information, and I was so fascinated by what I read that I continued reading late into the evening, not even bothering to prepare anything for my supper. Even after brushing my teeth and crawling into bed for the night, I couldn't stop thinking about how unfair life is for women, especially if we allow it to be. That little book provided me with the insight and emotional strength to realize just because my world seemed to have collapsed, I didn't need to collapse with it. It helped me recognize that I didn't fall apart when my parents died, and I certainly didn't need to fall apart now. It was time for me to move on and accept closure with what was and with the pearls of wisdom in this book, I might find the strength to find and live my new life.

26

THE WOMEN'S NEW ADVENTURE

"A woman with a voice is by definition a strong woman. But the search to find that voice can be remarkably difficult."

—Melinda Gates

True to her word, Martha came to the store the following morning, but the scowl on Carl's face told me he was extremely unhappy with her decision. So I kept my head down, pretending I hadn't noticed the tension between them. I was further surprised to see Martha had brought another bag of groceries with her and realized she intended to stay all day and cook their evening meal in the camper while we visited. While she cooked, I had the luxury of enjoying both her company and that of little Bernadette.

On the second morning, I made a point to be out in front of the store prior to when I expected them to arrive so I could help Martha carry in whatever she brought with her that day. I was impressed at how organized she was. She had her bag of grocery items propped up on the floor between her feet with the diaper bag slung over one shoulder and Bernadette in her arms. As soon as they arrived, I scooped

Bernadette up and relieved Martha of the diaper bag, thus freeing her to carry in whatever food items she brought with her. She began cooking as soon as we reached the camper, which again provided me with the pleasure of holding and cooing to little Bernadette.

"Did you have a chance to look at that book?" Martha asked.

"Yes, and I found it just as provocative and informative as you did."

"Isn't it a fascinating?" She browned the meat in the pan to begin its tenderizing process. "Since meeting you and reading that book, I've changed my mind about so many things. I never wanted to improve myself before, but now I really do. I want to be appreciated for who I am. I don't just want to be known only as Carl's wife or Bernadette's mother. I want something for myself too. Do you know what I mean?"

I smiled in acknowledgement, letting Bernadette's tiny fingers wrap tightly around my pinky.

"Don't get me wrong," Martha said. "I love Carl, but I want to be more than just a stay-at-home mom. I want equality and independence and to be respected for who I am as a human being, not just as a wife and mother. Does that sound selfish?"

"No, it doesn't sound selfish at all. In fact, it makes perfect sense. I don't know why it has taken me so long to figure that out, but I know exactly what you mean. But let's face it, Martha, the only way either of us will be able to feel any degree of freedom is to become financially independent. Money is what gives men their power over us. We women are vulnerable because we're financially dependent and legally bound to them."

Based on the reality of our limited financial independence, we brainstormed our options, finally deciding we could sell the services and skills we know, which in our case was to teach other women how to quilt. So we hand-printed flyers to advertise our lessons and hung them in and around town on bulletin boards inside the entrances of the Piggly Wiggly grocery store, the Five & Dime, the local coffee shops, The Kitchen on Cedar Street, and the church foyers of the Baptist, Catholic, and Lutheran churches and even in the lobby of the Pioneer Hotel down the street from us. And of course, Martha also taped one of the flyers to the front window of their gas station-convenience store.

"What's this, Martha?" Carl asked as he removed the flyer from the window that Martha had just put up.

"Miss Birdie and I are going to teach quilting lessons to some of the women in town."

"Not here you're not. We haven't even discussed this, Martha. You can't just go make up your mind about things like that without talking them over with me."

"Why not, Carl? Why can't I make up my own mind to do something with my time in what is also my store? It's not just your store, you know. It's *our* store, and it's my time."

"What has gotten into you!" he said rather than asked. "I hardly know who you are anymore. You're beginning to sound unstable. You know perfectly well that I've always made the decisions about the store, and you can't just decide to do something crazy like this without talking it over with me."

"Have you forgotten it was my daddy's inheritance that helped us make the down payment on this store? Have you forgotten that? And my name is on the deed for this store too, so I think I have the right to tape a small flyer on the window of *our* store."

Carl looked at her with shock, as I'm fairly certain Martha had never talked to him like that before. As baffled as Carl was by what had just happened, I knew he, like all the rest of society, had been brought up to think it was a man's duty to handle all business decisions. It was only a recent phenomenon for women to see the folly of that thinking. And technically speaking, Martha was probably correct. She very likely had as much right to make decisions about the store as he did, and just because they both referred to it as *his* store, didn't actually make it true.

But I knew the situation was delicate and very awkward, especially for me, because I also knew I had indirectly been the cause of their quarrel, and secondly because I needed to find a way to stay in the good graces of both of them in order to continue living in the camper. If either Martha or Carl asked me to leave, I had no idea where I would go.

I understood where Martha was coming from, but I also felt compassion for Carl, because I knew most of society expected new mothers to stay home with their babies. Poor Carl! He wasn't prepared for any of the changes he was seeing in Martha, and I wondered if she had shared any of what she'd read in Betty Friedan's book with him. Maybe if he knew where she was coming from, he might have been more understanding and open to the changes he was seeing in her.

Instead, I watched Carl's face blanch from the shock of seeing Martha re-tape the flyer to the front window of *their* store.

On the day we said our quilting lessons would begin, three women showed up.

The first was Dorothy Webber, a married woman with two married daughters. Her husband was an electrician. Then, there was Nancy Blanchet, a plumpish young woman with a pretty face, who'd recently married but didn't have any children yet. In many ways, she was still a child, and she told us she didn't think being a wife was any fun at all.

"It's boring being home alone all day doing nothing but dusting and cooking. And it's not like Garth is a barrel of laughs when he gets home from work either. He's mostly tired and grumpy when he gets home, and we hardly ever go out or do anything anymore. We don't even go to the movies like we used to when we were dating."

The third person was Janet Bauer, an already skilled quilter who was new in town and eager to meet other women. Janet had been a Home Economics teacher at Central High School in St. Paul. But when her husband was promoted to a managerial position at Alexander Lumber, she quit her teaching job in St. Paul so they could move near her husband's job.

The five of us could not have been more different, and yet we felt a kinship as we gathered in the camper. Immediately, however, it became obvious that the camper was going to be too small to do any quilting. It was barely large enough for the five of us to sit. We were going to need a larger space to work in.

"I have an idea," Martha said with a bit of a cocky attitude. "Follow me, ladies."

I didn't know what she was up to, but we dutifully followed her to the storeroom.

"What do you think of this?" she asked, turning around with out-stretched arms. "If we moved all the stock away from the center of the room and lined it up against one wall, we could set up our work-station out here in the middle. We'd need more lighting, and some tables and chairs, but maybe we will be able to think of something. What do you say? Do you think this would work?"

At first no one spoke, but I could see the wheels turning as the women began nodding their heads in the affirmative, thinking the storeroom might indeed become a plausible solution for us.

"I know who could help us with lighting," Dorothy said. "My hus-band is an electrician, and I think I could talk him into hanging a few lights for us. In fact, I just happen to know where there are some used and dented fluorescent lights sitting in the back of his shop, lights people returned for various reasons, because they either had scratches on them or changed their minds about purchasing them. Anyway, they're just sitting there collecting dust. They'd be perfect, and I think he may be happy to get them out of his way."

"While we're at it," Janet added, "the room could sure use a little paint to brighten it up a bit and give it a cleaner appearance. And I can supply the paint if we want to do the work ourselves, because I have several gallons of white paint sitting in the corner of our base-ment. I can't imagine what the previous owner planned to do with it, but I hated the idea of putting it in the trash when we moved in, so it's all still sitting there. What do you think? Are any of you interested in painting the room? It sure would look a lot brighter and cleaner."

The following day, we five women donned overalls, tied our hair up in scarves and began giving the room a facelift. First, we moved all the store stock to one wall. Then we crawled up on chairs and boxes and began painting the walls. On Saturday, Dorothy's husband arrived with a ladder. He removed the three 60-watt ceiling bulbs and installed three slightly dented industrial fluorescent lights.

"Good God," Carl said when he stuck his head into the storeroom. "A person is going to need sunglasses to be back here."

We all laughed. Even Carl found humor in the situation.

On the following Monday, we began setting up our new workspace with folding chairs and card tables the women brought from home, but quickly we discovered the card tables weren't large enough, tall enough, or stable enough to work on.

"I'll talk to my husband about building us some solid tables," Nancy said. "He owes me big time for making me move here, so let me see what I can do."

A few days later, Nancy's husband and two other men from the lumber yard brought wood, nails, and hammers, and built two strong tables for us to work on. As they were leaving, one of the guys asked us how we liked the bear out in front by the gas pumps.

"I for one like it very much," I said. "Did you carve it?"

"No, not me," he said, "but one of the old guys down at the shop carved it years ago, when he was young and wild. It was a huge tree that had been hit by lightning. Crazy old coot still talks about how it would have required taking up all the cement around it to remove the root of the tree, so he took it upon himself to stand on a ladder with a chain saw and carve it into a bear."

"Is his name Wilkes?" I asked.

"Yeah! How did you know that?"

I smiled and explained that the name WILKES is carved into the bear's foot. "I'm rather fond of that bear," I said. "In fact, that bear and I have a rather cherished relationship."

He looked at me quizzically but didn't ask for an explanation.

A few days later, two more women asked to join our group: Nadine Colbert, a recent widow and Betsy McGiffin, a mother of three school-age boys plus a toddler. Betsy's husband worked at the Edsel Garage next to The Kitchen on Cedar Street.

Our eclectic little group might never have sought out each other's company under any other circumstances, but here in our newly formed quilting group, we not only got along, but we discovered we complemented each other's strengths and weaknesses, as the women began sharing all sorts of things: rides, local news, foodstuffs from their homes and gardens, and opinions, lots and lots of opinions.

Before the women left at the end of each day, they'd occasionally made small purchases from the store: a can of beans, a box of pasta, tomato paste and sometimes they'd get gas for their car. And it was those purchases that helped appease Carl. After all, we were using the backroom of the store rent free and so far, he hadn't mentioned anything about asking us to pay rent or contribute to the heat or electric bill.

One night before he and Martha left, I overheard Martha ask Carl if he had ever considered stocking school supplies. She said, "Betsy is planning to stop at the Five & Dime to pick up school supplies before she goes home tonight. I know she would have preferred buying those things here and avoid the additional stop. And I think some of our gas customers might prefer to make this a one-stop situation too, because all the families with school-age kids need to buy school supplies someplace. So I was thinking, why not let them buy them here when they get their gas?"

Carl must have given her suggestion some thought because that following week he began carrying a limited number of school items: three-ring notebooks, paper, crayons, pencils, pens, and protractors. When those things sold out, he expanded his offerings. In October he added mittens and knitted hats to a portable stand near the register.

One night Martha said, "Have you considered asking one of the farmers to bring in pumpkins? You could keep them out in front. And I bet the parents will get gas while their kids pick out their Halloween pumpkin. We could even sell a few Halloween costumes. And we might want to add snow shovels, and maybe even a few Christmas decorations as it gets closer to the holidays."

Gradually, Carl seemed to value Martha's suggestions. Still, I sensed he found it unnerving to think Martha, being a woman, could possibly possess any business sense.

One day, while working on a quilt together, Nancy told us about a large easy chair she and her husband recently inherited from his grandmother. "It's comfortable," she said, "but it's ugly as sin. I have a blanket covering it, but that just makes the whole room look messy. I don't know what I'm going to do with it."

"Is it structurally sound?" I asked.

"Yes, it's in great shape. His grandmother was just a tiny little thing, and I'm not sure how often she even sat in it. But it's pink and flowery with swans on it." She scrunched her face to emphasize how distasteful it was. "Neither of us likes it. It should be in a nursing home instead of in our living room."

"Have you considered reupholstering it?" I asked.

"Gosh, that would be nice, but I wouldn't know where to begin."

"Well, I could show you, if you want me to. And I'd be happy to help you with it too. I haven't done any reupholstering for a long time, so it would be fun."

"Fun? You reupholster furniture, and you think it's fun?" Nancy giggled. But after a moment's thought, she said, "Actually, I think it would be fun too."

As we talked, I could see her excitement grow.

"I'm going to ask Garth to bring the chair in after work tomorrow," she said.

But she didn't wait until the end of Garth's workday. She and Garth brought the chair in the following morning when he dropped her off at the store. I measured it and let her know how much fabric the job would require, and she brought the new fabric in with her the following day.

I was surprised by the fascination of the group, as they were all captivated by the concept of reupholstering, as it was something they considered rather avant-garde.

"The process of reupholstering," I said, "can be frightening the first time you try it. But it's actually straightforward once you get the hang of it. First, we need to completely remove the present covering, but we need to carefully label each piece as we go because that will be the pattern for the new fabric."

I watched the women carefully follow my instructions as they undressed the chair, stripping it down to its cotton stuffing, and then gradually redressing it in its new fabric. The entire process took no more than three days from beginning to end.

"I can hardly believe it." Nancy beamed in awe at her newly refurbished chair. "I love it now."

"I just had a great idea," Martha said. "There's no reason for us to limit ourselves to quilting and knitting. We could do reupholstering, and I bet we could earn a *lot* of money because that's something hardly anyone knows how to do. People would be thrilled to pay us to do that for them!"

"That *is* a great idea!" I said. "I think you're really on to something, Martha! Let's talk about that some more."

And talk we did! We discussed who was the most skilled at each of the different tasks, and we agonized over what we would charge, but everyone agreed: reupholstering could indeed be a lucrative business because hardly anyone knew how to do it, and yet everyone knew of someone who had tired furniture that could benefit by a facelift.

"If we are serious," I said, "We will need a heavy-duty sewing machine because our small Singer here won't hold up to handle heavy fabrics in the long haul. Unfortunately, those machines are expensive, very expensive!"

"Hey, maybe one of you could find that Dan Cooper guy," Betsy said. "You know, the guy who strapped $200,000 to himself and jumped out of a commercial plane with a parachute. If we could find him, he could spare us enough to buy a sewing machine."

"Get serious, Betsy," Janet said. "What we need is a start-up loan."

"I am serious," Betsy said. "They're still looking for the guy. I heard it on the news last night."

"Well," Janet said, "until you find this Dan Cooper guy, let's explore our other options. I think we should write a business proposal that we can take to the bank."

"I don't even know what a business proposal is," Nadine said.

"I'm not sure either," Janet said, "but I think I'll stop at the library tomorrow and see what I can find out."

The following morning, before coming into the shop, Janet checked out several books on the topic. She read the pertinent parts aloud, thus allowing the rest of us to continue knitting and quilting as we listened. Throughout the day, we discussed the plan by analyzing our needs and the money needed to meet those needs. After much discussion, I put pencil to paper and began writing our business proposal. That evening I took it upon myself to refine it and brought it to the group the following morning. Nancy was the strongest at checking sentence structure and punctuation, so after honing it and making our proposal as professional as we could, Martha made an appointment for the two of us to meet with the local bank president.

On the day of our meeting, we prepared ourselves as best we could. We dressed in low heels, freshly ironed cotton dresses, and new pantyhose with no runs or snags. We arrived at the bank a little early to ensure punctuality. Martha nursed Bernadette well in advance of our appointment, knowing no one liked a fussy baby. She wanted Bernadette to sleep contentedly on her shoulder during the entire meeting.

"May I help you?" A young man, who was barely old enough to shave and was wearing an ill-fitting blue suit that was very likely a hand-me-down, asked as we stepped into the bank lobby.

"Yes," I said. "We have a 10:30 appointment with Mr. Slank, the bank president."

"Well, in that case, I'm sure Mr. Slank will be with you shortly. Please be seated and I'll let Mr. Slank know you are here."

We were kept waiting a full ten minutes after our scheduled appointment time. At 10:40, the young man beamed at us and escorted us into the president's exquisitely furnished office.

"Good morning, ladies," Mr. Slank purred as he motioned to a pair of chairs in front of his highly polished desk. "What fine and worthy charity brings such beautiful flowers as you two lovelies to my office today?"

I waited until he was seated before I tried to answer, but before I could speak, he flashed a plastic smile in our direction. "You know, the bank is always interested in helping the community with its little charities. But just because it's a bank doesn't mean we print money, you know."

He chuckled at his own cleverness, oblivious that we didn't find him the least bit funny or charming.

"I know you already understand that." He chuckled again, probably thinking we dim-witted women didn't understand his little joke. "But I still may be able to help you by making a small donation, if that would help your cause. Now, exactly what charity are you here for today?"

"Oh, we aren't here to solicit funds for a charity," I said, trying to appear as if I was used to talking to bank presidents all the time. "We're here as representatives of a group of women who are beginning a small business. And we are here today to request a start-up loan for that business."

Mr. Shank's friendly façade dropped from his face, as I can only assume he was trying to understand what I had just told him.

When he didn't speak, I went on. "We do reupholstery work, and a little sewing and quilting for hire, and we need to take out a loan to purchase a heavy-duty sewing machine."

Still, nothing came from his mouth, so I continued. "We need an industrial sewing machine. Simply said, Mr. Slank, we need the money to purchase one, but we can't earn money if we don't have one. So it's sort of a catch twenty-two."

He took a deep breath, exhaled, and leaned back in his chair, looking for the first time at the multi-page document I had handed him. He rubbed his chin as he studied the first page and then began flipping through the document, scanning the other pages.

"We're very serious about this," I said when I saw he'd stopped reading. "And the sooner we have the machine, the sooner we can pay back the loan."

He looked up at me, this time with a deadpan expression, as if he was seeing me for the first time.

"The first page," I said, "is our business plan, and the second page shows what we predict we could earn over the next two years, after we get the machine. We figure we could pay off the loan within two years."

I leaned back, waiting for him to say something. When he didn't speak, Martha said, "I think the type of loan we're asking for is called a *Start-Up Venture Loan.*"

Mr. Slank blinked a few times but remained silent. I saw the muscles in Martha's face clench, sensing how nervous she was and offered comfort with a smile and a gentle squeeze to her hand that she was rubbing onto the side of her skirt. I knew she was trying to avoid talking in fear of waking Bernadette, who would very likely begin crying when she found herself in an unfamiliar place.

Mr. Slank looked at the proposal a second time, rubbed his chin again, and cleared his throat. I had no idea what he was thinking. Finally, I couldn't stand the silence anymore. "We need a thousand dollars, Mr. Slank. I know that's a lot of money, but commercial machines are expensive, and if at all possible, we would like to get the money today. Because we can't even get started until we get a heavy-duty machine. As you can see on page three, a commercial machine costs nearly $600, but we also want to purchase a couple of smaller,

less expensive machines for other sewing projects, but we don't antici-
pate them to be our biggest money makers."

Mr. Slank remained silent, appearing to almost hide behind our
proposal.

"We've researched all of this very carefully," I said. "If you want to
see that information, I could show that to you as well."

I had presented our case as professionally as I could and instinctively knew I needed to stop talking, so I glanced in Martha's direction, giving her my best *"be confident, Martha"* smile. Then I leaned
back in my chair, determined to wait for him to say something, anything at all.

Finally, he lowered the document.

I smiled, trying to read his ruddy face. *Did I see respect? Was he impressed by how carefully we had thought through each and every detail?*

"Well, well, well," he finally said. "I see you've given this little project of yours a lot of thought. How do your husbands feel about all of
this? Do they approve?"

"Mr. Slank, this isn't a little project. It's a business venture, and it
has nothing to do with our husbands."

"Ladies, what you don't seem to understand is the only way this
bank would even consider loaning you money is if your husband requested the loan, and even then, we'd need some collateral. We don't
make loans to women just because they think they want to start a little
side business. Surely you know that. Don't you?"

"No," I said, "we didn't know that." We left the bank feeling confused and defeated.

That night, after the others left the shop, I kept chastising myself,
because I of all people should have realized there was no chance of
women getting a bank loan. How could I have forgotten about my
experience of trying to get my parents' insurance money when they
died.

I gathered my cleaning supplies and scrubbed the toilets with a
vengeance.

27

DON'T UPSET
THE LADIES

*"Woman must not accept; she must challenge. She must not
be awed by that which has been built up around her. She must
reverence that woman in her which struggles for expression."*

—Margaret Sanger

The group was shocked to learn we couldn't get a loan, at least not without having a husband cosign for us. When Martha explained how men could secure similar loans without the permission of their wives, and sometimes not even with the wife's knowledge, the group became even more incensed.

"No freakin' way!" Betsy, the spunkiest of our group said. "They can't treat us like that! We're 50 percent of the population and I think it's high time the men begin to realize that. It's the twentieth century for heaven's sake. We aren't second-class citizens, not anymore anyway. So how the heck does the bank think they have the right to prevent us from getting the money we need to start a business just because we're women."

"That's right!" Janet said. "With the passage of the 19th amendment we've been able to vote since 1920. And a lot of women have educations and careers too, so we sure as heck ought to be able to apply for a bank loan the same way men do!"

"Let's make a stink in front of that bank," Betsy said. "It'll be fun!"

"That's a great idea!" Dorothy said. "We should picket in front of the bank and let every woman in town know that women are being discriminated against at our local bank."

"Right on!" Nancy said as the group became more and more fired up. "Every woman ought to know about this, because as women we tend to trust our men to do everything for us. But if we don't pay attention to what's happening right under our noses, who will? I bet ninety-nine percent of the women in this county don't know they couldn't take out a loan if they wanted one. We've all been lazy about not knowing these things, and picketing would help other women wake up too. We give away our rights without even knowing it, simply because we aren't paying attention."

Those sentiments were shared by each of us. We tossed our displeasure about with great exuberance and talked more about moving forward with Nancy's suggestion to picket. Yet not a single one of us had thought through the physical logistics of actually doing such a thing. Neither did we think about the fallout or the backlash from such an action. We were, at that point, simply expounding on the unfairness of the system by expressing our disappointment the only way we knew how, by grumbling about it. But all of a sudden, the idea of picketing caught fire in our bellies, and we decided we would do *exactly* that. We would picket and make our grievance be heard.

That following Saturday morning, we met in front of the bank with hand-printed signs taped to mop handles and kitchen brooms. Each of us carried a sign with a different version of our protest against the unfair treatment of women by the bank. The event quickly became the buzz in town, and when Gene Gilmore of the Owatonna Press learned of it, he came out to snap pictures and interview us as we marched. We made him work for his interview, though, because none of us had any intention of lowering our signs or walking slower while he asked his questions and wrote our answers on his clipboard.

Back and forth we went, marching with gusto about the injustice of the bank having refused our request for a loan, and for all the injustices done to women over the years. Our fury smoldered deeper with every step while Mr. Gilmore recorded our comments on his clipboard as he struggled to write while walking next to us.

The following morning, there was an impressively large article with photos of us carrying our protest signs on the front page of the newspaper.

"Martha, do my eyes deceive me? Oh, is that you on the front page of today's newspaper? I guess it's you all right, because there's your name, right there for everyone to see. Good God, woman! What were you thinking?"

"I was thinking I don't think it's fair that you could get a bank loan and I can't. That's what I was thinking!"

"Martha, there are only three times in a woman's life when her name ought to be in the newspaper: once when she is born, once when she gets married, and lastly when she has died. No other time, Martha. There are no other times when your name should be in the newspaper. Do you understand? Have I made myself perfectly clear? And to have your picture plastered on the front page! Good God, woman! It's disgraceful!"

"What are you talking about? That kind of thinking, Carl, is so old-fashioned! Betty Freidan would never accept that!"

"Who the hell is Betty Freidan and what does she have to do with it? Is she one of those women you were marching with?"

"No, she wasn't actually marching with us, at least not in person. But she has everything to do with it, Carl. She's the author of *The Feminine Mystique* and she's a very smart woman. She's opened my eyes to so many things. I'll never be the same again after having read her book."

Carl threw his hands in the air and walked away. "I can't deal with this lunacy, Martha, and that's what it is. It's just plain lunacy. I don't know what's come over you. You should be content to stay home and take care of our baby instead of out there on the street picketing a bank. *A bank*, of all things! Not to mention exposing our baby to all this nonsense. It's just crazy, Martha. Crazy! Do you hear me?"

28

WHAT'S NEXT?

*"It was we, the people; not we, the white male citizens;
nor yet we, the male citizens; but we, the whole people,
who formed the Union. Men, have their rights and
nothing more; women, their rights and nothing less."*

—Susan B. Anthony

On Monday, when everyone returned to the sewing room there was no attempt to do any sewing, knitting, or embroidery. Instead, the women vented about the fallout they each received at home as a result of our picketing the bank. While still elated with their courage for having done it, they were furious about the lack of support or understanding from their husbands. They sounded more disturbed by their husband's attitudes than they were by the bank's stance on the matter.

Dorothy said she never realized how powerless she was just because she was a woman. "And to top it off," she said, "Jerry doesn't even seem to understand what I'm talking about. How can he not see how disappointing it is to be treated like a second-class citizen just because I'm not a man?"

"I hear you, Dorothy," Nancy said, "but don't think you're the only one with a nincompoop for a husband. Mine was nearly unhinged about it. Most of the time I can hardly get two words out of him, but he had plenty to say to me over the weekend. He chastised me on and off all weekend, as if I was a puppy needing to be housebroken. You would have thought I robbed that bank instead of merely demonstrating in front of it! I've always thought of Garth as being pretty easygoing because normally he hardly ever contributes to a conversation, so this was an eye-opener for me. In fact, now that I think about it, I can almost laugh at how he struggled to spit out his words. At first, I thought he was having a heart attack or a stroke because he started to sputter. Then, he began repeating over and over how embarrassed he was to see my picture in the paper. Embarrassed! Can you believe it? Him? My husband, embarrassed? I didn't think there was anything he could ever be embarrassed about. In fact, I didn't think he even knew what being embarrassed felt like, because I'm usually the one who's embarrassed by him. He wears those same old baggy jeans every place he goes, the ones with all those loops for his electrical tools. And he hardly ever talks to anyone or puts any effort into being cordial or even tries to have a social conversation. I'm constantly helping him in social situations, because to tell you the truth, he's ignorant when it comes to talking with people, or about anything other than electrical things. All he knows about is electricity and connectors and things like that. He said he was embarrassed. My eye! He hardly ever shows any emotions about anything at all. If it doesn't give off an electric spark, I guess it's not worth talking about, so now all of a sudden, he's embarrassed? Give me a break!"

"Mine was upended too," Betsy said. "But he wasn't angry. He just thinks this whole thing is a little nutty. He told me I was acting like a 'stupid woman'. *Stupid woman*! Can you believe it? Those were his exact words. Just because I'm a woman, it's stupid to feel strongly about something. I told him to shut up because his attitude was pissing me off!"

"Carl wasn't happy about it either," Martha said. "He was concerned about the men in town boycotting the gas station because of it. I suppose in some ways, Nadine and Miss Birdie are the lucky ones because they don't have husbands to contend with."

I was startled by Martha's statement, because even though we all knew Nadine was a widow, no one had ever broached the topic of my either having or not having a husband. Martha should have known differently, because I told her on the first day that we met that I was waiting for my husband.

I wonder, could Martha have forgotten? Or did she think I made that up? I suppose if she forgot our earlier conversation, she may have assumed I'm a widow too, especially since I'm still wearing my wedding band. I know I should explain my situation, but I'm not sure what I'd say because, quite frankly, I'm not sure I understand it myself. All I know is I still feel like a piece of discarded trash, and that's not an easy thing to share with anyone. Anyway, anything I'd share with them right now would only detract from the situation we're facing with the bank.

If the husbands thought showing their disapproval might slow us down, they were sadly mistaken. If anything, their condemnation added fuel to everyone's anger and supplied greater justification for all of us to forge forward. Individually, I suspect, any one of us would have backed down. But collectively, as a group, we found the courage and the determination to no longer accept a second-class status. It wasn't just the business aspect that was upsetting. It was a whole lot more. It was the realization that because we were women, we weren't taken seriously. We wanted equality, and we wanted the right to be heard and to be respected for who we were. After our bank experience, I knew none of us would ever be satisfied to be invisible or silent ever again. We not only wanted equality for ourselves, but also for our daughters and all women.

I wasn't sure what the group was going to do next, but I knew not a single one of us would ever be willing to remain passive by licking our wounds and quitting what we had started. We were ready for change, and as a group, we were determined to start it.

29

BACK TO BUSINESS

You can have unbelievable intelligence, you can have connections,
you can have opportunities fall out of the sky; but in the end, hard
work is the true, enduring characteristic of successful people.

—Marsha Evans

"Well, that's all good and fine," I said. "We can sit around here all day grumbling about the unjustness of things, but if we're serious about launching this business, we still need to find a way to get our hands on at least one heavy-duty sewing machine. So if we can't do that, there's not much point in any of this."

"Miss Birdie is right!" Martha said. "Does anyone here think they could ask their husbands to borrow the money on our behalf?"

Well, that had to be the silliest sentence I'd ever heard coming from Martha's mouth because the previously noisy room, the room that seconds ago was ready to take on the world, had suddenly become eerily silent. What had previously been a room of boisterous brave women had morphed into a room of wimpy mutes. You could have heard a hairpin drop. Each woman in the room knew the answer without having to broach the question further. Women simply didn't begin businesses, and husbands didn't go out on a limb to help them do it.

"OK," Martha said, "I guess that's a resounding no!"

Gradually, a soft buzz of voices could be heard as the women acknowledged what each of us already knew. First and foremost was the fact that none of them could rely upon their husbands for help, and yet, I realized they weren't entirely ready to give up either. They wanted to search for other options.

"Maybe we could all donate our income from our sewing and knitting until we've saved enough money to purchase a machine," Dorothy said.

"That might work," Janet said. "I've got a little money set aside from my teaching days and I could probably make the down payment on a machine. Then we could make monthly payments with our earnings until the machine is paid off, and you could reimburse me after we're making some money."

Dorothy slowly stood, appearing to be contemplating whether she wanted to say something or not. When all eyes were on her, she said, "There's something you don't know about me, and I'm not particularly proud to be saying this, but I have two grown daughters, who have no idea how deprived they are. I'm ashamed to admit I've never taught them anything about gender equality, because, quite frankly, I didn't even know what the words meant until now. So I guess what I'm about to say is this: since I don't have any young ones at home anymore, and I've got plenty of time on my hands, I really want to see our business get launched. That's why I wouldn't mind using my own money to buy a sewing machine."

Softly spoken, elderly Nadine said, "I could contribute something too, just 'till we get the first machine paid off. Then you could reimburse me later, if that would help?"

"I wouldn't mind contributing something toward it too," Nancy said. "John gives me plenty of money for household expenses, but we don't have any kids yet, so I only have two mouths to feed so I could just scrimp a little on my food purchases for a little while and contribute something too."

"You guys are great!" Martha said.

"Hey," Betsy said, beaming with a big smile, "What if we started selling baked goods, homemade jellies and small sewing and knitted projects right in front of the bank? The sports teams my boys play on have sales like that to raise money for all kinds of things, like ice time for hockey practice, and the softball and baseball teams raise money for bats, balls, and uniforms, stuff like that. Anyway, they raise money for whatever they need, and people are happy to contribute because they know it goes to a good cause. I bet if we got the word out that we're trying to raise money to start a business, we could do it that way.

The room nearly exploded with positive vibes and exuberance as they explored that possibility.

"I bet women will be happy to support us," Betsy said. "Especially when they get wind of the fact that the bank wouldn't give us a loan just because we're women."

They all loved Betsy's idea. All hands were on deck as the saying goes.

We allowed ourselves two weeks to build up our salable inventory. Then, on the designated Saturday, we met in front of the bank at 9:00 a.m. The women brought card tables from home, covered them with pretty hand-embroidered tablecloths, and placed our salable items out. We taped price tags on the front of each item. We offered hand-knit mittens with matching hats and scarves; pumpkin, apple, and custard pies; chocolate chip, oatmeal, and sugar cookies; fig klatches and an assortment of breads: potato bread, egg bread, rye, and pumpernickel. And Nadine baked cinnamon rolls earlier that morning and brought the entire tray of them to sell while they were still nice and warm.

Our tables looked great, and I was proud to be a part of the group, as they'd all gone the extra mile to ensure our success. Nadine's cinnamon rolls were the coup de grâce because they smelled so fantastic.

Of course, none of us ate any of them, because they were to be sold, but I was fairly certain they were every bit as good as the ones George's Auntie used to make, which caused me to wonder what she would have thought about all of this if she were still alive. I suspect she would have been supportive, and I'm pretty sure she'd be rolling over in her grave if she knew what George was pulling.

We had folding chairs set up behind each of the tables, thinking we'd need them as we waited for customers. But there was never time to use them because we were immediately busy with customers eager to purchase what they deemed bargains. Some even asked to see what else we had in our boxes and bought things before we had a chance to put them up on our tables. We sold everything within an hour.

The Press arrived just as we were packing up to go home, and the headline in the local paper the next morning read: "LADIES, FIGHTING BACK!"

We thought it was a wonderful article, and we were very pleased to see it on the front page again, as it was exactly the kind of media support we needed to get our message out, knowing it would help stir indignation in the hearts of any woman who read the article. Zealously we worked all that following week to produce more inventory. We stitched new lap quilts, knitted hats, scarves, and matching mittens, feverishly working to produce salable items for the following Saturday. On Friday the women stayed home to bake pastries and fresh bread for the next day's

We were shocked to see women in front of the bank before we even arrived that following Saturday. All were eager to buy something and show us their support, and again, everything sold out. Some women even slipped rolled money into our hands, giving us small donations with words of encouragement. It was heartwarming to know the female population was behind us, cheering us on for success.

But Mr. Slank, the bank president, was *not* happy about what he saw going on in front of his bank. And on this second Saturday, he was ready for us. He strutted out the front door, marching up to us with great exuberance, seemingly incensed by our selling goods in front of his bank.

"You women," he said, "are not only an embarrassment to yourselves but to this community as a whole. Good God, where are your husbands? Why are they allowing you to do this? You ought to be ashamed of yourselves, out here selling things like a bunch of lowlife gypsies. Go home!"

When we didn't move, he put his hands on his hips and said, "Pick up your stuff and leave before I call the police. If you're not gone within the next few minutes, I'll have them arrest you for loitering."

We mostly ignored him, which seemed to anger him more than if we'd responded because his next tactic was to try to shoo us away as if we were a bunch of stray cats.

On the third Saturday, Mr. Slank addressed us again. This time he came armed with a thick book and loudly read the loitering laws to us. He told us he had every right to call the police and have us arrested. He said he was trying to be a good guy by simply asking us to be reasonable and pack up and leave. But, when the shoppers heard him, they booed him, which caused him to quickly retreat into his bank.

With the female half of the community behind us, our sales effort continued in front of the bank every Saturday morning throughout the rest of September and well into the middle of October. Each week the crowd was larger and everyone who came supported us by ether making purchases or slipping money directly into our hands. By late October it was too chilly to be standing outside selling things. But by then, we had earned enough to pay the entire cost of our first heavy-duty sewing machine.

We paid cash for it and even had enough to cover the delivery fee. When the machine arrived, we rejoiced with a pride that none of us had ever experienced before. We had accomplished something so revolutionary that we could hardly believe we had done it. Never before in our lives had any of us thought about entering the male world of commerce, and knowing we had done it was nothing short of exhilarating!

30

JASON'S ADJUSTMENT

Back on the farm, Jason's days felt pointless, long thankless hours of drudgery, toil, and endless tasks of more work to look forward to. His nights were joyless. If it wasn't for the necessity of feeding the pigs, chickens, and the two cows, he may have considered staying in bed forever. But the animals needed him. Their pens needed to be cleaned, the eggs needed to be collected, the cows needed to be milked, and all the animals needed fresh food, water, and bedding every day. Life on the farm was demanding, never silent and never done. But all the sounds were those of animals. There were no human voices, and that made the farm feel empty and lonely. Like a robot each morning, he tended to his chores before leaving for school, which had become the highlight of his day, because at school he was at least able to hear human voices. Now that his father was dead and buried, all hope of finding his mother seemed lost. She was simply gone, poof, evaporated from his life. The few pictures he found of her were old, from back when she was young. But he gave them to the sheriff anyway, for the purpose of making a missing person poster.

"Do you think there is any chance your mother may have disappeared on purpose?" Sheriff Hicks asked as he gazed at the attractive young woman in the photo he held in his hand. "You know, she may have just gotten fed up with the whole idea of living on the farm. Maybe she decided to make a new life for herself someplace else, you know, someplace a little more comfortable or exciting for a pretty woman."

The sheriff's words curdled in Jason's ears, leaving a huge silence in the sheriff's tiny office.

"You know," the sheriff said when Jason didn't respond, "not all women are content to be living on a farm their whole life. I'm sure you know that, don't you? Were your parents having an argument about something? Could that have been what caused the accident. Any little shred of conversation that you can remember might help."

Jason tried to recall anything that might lend some light to the puzzle. He remembered the instructions his father kept repeating, and he could almost recite word-for-word the conversation he had with his mother about her chickens. He also held a vivid memory of watching them drive away down their driveway.

He knew his mother wasn't particularly happy about making the trip, but would she up and leave? No, he was pretty sure she wouldn't do that. Besides, she made just the right number of meals for the entire length of the fair. If she didn't plan on returning, wouldn't she have made more meals, or no meals at all?

"*No!*" Jason said a little louder that what he intended. "I don't remember anything that would make me think my mother left on her own accord. She just wasn't like that, and furthermore, I don't appreciate having you suggest such a thing."

As Jason spoke, he felt his anger build. "Actually," Jason said, "I resent your implications! Not for one single minute would I have any reason to think my mother wanted to get away from the farm. She would never leave of her own accord. Do you know why? Because I've never heard my parents fight or argue about anything! Not anything at all! Mom never argues with Dad! She always does exactly what he asks of her. And besides, my mom loves the farm, and she loves me, and she loved my dad. My mom would never intentionally abandon me. She loves me! Do you hear what I'm saying? *My mother loves me!*"

Jason was almost screaming and crying all at the same time.

"Okay, Okay," the sheriff said, holding his hands up in a gesture of submission. "I just don't know what else to tell you, that's all. I just wanted to throw that out as a possibility, just to see if you thought it might provide any answers or clues for us to follow. Meanwhile, I'll get the missing posters put up in the post office, and we'll see if they bring in any information. But that's about all I can do."

Jason stood and stomped out of the sheriff's office with heavy feet and a wounded heart. He was angry and he was confused, but he wasn't entirely sure who or what he was angry with. Was he angry with his dead father? His missing mother? Or was he angry with the sheriff? And what should he do with all that anger?

On a parting note, the sheriff said to Jason's exiting back, "If you think of anything that might help, give me a call. And if I get any information or leads, I'll call you."

Normally, September and October were Jason's favorite months. Early autumn was when the farm tasks were their lightest and the Minnesota landscapes were their most glorious. It was the time of year when the oak leaves turned red, and the elms became varying shades of gold and amber. It was also when the evening temperatures were comfortable. It was the time of year when Jason and his father would typically sit outside on the front porch at the end of the day, each with a soda or a beer while discussing various farm matters and simply enjoying each other's company. They would sit there for hours, with neither of them saying much more than a few words. They'd listen to the hum of the nighttime insects and in the process, Jason felt contentment. Occasionally his mother would bring out pieces of freshly baked cake or apple pie for them to enjoy as they sat there. But now, when he sat on the porch, he was alone. There was no conversation, no cake, and no apple pie. There was only the sound of the crickets, a whole lot of emptiness and unanswered questions.

The favorable autumn months and temperatures didn't stick around long. They never did in Minnesota, not in a state that bragged of having four seasons. Soon it was winter, which is the only season that seemed to last forever. Winter was cold, and the nights were even colder and there were fewer daylight hours to complete the farm chores.

After Jason fed the animals each evening, he returned to the empty quiet house, and that was when the sheriff's words crept back into his head.

Could what the sheriff said possibly be true? Could Mom have chosen to disappear? Would she do that? Would she intentionally leave me alone on the farm?

He didn't think she would, but as time passed with no answers, the plausibility of it festered. And as the days grew increasingly shorter, and the nights became longer, colder, and emptier, he began giving credence to those thoughts. What else could he think? She wasn't officially dead, but she was nowhere to be found. The only reality was Jason was alone with his nagging thoughts.

He continued doing all the farm chores because the animals required it of him. He also kept up with his studies because what else did he have to do with his evenings? And he kept up with football because that was his only joy.

An outsider might marvel at how well Jason was adjusting, how busy and productive he was with his time. But what that outsider could never have seen, was how lonely Jason was, how he ached for the small family routines he'd taken for granted. He particularly missed Sunday mornings when he and his dad read the sports pages together and his mom would say, "Honestly, you two! Put something on. You look like a pair of Neanderthals sitting around in your underwear."

What he wouldn't give to hear her scold him again. Now he could sit in his tidy-whities all day, every day of the week, and no one would care. He also missed seeing his mother all dressed up before she drove off to church on Sundays. And he missed smelling her perfume too.

In fact, he missed everything about his former life, especially mealtimes when they'd discuss the health of the animals or the farrowing of another litter of pigs. Now there was no one to help him decide anything. He was entirely on his own.

But the thing he missed most of all were the wonderful aromas that used to waft from the kitchen. Jason loved the smell of freshly baked bread, apple pies, and all the other things his mother routinely made. Sometimes he felt living life without his family wasn't worth living at all.

After football practice one day, Billy Dixon asked Jason if he wanted to take his place cruising chicks with Gordon DeFeo.

"Gordon's got a snazzy souped-up Mustang," Billy said. "He's removed the muffler and replaced it with some really cool straight pipes, and it sounds like thunder, man. And the girls really seem to dig it."

"Cruising chicks, huh?' Jason said. "Well, how come you're not going with him if it's so cool? Besides, Gordon didn't invite me."

"That's because Gordon asked me to invite you for him because Gordon's not allowed to come into the locker room. He'd come in here if he could, but only the football guys are allowed in here, you know that. Anyway, I usually go with him, but I can't tonight because my mom's picking me up right after practice for an orthodontist appointment."

"I don't know, that kid's weird. Why would he ask you to invite me, and why isn't he inviting one of his friends instead of me? We hardly know each other."

"Because he likes having football jocks with him. He thinks it's cool for us to show our muscles to the girls. Oh, and one more thing, he doesn't want you to call him Gordon. You're supposed to call him Flash."

"Flash? I'm supposed to call him Flash?"

"Yeah. He likes the girls to think his nickname is Flash."

"What's with that kid and his names for everyone? He calls you Sod Butt right to your face and you let him do it. Why do you tolerate that? He has no right to do that!"

"I know. He calls me Sod Butt because my parents own a sod farm. For some reason I guess all those names make him feel bigger or something. I don't know why he does it, but it doesn't bother me. When the girls ask me about it, I just explain that my parents own a sod farm. I tell them that's how I got my muscles and broad shoulders, which is pretty much the truth, because I've been lifting rolls of sod ever since I can remember. You know he calls you Pig Boy, don't you?"

"Yeah, I've heard him say that a couple of times and I don't like it at all. I don't like any of the name calling thing."

"But will you go with him tonight?"

"I don't know. What do you do with him?"

"Well, he drives up and down Main Street with the top down on his Mustang and he lets the pipes make a little rumble once in a while. We go really slow, and we watch for chicks. Sometimes we go up and down the street several times before we find a pair willing to talk to us. We just drive from one end of Main Street to the other. We turn around at the DQ at one end and the A & W at the other. The best girls are those from the Catholic High School, because they don't have boys in their classes so there're usually looking for boys. They seem to think we're hot stuff. And they know how the game works too. They usually walk in pairs, so it works out pretty well.

"Last night we picked up two named Sandra and Linda. Man alive, that Sandra was a looker. She had her little navy-blue pleated skirt hiked way up high above her knees, and when she sat in the back seat, I swear I could almost see all the way up to her you know what. She was so hot! We stopped in the A & W and ordered four Black Cows. When she sipped the root beer from her straw, I thought I'd die watching her, because she puckered her little pink lips around that straw so cute, and she looked at me with the biggest most beautiful blue eyes I've ever seen. I didn't know where to look at her. I loved looking into those eyes and I loved watching her lips on that straw, but I couldn't help watching and waiting for her knees to come apart just a little. Man alive, it was wonderful! I had to keep my jacket on my lap the whole time because I was afraid that I might embarrass myself, if you know what I mean. Sandra. Isn't that just the most wonderful name you've ever heard? Sandra."

"Did you get her phone number?" Jason asked.

"No, because I'm a dope! That's why I need to go with Gordon more often. He's smarter about girls than I am. I didn't even think about it at the time. Not until after we dropped the girls off did it even occur to me that I should have asked her for her phone number. I don't even know her last name. All I know is that she's just the hottest, most gorgeous girl I've ever seen, and her name is Sandra. I sure hope she'll come back to Main Street again. In fact, if you see her tonight, maybe you could get her phone number for me? Would you do that for me, Jason?"

"If I go with Gordon, and if he can show me which girl is Sandra, you want me to ask her for her phone number? Is that what you're asking?"

"Yeah! Will you, do it?"

"Okay, I guess I could do that," Jason said with some reluctance.

""You're a good friend, Jason. Thanks. So I can tell Gordon you'll go with him tonight?"

"Alright, I'll go just this once because I'll look for Sandra for you." Jason cuffed his buddy lightly on the shoulder. "You'd better get out of here and get to your orthodontist appointment. Tell Gordon I'll be out shortly. I want to catch a shower before I leave here."

After Jason showered, he walked out the gym door and entered the school parking lot. Sure enough, Gordon was parked as close to the door as he could.

"Hey, Pig Boy, over here," Gordon said.

Jason walked over to the car, tossed his gym bag to the floor of the front seat, and got into the car.

"Let's get something straight right here and now, Gordon," Jason said. "I'll cruise up and down Main Street a couple of times with you, but you're going to call me by my name. Got it? I'm Jason, not Pig Boy. Have I made myself clear?"

"Sure, sure, fine, but you have to call me Flash! Are you okay with that?"

"Flash. You don't want me to call you Gordon? I'm going to refer to you as Flash. Is that right?"

"Right, my name is Flash from here on."

"OK, Flash. Let's do this." Jason said.

Flash pulled out from the school parking lot and headed to DQ. He circled slowly scanning for girls while causing his car to rumble a couple of times. No unattached girls were seen, so he pulled back out onto Main Street and motored slowly and loudly in the opposite direction. There was a group of six or seven girls licking ice-cream cones on the corner near the stoplight at the intersection of Main Street and Community Avenue. Several of them giggled and waved at the boys while Flash continued driving slowly down Main.

"Hi, girls," Flash said with a syrupy grin.

"Stupid chicks," Flash said under his breath. Don't they realize we can't pick them up if they stay in large groups like that? They have to break up into pairs. That's how it's done."

"Do you do this every night, Gordon? I mean Flash?"

"Pretty much."

"Doesn't it get old after a while?"

"Old? No! Why would it get old? There's always a fresh group of girls."

"That's what I mean. Don't you ever want to get to know any of them? Do you just cruise out here every night and show off without making any actual friendships?"

"Well, Sod Butt met up with this Sandra chick last night, but he didn't even think to ask for her phone number. So you tell me how important it is to make a lasting friendship. There's a pair up ahead. Get ready, Jason. If they have some decent knockers on 'em, we're gonna pick 'em up." Flash gunned the engine a couple of times to make his car give off a loud rumble.

Flash drove very slowly next to the curb where the girls were walking. "This here is Jason and I'm Flash. What're your names?" he asked the girls who paused.

The girls giggled and the tall brunette said, "She's Barbara and I'm Anne spelled with an 'e.' Just like that girl in the *Anne of Green Gables* only her hair was red."

"Well, Barbara and Anne with an 'e,'" Flash said. "We were thinking of getting a couple of Black Cows at the A & W. Would you be interested in joining us?"

The girls giggled some more and eagerly climbed into the back seat of Flash's car.

"I like your car," Barbara said.

"Thanks," Flash said. "I like it too."

"Have you had it long?" Anne asked.

"Got it last year," Flash said. "You girls from the Catholic school?"

"Yes," they both giggled in unison. "Guess you can tell because of our uniforms."

"Yup, kind of figures."

Flash pulled into the A & W designated parking areas. A young girl in a brown and yellow uniform appeared with a pencil and small green tablet.

"Whatcha want?" she asked, snapping her gum while twirling her ponytail with the pencil in her hand.

"We'll have four Black Cows," Flash said.

"OK, four Black Cows coming right up."

"I'll also have a cheeseburger and fries," Jason said. "Do you girls want anything else?"

"Sure," Barbara said, all smiles. "I'll have the same as you."

"Me too," Anne said.

Flash gave Jason a menacing side glance and turned the radio up a few decibels. "That's not how this is supposed to be done," he growled through gritted teeth at Jason. "Didn't Sod Butt explain anything to you?"

"Nope," Jason said, making no attempt to cover up the conversation. "All I know is that I'm mighty hungry after football practice, and a cheeseburger and fries sound really good to me right now."

Flash grimaced and turned the radio a little louder. "Do you have enough cash on you to pay for all this food you just ordered?"

"Sure. I've got it covered, man. Don't sweat it there, little guy."

Flash was furious! He didn't appreciate the humiliation in front of the girls. Moments later the carhop struggled over to the driver's side of the Mustang with a heavily laden tray of food and drinks. Flash adjusted his side window to accommodate the carhop so she could clip the tray to his open window. Each Black Cow was a combination of vanilla ice cream with frothing root beer poured over the top in heavy glass mugs, still frosty from the freezer. Fat straws and long handled spoons were placed in each one. The cheeseburgers were wrapped in yellow paper oozing with grease and the steamy hot fries were packaged tightly in small cardboard boxes.

Jason reached across Flash to pay the entire bill by peeling off a twenty from the wad of bills he had in his pocket. He had cash with him that day because he'd planned to stop at a neighboring farm after school to arrange for a load of hay to be delivered to his farm as bedding for the pigs, but now that task would be postponed 'till tomorrow.

Flash passed the food to the girls, but it was Jason who the girls began paying attention to. The four of them made light small talk while listening to the radio and eating. Then Flash drove back down

Main Street and returned the girls to the same place where he'd picked them up.

"Goodbye," both girls said, batting their eyes in Jason's direction.

Gordon's attitude remained pleasant until after the girls exited his car. But as soon as the girls were gone, Gordon's attitude changed. He became stone silent as he drove back to the high-school parking lot with visibly clenched jaw muscles. He pulled up to Jason's motorcycle, put the car in park and said, "Don't ever pull that on me again!"

"What are you talking about, Gordon? I called you Flash, just as you instructed."

"I'm not talking about that! I'm talking about the food you ordered. That's not how it's supposed to be done. You're supposed to order something cheap. The girls know how the game is played. They will order exactly the same thing we order because they know we're going to pay for it. You're supposed to pay me back half the bill after I pay for it initially, and then I charge you a little extra for the gas. That's how it's supposed to be done!" He continued shouting. "You're such a dumb fuck!"

"Oh, now let me see if I have this straight," Jason said. "You get to play the big man by pretending to be called something you're not, and you pretend you're paying for whatever is ordered while you've already controlled what each person will actually order. And then, when the girls are out of sight, the poor schnook who's sitting in my seat is supposed to pay you half the bill plus a hefty portion of the bill to help pay for gas. Is that how it's supposed to work? Well, take a look at yourself, little man. You're a little guy with a big ego in a car you didn't earn because your daddy bought it for you. I don't ever want to be a part of your stupid little game again. You got that?!" Jason grabbed his gym bag from the floor by his feet, got out of the car, and slammed the car door. "And just for the record," he said leaning in the side window, "girls are people too. They aren't toys for you to play with. And another thing, assigning derogatory nicknames to people does *not* make you a bigger man. It only shows how insecure you are with yourself. If your game is to try to make the other guy look bad because of a label you put on him, you need to realize that it only reflects on what a jerk you are, Gordon. Billy, by the way, is not a Sod Butt. He's a square shooter and an all-around good guy who deserves to be called by his name. Friends, true friends, don't crap on their friends, Gordon."

With those parting words, Jason strutted over to his motorcycle without looking back at Gordon who was already peeling out of the parking lot laying rubber.

Jason strapped his gym bag to the back of his motorcycle and began driving home feeling good about himself for having addressed the name calling thing with Gordon. It was something he'd wanted to tell that kid for a long time.

He still had a lot to do when he got home, and he hoped he would be able to get it done before dark. But, even if he had to work a little after dark, he felt that staying late with Gordon and dealing with his name calling made it all worthwhile, so worthwhile that Jason actually began chuckling.

I'm still going to have to get the bedding for the pigs, but I can do that tomorrow. Putting that little creep in his place was worth it. God, I hope I never have to hear the name Pig Boy again.

Yet, he knew the pigs would be hungry when he got home. They would be waiting for him.

31

MISS BIRDIE'S LEADERSHIP

"Because I am a woman, I must make unusual efforts to succeed. If I fail, no one will say, 'She doesn't have what it takes.' They will say women don't have what it takes."

—CLARE BOOTHE LUCE

As I reflected on our little business, I realized how fortunate we'd been to have had those newspaper articles written about us, because they provided the best advertising we could possibly have had, and it was free. And with our new sewing machine humming along like an efficient train engine, our little business was up and running before we were totally prepared for the onslaught of work requests. The demand was staggering, with way more orders than any of us expected because the news articles had inadvertently done all our advertising for us. With very little earlier thought given to what hours each of us would work, or how we would equitably distribute the earnings, our little business was launched with numerous growing pains that needed to be addressed.

The ladies were used to coming into the shop whenever it fit their individual schedule, but now that we were a business, we had to look at that again. For instance, not until after Betsy's boys left for school was Betsy able to pack up her baby and head to work. But Martha was at the shop working several hours earlier than anyone else because she came in early each morning with Carl. Nancy came in early but left early when her husband picked her up at the end of his workday. And Nadine and Dorothy came in together because they carpooled. Then, Betsy had to be back home early to meet her boys when they returned from school. Thus, each one arrived at whatever time worked best for them and fit their individual situation. With the varying start and quitting times, we needed to decide how to make the running of the business fair and equitable for everyone.

"I don't think," Betsy said, "someone who's busting their butt working on a big reupholstering project should be earning the same as someone who's sitting in a rocking-chair knitting all day, no matter what hours they're here working."

"Yes," I said. "I agree with you. That make perfect sense."

"But, then again," Martha said, looking directly at Betsy, "I don't think someone who doesn't get here in a timely manner should be paid as much as those of us who are here early each morning either."

"That's also a valid point," I said.

"Hey, I get here as soon as I can," Betsy said. "I got kids to get off to school and then I have to pack up the baby. So don't go giving me any crap about that. Besides when I get here, I bust my ass off."

"Okay, ladies," I said. "You all have valid points. Now let's look for solutions that would be fair for everyone."

After a lot of discussion, we decided we would run the business as a co-op, where no one took a salary so it wouldn't matter what hours anyone worked. We would each take a part of the profit from whichever project we chose to work on, leaving a percentage of each project in the business coffer to cover overhead and supplies. That way, those who took on more labor-intensive projects could earn accordingly, while the lighter jobs such as knitting, would reap a smaller profit. Those jobs would take a smaller payment, but that would be their choice.

We appointed different zones in the room for each activity. We designated one area for quilting, another for reupholstering, and a third area was a quiet zone with rocking chairs for knitting and for the babies to nap and play in the playpen. With our pooled S&H Green Stamps we bought an electric coffee pot, and Nadine donated a small table for it to sit on. And of course, it was also where we could contribute fresh baked items anyone wished to share with the group on any particular day. That seemed agreeable to everyone, and our business once again became a cohesive cooperative effort in every sense of the word.

Martha's and Betsy's babies grew up together, side by side in the playpen. And when they began crawling, they seemed to enjoy playing together, first by bopping each other on the head with their toys but eventually learning to share with only an occasional punch by the other. While the babies played, the women worked and discussed an assortment of topics. They kept one another informed about local issues as well as national and world matters. Sometimes they didn't chitchat at all and chose to listen to the radio. But no matter what they did or didn't discuss they kept their hands busy and working.

"Did any of you see the Post magazine this month with Elizabeth Taylor on the cover?" Dorothy asked. "Finally, a woman is featured on the cover of a magazine."

"Really? I wonder what she had to do to get on the cover?" Betsy asked and raised an eyebrow.

"Good grief, Betsy! What are you implying?" Dorothy said. "Get your mind out of the gutter. She was on the cover because of the *Cleopatra* movie she was in, and, by the way, I heard it's a great movie. Did any of you see it?"

"No," Nancy said, "who am I going to go to a movie with? Not my husband, that's for sure. If it's not about football he's not interested."

"Well," Martha said, "what's keeping us from going to see a movie once in a while? If we wait until our husbands take us, we'll never see any of them. Why don't we go with one another? And if we went in shifts, we could always make sure someone is left in the shop, and Betsy, you and I could take turns taking care of each other's babies."

Everyone liked that idea and a few actually did go to see *Cleopatra* together.

Later that month there was a big front-page article in the newspaper saying that the Viet Cong had recently won their first major victory.

"That's a bunch of hogwash," Betsy said. "No one *ever* wins anything fighting in a war. If you ask me, war is just a bunch of bigshots playing big boy war games."

"Well, no one asked you, Betsy," Dorothy said.

We all noticed how Dorothy had begun censoring Betsy. While I felt some of Betsy's outbursts were a bit overly boisterous, I was more disturbed by Dorothy's reprimands.

"My husband," Dorothy said, "feels a refined woman should keep her thoughts to herself. He said women need to be vigilant about what they say, especially if they offer opinions about topics that may differ with what their husband thinks, and you, Betsy, you never seem to practice anything remotely near to that."

"Hey," Betsy said. "I'm not with my husband right now, so I can say any goddamn thing I want. And you can too if you ever decide to let yourself cut loose a bit. So let's just try to get along. Okay? Anyway, as I was saying, my younger brother was sent to Vietnam, and from what I hear it's a living hell over there. It's hot, humid, and full of insects. Our guys never know where or when the Viet Cong are going to show up. In one of his letters, he said the Viet Cong seemed to pop up right out of the ground, and then they'd disappear back into the ground just as quickly. He said the helicopter pilots were even having trouble getting in and out when they needed to pick up the injured. Seems to me we don't have any business being there in the first place! It's not like World War II when everyone knew what we were fighting for. Not even the bigshots in Washington seem to know what we're doing there. And a lot of our guys are getting killed and injured for no reason at all!"

The group heard Betsy expound on many things before, but this time she was not only a lot more articulate, but most of the group shared her convictions. Everyone clapped in agreement, everyone except Dorothy. But I could see from Dorothy's expression that she was thinking about what Betsy had said, not only about the Vietnam war, but also about the prospect of forming her own opinion about things.

Martha put her arm around Betsy and said, "You're absolutely right on that. One hundred percent!"

A few days later Betsy came to work wearing bell bottoms and a tee shirt with *Bombing for Peace is Like Fucking for Virginity*, printed on the front of the shirt.

"Good grief," Nadine said. "You could get arrested for wearing that. Where did you get it?"

Betsy beamed, obviously feeling just the right amount of naughty. "My brother sent it to me from Vietnam. His letter said he bought it from a little Vietnamese guy who had set up a portable print shop, right in the jungle near their camp. His buddies were buying them as fast as the guy could print them, and they were sending the shirts home to their wives and girlfriends. He bought this one for me. I think the ink must have still been wet when he bought it though because it's a little smudged right here. But I don't mind. It's just part of the character of the shirt. He also said he hates it there!"

32

ESTABLISHED CREDIBILITY

*"When we do the best, we can, we never know what miracle
is wrought in our life, or in the life of another."*

—HELEN KELLER

Early on our customers were mostly women: mothers and grand-mothers who commissioned quilts or knitted baby items. A few of the mothers brought their daughters into the shop to have prom and party dresses made for them, and there was a bride who wanted us to make her wedding gown, veil, and her five brides-maids' dresses. But there was only one request for a chair to be re-upholstered, which was rather disappointing because we had hoped the reupholstering side of our business would become our mainstay. But one day, out of the clear blue, a handsome young man dressed in a business suit entered our shop. I looked up when I heard the door open and saw him look around nervously, as if he wasn't sure how he'd gotten there or why he'd come. I assumed he was lost, and I only briefly looked up when I asked if I could help him.

"Good afternoon," he said almost apologetically, realizing his entrance had interrupted our work and stopped all conversation as soon as he entered the room.

I removed my glasses, set them on the cutting table where I'd been helping Nadine pin a pattern to a slippery fabric, and walked over offering my hand just as if I was a man in his business world.

"Yes, good afternoon," I said. "I'm Miss Birdie. Is there something I can help you with?"

"Well," he said, pausing as if he was rethinking why he'd come. After a brief hesitation he got to the point. "Word around town is that you know how to reupholster things, and since I was passing this way I decided to stop in and ask."

"Yes, you've come to the right place. Do you have something that needs to be reupholstered?"

"Maybe. Do you do car seats?"

"We haven't actually done any," I said, trying not to show how surprised I was, "but that doesn't mean we can't do them. Do you have a job like that for us?"

"I think so. You see, I've just inherited a 1931 Ford Model-A Coupe from my uncle. It's a pretty special car in its own right, plus it has a lot of memories for me from when I was a kid. Toward the end, the old guy didn't take very good care of it, but now that it's mine, I'd like to fix it up. I can work on the exterior myself, get her all shined up so she looks spiffy on the outside, but there's not much I can do about the cracked and torn seats. If you think you can do something about them, I'd pay you handsomely for your trouble."

After a bit more discussion we decided it would be best if he picked out automobile grade fabric in the cities, but prior to picking it out, I suggested he bring the car into the shop so I could do the measurements to figure out the amount of fabric he would need. We agreed upon a date, time, and cost for doing the measurements, and I told him I could give him an estimate at that time for the entire reupholstery job.

Once word got around that we could work on car interiors, our credibility exploded. Carl told Martha all the earlier jokes and speculation about when and how our little business venture would fail had stopped, because apparently the men no longer wanted us to fail. Instead, they wanted to use our upholstering skills for their cars, which once again piqued the interest of the Press.

"Good morning, ladies! Do you remember me?" Reporter Gilmore entered the shop unannounced, scanning the workroom with his professionally trained roving eyes. "I thought I'd just pop in to see how your little business is doing."

He, of course, captured the attention of all of us.

Before any of us could stop him, he brazenly roamed around the room, scrutinizing the various projects we were working on. I saw his brow wrinkle with the tip of his head as he stared inquisitively at the reupholstering project Martha was working on at one of the tables. I figured he very likely had never seen a partially naked chair with stuffing hanging out of it before. Next, he sauntered over to gaze at the sheer fabric Janet was cutting for a bridal veil on the other table. And he tipped his head with interest when he saw the wool plaid fabric Dorothy was pinning to a pattern at the opposite end of the table from where Janet was working. He looked somewhat startled when he first noticed Nadine, who was sitting quietly hand stitching quilt squares in one corner of the room next to a very large bolt of blue mohair car fabric waiting for me to begin reupholstering the young man's car seats.

But then, I saw genuine surprise on his face when he saw the playpen with the two toddlers in it. Stewart was busily sucking on his binky, while Bernadette was swinging a rattle in the air. Both babies stared back at him with big inquisitive eyes. Betsy was sitting next to the playpen knitting, her needles clacking along at record speed with yarn disappearing at one end and growing out the bottom into a panel. Mr. Gilmore's eyes left the babies, and he greeted Betsy with a smile and a nod similar to the one he'd given Nadine. Betsy reciprocated in kind.

"Interesting! Yes, very interesting," he said. "This is quite a little operation you have going here. Would it be okay if I snapped a few pictures?"

Without waiting for me to answer, a flashbulb popped, temporarily blinding most of us and causing the toddlers to become a crying duet.

"Sorry about that, little ones," he said leaning over the playpen.

But seeing the strange face leering at them after the startling flash only caused the children to bawl louder, triggering the automatic reaction of putting up their arms, wanting to be lifted to the safety of a familiar lap.

Betsy set her knitting down, swooped in and lifted both babies to her lap to offer the children comfort before picking the needles back up to resume her knitting.

"Amazing," he said. "Simply amazing. Wouldn't have believed it if I didn't see it with my own eyes."

"There's nothing amazing about it, Mr. Gilmore," I said from where I was standing behind the account books. "Women have been multitasking their whole lives. Men just don't seem to notice it."

He nodded and said, "Hmm, interesting. Yes, very interesting. May I quote you on that?" He didn't wait for me to answer and scribbled notes onto his clipboard. "Let me ask you something. Are you all soured by the men folks of the town? Seems to me they've treated you pretty unfairly. Would that be right?"

"Oh no," Martha said. "What makes you think that?" Unbeknownst to her, she was still holding her scissors in the air, which could have been interpreted as a rather threatening pose.

The reporter took a few steps back and said, "Well, it seems to me the men weren't very supportive of you back when you were picketing the bank."

"We were just trying to earn enough money to purchase the equipment we needed, Mr. Gilmore," Martha said. "But if it weren't for the men who helped us, we wouldn't have this business at all. You see, my husband is very generously letting us use the back of our store. And Janet's husband built us these solid tables that we're working on. Dorothy's husband installed all the lighting, so we'd have enough light to work with. And you, Mr. Gilmore, you helped advertise our business for us with your news articles. So you see, we're not in opposition to men. We just want to collaborate with them as equal partners. If you want a quote, there's your quote, Mr. Gilmore. We just want to be treated as equals, as partners with the men."

"Humm," he said. "Good quote! Very good quote!" He scrawled as fast as he could on his clipboard. "What about your housework duties? Are you all able to keep up with the cooking, cleaning, and laundry when you're here so much of the day?"

Betsy piped up from the rocking chair in the corner. "Oh yes! I just work more efficiently now. I get great ideas on how to shorten up my household chores, and my children are happier too. I pack my kids' lunches and get my housework done as quickly as possible each morning. Then I pop on over here with my little guy who isn't as cranky in the morning anymore. I think he was as bored as I was when we were home all day. Now he cooperates with me. We don't even have power fights over breakfast anymore, and he never has tantrums about getting dressed. We just get up, do what needs to be done, and hurry on over."

Mr. Gilmore was busy documenting every word on his clipboard. On the following Sunday, the article with several photographs was published on the society page:

"Women Want to be Treated as Equals to Men."
By reporter, Gene Gilmore

The ladies, Janet Bauer, Nancy Blanchet, Nadine Colbert, Betsy McGiffin, Dorothy Webber, and Miss Birdie, who picketed and sold items in front of the bank last fall have their business up and running. During my entire interview with the women, not one missed a beat.

They continued to sew, knit, and talk, and talk they did. These women have ideas and opinions on every topic you can think of. They talked about their projects: how best to lay out the fabric, how the fabric can provide alternate appearances, and who will do which tasks on any given assignment. They talked about politics: politics of the town, the nation, and the world. They talked about what they were serving for dinner, and they shared recipes. They talked about fashion, the latest haircuts and current clothing trends. They were well-informed, well-organized, and well-spoken on every subject I brought up. The one who was knitting could talk, knit, and hold two babies in her lap at the same time. The faster she talked, the faster the needles seemed to clack along as the yarn disappeared along the shafts of the needles.

The toddlers typically played in a playpen where they were safe and were happy because their mothers remained nearby.

This reporter is happy to report that these women have become independent and self-sufficient, and they feel great about themselves and the money they are earning.

"My husband," one woman said, "wasn't happy about me spending so much time at the shop at first, but now he's changed his tune because he sees how good it's been for our whole family."

Miss Birdie, the leader of the group, reinforced that by stating, "The shop has become a lucrative business and it's begun to earn good money. And that has benefitted each of the families and the husbands can see that. Each woman only takes on the projects she feels comfortable and capable of doing."

"Yes," Betsy added, "and my husband can see how much happier we are now that we're not at home all day with no one to talk to. Even my baby enjoys coming here."

"Men are beginning to realize that we aren't out to compete with them. We simply want to partner with them and be respected for who we are," said another.

So, there you have it folks: The follow-up story to the protest held in front of the bank.

Their business is called NEEDLES, THREAD & CLOTH and they're located behind the combination gas station and convenience store, directly across from the Pioneer Hotel on East Main and Oak

Avenue. You'll know you're in the right place when you see the large wooden bear. No appointment needed; just stop in and discuss your project with them. Someone is always there, Monday through Friday, 9:00 a.m. to 4:00 p.m. They'll happily tell you what your project will cost and when you can expect it to be completed.

I wondered if Mr. Gilmore had any notion about how impactful his article was on our business. Because over the next few weeks, our commercial endeavor exploded with requests. I was overwhelmed with the unexpected burst of new customers, which prompted me to call an emergency meeting because I didn't know if I dared to accept any more orders.

"Clearly," I said, "we need to look again at our strategy because I'm being asked to schedule more work than I think we can complete within the two-week turnaround we've been promising. While rapid growth is nice, we still need to find a way to meet the demand, and quite frankly, I don't know how we're going to do it."

After a lot of discussion and an evaluation of each part of our business, we decided the knitting projects were simply too time-consuming and weren't lucrative enough to warrant taking up shop time for them. We decided we would concentrate our efforts on the quilting projects and the reupholstery side of our business because they supplied the biggest monetary payback. Those who had already accepted knitting commissions decided they would work on them at home during the evening hours when they watched television with their husbands. That way, all hands were able to be used on the cutting tables and sewing machines for the quilts and the cording of the upholstering projects during the daytime hours.

"Our customer base is changing too," I said. "Men have begun commissioning more jobs, big jobs that pay well."

A few days later a burly man parked his motorcycle in front of the store and approached Carl, who was standing in his usual spot behind the counter. "Where's those ladies who do that reupholster-ing stuff?"

"They're out in the back, just past the beer cooler."

Carl watched the bow-legged guy hike up his belt buckle before strutting toward the back of the store.

"Hello, ladies!" the guy said, sticking his head around the corner into our working area.

We all stopped what we were working on in order to gape at him, a bulky man of short stature with the biggest, bushiest, reddish-brown beard I had ever seen. His little bow-shaped lips seemed almost femi-nine, snuggled inside all his facial hair. I tried to compose myself and walked over to greet him.

"I'm Miss Birdie," I said extending my hand. "May I help you?"

His huge hand, more like a paw with sausages, totally consumed mine as we shook hands.

"Well ma'am," he said, removing his hat and exposing a shiny bald head, "I read an article in the newspaper about ya'all and was just kinda wonder'en if you can reupholster a motorcycle seat. You see, ma'am, the one I have is torn up pretty bad, and it's getting down-right uncomfortable when I take my bike on long runs. I don't need it to be no real leather or anything that's too hard on my wallet, if you know what I mean. But I thought maybe something like that new look-a-like leather might work out mighty fine if you catch my drift."

"Are you talking about Naugahyde?"

"Yeah! I think that's what it's called. It looks like leather but it's not real leather. I saw some over at the Five & Dime last week. It weren't too terribly expensive neither."

I invited him to bring the motorcycle around to the back door so I could assess the cost of his project. Immediately I realized it would be a simple project. We settled on a price, and he agreed he would be the one to remove the seat after he picked out and bought the Naugahyde. On the day he brought the fabric in to me, he said he planned to grab a little lunch and a couple of beers down the street while I did the job for him. So he removed the seat, and I did the entire job for him on that same day. He was able to ride his motorcycle home that afternoon.

In November, Bell Telephone introduced a new type of telephone, something they called "dual-tone multi-frequency" technology, or touch-tone dialing. Some people referred to it as push-button phones. When we learned the telephone company planned to replace all the rotary dial telephones with the new system, we decided it was a good time for us to get our own business phone for the workroom. That way, we wouldn't have to rely on using the payphone out by the bathrooms to call our customers to let them know their projects were ready for pickup. The phone was another step toward legitimizing our business.

33

THE TENSIONS OF SUCCESS

"Any woman who understands the problems of running a home will be nearer to understanding the problems of running a country."

—Margaret Thatcher

"Well, look who finally decided to come to work," Dorothy said when she saw Betsy blow into the workroom a little later than normal, with Stewart perched on her hip.

"Are you talking to me?" Betsy said. "Because if you are, you better take those words back before I shove them down your throat."

"Yes," Dorothy said. "I am talking to you! You're late, again! You've been late every day this week. I don't know who you think you are, maybe some sweet little princess sleeping in while the rest of us are working our fingers to the bone trying to get these orders out."

Betsy pulled the snowsuit off little Stewart and thrust him into the playpen with such gruffness that she caused her own child to cry. "Now look what you've done. You've gotten Stewart all upset!"

"No!" Dorothy said, "I didn't upset your kid. You did that with your rough handling of him."

"Stop it! Both of you!" Nancy said. "You're both sounding like a pair of alley cats. It's not only upsetting the babies, but your bickering is giving me a headache, and I'm so far behind with my orders that I can hardly sleep at night as it is. I sure don't want to listen to Stewart crying and the two of you arguing on top of it."

"Ladies, ladies," I said, tapping the handle of my scissors on one of the worktables. "Do you know what's happening here? We're all feeling stressed because we're trying to meet deadlines for orders."

"No kidding," Martha said. "I'm already two days behind with this sewing job and I haven't even begun on a couple of other commitments I've made for after this one. It's getting so bad that it's keeping me awake at night, and I think it may be giving me an ulcer too."

"I hear you," I said. "I hear all of you, and I'm beginning to feel the pressure too. But do you realize what we're complaining about? We're complaining about our success, yes success. We've made this into a thriving high-demand business, not just a hobby club anymore, and you did that! We've all done that. We've made this happen. Together, we've made this business successful, and together we will either succeed or fail. But what we are *not* going to do is keep picking at one another!"

I took a deep breath, realizing I'd never talked that boldly to anyone before in my entire life. I didn't know what I was going to say next, but I knew I needed to be careful because everyone's emotions were running high.

In a softer kinder voice, I clarified by repeating, "What we are all feeling is the stress of success, and I agree with you. We do need to talk about it, but we need to talk about it together, as a group, not in an argumentative way but in a manner in which we might actually find a solution. Remember, it's because many of you have other responsibilities at home that we all agreed to work the hours that best suit your individual families. Remember? And we all agreed to let the moms among us bring their babies with them."

They mumbled, nodding their heads and acknowledging their agreement with each other.

At noon, all tempers had mellowed, and Martha turned the television on low, wanting to keep the noise down while the babies napped, just as she'd been doing for the past several weeks. The women each settled into their typical viewing positions with their sandwiches, salads, or oranges they peeled in their laps in front of the television we'd recently bought so we could watch the mid-day news.

That day there was a special report about two girls who had gone missing in Sioux City.

Apparently, the girls told their parents they were going roller skating, and because they were considered *good girls* who didn't drink or do drugs, one was allowed to take her grandfather's beloved 1960 Studebaker. But apparently the girls changed their plans, and attended a party hosted by the senior class near some gravel pits. The girls went missing without a trace. There was speculation about foul play, but no remains were found, and all interviews by the police ended in dead ends, which gave pause to the notion that the girls may have disappeared together intentionally.

"Well, that's pretty depressing news," I said. We all agreed, and I turned the television off.

"It sure is," Martha said. "Makes you wonder how it's even possible to disappear, doesn't it."

I chose not to comment about how easily my scoundrel husband managed to disappear.

34

JASON'S NEW REALITY

*"Depression is like drowning, except everyone
around you is breathing."*

—Unknown

Jason was feeling more cantankerous and frustrated every day. The smallest irritants morphed into major frustrations. The burden of trying to keep up with his studies, meet the demands of the farm, and still keep up with the demands of the football schedule consumed more of him than what he had to give. He continually berated himself for not doing better, better with everything. He wondered if he should be changing the animals' diets in the winter but didn't have a clue about what it needed to be changed to. Neither did he know what to do with all the eggs, finally deciding he'd just eat them, as they were available and simple to prepare. But if he never ate another egg in his life that would suit him perfectly.

Football was the only activity that offered him any degree of pleasure, but even that was blemished with guilt because of the time it consumed, time he felt he should be devoting to work that needed to be done on the farm. During one of the practices, when his coach had them running laps, Jason used the time to clear his head. At first, he fantasized about how much he would have liked having his father watch him play football, knowing how proud his father would have been of him. He also thought about some of the management aspects of the farm, finally realizing he could lighten his workload if he sold some of the pigs.

"Okay, guys, good run today," his football coach said. "Go hit the showers and be back here same time tomorrow."

Well, that was fast! I'm beginning to get into this jogging thing. I not only lost track of time, but I had a lot of good thinking time while I was doing it.

The very next day Jason took several of the pigs to the local butchering plant. He didn't know if he got the best price for them, suspecting his dad may have negotiated a better price in St. Paul, but Jason didn't have the luxury or the time to take the pigs to St. Paul. Nor did he have his father's negotiating skills. Jason was just happy to have sold them at the offered price. Not only did the sale result in fewer pigs needing his care, but it also provided him with working cash for other farm expenses.

After all, winter was quickly approaching, which meant he needed to prepare things for the long, cold days ahead. Among other things, he needed to pull out the rubber watering trough because the rubber would expand when the water froze on the surface. He would just have to remember to break the surface ice each morning.

That evening, after feeding the animals that were left, Jason trudged up to the house contemplating what he would make himself for dinner. *Anything except eggs.* He opened the breadbox, found two heels of Wonder bread, and slathered them with peanut butter and his mother's apple jelly. Then he carried his sandwich into the living room, where he turned on the television. He adjusted the rabbit ears and sat in his father's chair, ready to enjoy one of his shows. There were several he enjoyed: *Gunsmoke, Wagon Train, Have Gun Will Travel* and *Rifleman* were a few of his favorites. That night *Gunsmoke* was scheduled to air, with Matt Dillon, the wise all-knowing sheriff. Festus, the confused sidekick, was the character Jason felt most akin to. Much to Jason's disappointment the program had been bumped by a national news announcement about two teenage girls who had recently disappeared.

"How terrible," Jason muttered to himself. "I know exactly how the families of those girls must feel."

He stared at the television screen, set the crusts of his sandwich down onto the small table next to his father's chair, and felt a renewed sorrow wash over him.

"Disappearances are such a whole lot of sadness," Jason said to his empty living room.

35

BETSY'S DISCRIMINATION REVELATION

*"I could not, at any age, be content to take my place
by the fireside and simply look on. Life was meant to
be lived. Curiosity must be kept alive. One must never,
for whatever reason, turn his back on that life."*

—ELEANOR ROOSEVELT

We had all become accustomed to Betsy's outbursts as she breezed into the shop in a new state of chaos and confusion each morning, but on this particular morning, she appeared to be extra flustered. She crashed through the door, letting it slam behind her, with little Stewart parked on one hip, the diaper bag slung over her opposite shoulder, and her Newport still hanging on her lower lip. She plopped the poor little guy into the playpen, ripped off his mittens, hat, and snowsuit and stuck a binky in his mouth just as he was about to howl. No one was surprised when he spit it out and cried in protest at his rough handling, but Betsy distracted him by placing his favorite toy within his reach, a push-toy on a stick that lit up and made beeping noises. I hated that noisy toy, and more than once I was tempted to destroy the sound mechanism in it. Unfortunately, I couldn't figure out how to do it, so the toy continued its noisy life, and quite frankly compared to hearing Stewart's healthy lungs, there were times I was happy for the toy.

We greeted Betsy with our usual good morning, as each of us continued working on our own projects, all of us in our own way trying to ignore Betsy's mood.

"Yah, yah, yah," Betsy said. "Good morning to all of you too, and in case any you are interested, my baby sister just up and eloped." She shrugged dramatically and hung her coat on one of the hooks behind the door.

No one commented but I caught the roll of Nadine's eyes, knowing she was thinking *here we go again with another of Betsy's dramas.*

Betsy continued orating as she stuffed the butt of her cigarette into the nearest ashtray. "I met the guy she married a couple of times. He seemed nice enough, clean cut, good manners, and really good looking." She gave us a quick wink and a little swing of her hips. "Pretty buff too. Anyway, I knew Sis liked him a lot, but when he got drafted I kind of thought she'd forgotten all about him when he was sent to boot camp because she began dating a lot of other guys." Betsy gave us another shrug. "But I knew Sis wasn't serious about any of the new guys because she'd see them once or twice and then they'd just disappear. But I had no idea she still had the *hots* for this Buck dude."

Betsy managed to command the attention of every one of us, which I hated because it slowed everyone's work down. She even captured my interest because listening to Betsy was like watching a live soap opera. I saw Martha set her sheers down on the table where she'd been cutting the fabric for a bridesmaid dress, and I put a paper clip on the page where I'd been working in the account book. Nadine and Dorothy stopped removing the fabric from a chair they'd been working on, and each of the others stopped what they were doing while Betsy droned on. "But, I guess Sis didn't forget about him at all, because as soon as he came home to visit his parents after boot camp, he and Sis just tossed their clothes in his rusty Plymouth and they drove all the way to Huntsville, Alabama, where he's stationed."

"Really!" Janet said, breaking out into laughter. "Well, there's no telling what we women will do when we think we're in love."

"Yeah, I know," Betsy said. "But that's not all of it. When they got to the Redstone Arsenal base in Alabama, they got married. Just like that! They didn't say anything to anyone, didn't have a party or nothing."

"That had to be a big surprise for your parents," I said. "How are they taking it?"

"My mom's having a hissy fit and my dad, well, he had only one comment and he hasn't said another word since."

"What did he say?" Martha asked.

"Dad said something about having one less wedding to pay for, and now he just sits in his chair with a stupid smirk on his face, and he doesn't say anything at all. When either me or Mom try to talk with him about it, he just says, 'Don't want to talk about it, she's made her choice and what's done is done'!"

"Aw, honey, it'll be okay," Martha said and walked over to give Betsy a little hug. "Try to be happy for them. They're obviously in love, and you know how love is. If it works for them that's all that matters. I know it doesn't always seem to make any sense, but that's just how love is. It is what it is! You know what I mean. Sometimes there's just no explaining it, but you sure know it when you see it and feel it."

Betsy accepted Martha's hug and when she saw the rest of our smiling faces, she said, "God, I appreciate you guys! But let me tell you the rest because that's not the worst of it. The thing is, I can hardly believe what's going on in Alabama. That's why I brought her letter with me, because I know you'll all be interested in it. The discrimination in Alabama is horrible. I've never paid much attention to stuff like that before, not until we couldn't get our loan. But now, I'm seeing discrimination all over the place, but wait until you hear what it's like down there."

She removed her sister's letter from her pocket and began reading.

December 1963
Dear Betsy,

We arrived in Alabama, and it's warm here. The grass is green, but the dirt is almost red. You would never know it's winter here. Everything here is different, which is good in some ways, but really bad in others.

We have a two-room apartment in a very old brick home that used to be an old plantation house. It was probably once a fancy place, but today it's pretty sad and run down but it's all we can afford.

Buck took me to the Army base commissary to buy food, but I didn't really know what to buy because, as you know, cooking isn't exactly what I do, so I bought a cookbook with pictures.

The commissary has check-out counters just like our Piggly Wiggly stores, but there are big reddish-brown cockroaches crawling all over the food. The cockroaches run right down the conveyor belt where the food is being checked out. I kept swishing them off with the back of my hand, the best I could, while trying not to actually touch them. The check-out girl acted like she didn't even see them. She said, "You-all must be from the Nooooorth."

"Yeah!" I said. "I'm from Minnesota! And we don't have cockroaches running around on our food up there!"

She told me, with a real uppity attitude, that I'd get used to them. Can you imagine her saying that to me? She acted as if it wasn't a big deal. Can you imagine that?

But I know I won't ever get used to them. How can anyone get used to living with bugs? It's disgusting! Anyway, Buck and me, we cooked together that night and our dinner didn't turn out too bad. Who knows? Maybe, I'll become a really good cook. We don't have much money because we have to pay rent and stuff, so I decided I'd look for a job right away. The very next morning, I walked to the town square, which is only two blocks from our apartment where we live. I saw a notice on a bulletin board advertising jobs for cotton pickers. I thought that would be a lot of fun and a great southern experience, so

I got myself all prettied up the next day and showed up at the hiring depot real early, just like the advertisement said.

When I got there, there was already a line out the front door, so I just got in the back of it and waited my turn. I felt a little funny because I was the only white girl there and everyone kept looking at me, but I held my head high and pretended like I didn't notice them staring at me. I wore my pretty blue sundress and new white sandals, and if I say so myself, I looked really good. Some of those standing in line didn't even dress up for the interview. The men were the worst. They wore raggedy jeans and looked awful. Some even had mud caked on their knees. I have to say, the line moved pretty fast. There were groups sent off to different trucks parked around the town square. When I finally got up near to the front of the line, I realized how hot and sticky it was in the hiring room. There was a big fan blowing in the corner, but the fan was pretty much useless because all it was doing was blowing hot body odor. The man doing the hiring was a big fat white guy, and he had sweat trickling down both sides of his fat pinkish face. He had on a light blue short-sleeved shirt with big dark circles of sweat rings under both arms.

When it was finally my turn, he said, "Neeext," and held out his hand without even looking up. I handed him my application and when he looked at it his eyes slowly looked up at me. I smiled as pretty as I could and said, "Good morning, sir."

"Le'me see yo hands," he stated angrily.

I held out my hands, and he shouted, "Get on out-a here before I woop ya. What do ya think you're doin? You think you're some cute little bitch whose gonna make a big name for yourself with some discrimination statement or something? Well, not on my clock you ain't!" You should have seen him, Betsy! It was a really creepy experience.

I was afraid he might stand up and hit me. That's how mean he looked at me. But I didn't even know what he was talking about. I just went there to apply for a job.

I left as quickly as I could, thinking about my job interview all afternoon. I could hardly wait for Buck to get home so I could tell him about it, but Buck didn't give me a kiss or ask about my day or anything when he got home. He just asked in a real mean way if I had dinner ready. I told him not yet, but I began cooking something right away. I wanted to tell him about my day before I started cooking, but he was in such a bad mood I didn't dare say anything. So I just cooked.

He told me to hurry up with the dinner because he had to get back to the base. Then, he told me in a really angry voice that he had to clean the latrines that night because he couldn't control his wife.

I honestly didn't know what he was talking about, but then he told me he was being punished because I applied for a day labor job that's intended for the niggers!

"Do you mean the black people?" I asked.

Betsy, I had no idea there were certain jobs just for the black people? Did you know that?

The next day I walked around the town square again and that's when I discovered there are even separate toilets, one for white women and another one for black women. And it's the same for the men, one for whites and another for blacks. Can you imagine? It just doesn't make any sense at all.

I don't think I like it here, Betsy.

Love, Sis

"Anyways," Betsy said as she refolded the letter, and returned it to her pocket. "I know Sis's letter is long, but it started me thinking about a lot of things. It especially got me thinking about discrimination and disrespect. It's not as bad here as it is in the South, but we have it here too. The thing is, we all just sort of get used to our own discrimination. It took reading about how bad it is in the South, which by the way I think really stinks, to help me see it for what it is. Because those people in the south must think what they're doing is perfectly normal, because if they didn't, they wouldn't tolerate being treated like that. So it must seem natural to them, and that's my point. Because if you think about it, we don't recognize our own discrimination as being unfair because the racial segregation in the South is so much worse, and we've grown up with our discrimination."

I couldn't imagine where she was going with this story, but she definitely had my undivided attention.

"When we were trying to get our loan," she said, "I don't think Mr. Slank ever thought he was being discriminatory by refusing us a loan just because we were women. To him it was normal, just the way he thought it was supposed to be. And our husbands didn't think it was discrimination either, because they were brought up thinking women shouldn't work or run a business. It's just the way it is here. And quite frankly, until I met all of you, I thought that was how it should be too.

"But, when I began thinking about it, I realized there are all sorts of things that discriminate against women right here in our own town. I used to accept the idea that married woman with children shouldn't work. And I also accepted the idea that if by some chance a woman did work, she would be paid less than a man doing her same job. Do you see what I'm talking about? All of that is discrimination."

I knew we all thought Betsy was somewhat of an airhead, but that morning I found myself changing my opinion of her. She may not have as much formal education as the rest of the group, but I was amazed at her wisdom. And I think everyone else in the room was impressed with her as well, because everything she said was absolutely true.

At the end of the day, when I sorted through the day's work and evaluated our progress, as I did every afternoon after everyone left the shop, I was happy to see that in spite of Betsy's drama that morning, it had been a fairly productive day. Most of the orders were being completed close to schedule, and I could see how the women had begun working together as a team. They talked among themselves and shared personal things with one another, but they worked while they talked, and in so doing they'd become supportive of each other. And if anyone had asked, I'd have to say I was enjoying my leadership role in our little business more and more each day too. Not since my college days did I feel this kind of pride or sense of purpose in life.

Heck, I'd even gotten used to being called Miss Birdie, and if I'm honest I'd have said I'm genuinely happy here.

Could it be that I never wanted to go back home?

I dumped the coffee grounds into the trash basket, cleaned the pot, and rinsed the used mugs before setting them upside down on a clean towel to let them dry overnight. After finishing with the coffee area, I swept the floor and removed all the scraps of fabric and any loose tacks that could become a hazard.

For some unknown reason, while sweeping, I began pondering the value of hugs and all the missed opportunities I'd had to show Jason how much I loved him. I missed him, but I was also upset with him, because I couldn't understand why he hadn't contacted me.

Maybe I'll call him again this weekend, and I'll try not to scold him. I'll just tell him I love him and that I miss him. Yup! That's all. I'll call Sunday evening, just before The Kraft Theater comes on. That way our conversation will be fairly brief because I know he and George will both be eager to get to the TV before the program begins.

That Sunday Jason rushed to finish his chores so he could be back at the house in time to get washed up, prepare his dinner, and turn on the television. He slipped a couple of chicken pot pies into the oven and was in the process of adjusting the rabbit ear antenna when he heard something creak on the back porch.

Who, he wondered, would be coming over unannounced on a Sunday night?

Then he heard the boards creak again, even louder than before.

Jeez, it sounds like someone who is really heavy.

Reluctantly and with a feeling of dread, he cracked open the kitchen door, unsure of who or what he was about to encounter. "Priscilla! What are you doing here?"

There Priscilla stood, resolute and determined to enter the kitchen. She pushed her way past Jason with the ease of a bulldozer.

"Oh, no you don't!" Jason tried to turn the pig around. "You have to get out of here and go back to your pen."

But Priscilla, all four hundred plus pounds of her, made it perfectly clear she had no intention of going anyplace. No indeed! She remembered the warmth of the kitchen from when she was a wee piglet, and she was determined to enter the kitchen and bed down for the night.

"Who do you think you are? You're a pig, remember? Pigs live in pig pens. They don't live inside houses, not since you were tiny anyway. For cripes sake! I'm arguing with a pig!"

But Priscilla was having none of that conversation. She'd already decided she was entering the house and now her only decision was to select the location where she would bed down for the night. She scouted all the corners of the kitchen while Jason tried to coax her back out the door. Just then the telephone rang, and Jason tried to reach over Priscilla to answer the phone, but Priscilla remained in front of him, blocking his every move. He felt like he was trying to out-maneuver a 400-pound moving tractor, and not until Priscilla selected her preferred resting place was Jason able to reach the telephone.

"Hello!" he said breathlessly into the mouthpiece, sounding every bit as irritated as he felt. And as he said this, Jason heard a click followed by a dial tone, knowing whoever it was had already hung up.

Meanwhile Priscilla gave out a contented snort, making it perfectly clear she had made her decision and had no intention of moving.

When Jason heard *The Kraft Theater* theme music, he stated with as much authority as he could, "Okay, Priscilla. You win for now. You can stay here tonight, but you have to leave in the morning! You got that?"

Ignoring everything Jason said, Priscilla gave another contented snort and went to sleep.

Jason removed his pot pies from the oven and carried them out to the living room. He closed the kitchen door securely behind him and settled into his father's chair, where he ate his dinner and watched his program.

After the show ended, he returned to the kitchen, set his fork in the sink, and tossed the potpie tins into the trash before calling Jessica on the telephone.

"Hi," he said. "Did you call earlier?"

"No," she said. "Why? What made you think I called?"

"Well, the phone rang when I was dealing with one of the pigs and when I was finally able to reach the phone no one was there. I just thought it may have been you who called and hung up when I didn't answer in time."

"No, it wasn't me, probably just a wrong number."

"Yeah, probably."

"Is everything okay, Jason?"

"Yeah, sure, everything's fine. Why do you ask?"

"Well, because you sound kind of strange, like there's something else that you want to tell me. Are you sure there isn't something wrong?"

"Well, I do have a little situation. The thing is, Priscilla, the biggest pig, decided to move into the kitchen tonight."

"The pig decided to do what?" Jessica was unable to withhold her laughter.

Jason began to see the humor in it too when he heard Jessica laugh, and he told her what had happened. "Well, she weighs over 400 pounds. So she pretty much does exactly whatever she wants to do."

"That's the funniest thing I've ever heard! How are you going to get her out of there?"

"I don't know. That may be a problem, but I figure she'll want to eat tomorrow so I'll just have to lure her out with food. But if I have any trouble, I may be a little late for school. I'll just have to see how it goes."

"What if she makes a mess in the kitchen?"

"Yeah, well contrary to what people think, pigs are pretty clean creatures. So I don't think she'll do that. But if she does, I'll just have to clean it up."

"Jeez, Jason! Good luck with that!"

"By the way, don't tell anyone at school about this. Okay? This is the kind of thing some of the guys would never let me live down. There's already a guy who likes to call me pig boy, and this would just give him a whole new story to ride my ass with."

"No problem, Jason. It'll be our secret."

"Thanks, I appreciate that."

"Good night, Jason."

"Goodnight, Jessica. See you in the morning."

36

BETSY'S VISION
OF INJUSTICE

*"We don't develop courage by being happy every day. We develop
it by surviving difficult times and challenging adversity."*

—BARBARA DE ANGELIS

Betsy was still trying to get used to the fact that her sister was
married when she received a jarring phone call from her
parents.

"Betsy," her mother blubbered into the telephone. "We got a special delivery telegram from the State Department and . . ."

Betsy transferred Stewart to her other hip so she could put the
phone up closer to her ear.

"I'm sorry, Mom, I'm struggling with Stewart right now and you're
not speaking very clearly. I didn't hear what you said. Would you repeat it?"

Then Betsy realized her mother was crying, saying something
about her brother Bobby and the State Department.

"Mom! Mom! Stop crying! What happened? What are you trying

to say? Is it about Bobby? Has he been hurt? He didn't get killed, did he? Oh Mom, please don't tell me Bobby's dead! Is he?"

"We don't know," her mother managed to blurt out in a gulp. "We don't think he's dead, not exactly anyway, but, but he's . . ."

"But he's what? Mom! What did it say?"

When her mother broke down sobbing Betsy realized her mother was passing the telephone to her father.

"Betsy, honey," her father said. "Your brother is missing in action."

"Missing in action? What does that mean?"

"He's lost, honey. He's lost someplace in Vietnam. The State Department doesn't know where he is and, well, we can't figure out how the Army can lose a full-grown man, but apparently, they did. That's all the letter stated. It just said, 'Missing in Action.' One sentence! That was all. One single sentence with no explanation. Nothing about where he went missing, nothing about what he was doing, and nothing about who was the last person to have seen him or anything. Just 'We regret to inform you that Private Robert Williams is missing in action.'"

"Does the Army think he's dead?" Betsy asked. "Is that what they think?"

"I don't know what they think, honey. They may think he's dead or they may suspect he's deserted."

"Deserted? Bobby would never do that! He just wouldn't! It's not who he is! Don't even think that! No one better ever say that!"

"I know, honey, but it may be better than thinking he's dead. But you're right. I know your brother would never go AWOL. He's never walked out of a difficult situation in his life, but sometimes I kinda just hope that's what he did this time, if you know what I mean. But what do I know? I don't know anything, honey, and that's what's making this so difficult."

When Betsy hung up the phone, she kicked the wall, feeling as if the world might actually have ended, and in some ways, she wished it would. At least then she'd have something to fight. But this. What was missing in action? What did that even mean? She wanted to cry and be angry with something or someone all at the same time. But she knew that would be about as productive as trying to catch baby formula when it spilled on the counter.

She thought she might feel better if she could scream at someone. Anyone or anything would do. But hearing the statement *Missing in Action* was a pointless misery.

Like a robot, she packed the diaper bag with diapers, a bottle, a pacifier, bib, jars of baby food, and a spoon. She stuffed Stewart into his snowsuit and propped him up with blankets on the front seat of her car. Then, she got behind the wheel of her new secondhand Edsel and drove to the shop, the same as she did every morning. Parking near the side door, she slung the diaper bag over one shoulder as she always did. She picked up Stewart and slammed the car door behind her before stomping through the shop door, letting it slam behind her. She thrust Stewart into the playpen, removed his snowsuit and stuck a pacifier into his mouth before he could cry, and handed him a toy, a less noisy one this time. But we all noticed how gruff her actions were.

The shop became quiet, very, very quiet as we all pretended to be concentrating on whatever task we were doing. I continued working in the accounts book and wrote out a few customer invoices, but I was having a difficult time concentrating with Betsy in such a mood. I watched her from the corner of my eye and waited to see what would happen next. She almost didn't even look like herself because her face, which was normally a ray of sunshine, was hard and stern.

Timidly a few of us said, "Good morning," but none of us was brave enough to inquire what was wrong. Instead, we each pretended we weren't aware of her mood and continued working because she was acting like a caged animal ready to eat the first person who spoke to her. I assumed she'd had a fight with her husband, and I wasn't eager to hear about a domestic dispute, so I, like the others, kept my head down and continued working on the account book.

Finally, she said, "Do you all remember when I read my sister's letter and we talked about discrimination? Well, today I learned about something a lot worse."

At that point, we all stopped and looked up to hear what Betsy was about to announce. I couldn't help but marvel at how skilled she was at waiting until she had everyone's undivided attention before launching into telling us whatever it was that was bothering her this time.

"Today," she said, "I learned my brother is missing in action."

As soon as she said this, I heard gasps and saw the women's hands fly up to their mouths.

Before any of us could speak, she continued. "You probably don't know this, but I got pregnant when I was only sixteen, because Jimmy and me, we played around in the back seat of his jalopy when we were in high school and I got pregnant. I had to drop out of school, but Jimmy's a square shooter and he married me anyway. We've got four kids today and life hasn't been easy for us. But I understand why that is, and I accept my responsibilities for that because Jimmy and me, we did that to ourselves. But Bobby, my baby brother Bobby, he's always been smart. He's done everything right. He finished high school and he never got in any trouble at all. He was going to college part-time while he worked at the assembly plant when he got drafted. He didn't want to go to war. He didn't even believe in this war, but Uncle Sam said, 'I Want You' and that was that! He was sent off to boot camp and then to Vietnam. And now he might be dead. Now that's what I call really, really shitty! To have to maybe die for something you don't even believe in, is just plain unfair!"

Betsy finished that statement by pounding her fist on the cutting table, causing the scissors resting on it to jump and rattle.

Martha walked over and put her arm around Betsy's shoulder. "What exactly did the letter say, Betsy? Did it say your brother was killed in action?"

"No, it said he was, *missing in action.*"

"Well, honey, that doesn't mean he's dead. I know it's horrible frightening news, but there's still hope. You've got to keep having hope, sweetheart. I'm sure your brother would want you to think as positively as possible."

"Yeah, I know you're right," Betsy said, "but it's so hard, and right before Christmas too."

The tears Betsy had been trying to prevent from surfacing erupted into a flood, causing two streams of black mascara to run down her face. "Hand me one of those handkerchiefs, will you?" Betsy asked, motioning toward the stack of beautifully embroidered handkerchiefs she'd been working on. Martha picked one off the top of the pile and handed it to Betsy.

"Honey, aren't you embroidering these for a client?" Martha asked.

"Yeah," Betsy said. "I'll just have to make a couple more." She blotted the mascara with one of her beautiful creations.

After a few moments, Betsy was able to get control of her emotions. She blew her nose and wiped her eyes with the fine percale handkerchief, never imagining she'd ever use anything so fine or delicate for her own personal use.

"Thanks for listening to me," she said, "and for being so kind and understanding too. I think it was a mistake for me to come to work today. I think I need to take a couple of days off if that's okay with all of you."

"That's a good idea," Martha said, giving her another hug.

"Yes," I said. "Give yourself a little time to catch your breath, and who knows, you may hear better news in a few days."

"I sure hope so," Betsy said. "I think I'm going to spend a few days with my parents. They don't live far from here, and I want to be with them, at least until Christmas. And I can work on my knitting and embroidering while I'm there."

With that, Betsy gathered up the supplies she would need. She returned Stewart to his snowsuit, and they left the shop without another word.

The shop remained unusually quiet after Betsy's departure, as each of us seemed deep in our own thoughts. I slipped out of the work-room, needing a little time to reflect, realizing that Jason would be turning eighteen soon. I found it shocking to realize the government would consider him a man and require him to register with the Draft Board. At first, I wondered if he'd even know he was supposed to register, and then I pondered what would happen if he purposely neglected to register. Would the Army be able to locate him? And if they did find him would there be some kind of a penalty for not registering.

Maybe the penalty would be better than being sent to Vietnam.

I realized all my conjectures were foolish and futile because I knew George would make sure Jason got registered in a timely man-ner. In fact, George would very likely go with Jason to make sure all the paperwork was filled out correctly. Still, the mere thought of my boy being sent away to fight in Vietnam sent shivers up my spine.

In many ways, I found it hard to believe Jason was old enough for the government to even consider him to be a man, man enough to be sent to fight a war, a war that had been going on for six years. To me, he was still just a boy, my boy, my only child. And as Betsy so aptly stated, most of us didn't know why America was in this war. Why were we sending our young men to fight and die in jungles that we had never heard of, and in places I didn't even know how to spell? After all, this was nothing like WWII when we knew and understood exactly why we were fighting.

I felt a cloud of depression sweep over me, and guilt too, because in spite of worrying about Jason, I realized I didn't really want to re-turn to the farm. I was content and happy right where I was.

After everyone left, I shuffled around in the storage cabinet, look-ing for a fresh box of tea. Finding one, I opened it and placed the new bags in the container next to the teapot before making myself a fresh cup. The warmth of the cup was comforting on my arthritic knuckles. I slipped on my coat and carried the cup outside with me, where I sat on the bench next to the bear.

"Hello Wilkes," I said to the bear as I sat next to him. "It's a little chilly out here today, isn't it? You do remember me, don't you? Of course, you do. You and I have always gotten along just fine, and you're a pretty good listener too, no interruptions or anything like that."

I sipped my tea and found it still a little weak, so I jiggled the string a couple of times with my hands still wrapped gently around the warm cup.

"What do you think, Wilkes? Should I try to call Jason again? Part of me wants to talk to him, you know, because I'd like him to know I think about him, and I miss him a lot. But another part of me is still angry with him for not coming to get me or for not even checking on me."

I paused and sipped my tea, still finding it rather weak, so I jiggled the string a couple more times.

"And yet, I have to admit, if he did come to get me, I'm not sure I'd want to go back to the farm, because I'm really enjoying my life here." I paused as I let that thought settle. "I suppose that makes me a terrible mother, doesn't it?"

I took a sip of tea feeling like I must be the most awful mother that ever existed.

"You know Wilkes, the ladies here are a pleasure to be with, and I'm loving the challenge of running this little business with them, and I'm proud of what we've accomplished together. Is that terrible of me to feel that way? What do you think? Does that make me an awful person and a horrible mother?"

I dunked the tea bag up and down again before taking another sip, contemplating the issue of pride.

"The church teaches us not to be prideful, but somehow, I don't think all pride is bad. What do you think? Aren't we taught to do our best, and isn't it pride that makes us want to do our best at whatever we do? Why would anyone try to work toward anything at all if they couldn't be proud of their accomplishments? Surely, you have to agree with that."

I took another sip, enjoying its robust delicate flavor.

"You know, Wilkes, the world isn't perfect, "and I know you understand what I'm talking about because you have to sit out here day and night all by yourself. But you've adjusted to it all pretty well, haven't you! I don't know how long you've been out here, but you've remained strong and resilient, that's for sure. You're an inspiration. Do you know that? And somehow, I've got a hunch you're a pretty proud chap."

I took another sip of tea and rested my head against the bear's torso.

"Do you remember the first time I sat on this bench with you? It was really hot that day and I was so afraid and lonely. But I'm not afraid anymore. In fact, I feel stronger and more in control of myself than I've felt in years. And I'm not lonely anymore either because I have friends here, real friends, friends who genuinely care about me.

I extended my legs and took another sip before leaning back against the bear's chest, contemplating the problems of life, particularly my life.

"What do you think Wilkes? What should I do about Christmas? It'll be here soon enough you know, and I don't know what I should do about a gift for Jason. Do you think he'll be expecting one from me? After all, I have no idea what nonsense George has put in his head, which makes me think he may not want to hear from me at all. Actually, in some ways, I'm not sure if I want to take any of my hard-earned money to buy him anything anyway, because I'm barely able to live on the little I earn. And I certainly don't have anything extra to go squandering on some ungrateful person. The more I think about it, neither of them deserves a gift! I'll bet you anything I don't receive anything from either of them!"

My tea had turned cold, so I tossed the last of it on the pavement and patted the bear's leg.

"It's always nice talking to you there, my old friend. You've been a big help. I'll come back again sometime so we can have another little chat."

With that, I stood and went back inside to the telephone, fully intending to give those guys a piece of my mind! I lifted the receiver and dialed the farmhouse phone number. I didn't know which of them might answer, or for that matter, what I would say when one of them picked up the phone, but I felt as if I needed to get some answers. While listening to the ringing, I felt myself soften, hoping it would be Jason who answered. Knowing if I could just hear his voice, I'd feel better. After all, eighteen years or not, he is still my baby.

I listened to each ring with sweaty hands and a thumping in my chest, but no one answered, so I gave up and returned the phone to its cradle.

Maybe I'll just write Jason a letter, that might make more sense. I could form my thoughts better and tell him. Hmm, what would I tell him? That I love him? That I hope he doesn't get drafted? That I forgive him for leaving me here after his father dropped me off?

I'll have to think about that.

I gathered up my cleaning supplies and got to work, knowing the toilets wouldn't clean themselves.

37

THE PILL AND JUSTICE FOR ALL

"We ask for justice, we ask for equality, we ask that all the civil and political rights that belong to citizens of the US be guaranteed to us and our daughters forever."

—SUSAN B ANTHONY

Betsy didn't stay away from the shop for more than a few days. She told us she missed us and that she felt better when she was working. She also told us she needed to keep working in order to make her car payments on her secondhand Edsel, the one her husband bought for her from the Edsel garage where he worked. "Besides," she said, "I want to earn money for Christmas this year, not only for my kids but for my parents too. There have been far too many Christmases at our house when there wasn't much more than new underwear wrapped up under our tree. This year I want to splurge. I'd like to be able to bring a little joy to my family. Maybe a festive gift opening will ease the worry we're all having over my brother."

Once Betsy got all her news shared with the group, she got down to work, which meant all the rest of us were able to get some work done too. The day flew by, and before I knew it, the women were packing up to leave for home.

I usually got busy sweeping the floor and returning supplies to their proper stations as soon as everyone left, but tonight I felt tired and decided I needed a little pick-me-up before I began my regular chores. I poured the last of the strong coffee from the pot into a clean cup and sat down to reflect on the fact that Christmas was nearly upon us. I knew I'd been trying to ignore the holiday, but when I heard Betsy talk about how important it was for her to buy gifts for her kids, I began thinking about knitting a pair of gloves for Jason. With renewed determination to talk to him, I went to the phone and called the farmhouse, and was shocked when he answered on the second ring.

"Hello," he said. But instead of talking to him, I froze. Not a single word slipped from my lips. I had dialed that number so many times with no results that I was completely unprepared for Jason to actually answer. My heart began to pound, and I couldn't get over how grown up and deep his voice had become. He sounded confident and I wondered if he was happy. I wanted to know those things and more, yet I couldn't bring myself to talk or to ask.

"Hello," he said again. "Is anyone there? Hello?"

Gently, ever so gently, I returned the phone to its cradle without speaking.

38

MISS BIRDIE AND NADINE

"Christmas isn't a season. It's a feeling."

—Edna Ferber

"Today is the first anniversary of the death of Nadine's husband," Martha shared with me that morning. "She seems to be managing pretty well, but I thought you would want to know just in case she's extra sensitive today, since this will be her first Christmas alone. If we see some unusual behavior, I think we should cut her a little slack, although I don't think we should talk about it unless she brings it up."

I nodded my understanding because I didn't want anyone to ask me about my family either. Besides, Nadine was always quiet, the least verbal woman in our group. She barely talked about much of anything at all, which was why I was so surprised when she asked me if I'd be interested in accompanying her to church on Christmas morning.

"I know you don't have transportation," she said, "so I'll be happy to pick you up. Truth be told, I've been a little lonely since my Fred died, and this will be my first Christmas without him, so I'd really appreciate having someone attend the service with me." Without giving me an opportunity to respond, she continued. "And then, if you'd be okay with it, I thought we could go to The Bellowing Moose for dinner after the church service. What do you think? Would you be interested in doing that?"

"Are you kidding?" I finally said, finding an opening to respond, while thinking how uncharacteristically friendly she was being toward me. "I'd love to go with you. I hear the others talking about The Bellowing Moose all the time, but I've never been there."

"Well, it's a good restaurant and they usually serve a big buffet on Christmas. The first seating is at 1:00 o'clock. Fred and I used to go there on special occasions like birthdays or our anniversary, things like that, and we've never been disappointed with the quality of the food. Of course, they're a little on the expensive side, so we would each have to go Dutch treat. Would that be okay with you?"

"Yes, of course. That wouldn't be a problem at all."

I was elated with the invitation, so much so that I couldn't stop grinning and bobbing my head up and down like one of those new bobblehead dolls.

"We can even order a glass of sherry if we're so inclined. It just seems to me that a little sherry might be in order on Christmas. What do you think? You do drink sherry, don't you?"

I almost wept with joy at Nadine's invitation, as I could hardly remember anyone ever showing me such a kindness or special consideration. Not even Martha gave me a second thought with the upcoming holidays. Of course, I understood how awkward it would be for her because of Carl, but it still didn't diminish my loneliness.

"Yes," I finally managed to blurt out. "Yes, I do drink sherry, but I haven't had a glass in such a long time that I've almost forgotten how it tastes. But that doesn't mean I don't enjoy it. And yes, I'd love to join you! In fact, I really appreciate your invitation."

"Good," Nadine said. "I'll pick you up a little before 10:00 a.m. That will give us plenty of time to get a good seat at church because I like sitting up near the front so I can hear the minister. I hate to admit it, but my hearing isn't as good as it used to be anymore. And the service will end plenty early enough for us to get to the restaurant in time for the first seating, because if we don't get there early, we could end up waiting in line for what can feel like forever."

"That's perfect. I'll be ready by 9:45, and again, thank you. I'll look forward to it!"

On Christmas morning, I woke to the first dusting of this winter's snow and dressed in my new burgundy wool dress, the one I'd recently made by cutting apart a fat ladies' dress I'd found at the Salvation Army. This would be my first occasion to wear it. I also donned a fresh girdle and a new pair of nylons, as I wasn't about to wear nylons with snags in them for this festive occasion. I applied a little rouge and pink lipstick and finished up by adding a holiday pin to my collar, the pin I'd purchased for 69 cents at the same Salvation Army store.

I was ready a full fifteen minutes before Nadine was scheduled to pick me up, so I slipped on my new secondhand winter coat and donned the hat I'd purchased from the Goodwill, the one I'd spruced up with a pheasant feather, altering its appearance enough so I hoped the original owner wouldn't recognize it. Then I slid a silky scarf around my neck to protect my skin from the rough wool and slipped on a pair of white gloves before walking outside.

"Hello, Wilkes," I said, sitting next to the bear on the bench. "It's me again."

I found myself staring at the clumps of cauliflower clouds sliding low across the winter sky.

"Aren't those clouds interesting, Wilkes? What do you think causes that? The cold air? The wind? I don't suppose you know either, do you?"

I was amazed to see how rapidly the clouds were changing shape as they skimmed across the sky, wondering if they were the forbearers of a coming snowstorm.

"Guess what, Wilkes? I've had an invitation to go to church with one of the ladies, and then we're going out for dinner. What do you think about that? Well, I just thought you might want to know about it, because I think it's very nice of her to invite me. In fact, it may be the nicest thing that's happened to me in very long time."

I couldn't stop myself from smiling because I felt so glamorous sitting there in my newish dress-up clothes.

"Look at that, Wilkes. Do you see that red cardinal over there? The one pecking at some food someone spilled on the pavement. I've always liked cardinals, even though I know they're considered to be obnoxious birds. It's hard to believe such a beautiful creature can be such a menace to its fellow birds. But I guess it can be that way with people too. We can't always tell who's going to be nice or untrustworthy just by looking at them. I suppose Margaret Peterson is like that cardinal. She looks all jovial and harmless on the outside with her incessant chatter and her jiggling bosoms, but under that dyed hair of hers she's just another husband stealer."

I heard myself huff as visions of Mrs. Peterson with George jumped into my thoughts.

Nope, I'm not going to let those people ruin this day for me. I want to enjoy myself, without thinking about them, so I'll just change the subject.

"I suppose you'd like to know what I've decided to do about Jason's Christmas gift, because that was the last conversation we had together. Well, just to let you know, Wilkes, I knitted a pair of gloves for him, pretty nice ones too. I used double-ply yarn to make them really warm, and I mailed them a couple of days ago. I put a lot of scotch tape over the return address because I want to make sure he knows where I am in case George hasn't told him. I think when he receives my gloves, he'll want to come and get me, no matter what George may have told him. Actually, I'm surprised I haven't heard anything from him yet because it's not like Jason to hold a grudge. But as I said, I expect I'll be hearing from him any day now. Well, that's all the information I have today. We'll have to chat more another time, Wilkes, because right now I see my ride is coming."

I gave the bear's big knee a little tap and stood up from the bench.

Instead of the typical Christmas sermon, the minister chose to give a sermon about the importance of family unity during the holidays. I listened to the quotes he used from the Bible, but instead of making me feel better, I found myself wanting to argue or debate each point.

"God created humans to live as a family unit," the minister stated. "Colossians 3:13, says, *'Bear with each other and forgive one another. If any of you has a grievance against someone. Forgive as the Lord forgave you.'*

"In Corinthians 13:4-7," the minister read on, *"We learn love is patient, love is kind. It does not envy, it does not boast, it is not proud. It does not dishonor others, it is not self-seeking, it is not easily angered. It keeps no record of wrongs. Love does not delight in evil but rejoices with the truth. It always protects, always trusts, always hopes, and always perseveres.*

"And in Proverbs 11:29 we learn that whoever brings ruin on their family will inherit only wind, and the fool will be servant to the wise."

Well now, isn't that a lot of poppycock! George didn't inherit the wind. He inherited two entire farms, a farm my parents' insurance money purchased for him and now it looks like he's connived his way into getting Margaret Peterson's farm as well. And if I'm to be considered as the servant, I clearly do *not* feel very wise because I'm barely surviving, and it seems a wise person wouldn't be finding themselves in this situation. I suspect Nadine didn't feel any more uplifted by the minister's sermon than I did, because as a new widow, she's trying to adjust to being without a family, while I am trying to become less bitter about mine.

In spite of the lack of inspiration from the sermon, we did enjoy the opportunity to sing the old time-honored Christmas songs.

"Joy to the world, the Lord has come."

I'd forgotten how much I enjoyed singing at church, realizing that was the thing I enjoyed the most about going to church. I even considered joining our local choir at one point, but I never did because when the choir director learned that I didn't sing alto he didn't seem very interested in adding one more soprano. So I never bothered to join. But the thing that pulled my heart strings the most in today's sermon was learning about the orphanage right here in Owatonna, with all those poor children who could benefit by warm mittens, caps, and scarves. Now that's something I can feel good about contributing to, and I promised to begin knitting mittens and scarves for them at night when I watched the evening news.

After church we walked to The Bellowing Moose where we partook in their magnificent Christmas buffet: prime rib with au-jus and horseradish sauce, turkey with sage dressing and cranberry sauce, pork roast with applesauce, mashed potatoes with gravy, sweet potatoes, and baked potatoes with sour cream. There were so many items to choose from that I found it difficult to make my selections. There was also an assortment of vegetables and salads. Just when I didn't think a meal could be any more delicious, a waiter appeared at our table with hot popovers, delivered directly from the oven before the steam could escape, which would cause them to collapse. What a feast! And not only did Nadine and I have a glass of sherry, but we each had two. It was indeed a feast for both of us!

"Fred would have really enjoyed this meal," Nadine said, sipping her second glass of sherry. "He would have loved all these different kinds of meat. He wasn't much of one to eat sweets, but my-oh-my, he did so love his meat."

I smiled. "This is the first time I've heard you talk about your husband. Do you miss him terribly?"

"Sometimes I do, but after he retired, he began drinking and he became a different person. Toward the end, he wasn't my old Fred anymore. At first, he started putting a little whiskey in his morning coffee, but before I knew it, it was the other way around. He was putting a little coffee in his whiskey. Anyway, there's not much point in talking about it because it isn't going to bring him back or change a single thing now, is it?"

"Ahh." I nodded in understanding.

"How about you?" she asked. "Why don't you talk about yourself?"

"I don't know. I guess I'm just not the talkative type, at least not about personal stuff. I'm probably more of a listener than a talker when it comes to things like that."

Unbeknown to me and several days before Christmas, when the mail was at its heaviest, the Owatonna postal carrier who'd been a fixture in the community for years, drove into a whiteout on one of the most remote sections of rural road where there was a blind curve. He drove directly into an oncoming bus, loaded with a school band going to a performance. The flimsy postal wagon was demolished, spewing gasoline on the road, and saturating the undelivered mail remaining in his truck. He died before the ambulance arrived to take him to the hospital. Several of the teens were also taken to the hospital and treated for bumps and bruises. Two had broken arms, but all, except for the postal carrier survived the crash. Even the instruments were safe because they were in a separate truck following the school bus.

Two weeks after Christmas, the package with the hand knit gloves I knitted for Jason, was returned to me. The delivery address was smudged, and I was puzzled over the fact that the entire package smelled of gasoline. Only the return label, the one I'd covered with several pieces of scotch tape, was intact and legible, which allowed the package to be returned to me.

I wondered if George used gasoline to deliberately smudge the address, and put it back in the return mail before Jason was able to see it? I wouldn't be surprised by anything he did anymore.

Over the next few weeks, my friendship with Nadine grew, and as the weeks rolled into months, we found ourselves spending more and more time together. The community began treating us as a pair, as if we were sisters, and Sunday church service became a regular occurrence for us, followed by an early afternoon dinner either at The Kitchen or the Bellowing Moose. Before making our decision where we would eat, we typically studied the menus posted outside the doors of each restaurant, carefully scrutinizing what each establishment offered that day. The decision sometimes became weighty, as The Kitchen had good home cooked food and was a lot less expensive but also less festive than the Bellowing Moose. During hunting season however, The Kitchen offered venison and duck, which we assumed had been shot by one of the local residents.

Occasionally after dinner, we shopped for treasures at Pearl's Books, if it was open. Or we looked for quality clothing at the Salvation Army, clothing we could pick apart and make into something new, as we were both experienced with the concept of gleaning new garments from existing old clothing.

39

JASON'S LIFE MOVES ON

"I've come to believe each of us has a personal calling
that's as unique as a fingerprint – and the best way to
succeed is to discover what you love and find a way to
offer it to others in the form of service, working hard and
also allowing the energy of the universe to lead you."

—Oprah Winfrey

"**J**ason," Mrs. Peterson said into the phone, "I'm glad I caught you at the house because I'm calling to invite you to join us for Christmas dinner. That is, if you don't already have other plans."

"Gee, thanks! That'd be great! I don't have any other plans at all. Should I bring something, maybe an apple pie or something?"

"Oh, my lands, Jason. Really? That would be perfect! Would you mind picking one up at the Piggly Wiggly?"

"Well, I thought I'd just make one, if that'd be okay with you, because I stuck a bunch of apples in the freezer that I should probably use somehow. Because I don't know how long they'll be any good."

"Jason, you surprise me more every day! What would you do about the crust?"

"Well, do you think it'd be too difficult to just follow one of Mom's recipes?"

"Why don't you just spoon a top crust onto it, Jason. That will be a lot simpler, and I'll pick up some ice cream to go with it. That should work out just fine. I thought I'd make a turkey so apple pie à la mode would be very nice with it."

The invitation to spend the holiday with the Petersons was nothing short of exhilarating and provided the additional bonus of having someone to purchase a Christmas gift for. After all, what was Christmas without being able to give someone a gift?

The following day he visited the local jewelry store as soon as the coach dismissed the team. He'd never been in a jewelry store before, but he knew his mother liked jewelry, so he assumed Mrs. Peterson and Jessica might like it as well.

He parked his motorcycle in front of the store and was surprised to discover he couldn't just open the door and walk in. He had to ring a doorbell and wait to be admitted. Once inside he was overwhelmed by what he saw: multiple rows of glass cases, each displaying an assortment of rings, earrings, necklaces, bracelets, cufflinks, tie tacks, and stone-studded pins.

As soon as the clerk saw his confusion, she quickly tried to put him at ease by asking what his budget was and what type of purchase he had in mind. Then she helped him select a modestly priced necklace for Mrs. Peterson, similar to those he remembered seeing his mother wear. And for Jessica, she helped him select a pair of pearl earrings. He was greatly relieved when the clerk suggested she gift wrap his gifts for him, and right before his eyes he watched her transform the two small boxes into something exquisite.

"Some lucky girl is going to really enjoy these pearl earrings," she said as she handed both wrapped gifts to him.

On Christmas day Jason drove his motorcycle to the Petersons' farm, parked it in the barn, and walked up to the back door and knocked. As soon as Jessica opened the door, Jason's stomach let out a loud rumble, caused by the marvelous aroma of the roasting turkey.

"Gosh, Jason, you sound really hungry!" Jessica said, and they both laughed.

Mrs. Peterson's Christmas feast was exactly that, a feast, followed by Jason's apple pie, which was surprisingly tasty in spite of the tough clumps of crust Jason had spooned on top. But it was Mrs. Peterson's scoop of ice cream that made the crust irrelevant, as the crust was then more like a crispy cookie on top.

After dinner, they played Scrabble and chatted.

"Did you hear about old man Cuthbert?" Jason asked.

"Yes," Jessica said. "That was so shocking! He's been our postman my whole life." She looked up from the Scrabble board. "It sort of creeps me out to think he died out there all by himself in the cold while delivering Christmas cards and gifts."

"Yeah," Jason said, "I heard some of the band kids talking about it the other day. I guess it was pretty traumatic for everyone because the school bus just plowed right into him. You know, those postal trucks are really flimsy. They don't have much protection for the driver at all."

"I heard that he was on the wrong side of the road," Jessica said. "Apparently, he was reaching up into one of those rural boxes and never even looked for oncoming traffic."

"That's what I heard too," Jason said. "The school bus driver was pretty shaken up, but I don't think it was his fault. He never saw him 'till it was too late. I heard a lot of mail was lost because the addresses got so soggy and wet."

"I think we should be talking about something else," Mrs. Peterson said, "because it's too nice of a day to dwell on misery. Anyway, what's done is done, and there's no point in rehashing what can't be undone."

"You're right," they both agreed. "It is too nice of a day to talk about how Mr. Cuthbert died."

With that, they returned to their Scrabble game, while Jason glowed with his little secret of having successfully hidden his gifts for Jessica and Mrs. Peterson under the Christmas tree, knowing they would find their gifts later. He was delighted with his little secret Santa gifts.

But, if you asked Jason, the innocence and happiness of the holiday didn't last long enough, because he was back to all the same routine drudgery the very next day.

And when school resumed, all the talk among his senior guys was about the draft and the Vietnam War. No one, not a single one of Jason's friends was eager to go to war. Yet, he and all his buddies knew it was a requirement to register for the military draft prior to their eighteenth birthday. And as soon as they were registered, they were at once eligible to be drafted for military duty. The only thing that would prevent an eighteen-year-old male from being drafted was going to college to study something of dire importance to the nation. And even that had no guarantee.

Based on what Jason heard on WCCO radio, there were a lot of families upset about this war. He scheduled his work so he could be working in the barn when those talk shows were being broadcast. And as of late, everyone seemed upset and opposed to this war, which caused Jason to wonder if this war was worse than all the others. Or he wondered, if this war just seemed worse because he was of draftable age.

One of the newspaper headlines last week said 16,000 Americans had already died in South Vietnam and had come home in flag-draped coffins. Another article reported on war protests taking place on college campuses, not just by students and young people, but by the parents as well. Jason knew of people in his own community who talked openly about sending their sons out of the country, sending them to Canada to avoid being drafted. But there were mixed feelings about that as well because the act of sending one's son to Canada would make him a draft dodger, which wasn't considered an acceptable alternative either. Answers and solutions weren't easy for any of the families.

"Have you registered for the draft yet?" Billy asked Jason one day in the locker room.

"No, not yet, but I have to do it pretty soon because my birthday's coming up real fast. How about you? Are you registered?"

"No, but I've got to go soon too. My birthday is in February. But I think my old man will go down there with me when I do it. My older brother got drafted last year, and Dad went with him when he registered."

"Is your brother in Vietnam?"

"No, he's still in boot camp. He's just a year older than me."

"Well, my birthday is in January, so I've got to get my lonesome butt down there in the next few days."

Two days before Jason's eighteenth birthday, he walked into the Army Recruiting Station to get registered. He signed in at the front desk and sat in the waiting room on a metal folding chair with several other guys his age and their parents. As he sat there, he perused the room and read the posters taped to the wall.

One poster listed the different statuses of the men registering:

1-A Eligible for Military Service
1-AO Conscientious Objector; non-combat duty
1-O Conscientious Objector; alternate community service
2-D Disqualified
1-N Incapable due to medical, psychological, or unfit

Jason wasn't sure what some of those categories meant, so he pulled out the Farm Journal magazine he'd stuck in his back pocket to read while he waited in the reception area. He'd been finding it a challenge to keep up with all the latest farm developments, so he thought this would be a good opportunity to catch up on some of the articles he'd missed. This particular issue featured two articles of interest. One was about the latest techniques on how to treat different diseases that pigs were particularly susceptible to, and another offered ideas on how to increase production while decreasing costs. Because he'd rolled the journal so tightly to fit it into his back pocket, he fought with the pages to flatten them enough to be able to read them. In doing so he found a third article that interested him, one he hadn't noticed before. It was about the most recent guidelines on nutritional supplementation for swine. He was deep into reading the article when he heard his name called.

"Jason Herman Johnson, report to cubicle #22."

Jason stood when he heard his name and quickly scanned the room in search of the appropriate cubicle. He saw it was toward the end of the room and headed in that direction. Politely, he knocked on the side opening of the cubicle before entering.

"Jason Herman Johnson?" The uniformed man sitting at the desk asked, without looking up, as Jason entered.

"Yes, sir. I'm Jason Johnson," he said, with a slight quiver in his voice.

"Sit down, son. Did you bring identification with you?"

"Yes, sir. I have my driver's license. Will that do?"

The recruiter didn't respond or even look up. He continued writing on a paper on the desk in front of him while extending his left hand, expecting Jason to hand over his driver's license.

"Did you bring a parent with you today?" the recruiter asked.

"No, sir, I don't seem to have any parents anymore."

"How is that, son?" The Army recruiter looked up at Jason with a hardened expression. "How is it that you don't know if you have parents or not? Would you like to explain that to me? Because most people know if they have parents or not. So do you have parents, Jason Herman Johnson, or don't you? There's no seems about it. Where are your parents?"

Jason explained as best and as briefly as he could about his father's accident and the disappearance of his mother. The recruiter never blinked. He just stared stone-faced across the desk at Jason, while continually writing notes on the paper on his desk.

"Okay, I'm going to ask you a series of questions and I want you to answer them as quickly and honestly as you can."

The questions came fast and furious, as the recruiter scribbled Jason's answers on the paper in front of him: "Name? Address? Age? Medical information, such as childhood diseases and inoculations? What do your parents do? Do you have siblings? Are you planning on going to college? Are you married? Do you have children, either legitimate or illegitimate? Any venereal diseases such as: Gonorrhea, Syphilis, Chlamydia? How about mental illness?"

Jason wondered what the recruiter was trying to do. Was he trying to trip him up? Because much of what he'd already told him was asked repeatedly in a different manner or context.

"Look," Jason said in frustration with a louder voice than he intended. "My father is dead, my mother is missing, I'm not married, I'm healthy and I run a pig farm. I've already told you all of this. Why do you keep asking me the same stuff over and over?"

"Well, then tell me, son, tell me about this farm. How do you run it?"

"What do you mean? I just run a pig farm, like I said. I raise pigs and I have a few chickens and two cows. The farm is about five miles east of town. I don't know what more I can say about it."

"Do you run this farm by yourself? Or do you have people who work for you?"

"No, I do it by myself."

"Do you sell these pigs as food? Or is this farm a hobby?"

"Believe me, sir, farming is not a hobby. It's a lot of goddamn work. Excuse me for swearing, sir. But I'm just so frustrated right now.

Please, I'm sorry. Please, accept my apology. I don't usually swear." Jason took a deep breath and tried to begin again more calmly. "Yes, of course I sell the pigs. It's some of the best meat you can eat!"

"Can you verify any of this, son?"

"What do you mean verify it?" Jason asked. "How would I do that?"

"Well, do you have any deeds, or anything that can prove what you're telling me is true?"

"I suppose I could get the deed to the farm," Jason said. "Is that what you want? Or I can show you my checkbook, which would show you all the hay, straw, and vet bills I've paid. Would any of that help you?"

"Yes, anything to verify that you're the sole proprietor of a farm that helps feed the nation. That's what I need to see."

Jason pulled out his checkbook and showed him the purchases he'd made on behalf of the farm. He also showed him the deposits he'd made when he sold some pigs to the butcher. Then, he pointed out the check entry he'd written to the hospital where his father had been treated, the check he wrote to the ambulance that transported his father's body to the mortuary, and the check entry he wrote to the funeral home.

The recruiter pulled a couple of new forms from his desk drawer and resumed his writing. Then he stamped the papers with several official-looking rubber stamps and placed all the papers into a flat manila folder.

"Take these papers to the front desk and keep this one in your billfold. If all this information turns out to be accurate, you may find yourself exempt from military duty. Anyone who grows food for the nation is usually exempt. We'll be in touch. Have a good day, son." He shook Jason's hand and stood. "Next," the recruiter said loudly, indicating to Jason that he was dismissed and should leave his cubicle to make room for the next potential recruit to sit in the chair he'd just vacated.

Jason stood when the recruiter stood, and quickly exited the cubicle. The next young man began entering the cubicle Jason had vacated. The kid looked nervous, but he had his mother with him. That was a luxury Jason didn't have.

Jason walked up to the front desk with his manila file folder and left it with the uniformed person waiting for it. After leaving the recruitment office, he walked over to the parking lot, leaving footprints in the fresh dusting of snow. He brushed the snow off his motorcycle seat and drove directly home.

"Hello pigs!" Jason said joyfully that night as he fed them. "Do you know what? You look pretty darn good to me today! In fact, you're the most beautiful pigs I've ever seen!"

Priscilla came waddling over and let out a couple of loud snorts. "Yes, Priscilla, you too, old girl, in fact, you may be the best-looking pig of the whole lot. I actually love you, you big fat magnificent beast." He gave her an extra apple.

40

JASON'S 18TH BIRTHDAY

"The future belongs to those who believe in the beauty of dreams."

—ELEANOR ROOSEVELT

"Happy birthday!" Mrs. Peterson said, distributing an enormous mound of sweet potatoes onto Jason's plate. "Are things going any better for you now that winter is upon us?"

"A little, I guess." Jason speared another slab of pork loin from the platter. "I still battle to keep up with everything, but it has gotten a lot more manageable since I sold some of the pigs."

"If there's anything Jessica or I can help you with, you know, all you have to do is ask."

"I know. You and Jessica have been great. I don't think I could have gotten through any of this if it wasn't for the two of you, but I think I've got a better handle on things now."

"Actually," Mrs. Peterson said, "I was thinking, there may be something I could help you with come next fall, that is, if you don't want to pick all your apples. The Boy Scouts would be happy to come out and pick apples for you. They're always looking for service projects and then they could give the apples to the church Food Bank because there are plenty of needy families who would love to receive a bag of fresh apples. Same for any vegetables you may not want, before you plow the garden under."

"I'll keep that in mind, but actually anything that I grow too much of I can feed to the pigs. I was just too out of sorts last fall to think logically. This year will be better. I know it will."

The following morning, when Jason woke and looked out of his bedroom window, he was greeted by a blanket of blinding white snow. This wasn't just a dusting of white fluff, it was a foot deep blanket of magical, glimmering sparkles. The previously forlorn bare-leaved oaks and elms were dressed in billows of white upon barren angled branches, while the evergreens stood grandly embracing pockets of white snow in their arms. Winter had arrived.

Jason always felt exhilaration, in a childish sort of way, with the first snowfall and this year was no different. He dressed quickly, ran down the stairs, donned his warmest jacket, stocking cap, and gloves, and stepped outside onto the porch, taking deep breaths of the clean crisp air. Unearthing the snow shovel from the corner of the porch, he started to shovel, first the porch, then the stairs, and finally the long walkway where he carefully carved neat sharp edges. He was surprised when he heard himself singing, and then he did a most uncharacteristic thing for a near man. He threw himself onto his back into one of the snowdrifts, laughing as he slid his arms from side to side, making a snow angel impression just like the ones he used to make when he was a carefree kid.

With so little time left, he parked the shovel in a drift, tended to the animals, and gulped down a peanut butter sandwich he'd made with a couple heels of the Wonder bread he found in the breadbox, calling it breakfast.

Debating on the wisdom of driving his motorcycle to school on the slippery roads, he decided to take his mother's DeSoto. It was also a light vehicle, and it hadn't been driven in months, but he thought it would still be safer than his motorcycle.

He grabbed the shovel from the porch and tossed in into the back seat of the car before driving down his long driveway, stopping at the end to shovel out what the snowplow had pushed up into the driveway as it passed. Slowly, he navigated along the slippery country road, noting the height of the drifts. As he neared the Peterson farm, he saw Jessica standing at the bus stop, waiting for the school bus. She was swinging her arms and stamping her feet in an effort to keep warm.

"Hey, Jessica," he said from the car window. "Do you want a ride?"

"Yes!" she said, jogging across the road. She opened the passenger door, kicked the snow off her boots and got in. "Well, look at you! When did you start driving a car instead of your motorcycle?"

"It's Mom's car. I decided it would be safer and a lot warmer than the motorcycle today."

"Yeah, I'm sure." She held her hands up next to the car heater vents. "It's freezing out there today."

Jason smiled, noting how pretty she looked with ruddy cheeks.

"The school bus is really late today," she said.

Jason felt a little flutter sitting this close to Jessica because whenever he was at her house, they were on opposite sides of the table, and never alone, because Mrs. Peterson was always with them.

Suddenly, without warning when Jason wasn't concentrating, the car went into a spin. Jason frantically pumped the brakes in an effort to gain control, but to no avail. The car had no traction and didn't stop sliding until it wedged itself into a snowbank.

"Well, that was a surprise!" he said. "Are you okay?"

"I think so. I bumped my head, but my knitted stocking cap is so thick that it didn't even hurt."

"Me too." They both broke out into laughter.

Jason tried rocking the car back and forth by alternately putting it in drive and then reverse, but the rear wheels had no traction. They simply spun. He stepped out of the car to assess the situation, seeing one of the rear wheels was deeply buried in a drift. He opened the trunk in search of anything that might be of use and discovered his mother kept a blanket, a box of matches, a small bag of sand and chains in her trunk, chains he realized too late that he should have put on the car before he left his yard.

He shoveled as much snow away from the wheel as he could while Jessica watched and asked what she could do to help.

"Do you know how to drive?"

"A little. Why?"

"Well, I'm going to find a piece of wood to wedge behind the wheel and pour some sand around it to supply a little traction. If you could drive forward, I'll push."

Jason found a small tree branch, wedged it behind the rear wheel and poured the sand around it. Then he told Jessica to drive forward as he pushed. She started the car, put her foot on the accelerator, gradually revving it up faster and faster while Jason put all his weight into pushing the car, but the rear tires just kept spinning. Just when Jason was about to give up, one of the rear wheels grabbed the tree branch and hurled it back at him, ripping his pants leg and putting a gash down the front of his right shin.

"STOP! STOP! STOP!" He yelled.

Limping back to the driver's side of the car with blood dripping down his leg, he motioned for Jessica to move over so he could get into the driver's seat.

"What happened?" she asked.

"We're stuck and we're only digging ourselves in deeper."

She looked at him quizzically, noting his tone and was about to call him down about it, until she saw his leg. "Jason, you're bleeding!"

"I know, and I'm cold too."

"What are we going to do?"

"I don't know, Jessica. Sit here and wait I guess."

"Wait for what?"

"Wait Jessica. Just wait. That's all!"

He kicked up the heater and revved the engine to encourage more heat, but still they were cold, so cold that they huddled together under his mother's blanket, silently waiting, each with their own thoughts. They dozed off in a huddle and were both startled when a Highway Patrol officer knocked on the window and shone his flashlight into Jason's face.

Jason rolled down the window.

"Stuck, are you?" the officer asked. "You're the third one today. I've radioed for a tow truck to pull you back up onto the road, and I've asked them to put some chains on for you. I hope you've got enough cash on you to pay them."

When Jason got to school, he went directly to the nurse's office, where he waited in line for the nurse who was treating frostbite, chapped lips, and sprains from those who had slipped on ice. When it was his turn, she poured iodine on his wound, which stung something awful, before bandaging him, allowing his torn pants leg to flop in an unseemly manner.

After school, he still had his farm chores to do, because the animals didn't care what else had happened during Jason's day. But somehow the tasks seemed easier on that day because he was able to reminisce about the morning cuddle under the blanket with Jessica. He finished up at the barn and as he approached the house, he found Jessica was sitting on the porch steps in her full-length sheepskin coat.

"Hi," she said.

"Well, hi back at you. What are you doing here?"

"Nothing really. I just thought I'd check in on you to see how your leg is doing, and I decided I'd wait for Priscilla to come. She's more like a person than she is a pig, you know, and I'm fascinated by her."

"You're as crazy as she is." Jason laughed. "Do you want to come in or do you want to just sit out here and freeze your butt while you wait for her."

"Here's nice. It's just a little brisk, that's all. Actually, I like it when it's like this."

It wasn't long before Priscilla came waddling in their direction. With difficulty she dragged herself up the steps and stood before the back door staring at Jason, as if to say, "Well open the door there, bigshot. You know I'm waiting to go inside."

"Okay, Priscilla, you go on in and get yourself settled." Jason held the door open. "Come on, Jessica. You can help me cover her with her favorite blanket, and then I'll heat some wild rice soup for us. I made it over the weekend."

In February, Jason took Jessica to the Valentine's Dance. In March they went to the school Mardi Gras festivities. In June they graduated from high school, and in July, they married.

Ten months later a daughter was born. They named her Gertrude after the paternal grandmother neither of them thought she'd ever meet. And once little Gerti entered their lives, there was never a quiet moment in the farmhouse again. As her little lungs could be heard at all hours of the day and night. On the morning of Gerti's baptism, Jason paced in the back of the church, waiting for the minister to arrive while Jessica was changing Gerti's diaper in the lady's room.

"I've never been comfortable in this church," Jason told his mother-in-law as he paced.

"Aww, Jason," Mrs. Peterson said, "I suspect that's because it brings back sad memories of your father for you."

Jason nodded and continued pacing, eventually wandering into the vestibule where he scanned the church bulletin board. "Oh, my God!" he gasped. "Jessica!"

"What?" Jessica said and hurried from the lady's room with toilet paper still stuck to the bottom of her shoe. "What is it? What's happened?"

"We know some of these guys!"

"What guys? What are you talking about?" She walked over to see what he was looking at.

"These guys," Jason said, pointing to a bulletin board with three rows of names on it. "Look at who's on this list!"

Mrs. Peterson joined them to gaze at the bulletin board, all three of them standing like statues as they read the names of the fallen and missing in action, members who had formerly belonged to the church.

"They're our age," Jessica said. "This isn't just a bunch of old people we don't know. We went to school with these guys!"

"I know. Stewart Anderson was in my algebra class and Robert and Roger McLoughlin were twins on our football team. And oh my gosh, I especially remember Larry Johnson. He was in my history class. He was smart, and he kept up on all the current politics. He was nice too. It's hard to imagine someone our age can be dead!"

"Yes," Mrs. Peterson added, nodding her head solemnly. "This war has been hard on a lot of families in our community."

"It's a goddamn nightmare, is what it is!" Jason said.

"Jason!" Jessica said. "Don't swear in church!"

"Sorry." He reached over to put his arm around her shoulder. Together they continued reading through the list, and then Jason's eyes landed on the name of Gordon DeFeo.

"Oh, my God." Jason gasped. "This guy was a creep. He wanted everyone to call him Flash. I never liked him, but I'd never wish this on him. Actually, if I'm honest, I'd have to admit I was jealous of him because he had everything handed to him: a fancy car, parents with money, great clothes, the whole ball of wax. He used to call me Pig Boy and I hated him for it, and I'm afraid I wasn't very nice to him. Now I'm really sorry for that."

Jason leaned over and planted a kiss on Jessica's forehead as he reflected upon the wonderful life he had, knowing the farm he'd cursed on so many previous occasions had very likely saved his life.

Four years later, Gerti's little brother, Georgie, entered the world.

41

GERT

"No one can make you feel inferior without your consent."

—Eleanor Roosevelt

I hate to admit it, but I'm beginning to feel my age. I've always thought of myself as being somewhat invincible, thinking I could do anything if I put my mind to it. But more and more there are nights after everyone has left when I find myself having to sit down and rest before I begin my evening chores. Tonight is one of those nights when I can't seem to get myself motivated. I have coffee cups to wash, a floor to sweep, bathrooms to clean, and shelves in the store that need to be restocked. And this is the night I usually wash and wax the floor. I'm dreading that floor polisher increasingly each week because it's just becoming too heavy for me. Sometimes I wonder if the day may come when it will begin pulling me around the floor instead of me in control of it.

Won't that be a sight!

If Bernadette ever sees that she'll probably think it is the funniest thing she's ever seen, and I suspect she'll want to take a ride on it. But only if she can wear her jeans.

Gosh, when she first started school, she had such a big meltdown over wanting to wear her jeans to school, insisting that she would *never ever* wear a dress again! None of us understood what her problem was, not until she explained how her dresses were preventing her from climbing on the jungle gym because her panties showed when she hung by her knees. Finally, Martha and I grasped the problem. As we thought about it more, we realized girls' clothing inhibited and delayed the physical development of all our girls, because while boys were regularly strengthening their core muscles on play equipment, our girls were falling behind by virtue of their dresses.

I was glad when Martha allowed Bernadette to begin wearing shorts or some kind of slacks under her dress because that enabled her to climb and play on the school equipment. Even at that though, she had to contend with a skirt in her face if she hung upside down.

It was Bernadette who woke us up to a lot of issues we women hadn't thought about, because it wasn't long after the clothing issue that a second conflict rose its ugly head when Bernadette's kindergarten teacher, Miss Bonnie, asked Mr. Denzel, the school principal, to call a meeting with Bernadette's parents to discuss the problem. I wasn't surprised when Carl declined to go because he was such a wimp when it came to anything the least bit confrontational. He told Martha she should go without him, and she could just tell him about it, saying he didn't feel he should leave the store. That was so like him, and both Martha and I knew that was poppycock because I could have easily taken care of the store for a short time while he attended the meeting. We both knew he was just too chicken to attend.

So I ended up accompanying Martha to the school meeting. After all, Martha and I sat in front of the bank president together, so a schoolteacher and principal weren't particularly worrisome for either of us.

Actually, I found it a delightful opportunity for an outing away from the shop.

The first thing I saw when we entered the grade school was a large bulletin board filled with colorful drawings and construction paper letters indicating the artwork was created by the first-grade students.

Directly beneath the bulletin board was a row of hooks, all filled with an assortment of tiny little jackets and sweaters: little blue, brown, and pink jackets were all lined up next to one another. They looked so cute.

Martha led the way down the hall to the school office, where we were greeted by the secretary and invited to be seated on the folding chairs outside Mr. Denzel's office. We sat across from two boys approximately ten years old. Without having to ask, they told us they were there because they were caught writing bad words in the boys' bathroom. Martha and I glanced at one another, knowing we were both trying to keep stern faces, as we didn't want the boys to think either of us found humor in their prank.

As we waited, I couldn't help but think how different this was from the morning we waited to see Mr. Slank at the bank. So many things have changed since then. For one thing, neither Martha nor I are wimps any longer. As we waited for this meeting, neither of us felt any intimidation because we are different people today from the ones we were when we waited for the bank president. We have matured and are much more confident today than we were back then.

The boys were escorted into the principal's office before us, but they were only in there for a few moments. Both boys looked remorseful and sheepish when Mr. Denzel escorted them out of his office.

"Please, ladies," Mr. Denzel said, offering us his robust handshake. "I hope you'll accept my apology for having kept you waiting. When my secretary sets up my appointments, we never know what other situations may come up for me to deal with on any given day." He guided us into his office and invited us to be seated across from his desk, which was piled high with stacks of papers. There was a third empty chair next to Martha.

"I take it Mr. Olson won't be joining our meeting today," he said more than asked.

"Yes, that's right," Martha said. "He can't leave our gas station and store, so I've asked Miss Birdie to come with me today. I hope that's okay."

"Yes, of course. That's fine. We're just waiting for Miss Bonnie, Bernadette's teacher. She should be here any moment."

When Miss Bonnie arrived, introductions were made, and she took the third chair next to Martha. Martha explained again why her husband wasn't able to attend the meeting.

"That's fine," Mr. Denzel said again. "Miss Bonnie, would you tell us why you requested this meeting today."

"Yes, well here's the situation," she said, addressing her remarks to Martha. "Don't get me wrong, Mrs. Olson, Bernadette is a fine little girl. She's smart and she's polite and all that, but there is a problem during playtime. You see, we very carefully select toys we think will help our boys and our girls explore who they might become in the future. For instance, when the boys race the cars and trucks down little wooden ramps, and build tall pillars with large building blocks, they're learning a lot about weight and height ratio and the beginning of engineering principles. They don't know it of course, but it's the beginning of possible careers for some of our boys. I know this is only a farming community, but we never know who the next engineer might be now, do we? The same is true for the girls. We have a lovely walk-in playhouse, equipped with all sorts of tea sets. And we have several dolls with full wardrobes to give our girls an opportunity to gain experience dressing and changing a baby's clothing. We even have one of those new Betsy-Wetsy dolls from the Ideal Company, which they very generously donated to our school. When you feed her a bottle of water she wets her diaper." Miss Bonnie smiled. "The point is, our girls are learning all sorts of mothering and nurturing skills with the toys we provide for them, and I wanted to alert you to the fact that Bernadette isn't showing any interest in learning any of those skills. I'm very concerned for her. If we don't address this now, I'm afraid she may not acquire the skills she'll need to become a proper young lady and mother."

My inner gut seethed as I listened to her, and it took all my self-control to not interrupt her ridiculous speech.

"Anyway," Miss Bonnie said, "I'm rather concerned it may cause

Bernadette problems in the future as she begins to form her own identity."

"Thank you, Miss Bonnie," Mr. Denzel said. "I think you've stated the problem very well. So now I ask you, Mrs. Olson. What do you think we should do about this situation? Could you and your husband talk it over and explain to your daughter how important it is for her to begin playing with the girls' toys."

Martha was caught so off guard that she was speechless. But I wasn't. Oh no, not me. I heard myself saying, "What on earth are you talking about? Who is to say Bernadette may not want to become an engineer? Why can't she explore any interest she may have? And why can't she play with whatever toys she chooses to play with? You're acting as if a woman can't pursue a career if she wants one. All females don't have to become mothers you know. And some women may want a career and a family. There are choices today! You're looking at two women who will tell you that women can work, run a business, and have a family all at the same time. Women can marry and even choose to not have children if they don't want them today. So unless Bernadette is being rude, disrespectful, or disorderly in some manner I don't think Martha or her husband should even tell their daughter about this meeting. And I think you, Miss Bonnie, should bring your thinking into the future instead of promoting outdated ideas about keeping women in their homes making babies. You're acting as if the world is still like the 'Father Knows Best' television show. If you're trying to make Bernadette into a June Cleaver, I doubt that she ever will be that. You need to get with the times, Miss Bonnie, because the world is moving on."

I knew my own mother would have been appalled to hear me be so disrespectful to a teacher, but Martha wasn't shocked by what I said at all. She not only backed me up, but she set the principal straight as well. I was so proud of her. She told Mr. Denzel we wouldn't be taking up any more of his time on this matter. Then, she reinforced what I said by telling him she expected them to allow Bernadette to play with the toys of her choice and to allow her the opportunity to explore her imagination in whatever direction it took her.

I felt a little sorry for Mr. Denzel because I don't suppose he was used to having a parent challenge him about anything, let alone two vocal women.

Then, Martha wrapped it all up by saying, "if there is ever a genuine discipline problem with Bernadette, please feel free to contact me, but I don't ever expect to discuss this particular matter again."

With that we stood together, as if we'd practiced it, and exited the principal's office without shaking either Mr. Denzel or Miss Bonnie's hand, letting the door slam behind us.

42

SMALL VICTORIES
AND LARGE DOUBTS

"We have homework today," Stewart announced as he and Bernadette bounced through the shop door. "Can we use a corner of one of the tables?"

I smiled when I saw what Stewart had clutched in his hand, because it was the same type of wide ruled paper I remember seeing Jason practice printing on when he was Stewart and Bernadette's ages. I cleared the end of a table for the two of them to work on. After they printed the alphabet, both upper and lower case, they carefully folded their *homework* and set it aside to take with them to school the next morning. Then they brought out the game of *Clue.*

"Did the butler do it in the kitchen with a candle stick?" Stewart asked Bernadette.

"Yes," she said. "How did you figure that out so fast?"

Bernadette grimaced because the agreement between them was that whoever lost the game needed to be the one to put it away, by rounding up all the pieces and returning it to the game cabinet.

While she was doing that, Stewart was looking for what he could do next.

"You can sort our leftover bolts of fabric, if you want to," I said. "It would be nice to have them all sorted and lined up by color. But keep them clean, please. Don't paw at them if you have sticky fingers or dirty hands."

He jumped at the opportunity and ran to the playpen where we stored our inventory of bolted fabric. Not five minutes into the task he yelled out in pain.

"What happened?" we chorus of surrogate mothers all said at once.

"I got a staple in my finger," Stewart said.

"Don't bleed on the fabric," Bernadette said as she ran to the cabinet where she knew we kept a small first aid kit. She pulled out a bandage and ran back to Stewart to apply it to his bleeding finger.

"Thank you," Stewart said, smiling at her attentive tender care. "You're going to be a real good nurse when you grow up, Bernadette."

"I'm not going to be a nurse, Stewart," she said. "I'm going to be a doctor!"

All the ladies cheered.

As the children got older, and their homework became more challenging, I took it upon myself to help them with their math and science, as I'd always enjoyed both those subjects when I was in school. I also took pride in the fact that my skills remained current, and I enjoyed the opportunity to stay current. And of course, I was especially eager to help Bernadette develop an interest in math because neither Martha nor Carl seemed motivated to do so. Girls, I felt, needed a little extra encouragement to do well in those areas, and I was eager to do my part in making that happen for Bernadette.

On the children's tenth Christmas, we took money from our business profits to purchase ice skates for them. Stewart's hockey skates were jet black. Bernadette's figure skates were pristine white with little notches on the tips of the blades.

Of course, we knew the children would want to use their new skates at once after opening them on Christmas morning, so Nadine and I quickly changed our clothes after church. We bundled up in warm jackets that zipped up to our necks and pulled our knitted stocking caps down over our ears. I also added a scarf around my neck and pulled on warm wool mittens.

It was a perfect winter day for skating, as there was plenty of sunshine and the outdoor thermometer registered in the low teens, which kept the ice in great condition.

Nadine parked her car in the freshly shoveled lot, and we trudged on foot through the snowbanks in the direction of the wooden fence where the parents were already watching their children try to skate.

"Merry Christmas everyone," we said as we trudged through the snow to where the group was standing. "How are the skates working out?"

"Well," Carl said, shaking his head. "I don't think either of them are Olympic material, if that's what you're asking."

When I looked out on the rink, I was surprised to see how similar to ragdolls the children looked. Their legs and ankles wobbled back and forth, and their bodies flexed from side to side with their arms flailing about in every direction before falling. They'd no sooner picked themselves up before they'd fall again. It was a pitiful site.

When the children saw us, all lined up next to the rink, they clumped their way over toward us with their bent and wiggly ankles, swinging arms, radiant smiles, and ruddy cheeks. They fell several times before reaching us but continued laughing. They'd no sooner get back up onto their feet than they'd fall again while laughing each time. Neither of them was injured by the falling because their thick warm clothing padded and protected them.

When they finally reached our side of the rink, I offered instructions. "Kids," I said. "Keep the core of your body straight while alternating with opposite arms and legs. If your left leg is forward, then your right arm should be back so you can get a back-and-forth rhythm going."

"I didn't know you knew how to skate," Martha said, surprised.

"Sure," I answered, equally surprised by her thinking that I may not know how, as I'd assumed everyone knew how to ice skate. "I used to skate with my father when I was young. He had long racing blades and I think he learned when he was very young in Germany."

She looked so interested that I continued telling her about my father's skating skill.

"My father was really graceful on the ice. You would have enjoyed seeing him. We sort of danced together out on the ice. How about you? Don't you skate?"

"A little, I guess," Martha said. "But I've never been very good at it. I'd probably hurt myself if I tried skating today."

When Bernadette and Stewart heard me say that I knew how to skate they at once began chanting, "Skate, Miss Birdie, skate! Skate, Miss Birdie, skate!"

I laughed and explained I no longer owned skates. "Besides," I said, "That was a long time ago."

"Oh, man alive!" Carl said, chuckling in disbelief. "Are you really claiming that you know how to skate?"

"Yes," I said, more defiantly than what I intended. "I *do* know how to skate, Carl."

"I've got to see this. Come on, I'll rent a pair of skates for you."

"No, really," I said. "That's very generous of you, but I don't think I should. It's been years since I've been on ice skates, and now that I'm older it's probably not a wise thing for me to do."

"Come on, Miss Birdie!" he said with more enthusiasm than I'd seen from him in years. "Let's see what you've got!"

"You're just itching to see me fall and make a fool of myself, aren't you, Carl?"

"Yup! I've got to see this. Come on. Let's get you into a pair of ice skates!"

I knew Carl didn't believe me when I told him I knew how to skate, and truth be told, I wasn't so sure I'd remember how to skate either. But I knew his offer to rent skates for me was a dare, a dare that for some foolish reason I couldn't resist.

"Okay," I said, hoping I wasn't about to make a fool of myself, or perhaps worse, break a hip or leg.

I was surprised to see how quickly Carl moved toward the warming house, because it was so unlike him to be eager to spend money.

"Come on then," he said motioning for me to follow.

Even Martha appeared surprised when she saw his excitement. Clearly, Carl had no intention of letting me escape his challenge, thinking he was finally going to see me fall on my butt.

Carl flipped his half-smoked cigarette into a snowbank before entering the warming house. When we got inside, he told the pimple-faced teen tending the rental stall, "This lady needs a pair of skates."

"What size do you wear, lady?" the kid asked.

"I'm not sure. It's been a long time since I've been in skates, but I wear a size 6 shoe."

The kid removed a pair of women's white figure skates from the bin behind him. "Here," he said, passing the skates across the counter to me. "Give these a try."

Carl peeled off the money for the rental, while I found a bench to sit on and put the skates on.

"These are a little big," I said. "Do you have half sizes?"

"Naw, just even numbered sizes. You wanna maybe try 'em with a pair of wool socks? I got plenty of socks for sale."

Carl groaned while forking over the money for a pair of woolen socks. "Can't let her quit now," I heard him grumble to the kid under his breath.

The socks did the trick, by supplying just the right amount of added cushioning to my foot and had the bonus of offering a bit of extra warmth. I tightened the laces around the tiny hooks and pulled as hard as I could, for extra ankle stability. When I stood, I clunked my way toward the rink on the wooden walkway, knowing the wood was there to prevent the blades from becoming dull. I was also nearly two inches taller on the skates, which for some reason added a feeling of confidence. When I reached the ice, I glided out onto it gracefully and skated over to where the children were still trying to remain upright. I knew I was smiling because I felt the cold air on my front teeth. "Come on, kids," I said. "Skate over to that bench. I'm going to fix your skates so they'll fit tighter around your ankles."

"That's too tight!" Bernadette complained as I pulled the laces tightly around the little hooks. "My toes are going to fall asleep."

"Good!" I said. "They have to be tight until you strengthen your ankles."

Stewart winced when I tightened his skates, but he refused to complain.

"Come on you two. Take my hand and mimic my motions. Take long gliding strokes, like this." I showed them, and together we went across the rink, and neither of them fell.

"Good, now let go of my hand and keep doing that same motion. I'll be right next to you."

Immediately I saw they were beginning to get the feeling of the motion, and it didn't take long before they were gliding with long smooth strokes around the rink with renewed confidence.

"Wow! Is there anything you don't know how to do, Miss Birdie?" Bernadette asked as we sashayed past her parents. Carl didn't say anything as we passed him, but I saw from his expression that he was surprised. And I'd like to think he might also have been a little impressed as well.

It had been a long time since I'd enjoyed a day as much as that one. Not only was it a joy to be outdoors in the crisp winter air and having the opportunity to skate with the children, but I have to admit, my biggest thrill of all was having impressed Carl, who I know didn't think I could hold my own on the ice. That silent victory was a delight.

But at the end of the day, when I was alone in the camper, my jubilance and smugness faded because I couldn't remember ever teaching Jason how to skate. Or for that matter, I couldn't remember teaching him anything, not even how to ride his bike.

I wondered who taught him those things. *What a horrible mother I must have been because I couldn't remember ever teaching him anything.*

43

HISTORY IS BEING
MADE EVERY DAY

---

*"You have to have confidence in your ability, and
then be tough enough to follow through."*

—Rosalynn Carter

As the business grew and thrived, I observed an increased pride within the group. And that pride spilled over to each of us as individuals. Even more surprising was the fact that all the earlier gossip about how we were doomed to fail because we were women had evaporated. No one seemed to expect our business to fail any longer. In fact, they not only expected it to remain open, but I think many in the community expected it to grow.

I was well aware of the fact that a big part of our success had been due to our low overhead, because Martha still refused to let Carl charge us rent, by pointing out how our business had increased visibility to both the store and gas station. Neither have we had any advertising costs, because the newspaper inadvertently provided us with all the free advertising we needed when we first started our business venture. And now, our customers have learned about us by word of mouth from other satisfied customers. So with no rent, no advertising expenses, and with satisfied customers spreading the word for us, our customer base continues to expand.

I'm also surprised, but secretly delighted, by how everyone looks to me for leadership. I'm not sure how that happened, but somehow by default I've become the glue who holds us together. And I must admit, I'm enjoying the role a lot. Yet no one was more surprised than me to discover how I've been able to instinctively smooth away small tensions before they morphed into larger problems. I'd like to think I've become finely attuned to each of the women's individual strengths and weaknesses, and I hope I'll be able to continue with that, because I need to capitalize on each of our individual talents while at the same time bolstering or strengthen any individual weaknesses. That may sound easy, but it's not, and I know I need to tread carefully, especially if I want to emphasize teamwork rather than competitiveness.

On the fashion front, when women's trousers became acceptable, Janet began wearing them to work. Soon all of us, with the exception of Nadine, cast aside our girdles, nylons, and pantyhose, opting to work in loose legged trousers. Not only did we discover we were more comfortable, but we were noticeably less tired at the end of the day when our girdles weren't constricting us all day.

"It's a no wonder men have had an advantage over women in the workforce all these years," we all agreed.

"You know," Martha told me one day before the others came in, "I read someplace recently that women's clothing was specifically designed to systematically denigrate women so we would become less than our full potential."

"Look at you, with the big words," I teased and told her I thought that was a bit of a stretch. But I could see she was having fun with the notion, so I listened and let her continue.

"No, this is for real," she said when she saw me smiling. "Just think about the old bustle, and the clothes that required women to ride a horse sidesaddle, and then there is the back zipper on women's dresses. Did you know that the long back zipper was designed to en-sure someone would always have to help a women get dressed? In particular with middle-class women, it is supposed to be the husband who helps his wife get dressed for special occasions. I guess it's sup-posed to represent a little foreplay."

"Where in the world did you read that, Martha?"

"I forget where it was, but the essence of it has stuck with me, and every time I think about it, I get angry all over again. What? Why are you looking at me that way?"

"I'm looking at you, Martha, because I can hardly believe you're the same woman I met a few years ago who told me she didn't like to read. Do you remember that? And here you are telling me you read a thought-provoking article about women's clothing habits? You amaze me!"

"Oh no," Martha said. "You and Betty Freidan are the trouble-makers because you are the ones who helped me see how important it is for women to be well-read and informed about things."

"Well, thank you," I said and curtsied. "I'm glad I've been such a big influence for you, and to answer your question, no, I don't think women's clothes are intentionally designed to keep us set back. But the reality is, women's clothing does sometimes do exactly that."

"Well, then tell me this," Martha said, "why didn't we wear slacks a long time ago? Why didn't we get comfortable years ago? The answer is because we didn't know any better, that's why. It took Bernadette's little tantrum about not wanting to wear dresses to kindergarten to open my eyes. Do you remember that?"

"Oh yes, I remember. And you're right, of course. Often times we women allow ourselves to be set up for failure, and it does seem to begin by wearing clothing that inhibits us when we're very young. Unfortunately, little girls don't even realize it. They just want to look pretty. And don't let me begin to get started on shoes. I cringe every time I see women wearing those spike heels with the pointy toes in church. They look so impractical and uncomfortable. Oh, I almost forgot. I wanted to ask you about something I saw in the latest holiday issue of McCall's. It features women's holiday trousers in soft, flowing silky fabrics. The idea is that they can be worn as evening clothes to cocktail parties and things like that."

"Yeah? Well, I don't know if I'd want to go that far. I'm happy to wear slacks for casual wear, but I'm not oblivious of the fact that they're not exactly flattering enough to begin wearing for dressy occasions."

"No, that's not my point. We haven't been doing much sewing lately, but these are so unusual that I wondered if you thought we'd begin getting requests to sew them?"

"I don't think we should get back into the business of sewing clothing. But I doubt that we'd get any requests for them anyway. When was the last time you heard of a cocktail party happening in this town?"

"I don't know. No one is going to invite me to a party, but I thought maybe you and Carl got invited sometimes."

"Oh, please!"

"Don't people in town have cocktail parties?"

"Well, if there are any, they sure haven't invited us."

"Okay," I said. "I just thought I'd mention it in case we got requests to sew them. That silky fabric they featured is really difficult to work with, and I'd just as soon not deal with it if we don't have to. It unravels easily, so we'd have to bind all the cut edges which would add to the labor cost, and as you know, it tends to walk and slide all over the cutting table. It's difficult enough to deal with fabric like that for sheer draperies. I've worked with it in the past for clothing, mostly for wedding dresses and stuff like that, and I hated every minute of it. Our best bet is to stick with the reupholstering and draperies. It pays the best and we're good at it."

"That's fine by me," Martha said. "Let's just turn down any orders if they come in."

"Good! I'm glad we're on the same page with that. We can tell the others when they get in today."

A few days later, Betsy bounced through the door wearing mustard colored stretch pants.

"Holy cow, Betsy," Martha said. "What are you wearing? Are those your pajamas?"

"Hell no," Betsy said. "These are called stretch pants. And let me tell you, they're mighty comfortable. I can bend, squat, and do just about anything in these. I'm going to be working on that big old floral sofa again today and it's a heavy honker. I'm going to need to be able to move and do a lot of bending while I work on that thing."

"Oh, my goodness!" said Janet when she saw Betsy.

"Lands alive!" gasped Nadine, bringing a hand to her mouth. "It almost makes me blush just to look at you. My husband would have had a heart attack if I'd have ever worn anything like that."

"Well, you're not wearing them," Betsy said. "And besides, your husband's already dead. So he for sure don't have no say in what I wear. So don't go spouting off about things you don't know anything about. These stretch pants are the newest rage and they're comfortable."

"Has your husband seen you in them?" Martha asked.

"Sure, he saw me. What's he got to do with what I wear?"

"Well, all your curves show, that's all," Martha said. "I can't imagine what Carl will think when he sees you."

"Well," Betsy said, "maybe he don't hafta look. These are the newest rage and they're comfortable." With a final harrumph, she headed over to the sofa she intended to work on that day.

44

TEN YEARS LATER ON THE FARM

"Wisdom isn't about accumulating more facts; it's about understanding big truths in a deeper way."

—MELINDA GATES

Five-year-old Georgie dragged an empty slop pail behind him and tried returning it to the front bucket of the tractor, where the pail had previously ridden to the pig pens when it was full. "Do you need help with that?" Jason asked.

"No, I can do it, Dad," Georgie said, struggling to push it up onto the tractor. "I'm almost all growed up now." He continued to struggle with the pail, but much too proud to accept his father's assistance.

Jason smiled, knowing Georgie was trying to mimic his every move, not unlike what he remembered doing with his father when he was his son's age. Georgie had been following Jason around the farm almost from the first day he could walk, carrying buckets much too large for him and helping with the farrowing and birthing of the piglets by guiding the newborns to the sow's teat. Recently, Georgie even attempted to milk one of the cows, but of course he couldn't get any milk because his hands weren't strong enough or large enough. But someday they would be, and in the meantime, Georgie tagged along and helped wherever he could, enjoying his time with his father, no matter what the task.

"Georgie," Jason said, "I was thinking, maybe you're big enough to go to the State Fair with me this year? Do you think you would like that?"

"Yeah, Dad! That'd be cool!"

"Well, it won't be all about rides and having fun, you know. There would be a lot of work to do, and I'd expect you to help me get the pigs settled. That means getting bedding for them, feeding them, and making sure they have fresh water."

"That's okay, Dad! I can help. I'm a big boy now."

"Okay," Jason said, helping Georgie push the large pail the last few inches up onto the tractor bucket. "Let's ask Mom tonight at dinner and see what she thinks of the idea. Okay?"

On the morning Jason was leaving for the fair, Georgie was full of questions, questions he'd asked many times before, but he asked them again and again, as young boys tend to do when they're both nervous and excited.

"Is Priscilla going with us, Dad?" Georgie asked at the breakfast table on the day of their departure. He only half listened to the answer because he not only already knew Priscilla would be going with them, but he was trying to get his breakfast of scrambled eggs into his mouth as opposed to having them land in his lap.

"Yes, Georgie. Priscilla goes to the fair with me every year. You already know that."

"That's good, 'cause I like it when I'm with Priscilla. Mom, can I have more orange juice?"

"Yes," Jessica said, "but are you sure you want more juice?

Remember, you're going to be riding in the truck for a long time today, so you may want to think twice about drinking more liquid."

"Oh, yeah," Georgie said with a big grin as he squirmed in his chair.

"When you've finished with your breakfast, son," Jason said, shoving his chair back from the table, "we'll be hitting the road right away. Are you all packed up and ready to go?"

"I don't know. Am I, Mom? Am I all packed?"

"Yes," Jessica said smiling at both of them. "You're both packed. I've put several changes of clothes in the duffel bag for each of you."

Jason kissed Jessica on the forehead before grabbing the duffel bag she'd packed for them.

"I'll meet you out by the truck, Georgie, just as soon as you're ready. I'm going out to get the pigs loaded. I'd like to hit the road as soon as possible."

Jason quickly slopped the pigs and loaded the ones who were going to market into the back of his truck. Then he loaded Priscilla, their pet pig who would be going along as a *show* pig. Priscilla's size and meat-to-fat ratio was so impressive that Jason felt he always got better prices for his other pigs when Priscilla was present.

Shortly after the pigs were loaded, Georgie and Jessica walked out to the truck together. Jessica kissed Georgie's forehead and opened the passenger door so Georgie could crawl up onto the seat. Jason and Jessica gave each other an embrace, and Jason said, "Give Gertie a hug from me, when she gets up."

"I will, she only has a few more days before school starts, so I thought I'd let her sleep in this morning."

With that, Jason got into the truck and drove off.

The early morning air was cool and crisp, but Jason knew that would change once the sun began peeking over the horizon. Meanwhile, Georgie's excitement about the trip caused him to squirm in his seat and chatter away nonstop.

"What's the Fair like, Dad? Are there lots of crazy rides? Kenny, my friend at school, said there is a big roller coaster that's really scary. Is that true?"

"Yes, there is a big roller coaster, and I guess it can be pretty frightening. Did Kenny ride on it?"

"No, he said he didn't want to, and all the kids called him a chicken. Will they call me a chicken if I don't ride on it?"

"I don't know, Georgie. Would that worry you if they did? You know, being grown up means you don't care what other people think. It's only what *you* think is right that's important. Do you understand what I'm saying?"

"Ah huh, I know what you're saying, Dad. But I don't think I'd be a chicken anyways, because I'm pretty brave you know."

"Yes, you are brave." Jason reached over to give his brave son's knee a kindly pat.

The slight chill that had been in the air when they left had quickly changed into a sticky, uncomfortable heat. Opening the windows didn't help because the air that poured in was hot, dusty, and noisy. That coupled with the monotony of listening to the tires on the pavement caused Georgie to doze off. Soon he was a mere lump of a boy crumpled on his seat.

Halfway into the trip, Jason pulled up to a gas station and said, "Wake up, Georgie. I have a surprise for you. We're about halfway there, and I'm going to stop here to use the bathroom and eat the lunch Mom packed for us.

Jason peeled the hardboiled eggs for both of them which they ate with the peanut butter sandwiches Jessica had packed for them. When they finished eating, Jason led Georgie over to the large wooden bear where he deposited their trash into the trash container next to the bear.

"Wow! That's crazy, Dad." Georgie gazed up at the carving with bronze glass eyes.

"It sure is!" Jason said. "You can climb on it if you want to. I've seen other kids do that."

"Nah, I'm too old for that, Dad. That's just for little kids. I'm almost six you know."

"Yes, I know." Jason said with a smile. "Six is nearly all grown up, isn't it?"

"Yup! But can I get some gum? The gum with the sports baseball cards in it? I bet they have different ones from what we have at our store."

"Sure, let's go have a look."

Georgie found the cards he was searching for and plopped the small package up onto the counter for his dad to pay for them. Jason dug in his pocket for his money, but stopped and began staring at the clerk behind the counter.

Seeing the clerk staring back at his dad, Georgie said, "What's wrong, Dad?"

When Jason didn't answer, Georgie began laughing because that's what Georgie did when he was uncomfortable or embarrassed.

Tugging harder on his father's pants leg, Georgie said, "It's okay, Dad. You don't have to buy the gum for me if you don't want to. Let's just go!"

45

GEORGIE'S FRIGHT AND JASON'S DISCOVERY

Georgie saw how strangely the woman behind the counter looked at them. It was sort of creepy the way she stared. Her mouth hung open and her eyes got big and sort of bug-eyed, reminding Georgie of the monster eyes in his Saturday morning cartoons.

"Let's go, Dad," Georgie repeated, tugging harder on his father's leg.

Georgie had seen stuff like this happen on *The Twilight Zone* and knew scarry things like this never ended well.

"Dad," Georgie repeated, pulling harder on Jason's jeans. "Let's go."

But Jason didn't move. He remained rigidly planted with both feet firmly rooted in front of the counter, with his right hand seemingly stuck in his jeans pocket.

"*Mom?*" Georgie heard his father say to the woman in a loud voice. "Is that you?"

"Yes, Jason. It's me." The woman answered in a mean tone. "Why are you here and what do you want?"

"What do I want?" Jason asked. "Is that what you just asked me? After all these years, that's what you have to say? You dare to ask me what I want? I want answers! That's what I want! I want an explanation, and I want to know why you are here and why you left me alone on the farm!"

"Surprise! Surprise!" the woman said. "This is where I live, Jason! This is where I've lived for the past ten years, ever since your father dumped me here! What do you think I'm doing here?"

Georgie didn't know what was happening, which caused him to become not only frightened but also very confused, because it sounded as if his dad was going to pick a fight with this strange woman.

"Let's just go, Dad," Georgie said again. "You don't have to buy me the gum."

But Jason ignored Georgie and remained firmly standing in front of the counter, looking more and more angry every moment that he stood there.

Then, Georgie saw the woman take a deep breath, the kind that dragon monsters take before breathing out fire. But instead of blowing out fire, she asked in a real mean way. "How is that scoundrel father of yours? I suppose he's feeling pretty wealthy and smart now that he has both farms?"

"Both farms?" Jason said. "What are you talking about. Father is dead! He died ten years ago, the same time you disappeared. And who dumped you here?"

"You know exactly what I'm talking about, Jason," the woman said. "This is where your father dumped me, left me to fend for myself with no money and not so much as a goodbye. I came out of the bathroom, and he was gone. So don't pretend you're surprised to see me."

She not only was yelling louder and louder, but she began shaking her finger in Jason's face all at the same time.

"Ten years, Jason! Ten years ago, this is where your father dumped me. Ten years, Jason! That's a long time so don't go pretending you're surprised to see me."

"But I am surprised to see you," Jason said. "Actually, I'm *shocked* to see you because I thought you were dead!"

Then, both of them became silent and glared at each other.

Finally, Jason said, "Look, I don't know what you're talking about. The sheriff and I searched for you after the accident, but we didn't know where to look for you. He even put up missing persons posters. Why didn't you just call me?"

"Oh, I called you Jason. I called every day. But I never got an answer, never got through the phone lines until the day of the big celebration party."

"What party?" Jason asked. "There has never been a party at the house!"

As soon as Dad said that the woman got angry all over again, and this time she began screeching.

"*Oh no! No! No! No!* You can't get by with that Jason! Not with me you can't!"

Georgie watched her shake her finger at his dad as she continued shouting at him.

"I heard it, Jason! I heard it with my own two ears. I heard Mrs. Peterson tell her daughter, Jessica, to put the main dishes on the dining room table and to take the desserts to the front porch table. I heard it all, Jason! Those were her exact words, words that have haunted me all these years."

"Goddamn it, Mother! That wasn't a party! That was Father's funeral!"

When Georgie heard his dad swear, he got so frightened that he burst into tears because he'd never seen his father that angry before. Then the three of them heard a splash, and when they looked down, they saw a puddle growing under Georgie's feet.

"I'm sorry, Dad," Georgie whimpered, wiping his eyes on his shirt sleeve. "I didn't mean to do it. I just got scared."

"It's okay, Georgie," Jason said in a softer, kindlier voice. "Don't worry, Georgie. It'll be okay."

Jason bent down and gave Georgie a hug and apologized. "I'm sorry if I frightened you." In a gentler, more compassionate voice Jason said, "it's not your fault, Georgie. It's mine."

"Dad, you said a bad word. You had a potty mouth."

"You're right, Georgie," Jason said. "I did have a potty mouth. I'm sorry. I won't do that again. Okay? Should we go back to the truck and get you some dry clothes? Come on, let's do that, shall we?"

"Will Mom wash your mouth out with soap?" Georgie asked as he let his father lead him toward the door.

"I don't know, Georgie. We'll have to ask her about that when we get home."

Just before Jason and Georgie exited the store, Jason turned toward the woman and said, "I'll be right back, Mother. Don't move! Stay right where you are!"

"What's going on out here, Miss Birdie?" Carl asked, looking flushed and confused as he rushed from the men's room. "Can't a guy have a few moments for a peaceful sit on the can around here? What's all the commotion?"

"That was my son and grandson," Miss Birdie said.

"You have a son?" Carl asked with a look of shock.

"Yes, Carl, I have a son, and apparently, he has a temper. He said he will be back in a few moments."

"What's he coming back for?" Carl asked. "He isn't getting a gun, is he?"

"I don't think so, but I don't want you to begin quizzing me about him right now. And I'll mop the floor later, after they've left. But not now."

46

GERT'S PEACE

"The day will come when men recognize woman as his peer, not only at the fireside, but in councils of the nation. Then, and not until then, will there be the perfect comradeship, the ideal union between the sexes, that shall result in the highest development of the race."

—Susan B. Anthony

When Jason returned to the store I noted how tenderly he kept his hand resting on his son's shoulder.

"Okay, Mother! It's time for some answers!

"We can't talk here," I said and led them both toward the back of the store.

"Where are we going?" Jason asked.

Without answering, I continued walking, expecting them to follow. I opened the workshop door, switched on the lights, and motioned for them to step inside.

"What is this place?" Jason asked, as we entered the upholstery workshop.

I noted his surprise when he saw it, knowing he'd have assumed the room would have been filled with stock for the store. But I avoided answering because I wanted to allow ample time for him to study the room more closely before I began explaining anything. He frowned when he saw two partially naked chairs, in the process of being re-upholstered, but then I noted how his eyes softened when he saw the small fabric squares on the tables. Just as I was about to explain, I saw a smile spread across his face, realizing he recognized that the table was covered with two partially finished quilts.

"This reminds me," he said, "of all the unfinished quilts you used to have spread across our dining room table at home when I was a kid."

My tension eased when he said that, and I felt a small smile. When our eyes met, I realized we were each feeling more congenial toward each other. But when he saw the wooden playpen in the far corner, I saw him blink with renewed confusion.

"I've been storing extra bolts of fabric in the playpen," I said without waiting for him to ask. "That is, ever since the children who used to be babies in it have grown up."

I tried imagining what this room looked like to Jason as he gazed at it for the first time, knowing it all must appear to be very strange indeed.

"This is what I do," I finally said. "I run a quilting and reupholstering business. Sometimes we make draperies too, but mostly it's reupholstery projects and quilts."

"We?" he asked. "Who is we?"

"Me, and five other women. We're women who enjoy doing something more than just being housewives."

With that bit of information, Jason scrutinized the room more carefully, and I wondered how what I had just told him was sitting with him.

"This looks like a really heavy-duty machine," he said as he examined our coveted sewing machine more carefully.

"Yes, it is, and it was expensive too. But it's essential to our business."

Then he chuckled and said, "I see you even have your little coffee area." He was looking at the coffeepot and pile of cups sitting next to it on the small table next to the upright metal cabinets.

Then, he and Georgie strolled over to the furthest corner of the room, where he stared at what must have appeared to be a graveyard of decrepit chairs and sofas, all piled on top of each other, each with a swatch of fabric pinned to it, along with the owner's name.

"What about those?" he asked. "They look like they're ready for a junk yard. Are they even salvageable?"

"Yes. They've obviously seen better days, but they'll be quite elegant again after we shore them up, add some new stuffing and give them a fresh covering."

Jason nodded his understanding and sauntered back to the center of the room, where he took a closer look at the unfinished quilts. "These are nice, Mom, really nice!"

"Thank you. I'll tell the ladies who are working on them what you said. We all work on different projects. And as I said, there are six of us all together. You'd probably find us a rather interesting group, because some of us are old, one is a new bride, and a couple of the women still have young children. When there's no school the children hang out here with their mothers. Two of them were practically raised back here in this room, ever since they were babies. That's how we got the playpen in the first place. But now, as you can see, it works out very well for our bolts of fabric."

"Wow! This is cool," Georgie said as he explored the corners of the room more closely.

"Take it easy there, champ." Jason reached out to rough Georgie's hair.

It tickled me to see the display of affection between them.

"This way," I said, guiding them toward the back door that led to the camper. "Careful where you step though, because sometimes there are upholstery tacks left on the floor back in this area, and they can go right through the soles of your shoes. So avoid stepping on them."

I saw Jason's look of surprise when he saw the mishmash of

unmatched chairs and the emerald, green mohair sofa that was parked in the corner nearest the back door.

"These just got finished this week. The owners will come by for them sometime this weekend. We need to get them out of here before Monday because as you can see, our workspace gets rather crowded."

"Mom, did you say you're in charge of all of this?"

"Yes. Well sort of. I provide the leadership for it, but it's actually a Cooperative. All the ladies who work here own part of the business."

"I'm impressed," he said. "It looks like, well, it appears to be very well organized."

"Thank you, Jason. I'd like to think that's true. Now, follow me. I'll show you where I live. But, first Georgie and I are going to unearth some Hot Wheels. That is, if you like Hot Wheels."

"Yeah! I do like Hot Wheels, and I have lots of them at home."

"I thought you might like them because the children here seemed to enjoy them when they were about your age."

I opened one of the upright storage cabinets and removed two 5-gallon plastic ice cream pails filled with an assortment of Hot Wheels.

"Here," I said, handing one of the buckets to Georgie and the other to Jason. "There's a lot of different cars and trucks in each of these."

Then I led them through the back door of the workroom and invited them into the camper where I'd been living for the past ten plus years.

"This is really cool," Georgie said as soon as he climbed up the two camper steps. "It's like a little house."

"That's what it is, Georgie. This is where I live."

I watched Jason hunch over to avoid hitting his head as he entered. "Sorry about the lack of headroom, but feel free to have a look around if you want to while I put the kettle on."

Jason ducked his head and stepped toward the bedroom while Georgie was already scooping cars and trucks out of one of the pails and lining them up on the imaginary roads on the quilt on my bed.

"I remember this quilt, Mom," Jason said from the bedroom.

"You remember it? That's the quilt I intended to enter into the fair that year."

"I don't suppose you ever got to enter it, did you?" Jason said, dwarfing the small camper table as he joined me at it.

"No," I said placing a tea bag in two cups. "I never did."

47

A RESOLUTION OF SORTS

*"What does it take to be the first female anything?
It takes grit. And it takes grace."*

—MERYL STREEP

Still licking the lollipop Carl had given him when they returned to the store, Georgie hauled the second bucket of Hot Wheels into the rear of the camper.

Apparently, he planned to continue using the pattern on my bedquilt as a car track. I winced when I saw how sticky his fingers were but decided to ignore it and clean up any stickiness later, thinking that if he occupied himself back there, Jason and I may have relative privacy to talk.

After pouring hot water into our cups, I set out a tin of oatmeal cookies that I'd baked the day before. "Tell me about your father's accident." I placed the sugar bowl and two spoons on the small table. "Where did it happen and what caused it?"

"It happened about a half hour east of here, out on county road 14, on the same day the two of you left for the fair. And the weirdest thing is, it didn't involve any other cars. There weren't even any skid marks. The mechanic said he thought the accident was probably caused by a broken axle.

"I don't understand. Why would the lack of skid marks imply that?"

"Because Dad never put the brakes on. He may not have even known what was happening. When I got there, I could see deep gouges in the pavement where the truck careened along on its side, but there wasn't a single skid mark."

I could see Jason was waiting for me to respond, but I didn't know what to say, so I just nodded my head and continued listening.

"Dad was trapped inside the cab of the truck, Mom. I guess the paramedics had a hell of a time getting him out. The only saving grace is that they said he was unconscious through the whole ordeal. So they didn't think he suffered."

I removed my teabag and placed it on the small saucer between us, feeling increasingly guilty for not ever questioning the possibility of George being injured or in trouble while still trying to understand the relevance of there not being skid marks on the pavement.

"Dad never woke up, Mom. I visited him every day at the hospital. I prayed that he'd wake up and tell me where you were, but he never did. He knew he'd been in an accident though because he kept trying to say comforting words to Priscilla. But I don't think he knew he was in the hospital. In fact, I think he thought he was still in the truck."

I felt tension building in the back of my neck, feeling worse by the moment as I listened to Jason tell me about George's accident and ultimate death.

"I'm so sorry, Jason," I said. "I truly am. All these years, I've made this whole thing about me, never questioning the possibility of your father being injured or in trouble. Please believe me when I say I had no inkling of any of this. I suppose the accident would have been broadcast on the news, but I never saw a television because I was pacing out in front waiting for your father to return for me. And then, when it got dark, I didn't know what to do. Out of necessity I ended up sleeping outside on that big wooden bear. And the next day, I finessed permission to sleep on a cot in that room where we have our business now. But back then, it was just a stockroom. I didn't see a television for a couple of years."

Jason leaned back and looked at me with a somewhat softened expression, seemingly seeing me for the first time. "That must have been a horrible experience for you, Mom."

"It was, Jason! It truly was!"

"But there's several things I still don't understand. For one thing, after the bed of the truck got separated from the cab, it skidded down the road for another 30 or 40 feet before it tipped over into a drainage ditch. Somehow, all the pigs got out uninjured and made themselves comfortable in a cornfield. When I got there, they were roaming around freely, as if nothing had happened, just chomping away on the corn as if the whole field had been planted just for them."

"A cornfield? Really?" I couldn't help but smile when I envisioned the pigs making themselves comfortable in a corn field. "That must have been a paradise for them. I bet they made a pretty big mess of it though."

"Yeah, you're right about that. The pigs loved it. But the farmer who owned the field wasn't happy at all. In fact, he was irate. I can't say I blame him of course, but honestly, he was really obnoxious to me when he learned they were my pigs. He clammed up and refused to talk to me. He just kept giving me the old stink eye and popped another piece of Juicy Fruit into his mouth. I don't blame him for being upset, but I do think he could have shown a little sympathy for what Dad was going through too. But what's so confusing, is that the pigs got out of the truck without injury, yet Dad was so badly injured that he died. How does that happen? It's never made any sense to me, and it still haunts me at times."

Neither of us spoke, each thinking about pigs, accidents, and a lot of should haves.

"And the other thing that never added up was that the accident took place a half hour east of here, not north which is the direction he should have been going. I could never figure out why that was. Why was he even there? It's way out of the way."

"I have no idea, Jason. None of this makes any sense to me at all. It didn't make sense then, and it doesn't make sense now. Shoot, for the longest time I didn't even know where I was. As I told you, I needed to find a bathroom and your father dropped me off here, and then he disappeared. I was irritated at first because I thought he was running errands. But then I began wondering if he was punishing me because I told him I wasn't keen on going with him to the fair. You know, your father never did seem to understand how much I dreaded seeing that intersection where my parents died in that fire. And I knew we'd have to drive right past it in order to get to the fairgrounds. But then, as the day wore on, I began feeling frightened, because I not only didn't know where I was, but at that time I thought I was totally helpless to take care of myself."

I saw Jason's expression soften as he reached over to gently hold my hand. So I took a deep breath and asked, "Do you think I might have been able to save him if I was in the truck with him, Jason?"

"I don't know, Mom. You might have died with him."

Neither of us spoke as we contemplated other possible outcomes. Then, I broke the silence and asked, "Did you take a good look at that huge bear carving out in front of the store?"

"Yeah, it's pretty impressive. In fact, I told Georgie he could climb on it."

As if on cue, Georgie wandered back into the kitchen. "Dad sometimes forgets that I'm almost six, Grandma. I had to remind him that I was too grown up to be climbing on things like that."

I was startled by Georgie's voice because I hadn't realized he was listening to us, which reinforced the old adage that *little pitchers do indeed have big ears.*

"Well," I said, "that's where I slept that first night. I curled up in the arms of that big bear and I slept there all alone in the dark, with frightening noises all around me. I fooled myself into pretending I was brave." I roughed Georgie's hair, similar to what I saw Jason do earlier. "Actually, I think I was just too stubborn to admit how helpless I was. But, like you, Georgie, I was too old to be sitting in the arms of a wooden bear."

"Gee, Grandma. I would have been a little scared too, and I'm almost all grown up, but I would have protected you."

I opened my arms and invited little Georgie into a hug, feeling my eyes water as I realized how much I'd missed by not being a part of this beautiful child's life.

Georgie wiggled out of my embrace and returned to the bedroom. I lowered my voice and said, "As soon as it began getting dark, Jason, I knew I should have called someone. But I didn't know who to call, and because I didn't know where I was, I wouldn't have been able to tell anyone where to come for me anyway. So I just kept kidding myself into thinking your father would be back for me at any moment. Then, I began thinking he might have decided to go to the fair without me for those fourteen days, that he may have reconsidered and concluded that I'd just be a burden to him. But I knew that didn't make sense either, because he could have just left me home in the first place. That's when I talked myself into thinking he might be going through some type of male midlife-crisis, and just wanted to kick up his heels without the encumbrance of a wife."

Jason looked at me with shock, but didn't say anything, so I went on. "I was so angry with him, and yet I didn't want to burden you with our problems because I didn't think it was right to involve you. But the irony was, I didn't know what was wrong. I stayed in an infinite loop of confusion, denial, and anger right up until he didn't show up to get me on Labor Day. Not until then was I forced to admit there was a larger issue. So when I called the house, and Mrs. Peterson answered the phone, and I heard what sounded like a party taking place, it all seemed perfectly logical that your father hooked up with her so he could combine the two farms into one."

With that statement, Jason looked at me with such shock and anger that his eyes felt like bullets.

"How could you even think such a thing, Mother?" he asked.

"Wait, Jason. Hear me out on this! Land was always important to your father. I know you may think that doesn't sound very kind of me to say in light of what has happened, but that's what I thought. I really thought this was all about land, money, and greed because that's why your father married me in the first place."

Jason leaned back and glared at me, as if daring me to explain myself.

"Please try to understand, Jason. Neither your father nor I had any family, because your father's parents died before we met, and mine died in a fire on the night of our first date. I was only twenty years old and had no way of supporting or taking care of myself back then. So when I learned there was an insurance policy belonging to me and that I needed a 'male overseer' in order to collect it, I asked your father to marry me. It seemed like the prudent thing to do at the time."

"What?"

"Jason, back then women couldn't have credit in their own name. Neither were we allowed to manage our own money. All banks and financial institutions back then required a *male overseer* for woman's financial matters, someone who would agree to be responsible for us if we defaulted on our obligation. It was that Equal Opportunity Credit Act that just passed in '74 that provided the flexibility for women like me to manage their own money. I couldn't have gotten my insurance money without marrying your father, and he wouldn't have been able to purchase the farm without me and my money. It was the perfect solution for both of us.

Jason shook his head in what I could see was confusion, anger, and hurt.

"Jason, I suppose our marriage was in many ways a mistake, but your father and I managed to work it out. But I was never really happy on the farm. I didn't like being around the animals and found it all monotonous. You were my only joy, but when you got older, you had your own interests and didn't seem to need me. I'm not cut out to be a pig farmer's wife. I lived in the Twin Cities up until I married your father, and ironically, I'm fairly content here in this little camper. I enjoy running this small business and coexisting with these other women."

Jason stared across the small table at me with what I could see was bewilderment and anger. I knew he had every right to feel that way, because in many ways it wasn't only me who had been abandoned. I had abandoned him.

We each sat there, neither of us saying anything for what seemed a very long time. Finally, he reached over and clumsily rubbed my shoulder, his version of an awkward hug.

"You know, Mom, I drove past this intersection every single day when I visited Dad in the hospital. Just think how different this all might have been if I had stopped in here just once and found you ten years ago. If I had done that neither of us might have gone through all the pain we've both experienced."

I nodded my acknowledgement and timidly asked, "Can I ask you something that's probably going to sound silly?"

"Of course."

I looked at him in earnest. "Who taught you how to ice skate? Was it me?"

"Ice skate?" Jason laughed. "I don't know who taught me to skate, Mom. I have no idea. It just seems like I've always known how. What does that have to do with any of this?"

"The thing is, I don't remember ever teaching you anything. I've taught Martha's and Betsy's children a lot of things. I taught them how to tie their shoes, how to skate, and I've even helped them with their arithmetic lessons. But I don't ever remember teaching you any of those things. So I've been thinking for the longest time that I must have been a terrible mother, and that was perhaps another reason you didn't want to come for me. And I suppose in some ways, I didn't blame you because I felt as if I deserved to be abandoned."

"That's not true, Mom, none of that's true! You were a good mother. You were kind, loving, and you never lost your temper. I would have come for you if I'd known where you were. I just didn't know where to look for you. I kept asking the sheriff for his help, but he was useless. The missing person poster he put up in the post office and police station didn't even look like you because I didn't have any current pictures of you in the first place, and the one I gave him got all grainy when it was blown up to be poster size."

"Well, what did I teach you, Jason? Did I teach you anything?"

"I don't know but learning to skate wasn't a big milestone for me. I've always had a good sense of balance, so skating just came naturally to me. You do realize I'd been walking on the boards in the pig pens since I was little, so I guess I just developed a really good sense of balance early on. I think that's what gave me an edge with football too. And I was driving farm equipment as soon my feet could reach the pedals, so riding a bike came easy too. I don't think anyone taught me, not really. I just took to those things naturally. And I got that small motorcycle when I wasn't even old enough to have a driver's license."

"Did I have any positive influence on your life at all, Jason? I need to know."

"Well, let's see," he said scratching the top of his head. "You taught me how to pick up my clothes so that I wouldn't be a slob. And you gave me the love of reading. Do you remember reading *Green Eggs and Ham* to me, and *One Fish, Two Fish*? I always loved those Dr. Seuss books. I found my old books way up on a shelf in my bedroom closet, and when the kids were small, I read those books over and over to them just like you did for me. I even tried to make all the same funny voices you used when you read them to me. But, quite frankly, the thing you helped me with the most were your financial ledgers. Your account books helped me enormously when I was faced with taking over the farm. They let me know what and how much food and bedding I needed to purchase for the animals and what times of the year to purchase them. And they let me know where you sold the eggs and milk, and how much you got for them. I could see right away how you were the business head of the farm. Dad loved the animals, but you knew how to manage it."

I smiled, remembering how I'd meticulously entered our expenses and income into the ledger books over the years.

"Thank you. I really needed to hear something positive because these past ten years I've thought horrible things about myself. I tried not to show it by putting on a brave face, but deep down inside, my stomach was always in knots when I heard people talk about their families."

"Oh, Mom," he said, letting all the tension dissolve as he burst into a big smile. "Jessica and I have a beautiful family. Besides Georgie, we have an eight-year-old daughter named after you, and she's going to be so eager to meet you. And we're expecting another baby in a few months. And I built a new hog house, so the pigs don't have to endure the cold winters anymore. And I've installed water pipes that run water from the house directly to the pig barn. So now I can pump directly into the pig's water trough."

Then, he paused and said, "Mom, if I come to pick you up, would you like to come and spend Thanksgiving with us this year?"

"Yes, Jason. I'd like that very much!"

"Grandma," Georgie said, materializing once again from the bedroom. "Are you going to bring me a present when you come to visit?"

"Do you want me to bring you a present?"

"Sure, my other grandma buys me presents all the time."

"Well, Georgie, I'm not really the present-giving kind of grandma. I'm more of the story-telling kind of grandma. Do you think you might enjoy that?"

"What kind of stories do you tell?" he asked.

"I have a great story about your grandfather when he put a snake in someone's bed. How about that story? Do you think you might enjoy hearing that one?"

"*Really?*" Georgie asked wide-eyed. "Did my grandpa really do that?"

"He sure did! And I'll tell you all about it when I come for Thanksgiving."

Jason laughed. "I think I might be interested to hear that story too, Mom." Then he started to chuckle.

"What?" I asked. "What's so funny?"

"Wait till you see Priscilla. She's huge!"

"Priscilla? Is Priscilla still alive? How can that be?"

"I don't know, but she is very much alive and she's enormous! Come on. Grab a few cookies for her and walk us out to the truck to see her."

With cookies in hand, I followed Jason to the truck that he'd parked at the far end of the lot where he'd found some shade under a large oak. I stepped up onto the rim of one of the rear tires and peered into the truck bed, where I was able to see several market-size pigs and one huge one. The huge one lifted its massive body and speed-waddled toward me, snorting the entire way. Immediately I recognized the marking on Priscilla's hind left quarter. What I used to refer to as a butterfly pattern on her back had grown to two large serving platters attached at the middle.

Priscilla gave out another snort, aggressively pushing the other pigs out of her way to greet me.

"Do you really remember me, old girl, or do you just want the cookies?"

After feeding Priscilla the cookies, I climbed back down from the truck and looked up with admiration at my tall handsome son.

"You've done extremely well for yourself, Jason. I'm very proud of you, and I'm also very sorry I wasn't there for you these past ten years. I truly am."

Jason's face took on a somber appearance. "Do you remember big Billy Johnson? His parents owned the sod farm, and he was defensive end on my school football team."

"Yes. I think so. Why? What about him?"

"Well, I always liked Billy. He was a really nice guy, a square shooter, not always the brightest guy on the team, but a good friend and a pretty good football player. He got drafted right out of high school and now he's *missing in action*. Everyone assumes he's dead, and of course his parents are devastated."

I listened, not knowing where Jason was going with this information.

"Mom, the war affected a lot of families in our community. Some of the guys I went to school with have come back with missing limbs. Others look okay physically but ended up with scrambled eggs for brains. Everything has changed, Mom. Nothing is the same anymore. My being on the farm is what saved me from the draft.

"Oh," I said, understanding what he was saying. "I'm glad the farm worked out for you, and you know you and Jessica are welcome to stay there for as long as you want."

"What do you mean?" he asked. "I don't ever plan on selling the farm."

"Well, now that your father is dead, don't I own the farm?"

"No, Mom. Your name was never on the deed. You never signed any of the papers. Dad owned the farm, and I inherited it from him. I own the farm."

POSTSCRIPT

I hope that you enjoyed reading *The Pig Farmer's Wife* and that this novel may have transported you to a time and place where you were able to feel the challenges and joys of women fifty and sixty years ago.

This novel aims to spark reflective thought and conversations about society's conflicting standards for women. Is there still an unspoken expectation that women sacrifice their careers for their husbands' advancement? Is it assumed that women resign from their position and willingly move to a new location when opportunity knocks on her husband's door?

Secondly, I built into the novel a situation when Gert learned how to read a map and thereby discovered where she was in relation to the farm and her son. Did you find it unsettling when she chose to remain where she was? Why is it more disturbing when we hear of a mother abdicating her maternal responsibilities than it is when we hear of a father walking away from his family obligation? Do we, as a society, hold women to a higher standard?

As we go to print, women's health issues are being challenged in southern states. In these instances, the courts are dictating the treatment options for women instead of allowing them to make decisions in consultation with their physicians. While this novel is set during a time referred to as *the second wave of feminism,* what label do you suppose society will place upon this present era?

Book clubs are loving _The Pig Farmer's Wife_ as they not only discuss what it was like for women fifty and sixty years ago but they reflect upon the conflicting standards for women today. If you would like to have a photo of your book group posted on my website, send it to lavonne.misner.author@gmail.com.

Discussion Questions

Discussion questions, for "The Pig Farmer's Wife" are available, free of charge, upon written request at:

lavonnemisner@gmail.com.

APPENDICES AND DOCUMENTATION

APPENDIX A
Birth Control History

Abstinence was the first form of birth control.

Masturbation or Outercourse sometimes referred to as "bundling," where couples slept together while wearing their clothing, thus being able to express affection without having intercourse.

Withdrawal or pulling out prior to ejaculation was promoted by the Catholic Church as far back as the 1800s.

Breast Feeding, although unreliable, is still used today.

Male Condoms made from linen sheaths were used by men since 1000 BC but were primarily used to protect themselves from syphilis. For increased protection, the Egyptians soaked the sheaths in a spermicidal solution, coincidently discovering this also prevented unwanted births.

In the 1700s London began selling condoms of various materials to single men actively engaged with prostitutes. In the 1800s the Goodyear Tire company used their rubber to make condoms, promoting them as "the material of choice," making them more acceptable to be used by married men.

Female Condoms were introduced in the 1920s as *diaphragms* or *womb veils* and worn inside the vagina and are sometimes still used today.

Birth Control Pills were introduced to the US in 1957 by Margaret Sanger, who was in her 80s, when she underwrote the early research necessary to create the first human birth control pill, called Enovid. The US Food and Drug Administration (FDA) approved it for contraception purposes in the early 1960s. But the pills were not readily used due to concerns of side effects. Not until Dec 14, 1965, when The Supreme Court (in Griswold v. Connecticut) ruled that married couples had the right to use birth control, was it ruled that birth control was protected in the Constitution as a right to Privacy.

As we go to print, The Food and Drug Administration approved the birth control pill called Opill, for over-the-counter sales without a doctor's prescription.

The IUD, or intrauterine device, *The Copper-T* and *ParaGard*, work by stopping a newly fertilized embryo from implanting itself and growing in the lining of the uterus. These were invented in the early 1900s and called *Stem Pessaries, intrauterine devices,* or *sponges.* Early sponges were often soaked in some form of spermicide such as iodine, alcohol, quinine, or carbolic acid.

Contraceptive Implants such as *Norplant, Implanon* or *Nexplanon* were created in the early 2000s. This form of birth control offers pregnancy protection for up to three years with the insertion of a rod in the upper underarm.

The Depo Shot or Patch has been used since 1992 and releases the same hormones as birth control pills, through skin or vaginal walls.

Permanent Sterilization is a surgical procedure involving cuts or clamping of the fallopian tubes. The male version is called a vasectomy.

Abortion, another form of birth control, has been available since the 1973 Roe v. Wade case, which protects a woman's right to abort her fetus. It is presently being challenged in several states and will likely be relooked at by The Supreme Court.

www.ourbodiesourselves.org
www.plannedparenthood.org

APPENDIX B
Working Women's Rights

In 1791 Alexander Hamilton wrote his Report on Manufacturers. In it he described new ways to develop industry in the United States. He felt one of the biggest areas of opportunity was cheap labor in the form of women and children. Soon afterwards, factories began hiring women to work in the textile mills. Young women entered the workforce out of financial necessity and willingly accepted salaries less than men in similar jobs. Society didn't question the lower pay for women, based on the assumption that the women would stop working after they married.

But male factory workers immediately viewed the female workers as a threat to their status, which was further exacerbated when advanced machinery and technology reduced the need for all skilled labor. As a result, men unionized to combat their declining status in the workforce.

Women were rarely included in the male unionization efforts; nevertheless, due to their sheer determination, women remained influential figures in early unionization efforts.

By 1844, women created their own union, called The Lowell Female Labor Reform Association (LFLRA). In a revolutionary action, the group's leader, Sarah Bagley, testified before the Massachusetts legislature. Until then, it was a nearly unheard action, because women at that time seldom spoke in public. The LFLRA stood up for labor issues like higher wages and shorter working days. Women also protested being forced to work on machines at increasingly accelerated rates, as they felt the accelerated machines "endangered their physical wellbeing."

After the US Civil War, the role of women in the workforce evolved again. Approximately, 600,000 American men died in that war, and hundreds of thousands more were injured. Women were required to enter the labor force in order to fill the factories.

During the Great Depression of 1929-1941 another setback

happened for women in the workforce. When unemployment rose to 25% the male-dominated unions revived their argument that only men should be entitled to jobs.

Not until America entered World War II in 1941 did the role of women in the workforce change, because when American men went to war, women were needed to fill the jobs previously held by the men. Six million women entered the labor force, filling jobs in heavy industry and other previously male-dominated industries. Even then, however, the women had no rights in the workplace which didn't go unnoticed by them.

They established (NOW), the National Organization for Women, which expressed their dissatisfaction with the Equal Employment Opportunity Commission's omission of sex in the Executive Order by addressing their concerns in a letter sent to President Johnson. It was signed by Kathryn F. Carlebach, Betty Friedan, and Caroline Davis, officers of NOW from its inception. The omission of sex in Executive Order 11246 was rectified in Executive Order 11357 on October 13, 1967.

https://catalog.archives.gov/id/133876152
https://www.archives.gov/files/women/now-ltrs.jpg

APPENDIX C
Credit For Women

Prior to 1974 financial discrimination against women was accepted as the norm. Credit cards were reserved for men. Only married women could get a credit card, and then only if their husband cosigned on their application. Single woman needed a male family member to agree to be legally responsible for the debts of that credit card. And mortgage lenders discounted a married woman's income, especially if she was of childbearing age.

In 1974 the Equal Credit Opportunity Act was enacted, prohibiting discrimination based on sex, marital status, or age in all credit transactions.

In 1975, the first women's bank was opened.

APPENDIX D
Other Discriminatory Practices

1: Until the Pregnancy Discrimination Act in 1978, women could be fired from their workplace for being pregnant.

2: Sexual Harassment in the workplace was not recognized by the court until 1977 when the Equal Employment Opportunity Commission (EEOC) was established. www.eeoc.gov

3: Katherine Virginia Switzer, an American **marathon** runner, author, and television commentator was the first woman allowed to run the Boston Marathon as an officially registered competitor in 1967.

4: Not until the beginning of the 19th century feminist movement was the premise of a husband's right to control marital intercourse challenged. The movement fought against a husband's right to control marital intercourse, singling out a woman's right to control her own body. Bertrand Russell, who was awarded the 1950 Nobel Prize in Literature in his book *Marriage and Morals* (1929) deplored the situation of married women. He wrote "Marriage for woman is the commonest mode of livelihood, and the total amount of undesired sex endured by women is probably greater in marriage than in prostitution."

5: Serving on a jury: Women were banned from any and all civic duties in United States courts until 1975. Among the reasons for excluding women were:

- They weren't fit to hear details of criminal cases, particularly those involving sex offenses.
- They would be too sympathetic to the accused criminals.
- They're primary focus should be that of wife and mother.
- And it was considered improper for men and women to be sitting close together for long periods of time.

Finally, in 1975, the Supreme Court struck down that ban.

6: Becoming an Astronaut.

There was never an official ban on female astronauts, but NASA's recruiting methods effectively blocked women from interviewing for the job, because they only accepted applications from military test pilots. And because the US military didn't accept women into pilot training programs, there were no women to interview.

Finally, in 1979 NASA hired the first female applicants to train as astronauts. In 1983, Sally Ride was the first female astronaut to enter space. As of this writing there have been 565 total space travelers, 65 have been women.

APPENDIX E
Right to Own Property

Prior to the 19th century, the common *law legal* doctrine was known as the law of *coverture,* which meant a married woman had little or no legal existence apart from her husband. Her rights and obligations were established by her husband and under his rule. She could not own property, enter into contracts, or earn a salary.

Not until late in the 19th century, after the rise of feminism in the mid-19th century was the *Coverture Law* substantially modified under *Married Women's Property Acts* passed in various common-law legal jurisdictions. Still, some forms preventing a wife from incurring major financial obligations, for which her husband would be held liable, survived in some states until the 1960s.

www.llibrary.hbs.edu
www.womenshistory.org.
www.merriam-webster.com
www.americanhistoryusa.com
www.amazingwomeninhistory.com

APPENDIX F
Jim Crow History

The segregationist philosophy of "Separate but Equal" was made famous by the 1896 Supreme Court decision "Plessy vs. Ferguson," in which the court ruled that the state of Louisiana had the right to require different railroad cars for black and white people. The Plessy decision soon had widespread adoption of segregated restaurants, public bathrooms, water fountains and other public facilities.

"Separate but Equal" was eventually overturned in 1954 in the Supreme Court Case "Brown vs. Board of Education," but Jim Crow's legacy continued to endure in some southern states until the 1970s.

www.legendsofamerica.com
www.encyclopedia.com

APPENDIX G
THE MILITARY DRAFT/ CONSCRIPTION

Historically, all American men, eighteen years or older, are considered eligible to be drafted by the Selective Service System. Most young men drafted during the Vietnam War were from poor and working-class families (25% poor, 55% working-class, 25% middleclass), many from rural towns and farming communities. Very few were drafted from upper-class families.

In response to criticism of the draft's inequities, on Dec. 1, 1969, the Selective Service system met in Washington DC to determine the order in which men of draft-eligible age (born 1944-1950) would be drafted, basing their selection on birth dates.

Three hundred sixty-six blue plastic capsules, each one containing birth dates (including February 29) were placed into a deep glass container. The capsules were drawn by hand, opened, and assigned to a sequence number starting from the number 1. The drawing process continued until each day of the year was assigned a lottery number. The lower the number, the higher probability men with that corresponding birthday would be called to serve.

The second lottery was held on the same day with 26 letters of the alphabet to determine the order of selection among men with the same birth date through the ranks of the first letter of their last, first, and middle names. "J" "G" and "D" were the first 3 letters, while E, B and V were the last ones drawn, which meant men with initials "JJJ" would be first, followed by JGJ and JDJ, while VVV would be last.

Since 1973 the US military became all-volunteer, but all US male citizens and immigrants living in the US, are still required to register with the Selective Service within 30 days of turning 18.

While women were not drafted, several did serve military duty in a medical capacity.

www.usa.gov
www.military.com

APPENDIX H
Military Farm Deferment

Bill HR 5916-6057 Farmer's Education and Cooperative, concerning the special no draft status of those who grow food for the nation, is known as a "reserved occupation" or an "essential" civilian job.

It is considered so necessary to a country's war effort that drafting men doing that job would be illegal because those jobs cannot be done by others. Neither can those jobs be abandoned. The men doing those jobs were required to continue working that job.

www.jstor.org

APPENDIX I
Women in Military

In 1916, The National Service School was organized by the Women's Naval Service for the purpose of training women for duties during times of war and national disasters. Loretta Walsh was the first woman to enlist in 1917, followed by more than 35,000 more women who served during World War I.

Women were not admitted into a US military academy however, until 1976.

www.army.mil
www.womensmemorial.org
www.military.com

APPENDIX J
Inequalities Today

There are 104 countries where laws keep certain jobs as "off-limits" for women. In Russia, there are at least 456 jobs that women are not allowed to perform (i.e.) carpenters, professional drivers, ship captains, etc.

Twenty-nine countries restrict the hours women can work.

There are seventeen countries that have laws limiting how women can travel outside the home, including Yemen, where a woman is not allowed to leave her home without her father or husband's permission.

Equatorial Guinea, a woman needs her husband's permission to sign a contract.

In Chad, Niger, and Guinea-Bissau, a woman needs her husband's permission to open a bank account. Up until 1964, this was also a common practice in the United States.

"The Moment of Lift" by Melinda Gates

APPENDIX K
Jungle Gyms and Outdoor Play Equipment

The benefits for children playing on jungle gyms and other play equipment has been well documented, as it helps children develop their large muscle groups, improves hand and eye coordination, and the ability to maneuver their bodies in smooth coordinated movements for effective balance.

When young girls were required to wear dresses to school, it had the effect of discouraging girls from playing on playground equipment because they didn't want their underwear exposed. This practice delayed the physical development of the core body muscles for girls, the very muscles they would later need for childbirth.

https://www.jpost.com>Special

APPENDIX L
The Life Expectancy of a Pig

The Guinness World Record claims Ernestine was the longest living pig on record. She lived 22 years and 359 days. She died July 11, 2014.

https://www.guinnessworldrecords.com>world-records

APPENDIX M
The St. Clair Broiler

The St. Clair Broiler, originally opened in 1956 by brothers John and George Boosalis, was a much beloved eatery in the Macalester-Highland Park community, located at the intersection of St. Clair and Snelling Avenues in St. Paul, Minnesota. The broiler remained open for sixty years, closing its doors in 2017.

APPENDIX N
Historic St. Clair Theatre

Liebenberg and Kaplan were the architects who designed the façade and marquee of the St. Clair Theater in St. Paul, Minnesota, in 1919. Their well-known art deco style façade was used for the front of more than 200 motion picture theatres in the upper Midwest.

The St. Clair Theater was opened in 1924 by Finkelstein & Ruben. In 1929 Byblis took it over allowing it to become part of the Paramount Pictures chain.

After the theater closed, the building served as a racquet ball club and a fitness center. In 2005 it was converted into a ballroom and dance studio, and as of this writing it is still a dance studio.

http://cinematreasures.org/theaters/9736/photos

APPENDIX O
Owatonna, Minnesota

Owatonna is a Minnesota town, rich in history with its Steele County History Center, Village of Yesteryear and Orphanage Museum. It is located south of the Twin Cities at the crossroads of Highway 14 and Interstate 35, snuggled along the Straight River.

Owatonna.org

OTHER BOOKS BY LAVONNE MISNER

"No More Monday's – a nautical odyssey"
A memoir of LaVonne's six-year sailing adventure
with her husband on their own 50-foot sailboat.

"Seasick Ants"
A children's book promoting the importance of
leaving creatures in nature undisturbed.